ESPERANZA

Daring to Dream Beyond Borders

Irving Tragen

Printed in the United States of America
First printing November 2024

ISBN 978-0-9653949-6-3 (Softcover)

Published by Arlington Hall Press, an imprint of the Association for Diplomatic Studies and Training.

Association for Diplomatic Studies and Training
P.O. Box 41839, Arlington, VA 22204

info@adst.org
www.adst.org

Voices of Change
A Tale from Central America

Book One: *Mañana Is Yesterday*
A gripping tale of political intrigue, familial loyalty, and the struggle for power in a rapidly evolving El Salvador.

Book Two: *Esperanza*
The inspiring story of a young Salvadoran woman who overcomes poverty and cultural barriers in pursuit of her dream to become a teacher.

Book Three: *Twilight of a Dream* (Forthcoming)
The convergence of characters and stories from *Mañana Is Yesterday* and *Esperanza*, culminating in the civil unrest that shaped El Salvador's future.

DEDICATED
TO
ALL OF US WHO DARE TO DREAM

WORDS OF APPRECIATION

Writing *Esperanza* has been a trip down memory lane through three decades in which my wife, Ele, and I lived in Latin America. As I wrote, I could almost hear my late wife sharing stories at the dinner table about her adventures in the markets and her experiences with the household staff who shared our homes with us. I also recalled conversations with fellow diplomats and friends from our host countries about the social structures and environments where we lived. To Ele and all those who helped educate me, I owe my sincere gratitude for giving me the knowledge to write this book.

To Lisa Terry, my special appreciation. Working from coast to coast—she in Northern Virginia and I in San Diego—she not only edited my text but also enriched it with her comments and suggestions. She reminded me that literary license cannot override immigration laws and worked with me to reshape the narrative to reflect reality, ultimately enhancing the storyline. Having worked together on editing and publishing my autobiography, *Two Lifetimes as One—Ele and Me and the Foreign Service*, collaborating with Lisa once again was a joy.

I am also deeply grateful to the Association for Diplomatic Studies and Training (ADST) for their support in editing and publishing *Esperanza*.

I am truly honored that this prestigious organization has once again extended its hand to me.

— Irving Tragen

CHAPTER 1

E speranza, her mother Flor, and her six-week-old son, José, huddled together at the bus stop along the dusty road from La Palma to San Salvador. The unpaved road kicked up swirls of dust each time an ox-drawn cart or truck passed by. Flor cradled the baby in her arms, keeping a watchful eye on four sisal sacks that held all the belongings they could carry. They were leaving behind the farm that had been their family's home for as long as anyone could remember.

Esperanza had been the driving force behind their move. She convinced her mother that there was no future for them in the community where their family had lived and been buried for generations. For her mother, leaving this ancestral land felt almost sacrilegious. She had been raised by her grandmother and mother, immersed in the folklore of their people. Her great-grandmother had been the revered *curandera*, healing their community with the herbs and plants that the gods provided. Although the *curandera* chose Esperanza's grandmother to be her successor, her grandmother struggled to master the healing arts, often forgetting the right mixtures and failing to achieve the desired cures. But Grandmother did absorb the *Gran Curandera's* skill in using those herbs and plants to enhance the flavors of every dish she cooked.

Esperanza's mother had little interest in the lore of herbs and plants, focusing instead on the soil and tending to the farm animals. Her grand-mother's cooking skills, however, were passed down to Esperanza. Her mother's true passion lay in the daily rhythms of farm life, which she cherished alongside her husband and children.

Once on the side of the road, her mother pleaded with Esperanza once more, "There is still time, my daughter, to reconsider leaving our El Nido. This has been our ancestral home for generation after generation. Our family found this haven after we were forced to leave the land of the *cenotes*—the sacred pools of our gods. The great shaman led us here after the terrible famine and pestilence that drove our clan from the *cenotes*. You know how our people wandered through lands controlled by hostile clans and over the mountains to this pristine mahogany forest where they set down new roots. Here was peace for our people. As the great shaman told our ancestors, 'This is the place chosen for us by the gods.'"

Esperanza just shrugged her shoulders. She knew the story well.

"This new land had been our haven. There were no hostile clans. It had a cool stream of fresh water and soil rich enough for the precious seeds our ancestors had so carefully protected during their long journey. By the grace of the gods, those seeds have given us corn, chilis, yucca, potatoes, tomatoes, chayote, and squash to fill our bellies, even to this day. Now, with our plantains, mangoes, chickens, and pigs, we live well and sustain ourselves. What more could we need?"

Esperanza just looked at her mother.

Her mother looked back intently as she continued her plea. "Our home is the legacy of the great shaman. He carefully arranged our village and gave us the very land on which our house still stands. He settled us so the trees would afford us through the ages protection against other clans who might become our enemies. He guided us in building homes of adobe and the hard wood. The great shaman blessed this land, and all who lived in it. He dedicated this land to us and pledged us to treat it well and show our love of the gods by living in peace together and not through human sacrifices. I don't want to leave my special place."

She paused, almost sobbing, looking straight down at the earth. Almost in a whisper to her daughter, she blurted out, "And we will lose the sight of the gods who rewarded us with this land. We shall lose the protection of the great shaman and his knowledge of the herbs and plants of the forest. We are abandoning him—he who gave us cures for his people's ills and delights for our well-being—and the seed for the divine indigo from whose core exuded the dark blue dye that the gods love. Oh, Esperanza, I wish I could change your heart."

Her mother looked up at her and made one last attempt, "We have been blessed living here. Even when cruel Spaniards came, El Nido was spared. Our shaman made peace with them, and in turn, we in El Nido remained free to raise our crops and trade our indigo. We have always lived as a special people, and despite the hard times we've faced recently, I do not want to leave this land to live in San Salvador."

Esperanza had heard these arguments many times over the past several months, but she found them empty in the face of her reality. She saw no future in El Nido. She saw a village dying without cash crops and its men forced to leave for seasonal farm jobs beyond the home villages—and then not returning. Only one uncle and his family had enough income from their modest indigo crop to keep his and her mother's family from leaving the homestead. Now, with her son, Esperanza had determined that they could no longer hold on to the past.

"Mother dear, those days are long past. In the time of your grandmother, someone in Europe found a chemical formula to produce the same color as the indigo dye, and our world collapsed. You lived through the bad times when the market for indigo plunged. The income for our families fell so sharply that they could not support themselves—and our men had to leave the indigo fields to find work and income. It was the sons who first began leaving, and many never returned, causing our families to fall into poverty."

3

"Now I have a son to raise and you to care for," Esperanza continued. "We are no longer able to take care of ourselves—except for the charity of my uncle. I do not want my son to live on charity now. There is no employment for me in El Nido. Three generations have passed since we had a shaman to lead us. His knowledge died with him. Great-Grandmother, the *curandera,* is gone, and you and Grandmother did not inherit her healing skills. El Nido is dying, and we are not dying with it."

CHAPTER 2

The bus from La Palma arrived a half hour late; Esperanza helped her mother mount the three stairs and then brought aboard their few possessions. Her mother, with the baby in her arms, navigated among the chickens and pigs and the suitcases already piled around the bus and found two seats near the back. No one offered a helping hand—all were too busy guarding their own precious goods. Esperanza, juggling her sacks, gave her tickets to the driver.

He asked her, "Where do you plan to get off?"

She said, "Soyapango. The Pension Romero. I understand that she is from La Palma and runs a nice place."

The driver smiled, "She will make you comfortable, but she charges for it."

Esperanza made her way toward the back of the bus to join her mother, past a score of farmers and their produce bound for some marketplace on the way to San Salvador. She had barely sat down when the bus began to pick up speed. She settled on the hard bench—down the hill to a new life.

The baby began to cry, and she placed her breast into her son's mouth. She seemed to feed him for an eternity before he quieted down and dozed off. Her mother took back the baby. He was named José after his grandfather.

Despite her stoic calm on the surface, Esperanza was churning in her mind and heart about the decision to leave El Nido. She stared straight ahead, almost afraid to face her mother. Maybe her mother had been right about not leaving El Nido. In her village, they counted. Her great-grandmother was the *curandera* most treasured throughout this region of Chalatenango—the master of herbs and plants that cured diseases and the most sought-after midwife. All the villagers treated her grandmother and mother with special deference as homage to the great *curandera*.

No matter that most of the girls her age were with babies—some were even expecting a second on the way. In her village, being a teenage mother wasn't a disgrace. Her mother could have stayed to help rear the child while she, Esperanza, found work nearby. She could read, write, and do arithmetic and had completed eight grades—at the top of her class. But where would she find a job? Certainly not in El Nido. She would have to try La Palma or Chalatenango City, but even for a menial job, high school graduates had a better chance. In Chalatenango, everyone knew that jobs were so scarce in La Palma or Chalatenango City that even those with high school diplomas often had to go to the capital, San Salvador, for work. So, why not go to San Salvador now?

She realized that, even though she had finished elementary school at the county seat as the top student, her only real talent lay in cooking. She had absorbed all her grandmother's recipes almost by osmosis—recipes passed down from her mother, the great curandera. How Esperanza had loved her grandmother, and what a void her passing had left! Esperanza had mastered all the traditional recipes, with the perfect blend of herbs and seasonings to awaken the taste buds. But where could she possibly make a living cooking these dishes in El Nido, or even in La Palma or Chalatenango City?

What weighed even more heavily on her was the terrible event that had happened nearly a year ago, after her first visit to Chalatenango City. She had completed all eight grades at the municipal school, but the nearest high school was in Chalatenango City. She graduated from the municipal school with the highest marks, and both the principal and her eighth-grade teacher encouraged her to enroll in high school. The principal even promised to help her get a scholarship and find a family with whom she could board in the city.

For Esperanza, it was a dream come true. She had told her grandmother that her greatest ambition was to become a schoolteacher. She loved learning—studying was a joy to her. She was fascinated by the world, the forces that shaped it, and the lives of the people and events that influenced it. Earning a high school diploma, a *bachillerato*, was her dearest ambition—the key to qualifying as a teacher.

The elementary school director arranged for her to have an interview with his friend, the director of the high school in Chalatenango City. He gave Esperanza not only a letter with two copies of the transcript of her excellent grades but also a note for his aunt in Chalatenango City, who had a spare room in her house.

On the day of the interview, Esperanza took the early morning bus to the city and was sitting at the door of the high school director's office well ahead of the hour of her interview. The director commended her for her grades and asked her about her goal in life. "A teacher," she said. He smiled. He then gave her a series of short tests. None of the questions phased her. After reviewing her answers, he placed them in a file along with her elementary school transcript and congratulated her on her acceptance to the high school. He also gave her a copy of the transcript for her personal records, as he only needed one.

Her visit with the director's aunt went just as well. The aunt was willing to let Esperanza stay in her spare room in exchange for a few *colones* per week, along with four hours of house cleaning and occasional cooking. The scholarship would cover the rent, and the housekeeping and cooking were no challenge for Esperanza. And the house! It had electricity, running water, and an inside bathroom—luxuries that Esperanza had only heard about. She was delighted—she had an almost unbelievable room to live in while she went to high school to become a teacher.

Everything seemed idyllic to the young girl when she got off the bus at the El Nido stop. She was walking happily along the dirt roadway to El Nido when it happened. Someone jumped out of the brush and tackled her, tore off her skirt, put his hand tightly over her mouth, and then ripped off her underwear. Before she could react, she felt a rod slam into her body. She felt him thrusting into her and smelled his alcohol-laden breath before she finally understood what was happening to her. Her mind went blank.

When she came to, she was alone. Her torn clothes were splattered with her virginal blood and some greasy slime. She pulled herself together, grabbed her belongings, and ran to the safety of her home. She was trembling with terror as she recounted to her mother what had just happened. Her mother helped clean her up, using some herbs to ease the burning pain in her daughter's thighs—and others to try to prevent pregnancy. Esperanza cried through the night as she saw her dreams imploding. She had an unsettling feeling that the drunken monster had impregnated her, a fear driven by both the pain and the terror she felt.

Days turned into weeks. She hoped, and she lost hope. She kept her feelings locked up inside herself. Then she found that indeed she had been impregnated by the drunken man. Who? She would never know. Why? He just had a need and took it out on her. The result was that her dreams were shattered.

When her mother and she were certain that she was pregnant, she decided she had to tell the director of the grade school and her eighth-grade teacher. They scoffed at her account of being the victim of rape. They blamed her for betraying their trust and quickly informed her that her admission to high school would be denied, and her scholarship application rejected. All she had left was the one transcript of her grades in elementary school. The man with the terrible, alcoholic breath had destroyed her future. She was deeply hurt and bitter. She hated all men.

With her hopes dashed, Esperanza carefully weighed the opportunities for her. If she just stayed in El Nido and lived on the farm, she would have to accept living a life like her mother—tending to the crops and farms animals and watching her children drift away. Oh, yes, she remembered what she learned in school—and what her grandmother had told her about the years, not so long ago, when El Nido and the neighboring farm communities had prospered from the cultivation of anil. As her grandmother described it, anil is the sacred plant of the gods—the plant from which the indigo was extracted—the sacred deep blue ink the gods used to communicate with their people. It is the plant that the great shaman brought with him when he led his people to El Nido.

As Esperanza learned in school, a German chemist in the late nineteenth century invented a chemical process to produce indigo blue, and the markets for the local production dried up. The demand for their local indigo declined so sharply that its production could no longer sustain the local economy. Other food crops could not earn the income needed for the once thriving farms, so the sons and daughters of El Nido and other anil-producing communities left their ancestral homes to find employment elsewhere. Jobs in El Salvador were few and far between, often limited to only seasonal labor in crop picking from Guatemala to Nicaragua. Sometimes sons and daughters would come home after a seasonal job, but more and more often they did not return. And El Nido and the neighboring villages saw not only increasing poverty but more and more broken families. Neither her teachers nor her grandmother could see a brighter future unless someone could find a crop, or a mixture of crops, to replace anil.

Her thoughts turned to her beloved grandmother. She recalled the stories her grandmother shared about the good old days, when their family and El Nido were prosperous and respected. Her grandmother was the daughter of the *Gran Curandera,* and her uncle was the shaman. Indigo

9

provided them with enough income to live comfortably and lead their people, not just in El Nido, but also in the surrounding villages—even as far as La Palma and beyond. Grandmother could afford to marry in the church and make charitable contributions to the poor. She had three sons and three daughters. Then came the decline of the anil crop. One by one, her children left to find work elsewhere. Only her oldest son, Esperanza's uncle, and Esperanza's mother remained. They lived as best they could, but they had had to eke out a living. They had no shaman to lead them; he died without leaving an heir.

Her dear grandmother tried to fill the shoes of the *Gran Curandera*. But try as best she could, she did not succeed. Even though the great *curandera* had shared her knowledge of the power of herbs and plants in curing and cooking, grandmother could only apply them adroitly to cooking. Yes, in her brain, she carried the age-old cures for her people, but she never seemed to make them work as expected. She tried to teach the cures and recipes to her daughter Flor, but Flor showed no interest in them. She preferred to work in the fields and tend the livestock and chickens.

During those difficult times, Flor worked alongside her father in the fields, raised the chickens, and milked the two remaining cows. Her son had his own family to care for and barely enough to meet their needs. Flor took care of her parents and remained in the family home. When her grandfather died, Flor worked alone until, at fourteen, she married another young teenager. She had never been married in the church, unlike her mother and grandmother, who could afford the dispensations and rites in the good days when indigo provided the extra income they needed.

When Esperanza's mother and father decided to marry, they had barely enough money to buy the food for the wedding feast. So, they took simple vows before their families—without the benefit of clergy. Her mother had six children; four died in childhood. Only Esperanza and her older brother, Diego, survived. Diego had to leave El Nido to find seasonal work, and for a year or two, he returned with some money. Then, he disappeared. Her mother still silently pined for word of him.

When Esperanza was three, her father died. Her mother doubled her efforts in the fields tending the livestock and chickens. Her grandmother raised her, taught her to read and write, and poured into her all the knowledge of plants and herbs that she had inherited from her mother, the *Gran Curandera*. She was often confused when it came to healing, but never when using plants and herbs for cooking. Every day, she spent hours with her young granddaughter, sharing the folklore of their people, the power of plants and herbs, and the importance of understanding the world beyond El Nido. Her grandmother walked with Esperanza to the county elementary school to enroll Esperanza when she was six, and she accompanied her every day to and from school until she became too ill to walk the kilometer or two. And every day after school, she gave her lessons in cooking. Her grandmother had been Esperanza's inspiration. When she passed away just before Esperanza's tenth birthday, Esperanza not only mourned her loss but also resolved to become a teacher in her honor.

Then Esperanza's life changed. She felt no one in her family was interested in her aspirations and dream of becoming a teacher. She thrived in school and earned the highest grades in her class, but her mother never asked her about her studies or her school experiences. Her mother seemed indifferent to her desires and needs. Her mother only encouraged her to become the family cook.

To Esperanza, that was not the life her grandmother had wanted her to live. Even before she was assaulted, she had started to question what her future would look like if she stayed in El Nido. Now there was no hope for further education. She could never become a teacher. What kind of a job could she find in El Nido or the neighboring communities? If she stayed, she would eke out a livelihood on a farm in a stagnant—if not dying—community. Her commitment to her grandmother and her lust for an education made her want for more.

Esperanza's rape had made her a realist. Her treatment by the school director told her not to expect understanding and help from others. She knew she had to rely on herself, and she realized that being a great cook in El Nido wouldn't provide the means to support a family. While she might prepare feasts for family and village events, there was no one willing to pay for them, and she needed an income to sustain her mother and son. She concluded that her future lay beyond Chalatenango, and her next step had to be the capital, San Salvador.

She did not discuss her emerging plans with her uncle or mother. She discreetly asked all the neighbors if they knew anyone in the capital. Yes, her uncle's aunt had a daughter, Carmen, who ran a restaurant near the great market of that city; but she had not contacted her for many years. Esperanza also learned of a woman who came from La Palma, Senora Romero, whose mother had been a patient of the great *curandera* and who ran a pension in the town of Soyaponga, a suburb of San Salvador. Esperanza made careful notes on each one with their names and addresses. *Ah*, thought Esperanza, *I can contact those two women, and they will help me secure a future for my family.*

These were the thoughts that crowded her mind as the bus crawled toward San Salvador. Esperanza repeated to herself: "I've made the right decision. I have to make it work."

CHAPTER 3

The bus ride was nearly six hours long—not for distance, but for the stops. At each town along the route, the bus took on and let off passengers, cargo, and animals. At each one, there were local women selling *pupusas, chicerones, panos de pollo, yucca frita, empanadas de frijoles,* and *elites locos* to eat and *horchata* to drink. Mother and daughter just looked. Esperanza had prepared her own lunch of *panes* and *horchata*—just enough to get to Soyapango. Her mother changed the baby, and Esperanza kept him fed.

When the driver announced the next stop was Soyapango, Esperanza organized the departure. She held her mother with the baby in arms in the seat until the pigs and chickens bound for the market or the abattoir got out the door. Then she led her mother down the aisle to the driver's seat. She thanked him for the ride and asked him for directions to the Pension Romero.

He gestured with his left hand that it was around the next left-hand corner and said, "There is a sign over the front door, if you can read."

Esperanza half-snarled, "Thank you. I can read."

To the right of the bus stop was a cantina with bright lights and loud music—and that horrible smell that reminded her of the night she was assaulted. Fortunately, the pension was straight ahead in the opposite direction. As they rounded the corner, she saw on the other side of the next block a sign that read "PENSION MORALES." In only a few more steps, they were at the front door.

Esperanza rang the doorbell. A middle-aged, full-bosomed woman opened the door.

"Yes," she said.

"We would like room and meals for a week," replied Esperanza.

The woman looked at the two countrywomen and baby. She saw that they were tan-skinned, both about five feet tall, and dressed in typical garb—rebozos, blouses, and skirts. She was about to shoo them away when something about the garb caught her attention. It reminded her of home, in Chalatenango, and the attire of the village people in Sunday dress. She looked but said nothing.

Sensing a problem, Esperanza said, "We have just arrived from El Nido. We found an envelope with your name and address on it in my grandmother's special box."

The lady in the door looked at the envelope and then nodded, "Come in. I think I have a room available."

"I have money to pay for the room and meals for a week," assured Esperanza, as she, her mother and son followed the lady through the door and down the hall to a table with a brightly lit lamp.

With soft music from a radio playing in the background, the lady sat down at the table and opened a register. She motioned for Esperanza to sign the register, "Can you read and write?"

"Yes, indeed," Esperanza smiled.

"Then write down your names and your home address."

Esperanza, in an elegant script, wrote her name and those of her mother and son and the name of their village. There were really no streets, only houses. Some close together, others quite apart.

The lady was considering which room to assign these nondescript guests—one in the rear of the second floor overlooking the backyard, or a front room on the same floor. Then, she glanced down and casually read the names: Esperanza Vasquez Choarti, Flor Choarti de Vasquez, and José Choarti.

She looked up, "Did you say you are from El Nido?

"Yes," said Esperanza's mother. "I have never left it until today. And, Señora, in the light, your face looks familiar. Were you ever in El Nido?"

"You are the family of the *Gran Curandera* Choarti?" she asked.

"Yes, she is my grandmother. I am named for her, Flor de los Angeles."

The tone and demeanor of the pension owner changed completely. She smiled warmly at them, "You are indeed welcome to my pension. I am from La Palma. I am here only because of the great *curandera*. When my mother was a young girl, she became very ill, and her mother took her to El Nido to see the *curandera*. That saintly woman took my mother into her care and, using her herbs and nostrums, cured her. My mother told me that the doctor in La Palma had said there was no hope. But when my grandmother brought her to the great *curandera* in El Nido, she said that there was hope—and the *gran curandera* proved the doctor wrong. It took months, but her herbs and plants saved my mother. The *curandera* would take no money for her cure, but my mother sent her and her daughter 50 *colones* a year every year until she died in 1930. The envelope must be from one of her annual gifts. Yes, my family is in debt to yours."

Holding baby José in her arms, Flor replied, "My grandmother's house has been my home all my life, until today. My grandmother, the great *curandera*, taught my mother and me how to use all the herbs, plants, and mixtures she used for her cures and cooking—but sadly, we could only use them in cooking, not for healing. We were not blessed with her powers."

The pension owner extended her arm to Flor and said, "My name is Marta Chavez de Romero. Flor, lay the baby on the table while I find a cradle to put him in."

As Esperanza looked on in total surprise, Marta crossed over to a closet and brought back a cradle. She placed it on the table next to the baby and then placed him in it. "There," Marta sighed, "He will be quite comfortable for now."

Marta then said, "Ladies, I know it is late, and you must be hungry. I will settle you in a room across the hall from mine. It has two good beds and a table for the cradle. It is close to the bathroom and shower." She picked up the cradle and led them a few more steps toward the back of the house.

She opened the door and turned on an electric light. Their home in El Nido had no electric lights. In fact, there was no electricity in all the village. In the room were two beds with mattresses, a table, two chairs, shelves for clothing and a bureau. At home, their beds were made of straw, and their bedrooms held only one chair and a well-worn homemade armoire.

"Ladies, let me show you the bathroom next door." She took them one door back down the hall to the bathroom. Flor had never seen one before, but Esperanza had—both at school and in Chalatenango City, in the house where she had planned to live during high school.

Marta cautioned, "You'll be sharing the bathroom with all the other guests on the first floor. Keep it neat and clean and never stay too long." Then she walked into the room and pointed, "This is the commode. You sit on it—don't straddle it or squat. Just sit. When you are finished, here is the paper to clean yourselves and this is the box into which you throw the used paper. And this is the chain to flush. Over there is a wash basin. See the bar of soap? Just turn on the faucet and you have water—be sure to turn it off when you finish." She turned around and pulled a floor to ceiling drape and showed them the shower. "This is the shower to bathe," she laughed, "you don't have to go the river while you're in my pension."

Esperanza's mother was overcome. She had never seen anything like the bathroom before. Esperanza sensed her mother's puzzlement and quietly said to her, "I'll help. We had toilets like this in my school."

Marta said, "I'll have some food prepared for you even though it is late, just something to tide you over to breakfast. When you are ready, just walk up the hall toward the front door. You will see the dining room lit up. Go in and sit down. The maid will be watching for you and will bring you some food. For me, I will say goodnight. We will talk more in the morning."

While her mother changed the baby, Esperanza unpacked. She then showed her mother how to use the commode and turn the faucet on and off to wash up. Afterward, Esperanza nursed little José before the two women headed to the dining room. Marta had arranged a *caldo de res*, a hearty beef soup with pieces of yucca, potato, chayote, and carrots, with warm tortillas on the side. It was a feast. The soft music continued to play in the background as they ate.

When they returned to their room, Flor seemed overwhelmed. She sat on her bed as if in a spell—she sat on a mattress for the first time in her life. Esperanza saw a strange look in her mother's face and asked, "Are you all right?"

Her mother shook as she said, "This is all so new to me. Here I am, far from the only home I've ever known, in a room much larger than my own. I'm sitting on a mattress that isn't made of my own straw, and I just had a meal we would only prepare for a feast day. Everything feels so strange. And there's been music playing ever since we walked in the front door."

"And the music—where does it come from?" mused her mother.

"That comes from a radio. My school had a radio, and we listened to news and music during some classes. We never had a radio in El Nido because we didn't have electricity—and no one could afford one anyway."

"A radio, yes, I heard someone mention that word, but I was never sure what the word meant," her mother mused. "Isn't it wonderful that you can listen to music all day long?"

The two tired women then lay down on their separate beds and soon fell sound asleep.

CHAPTER 4

B aby José woke both women before dawn. After tending to him, Esperanza showed her mother how to use the shower, and they both enjoyed cold-water baths. It was so much easier than walking to the stream and back in El Nido. They used plenty of soap to wash the grime and dust of the highway from their hair and skin.

Esperanza put on her best blouse and skirt because she planned to leave after breakfast to look for a job as a cook in a restaurant in the city. She had only enough money to pay for about ten days at the pension. Selling their chickens, pigs, and cherished belongings barely covered the trip expenses, bills, and a ten-day pension stay, so finding a job became her top priority.

Breakfast service began at 6:30 a.m., and Esperanza and her mother were among the first to enter the dining room. Near the door to the kitchen was a table with plates of fried yucca and fried plantains, a bowl of hot beans, and a basket of tortillas. There were also two urns—one with coffee and the other, water. The two women thought it a feast.

They were unsure about what they should do. So, they just stood near the entrance to the room and watched other guests take a ceramic plate from the sideboard and fill it with food. The women were surprised to see the men take more than one piece of any item—at home they never took more than one piece of anything,

Mother led the way. She took her plate and filled it with several slices of plantain, a piece of yucca, two large spoonsful of beans, and two tortillas. She then placed her food on an empty table and returned to the sideboard for a cup, which she filled with coffee. Then, with a shrug of her head, she signaled to Esperanza that it was her turn.

They ate slowly and silently. They said nothing, and their faces were stoic. They savored each mouthful. It was a dream breakfast. They hadn't been prepared for another feast. The luxury of just picking up the food and eating it quietly was beyond their expectations.

It was nearly 7:30 a.m. when they finished the last drop of coffee. Esperanza said quietly to her mother, "I must ask Señora Romero how to get to the Central Market in San Salvador. I need to find a job today."

Her mother looked sternly at her, "Yes, you brought us here and you said that you would take care of us."

Esperanza said, "Yes, Mother, I know what I must do."

Just then, the maid appeared at the door of the kitchen. She looked over the sideboard and table. Then, she reappeared with a tray of fresh food. Esperanza hurried over to her and asked, "Do you know where Señora Romero is?"

The maid eying the country bumpkin up and down before replying, "She's busy with the cook in the kitchen."

"May I go into the kitchen to see her?" Esperanza asked.

The maid replied, "I'll ask her," as she finished her task of placing fresh food on the table and then placing the already emptied plates on her tray.

Esperanza just stood frozen.

A few minutes later, Señora Romero appeared from the kitchen. When she saw that it was Esperanza who wanted her attention, she smiled and said, "What can I do for you?"

Esperanza half apologetically said, "Señora, I need to go to the Central Market to look for a job. I want to be a cook. I was told in El Nido that one of my cousins by marriage owns a restaurant near the Central Market, and I want to ask her for a job. I need the money to take care of my mother and son."

Marta looked at her and said, "Who are you going to see?"

"Señorita Carmen Delgado," was the reply.

Marta almost snorted, "She is one tough lady. I know her and know how hard she has worked to build that business. She has one of the most successful restaurants in the city."

"My uncle told me that she ran a restaurant near the Central Market, and that she had prospered using the recipes of the great *curandera*—the same recipes my grandmother taught me," Esperanza replied.

Señora Romero thought for a minute and then gave her precise information about the bus to take to reach the Central Market, how much she should pay for the bus ticket, and the specific location of the restaurant. She also indicated the street where she would find the bus back to Soyapango. "Be careful on the bus. There are many pickpockets and dangerous men who prey on young girls. Stay safe, and I wish you good luck."

Esperanza returned to the room to nurse José and freshen up for the bus trip to the market and the search for Carmen Delgado. Señora Romero noticed Esperanza's mother still sitting at the table. Feeling a pang of sympathy for the woman sitting there alone, she poured herself a cup of coffee and took the seat Esperanza had vacated. Smiling at Flor, she asked, "Did you sleep well? Enjoy your breakfast?"

Flor smiled back her yes. "Oh, Señora, how can I thank you? I feel so clean and comfortable. I am indeed very satisfied."

"Today will be a tough day for Esperanza. I know Carmen—she's a strong woman and not easily convinced. In the meantime, if you need anything, just let me know."

CHAPTER 5

E speranza caught the 8:30 a.m. bus, tense and on guard the entire ride. She got off at the stop Señora Romero had mentioned and headed toward the main entrance of the Central Market. Following the directions, she turned right, walked two blocks, and found the restaurant called "Carmen."

The front door was open, and the restaurant was bustling with breakfast customers. A large sign read, "Only paying customers enter through the front door. Others use the back." So, Esperanza made her way around the building to the back entrance, where garbage cans and waste cluttered the area. She cautiously pushed the door open and saw the kitchen stretched out before her. She stepped inside and approached a cook, who shooed her away. When she tried a second cook, he gave her a disdainful look, as if she were just a country bumpkin. Finally, a kitchen maid looked up and asked, "What do you want?"

"I am looking for my cousin, Carmen Delgado." Esperanza replied.

"Your cousin," laughed the maid. "Well, her office is around that corner." The maid looked at one of the cooks, "That's a hot one—her cousin."

Esperanza walked around the corner and knocked on the door that said "Manager" on it.

"What is it now?" said a shrill voice from the other side of the door.

"I am your cousin Esperanza Vasquez Choarti from El Nido."

"You are what?" the voice sneered. "That's a new one, I'll bet you are."

"I am your cousin Esperanza Vasquez Choarti. I just arrived from El Nido," Esperanza said very firmly, trying to keep her calm.

"Oh, you are?" said the voice on the other side of the door. "I doubt it but, come on in."

Esperanza opened the door and looked at the large woman with bright red hair sitting behind a large mahogany desk.

Esperanza was unsettled by the treatment and practically shouted, "I am Esperanza Vasquez Choarti, from our village El Nido in Chalatenango. I arrived here yesterday with my mother and my newborn son. My uncle told me about you, and I have come to ask you for a job as a cook."

"You are my cousin? Well, that's a good approach."

"Yes," said a very insistent Esperanza. "I am your cousin through my uncle. He told me that your mother was the sister of the *Great Curandera*, who was my grandmother. He told me that you learned all her recipes. My grandmother also taught them to me. Your uncle also told me that you were raped by a drunk near the cantina, and afterward, you left El Nido. Well, I was raped by a half-drunk farm worker on the road home from the county seat, and I left El Nido, too. Now, I need a job to support my mother and my son."

Carmen's tone changed as she took a closer look at her visitor. The young woman had the family features—she looked very much like her own mother. *Maybe she is telling the truth*, she thought to herself.

Esperanza continued in a matter-of-fact voice, "I have completed eight years of school in our municipal school and went to Chalatenango City to apply for high school. You see, I wanted to be a teacher. I passed the test and was approved for a scholarship and found a place to stay in the city. On the way home, I was raped by a drunk farm laborer. He took me by surprise as I walked from the highway to El Nido. I still remember his body odor and the alcohol on his breath."

Esperanza's whole body shook. It was nearly a minute before she could continue, "When I got pregnant, the men at the school blamed me for what that man did. Then, I decided that there was no future for me or my child in El Nido. I convinced my mother to come to San Salvador to build a new life and to take care of my son while I worked to support them."

Carmen fixed her gaze on Esperanza and said, "I think you are telling me the truth."

"Of course, I am. I am your cousin, and I need your help. But I can also help you as a cook. Like you, I know all the *Great Curandera's* recipes—they're engraved in my memory. The recipes for *sopas*, *platos*, and *dulces*, with just the right touch of herbs and plants to bring out the true flavors. I've been cooking for my family and the community since my grandmother passed. Let me show you what I can do."

Esperanza looked directly at Carmen as she confided, "I started making plans to leave even while the baby was growing inside me. I saved every *centavo* I earned from cooking dinners and helping neighbors with chores. I sold all our chickens and farm animals. I asked everyone if they knew anyone in San Salvador. My uncle's wife told me about you—how you left El Nido after your baby girl was born, opened a restaurant near the Central Market, and sometimes sent *colones* back to help them survive. The more I thought about leaving, the more I knew I had to meet you."

Carmen looked at Esperanza, now with real compassion in her eyes, as if she were reliving a dark part of her own life. The look was fleeting, as she quickly shifted back to the businesswoman she had become. "Esperanza, I'd like to help you, but I don't need a cook or even a maid right now. Yes, I want to help, but you'll have to wait until someone on my staff leaves—and they don't leave often because this is the best restaurant job you can get in San Salvador."

Esperanza looked downcast. This had been her best hope.

Carmen continued, "Where are you staying now?"

"We are staying in the pension of Señora Romero in Soyapango," was the reply.

Carmen rose from her chair and approached her young cousin, saying, "Can I lend you a few *colones*?"

Esperanza looked at Carmen with great determination in her heart as she blurted out, "I don't want charity. I want a job to take care of my mother so that she can take care of my son while I work."

Carmen said, "That I can't do today. But keep in touch with me. I will consider you for the next vacancy." She patted Esperanza on the shoulder as she showed her out.

CHAPTER 6

E speranza left the restaurant feeling despondent. She was angry about Carmen's reception and filled with doubts about her decision to leave the safety of El Nido. She blamed herself for putting not only her own life at risk, but also the lives of her mother and son. Yet, she knew she had no choice but to find a job.

So, she walked around the area of the public market and asked if anyone knew about a job opening for a cook. Most people just ignored her. A few said politely, "No."

She walked back toward the bus stop, looking for cafes or restaurants. When she came to the then most fashionable hotel in the city, the Astoria, she asked the doorman of the hotel, "Do you need a cook?" He just laughed at the country girl and told her to go on her way. At one of the cafes, the waiter suggested that she could make a few *colones* by having sex with him.

It was a contrite and weary traveler who arrived at the pension after 3:00 p.m. Señora Romero took one look at her face and immediately knew what had happened. In fact, knowing Carmen, she had expected this outcome.

She took Esperanza into the dining room and offered her a plate left over from lunch and a glass of horchata. Esperanza almost sobbed as she ate. Everything looked so bleak.

When she returned to her room, her mother offered comfort. "I remember Carmen as a difficult person. We never got along very well. After she got pregnant, she just shut us out. She kept to herself, and when her baby was born, she left on her own. No wonder she's so uncaring."

Esperanza sobbed. Her mother just looked at her, "Don't be so depressed. We still have enough *colones* to buy bus tickets back to our home. We can move back into our house. You can prepare the meals for our family and those in our community who need help. I can tend the chickens and pigs. My brother and I can work our fields together. We can raise José. It wouldn't be that bad a living."

The two ladies stoically went through the rest of the day. Esperanza nursed José. Her mother commented, "Señora Romero fed him some powdered milk about noontime, and he really seemed to like it. Did you know about this powdered milk?"

"Yes. mother, I heard about it in school, but we couldn't afford it."

At dinner, Señora Romero sat with them and tried to cheer Esperanza up, but to no avail. The young mother seemed to believe her world had fallen apart.

After an almost sleepless night, she resolved to try again. Maybe something would turn up. She resolved to ask Señora Romero for suggestions about where she might apply for a job as a cook. She also kept hearing the sneering voice with which Carmen had greeted her, and she promised herself that one day she would make Carmen apologize for her words. She kept telling herself that it was her duty to find a job, no matter how menial, to support her family. Her people never begged or accepted charity. Work was the ethic that bound them together. But reluctantly she conceded that her mother was right: if she didn't find anything in the next few days, they would have to go home to El Nido and exist as best they could. Then she dropped off to sleep.

She was dozing when she heard her son cry. Quickly, she jumped up to tend to him. She nursed him, changed his diaper, and watched him drift back to sleep. Determined to get an early start the next day, she grabbed the towel from the chair by her bed and, still in her nightdress, headed to the commode and shower.

As she emerged from the bathroom, she heard a lot of yelling coming from the kitchen. She hurriedly put on her blouse and skirt and went through the dining room to the kitchen. She had never been in that large space before. It was a sunlit room, with large windows, a long sink, a wood-burning stove, another large object with a door in its middle, cabinets along the walls, a refrigerator, a large worktable, and some chairs. She saw Señora Romero, her face red and angry, standing near the worktable.

"Are you alright?" she asked Señora Romero.

"Furious," she replied. "The cook arrived late, smelling of *aguardiente*. It is Wednesday, can you imagine? I expect it on Mondays when she's taken a day off, but Wednesday! She was a mess. I asked her what she thought she was doing. And I told her that she was in no condition to work. She screamed back at me that she was fine—as she half-reeled around the room. We screamed at each other, and I fired her. She sneered at me and weaved out. Now, I am here trying to figure out how to prepare breakfast."

Esperanza asked, "The same breakfast as yesterday?"

"Yes," Señora Romero answered. "The same every weekday. On Sundays, I also serve eggs."

Esperanza said, "I'll prepare breakfast for you. Don't worry."

She glanced around the room, taking in where everything was. In front of her stood a wood-burning stove, and nearby was another large appliance that Señora Romero identified as an electric stove. To her left was a large sink with a single faucet, and to her right were a refrigerator and several floor-to-ceiling cabinets. On the tables beside her were frying pans filled with yucca and plantain slices, along with a large metal pot of coffee. She had never seen such an array before. It brought to mind the simple wood-burning stove, worktable, and small bucket she used to carry water from the well back in El Nido.

"Señora Romero, could you show me where you cook the plantains and yucca? It doesn't look like there's enough room on the stove. Where do you brew the coffee? And where do you store extra yucca and plantains? Which cabinets hold the platters? Also, where are the knives to cut the plantains and yucca? I see the mortar for rolling tortillas, but where is the masa? Is there anything else you'd like me to prepare?"

Señora Romero was almost overwhelmed. She called the kitchen maid and told her to help Esperanza. Then, Esperanza went to work. The maid told her that the beans had been cooking since dawn—in the same olla that held the left-over beans from yesterday. Esperanza stared scornfully at the maid before tasting the beans to be sure that none had soured or were undercooked. Fortunately, they seemed fine and ready for the table. She put the frying pans of yucca and plantains on the electric stove as the maid showed her how to turn on and off the burners. She had the maid slice more yucca and plantains. The maid brought her three dozen already made tortillas from the shop around the corner—no need to roll out the massa and pat it into shape as she had done every morning in El Nido.

Within thirty minutes, Esperanza had breakfast ready on the serving table, and the pension guests were able to fill their plates, unaware of the crisis Señora Romero had faced earlier that morning.

After breakfast, with no complaints from the guests, Señora Romero was so relieved that she asked, 'Esperanza, would you work for me until I can find a new cook?"

"Yes, if you allow us to stay on in our room."

"Oh, yes," replied the pension owner. "Yes, that would be a good arrangement for now."

Esperanza smiled for the first time in many a day as she said, "I will be your cook as long as you need me."

Señora Romero smiled, drank another cup of coffee, and then added, "I am going tomorrow to the Central Market at ten. I would like you to join me."

Esperanza was very pleased as she informed her employer, "This morning I was unable to find several herbs and plants that I used in El Nido. They add flavor to the dishes. They are the ones used by the *Gran Curandera*. Please show me where you keep your herbs and plants, and please let me buy some if you don't have any."

After Señora Romero showed Esperanza her collection of herbs and plants, which she called spices, and made a list of the ones Esperanza noticed were missing, Esperanza ran to their room to share the good news with her mother.

CHAPTER 7

The next day, after breakfast service, Esperanza could hardly wait to visit the Central Market in downtown San Salvador. She was already waiting at the front door when Señora Romero appeared at ten. A taxi was parked at the curb, ready to take them. As they walked toward the cab, the pension owner remarked, "I usually go in my son Ricardo's car, but he's busy today, so we'll take this taxi. The driver is a friend of mine and very trustworthy. Always be cautious when taking a cab—some drivers are thieves."

She gestured for Esperanza to pick up the baskets and follow her to the cab. Señora Romero motioned for Esperanza to sit in the front seat next to the driver and place the baskets in the back seat, where she herself settled in. After locking her door, she said, "Chico, meet Esperanza, my new temporary cook. Now, take us to the Central Market."

As they settled into the taxi, Señora Romero continued, "I go to the Central Market three times a week—every Monday, Wednesday, and Friday. I know how many guests I have at the pension and how much food I need to buy. Today I have eight guests, plus your mother and you. I estimate what my guests will eat. Very few guests have lunch here, as they usually eat with their business associates downtown—often at Carmen's or one of the two good hotels, the Astoria or the Nuevo Mundo. So, I don't buy much for midday meals. Breakfast and dinner demand most of my attention. I've made my list, and I expect you to help me select the items, making sure I get exactly what I order and in good quality. I always go to the same market women—they know I won't tolerate any tricks."

It was a much shorter trip than the day before on the bus. No stops and not too much traffic—although horse carts and an over-laden truck did slow them down. The driver dropped them at the main entrance. As they alighted from the cab, Señora Romero motioned to one of the boys near the entrance to assist her. Esperanza retrieved the baskets from the back seat of the cab as Señora Romero said, "This is one of the boys who helps me each time I come to the market. He'll carry the baskets while you assist me with the selections."

They then swept into the market, Señora Romero leading the way. She went straight to a booth near the back of the first aisle, where an elderly lady greeted her. "Doña Marta, good morning."

Doña Marta smiled, "Good morning, Maria. I see you don't have a good selection today."

"Oh, you're mistaken—the carrots, potatoes, chayote, cabbage, and squash have never been better. And the green beans are freshly picked. You have an exceptional choice today."

Doña Marta started checking the items one by one, sparring with Maria over the quality and freshness. They were in their normal bargaining routine. "How much for the green beans—they don't look too fresh to me."

"Oh, but they are. They are only 80 *centavos* a bunch."

"Highway robbery," retorted Doña Marta, "I'll give 40 *centavos*."

They haggled to a price of 55 *centavos*. And then repeated the routine over each of the vegetables. It took nearly twenty minutes before the two ladies ended the charade.

When they left Maria's stand, Señora Romero turned to Esperanza and said, "Everyone in the market calls me Doña Marta. I think you should, too."

"Very well, Doña Marta. As you wish."

They moved from stand to stand. At each one, there was the same greeting for Doña Marta, the familiar bargaining, and, finally, a deal struck, followed by warm farewells. Doña Marta purchased oranges, papayas, mangoes, bananas, and plantains.

Esperanza added an additional stop to Doña Marta's routine by reminding her that she would need some spices. She led her to a stand with a broad array of green and red chilis, herbs, and spices. It was a stand that Doña Marta had not visited often, and she was leery about making a purchase. Esperanza insisted, "Doña Marta, to bring out the best flavors in the food you're buying, we need to use these chilis, herbs, and plants. I noticed you had very few of them this morning. My grandmother taught me how to use them in my cooking. I think we should buy some."

"Esperanza, they're expensive. We call them spices and peppers. I haven't used many in the food I serve because my clients might not like them."

"Doña Marta, I think I can make the food taste much better with just a few of them."

Begrudgingly, Doña Marta acceded, and they bargained for a mixture that Esperanza identified. Doña Marta paid the few *colones* and mumbled, "These spices better be good."

The last section of the market they visited housed live chickens, pigs, and goats, as well as freshly butchered beef and pork. Doña Marta greeted her usual butcher, "Your meat better be fresh and tender today."

He smiled and replied, "Doña Marta, you know me. The beef and pork came fresh from the slaughterhouse this morning."

"I bet," the pension owner scoffed.

Choosing good cuts of beef was new for Esperanza. In El Nido, when they ate meat, it was usually poultry or pork. Ever since the indigo market had broken, there wasn't much beef raised or sold in her area. Doña Marta knew her clients wanted beef as often as possible, and she served a variety of soups, stews, and special dishes that featured beef. So, her bargaining with the butcher was a longer process than her with the market ladies. She ended up buying several cuts of meat and a couple live chickens. She remarked to Esperanza, "There is enough space in the refrigerator for the beef to last for the rest of the week."

When they looked over the chicken, Esperanza was more knowledgeable than Doña Marta and saw one or two that she warned Dona Marta not to consider.

It was noon before the threesome departed the market with full baskets. Doña Marta led the way. She checked all the baskets and packages that her market boy was carrying and counted the number of live chickens in the wooden box he carried on his back. Esperanza carried all the chilis and spices in separate bags. As they reached the front door, the taxi driver drove up, and Doña Marta supervised the market boy as her purchases were carefully loaded into the taxi. Satisfied that everything was accounted for, she gave the boy a few *colones* and told the taxi driver to take them back to the pension.

When they reached the pension, Esperanza, with her bag of chilis and spices, jumped out of the front seat, rushed to the front door, and rang the bell. The maids were waiting, and they quickly emptied the taxi of its wares, including the chickens. Doña Marta re-entered her pension with the dignity of an owner.

That routine became Esperanza's adventure every Monday, Wednesday, and Friday while she worked as the cook at Pension Romero. They bargained with the same market women and butcher each time, haggling over the price of each item. The only change came from Esperanza's search for chilis and spices needed to give her meals their proper flavor. From that day on, Señora Romero became Doña Marta to Esperanza, her mother, and her son.

CHAPTER 8

On the return to the pension, Esperanza went into the kitchen with the maids to oversee the storage of the items they had purchased. The kitchen maid took the live chickens to a backyard enclosure. The two housemaids helped her locate the right place to store the vegetables and fruits. Esperanza searched for glass jars to store the spices she had persuaded Doña Marta to buy and quickly realized how little she knew about the kitchen where she was going to cook.

She realized just how different this kitchen was from the one in El Nido. Back home, she had a wood stove and a sink where she poured water from the *ollas* she'd filled at the village well. She had a few open shelves for storage, but no cabinets. She had never owned a refrigerator—she'd only seen one or two in stores at the municipal center and in Chalatenango City. She asked herself, "*What do you even store in a refrigerator?*" Then she puzzled over the strange device with counters on either side, something she had never seen before. She wondered, *What would I use that for?* Without thinking, she said aloud, "I am lost in this kitchen."

One of the cleaning maids mocked, "What did you say, Esperanza?"

"Oh, I am a little confused about the things in the kitchen," she almost apologetically replied. "This kitchen is so different from the one at my home in El Nido. I don't know what all the devices are used for."

They half-giggled, "Just ask Doña Marta."

Esperanza bristled.

The maid added. "You can't put away the vegetables without cleaning them. Doña Marta insists that they be carefully washed to make sure that there are no bugs in them."

"Oh, I never did that at home. Bring them to me at the sink, and I will wash them."

At this point, Doña Marta entered the kitchen and praised Esperanza. "You never know what devils have latched onto the produce in the market. Clean them well and kill anything you see moving." As she turned to leave, she said to Esperanza, "For lunch, I want you to make a dozen *panes*, a large bowl of beans, and a dozen *pupusas*. I don't expect more than four or five guests to be back for lunch. I am going to take my shower now and will be back in about an hour."

Esperanza drew a deep breath and went back to work scrubbing the vegetables.

Doña Marta returned to her two-room suite and private bath. She walked through her office and bedroom right into her tiled bathroom. She stepped out of her clothes, inspecting them carefully to make sure that she had not acquired any fleas at the market. She then folded them and put them into a large basket, which held all her clothes to be laundered.

She took a leisurely shower, reflecting on everything that had happened since breakfast. She felt grateful to Esperanza for saving her from so much work and stress after she had to fire the cook the day before. She noted how efficiently the young woman had stepped in to fill the gap and how satisfying the meal had been. Esperanza clearly knew how to prepare country fare, and she did it well. There wasn't much to judge her on yet, but it was a good start—especially after having to fire that drunken woman who called herself a cook. Then she recalled how especially flavorful the yucca and plantains had been that morning. *Hmm,* she thought, *I wonder what Esperanza did to them?*

She was also impressed with Esperanza's behavior at the market. She didn't fall for the market women's attempts to sneak in older carrots or beans, catching them and discarding the unacceptable pieces. She knew quite a bit about chickens and pork but seemed somewhat unsure when it came to selecting cuts of beef. One thing was certain, though—when the butcher tried to make a move on her, she quickly shut him down. Unlike the last cook, who flirted with every man in sight, Esperanza didn't seem to pay any attention to the men and boys at the market.

As she dried off and began dressing in clean clothes, she thought to herself, *Esperanza may not be up to the job—or maybe she is. Well, at least she doesn't drink or flirt with men. She'll be living right here, so I can keep an eye on her. I'll give her a week or two and see how she does. I have nothing to lose. I'll supervise the kitchen, give her daily menus, and teach her where needed. In the meantime, I'm getting a cheap cook—just room and board. I'm a businesswoman, and I never turn down a deal until I know it won't work.*

As she finished putting on her make-up, she said to herself, *I will watch Esperanza and help her where I can. I will also have a horchata or coffee with her mother in a day or so to find out as much as I can about my temporary cook.*

It took Esperanza over an hour to check and rinse the vegetables and then put them away. Then she prepared the luncheon fare. The kitchen maid just smirked in the corner, not offering any assistance. Doña Marta walked in just as Esperanza finished. She was genuinely pleased with the order in the kitchen and the array of food ready for lunch. She also noted how tired Esperanza looked, and she sensed that something was not quite right.

She smiled at Esperanza and asked, "Did you get any time to rest after the market?"

"Not much," she replied. "Between cleaning the vegetables, putting the food away, and preparing lunch, I was just about to ask for some time to nurse my son and freshen up."

Doña Marta screamed at the kitchen maid, "Did you help her?"

"Yes, I took the chickens to the coop," whispered the maid.

"You know it's your job to clean the vegetables and put them away—not the cook's. That's what you were hired to do. And you let Esperanza do your job? I'm tempted to fire you as well."

The kitchen maid cowered, and she knew from the look on Esperanza's face that she had made an enemy.

Doña Marta turned to Esperanza, "Thank you for helping me twice in two days. Go take a couple of hours of rest. I will hold your lunch for you while you rest and clean up."

Esperanza smiled, "Thank you," as she walked out of the kitchen. As she was exiting, she heard Doña Marta ordering the maid, "Put the *panes* and *pupusas* in the oven to warm up and prepare the *olla* for the beans. You know what your job is. Now get to it."

When she entered her room, she found her mother resting on her bed and the baby sleeping in the crib, "Mother, I think I should nurse José. I haven't fed him since before I went to the market."

"No need, my dear. Doña Marta left some powdered milk for me. I heated it on the wood stove in the kitchen while you were away, and José just gulped it down. No need to disturb him now. Just rest—you've had a busy day."

"I will take a bath first and then come back to rest."

She went to the bathroom, relieved herself on the commode, and then carefully removed her clothes. As she shook out her skirt, blouse, and underwear, she checked for fleas. She wiped her sandals with a towel before stepping under the cool water. The luxury of soaping herself felt indulgent.

As she bathed, she also assessed her situation. She had a temporary job and would not have to spend any of her small reserve on bed and board for as long as the job stretched out. It was not an easy job—long hours and real responsibility. She asked herself if she was up to doing it. She really didn't know what all those things in the kitchen were for. What is the refrigerator to hold? What is the stove that Doña Marta told the kitchen maid to use? How could she be sure that she had picked out the right spices for the dishes that Doña Marta wanted her to prepare? At the market, there were so many items she had never seen before. What were they for and how does one use them?

She pondered and then said out loud, "You have to explain to Doña Marta what you don't know and ask for her help. I can't ask that maid. She's out to get me. If I am to keep working and protect my mother and son, my only choice is to tell Doña Marta that I need her help."

It was almost three in the afternoon when Esperanza awoke and dressed. She went straight for the dining room and kitchen. Doña Marta was seated at one of the tables in the dining room, drinking a cup of coffee. She motioned for Esperanza to help herself to the leftover *pupusas, panes,* and beans. Esperanza brought her plate over to the table. Doña Marta nodded to her to sit down.

Almost as soon as she took her first bite, Esperanza admitted, "This morning, I realized just how much I don't know about being a cook. I don't really understand what everything in the kitchen is for. I've never had a refrigerator before, and I'm not even sure what to call the stove. At the market, I saw foods I've never seen, and I felt overwhelmed by the variety of meats at the butcher shop. I'm grateful for the chance to work for you, but I need your guidance—both in learning how to do the job and in organizing my work. Without your help, I'm afraid I won't be able to manage."

Doña Marta smiled inside, while she kept a poker face. All the luncheon guests had told her how delicious the luncheon had been. The new spices had improved the ordinary tastes. Whatever herbs and plants Esperanza had added to the selections on her simple menu, she didn't know. But she had also noted the improvement in the taste—and the businesswoman she was, she was going to take advantage of the situation.

She said, "Esperanza, eat your lunch now. I will work with you in preparing dinner and I will train you in the use of the items in the kitchen.

It may take us a few months to get everything in place, but I will help you."

CHAPTER 9

T he following morning, Esperanza was up at daybreak. She nursed her son, changed his diaper, and took a quick shower. In the kitchen, she gave the kitchen maid clear instructions and checked the stack of thirty-six fresh tortillas the maid had picked up from the shop around the corner. She inspected the fire in the wood-burning stove, which the maid had already lit, and tasted the beans simmering in the large *olla*. After adding some spices she had bought the day before at the Central Market, she instructed the maid to bring her the plantains and yucca and to slice them evenly for frying. Esperanza found the lard and placed some in each of the two frying pans for the plantains and yucca. She carefully selected the herbs and spices she would add as they fried. It was clear she was taking charge of the kitchen.

By the time Doña Marta entered the kitchen, Esperanza had the tray of plantains and yucca ready for the table. She also had a ceramic bowl full of beans ready. She was supervising the kitchen maid's grinding of the coffee beans to be used in the morning beverage service.

"Good morning, Doña Marta," she smiled. "I hope everything is to your satisfaction."

Doña Marta tasted the beans and was delighted by the fragrant flavor. Then, she took a cut off the plantain and then the yucca. Something new had enhanced their taste, too. She turned to Esperanza, "You added the spices you brought yesterday."

Esperanza nodded.

"Well, I certainly like the taste." She turned to the kitchen maid and said brusquely, "Go ahead, place the platters on the serving tables."

Esperanza was clearly pleased. She had prepared the meal in her way, and Doña Marta seemed pleased.

As she was leaving for the dining room, Doña Marta smiled at Esperanza and advised her, "After breakfast, I will show you around the kitchen area and answer your questions about the various appliances."

Breakfast went off without a hitch, and several guests praised Doña Marta for the flavorful food, "You added something to the beans this morning that made me take an extra helping."

Another said, "I have never tasted yucca any better than yours this morning."

Doña Marta beamed and determined to find out just what Esperanza had added.

When the last guest had checked out, Doña Marta re-entered the kitchen. "All went well today. The guests were pleased with the food."

Esperanza smiled in acknowledgment.

Doña Marta asked, "Do you want to take a rest, or are you ready for me to show you how the appliances work and answer your questions?"

"I would like to clean up and rest a bit right now, but I really want to know how to use everything in the room."

"We don't need to start preparing lunch until noon. So, why don't you take a rest for an hour or so. I'll give your mother some more powdered milk for José's midday bottle—he seems to like it. I'll be waiting for you in my office. It's the door across the hall from your room."

Esperanza nodded and left the kitchen. Doña Marta glared at the kitchen maid, "Get to work. Clean up the dishes and have everything in order when I come back in an hour." She turned and walked back to her office.

Shortly after ten, Esperanza knocked on the office door. Doña Marta closed her accounts book, rose from her desk, and walked to the door. She took Esperanza by the arm and led her back to the kitchen. She said to the kitchen maid, "You can take a rest. I am going to show Esperanza how I want the kitchen to run." The maid just turned and left as quickly as she could.

"Where do you want to begin?" asked the owner.

"Please show me how to use the stove and the refrigerator. I have never worked with them before," was the reply.

"Oh yes, they're some of the newest in the city. With the world at war, I can't replace them now, so you'll need to be extra careful when using them. Both came from the United States, the latest models from General Electric. My sons bought them for me in New Orleans just weeks before the US entered the war. In fact, they arrived only a day or two after the attack on Pearl Harbor."

Esperanza was quite surprised, as she hadn't heard about the war or Pearl Harbor. In El Nido, such events were far removed from their daily lives. Of course, she knew about the United States from her history and geography classes, and she remembered learning that New Orleans was a port in the Caribbean—she could even recall pictures of it.

Doña Marta began, "Well, the stove is electric. It is plugged into the wall. Whenever the power goes off, it stops working. You see here on top are four burners. You light each one by the dial here in front. Each dial lights a separate burner, and you can graduate the heat by turning the dial. Electricity is very expensive, so I only use the stove when I can't use the wood burner."

She took Esperanza's hand and placed it on the dial, showing her how to turn it on and adjust the temperature. "So, if you just want to warm up the tortillas, turn the dial up a little. If you need to fry yucca or plantains, turn it up higher. And to boil water, turn it all the way up."

Esperanza was flabbergasted. She had never seen anything like it. She tried to imagine how she would use it—it was so much more complicated than her usual wood burner.

Then Doña Marta opened the big door in the middle of the stove and announced, "This is the oven. You turn it on with this dial and you choose the temperature you want by moving the dial," Doña Marta demonstrated. "This oven is much better than a wood stove and you can roast and bake meat and potatoes at fixed temperatures that we can't really control on the wood stove."

Esperanza was speechless. She had no idea about the best temperature to properly cook meat or other foods. She remembered her grandmother saying low or slow, high and fast—but numerical temperatures, never. She merely commented, "Oh, Doña Marta, this stove is very complicated."

Doña Marta reassured her, "We will work together. I will show you what foods to cook on the old wood-burner and those better cooked on the electric stove. I will also tell you the right temperature for different foods." She started to move toward the refrigerator when she remembered to tell Esperanza, "I also have a roasting pit in the back area for roasting meat. You probably had one at your home in El Nido."

Esperanza sighed, "Oh yes. My grandmother taught me how to barbecue and roast meat and chicken as well as potatoes and other foods in the pit."

The refrigerator was another revelation. Esperanza was surprised by the variety of items, from meat and cheese to fruits and vegetables, that were stored in it. Doña Marta said, "The refrigerator keeps them fresh for days instead of spoiling and rotting when left out. I'll teach you how best to use the space available."

Then, Doña Marta opened the top door of the refrigerator and took out a tray divided into twelve cubes. It was ice. Esperanza had seen cubes of ice before at the grocery store near the school at the county seat, but she had never realized that they were made in a refrigerator.

Doña Marta noticed the surprise on the face of her temporary cook. She just smiled, "I will teach you how to make ice cubes and how to store them."

Then, they went to the screened-in cabinet, with several shelves. The cabinet stored most of the fruits and vegetables that they had purchased the day before. "Why don't you keep all the foods stored in the refrigerator?" asked Esperanza.

"Lack of room," responded Doña Marta. "These are the fresh items we bought yesterday. For our meals today, we will use some food from the refrigerator to avoid their spoiling, but mainly we will choose the fresh vegetables. It's a matter of avoiding as much loss as possible. You will learn in no time which food to store in the refrigerator and which to use."

Doña Marta went through all the other cabinets in the kitchen and in the small pantry between the kitchen and the dining room. Most of the shelves held plates and glasses, while a few were stocked with canned fruits and vegetables, often referred to as *del montes* in El Salvador. "It is the job of the kitchen maid to keep the dishes clean and put clean dishes and cutlery on the table. She also cleans and puts away the items we bring back from the markets. She, not the cook, cleans the floor and gets what the cook needs to work with. She is your helper—the cook tells her what to do and how to do it. You'll learn quickly. Now, take a rest. We will start lunch in about an hour. I am planning for chicken *panes* today, with some *pupusas*, a *curtido* of cabbage and carrots, and some fruit for dessert, I expect about five guests: your mother, me, and the maids. Not much to get ready. I'll give you the menu for dinner later."

As a very unsettled Esperanza took her leave, Doña Marta wearily went into the dining room to make sure that everything was in order before she took her morning rest and shower. She was really quite pleased with herself and the reaction of her new cook. Yes, she said to herself, "*I think I can train her to do it my way and keep her working for room and board for quite a few months.*"

CHAPTER 10

It was after 10:30 a.m. when Doña Marta entered her office, having just finished introducing Esperanza to the electric appliances and showing her where various food items were stored in the kitchen cabinets. She sat down at her desk to review her accounts, making notes on which guests had paid or still owed for their room and board. After glancing over the bills that needed attention, she took out her checkbook to pay some of them, while setting aside those she would pay in cash until she could open the large safe tucked behind a screen in the far corner.

Then she turned to the menus for the rest of the week. She took out yesterday's shopping list of meats, chickens, vegetables, and fruit and decided which to use over the next three days. She double-checked her occupancy schedule and estimated how much each guest might eat. She knew which ones would come back to the pension for lunch and which ones would leave early Saturday morning for home and those who would probably stay the weekend. Most of her guests went home for the weekend due to the relatively short distance between their homes and San Salvador. If they lived near the Pan-American Highway—the recently built paved lifeline—they could use the first-class bus service to make the round trip in just a few hours.

She leaned back in her chair and reflected on the events of the past five days. She remembered the bell ringing late Saturday evening, announcing the arrival of Esperanza, her mother, and her son. Her first instinct had been to turn them away, thinking her pension didn't cater to people like them. However, as she had looked at them, she had found herself saying, "Yes, I have a room available." What premonition had prompted her to do that? When she later learned they were Choarti, descendants of the great *Curandera*, she felt an obligation to return a family favor. Still, she had never imagined that Esperanza would be sent by some divine force to help her out of a kitchen crisis.

She half-smiled as she thought of the plight of Esperanza, and her rejection by her cousin Carmen—well, she had known Carmen for a few years and wasn't surprised. She was a businesswoman like herself—she had had a real rough time getting everything she has now, and she wouldn't take on a new hire, even for a relative.

Then her thoughts turned to her frustration with the still-inebriated cook and how Esperanza had stepped in last Tuesday morning to fill the gap. She remembered how well Esperanza handled the market, how overwhelmed she had seemed taking over the kitchen, and, more importantly, how good the food turned out. The guests had genuinely enjoyed the flavors of the dishes Esperanza served. Frankly, she couldn't remember the last time so many guests had praised her food.

"Maybe some special force led Esperanza to my pension," she said out loud to herself. "Well, I'm going to take advantage of her talents, and I am going to make it pay off. I'll teach her and make it last as long as possible."

Then Doña Marta got up and went into her bathroom for a leisurely shower in the warmish water of the March morning.

When she finished her toilette, she crossed the hall to the room where Esperanza and her family were staying. She knocked on the door, and Esperanza's mother answered. She put her finger to her lips and stepped out into the hall, quietly shutting the door.

"Esperanza is sleeping right now, and so is José," she said softly. "I promised to wake her when the sun is high so that she can get ready for lunch."

"When she wakes, tell her that I have the menu for dinner ready and will go over it as soon as she has prepared lunch." Then, looking at Esperanza's mother, she asked, "How are you getting along?"

"Oh, I am fine. This is such a new experience for me. I sit in the room all day watching José. The bed is comfortable. I enjoy the shower and facilities, but I am not used to sitting in a room all the time. At home, I get up at daybreak, tend to the chickens and pigs, prepare breakfast, and work on my plots—I am almost always outside and being confined to the room is not easy."

Doña Marta broke in, "Flor, you don't have to stay in the room. I have created a sitting area under the mango tree with comfortable chairs and a table. I built it for my guests, but they never seem to be around during the day to enjoy it. Please feel free to use it. I think José's cradle would fit on the table and you can watch him easily there."

Flor smiled, "I noticed the chairs under the mango tree when I looked out the window and thought how pleasant it would be out there. The room does get a bit warm during the afternoon, so I am grateful for another great favor from you. I will not cause you any problem and will come inside whenever one of the guests appears."

"I am sure that none of the guests would object to sharing the space with you. So, whenever you want, just enjoy the outdoors."

That afternoon, when lunch was over, Flor took the cradle with little José out to back open area. She was surprised at how large the space seemed, even though it was surrounded by a thick, nine-foot-high adobe-reinforced wall. The wall's top was covered with broken pieces of glass and metal to discourage intruders. As she looked to her right, she saw two small rooms that she surmised were for the maids; they were partly obscured by a couple of plantain trees, with ripening fruit. To her left, she saw the chicken coop that was near her bedroom window, with its wire fence that kept the birds in their place. She thought the arrangement under the mango tree was very inviting and thought that she would create something similar when she returned home to El Nido. She felt so cool in the shade of the mango tree and its neighbor, a tamarind. As she set the cradle on the table and sat down on the soft seat, she was delighted to see the yellow flowers of several hibiscus plants that Doña Marta had nurtured between the house and the sitting area.

As she settled into her seat, she heard the kitchen door close and looked up to see Doña Marta approaching her with the tray in hand.

Doña Marta smiled as she approached, "Esperanza has everything she needs to prepare dinner, and I decided to join you." She motioned to Flor that there was no need to get up, "I brought some horchata to keep us cool."

Doña Marta settled down on the chair next to Flor and filled two glasses, handing one to Flor, who smiled her appreciation.

After a short sip of the drink, Doña Marta commented, "I enjoy sitting out here in the afternoon. It is much cooler than being indoors. I have even become accustomed to the foul odors that come from the slaughterhouse and the animal pens a few blocks away. But they are earthly smells that one can learn to endure."

"I can't tell you how much I am enjoying sitting outside after five days in the room. The breeze is so pleasant, and the odors remind me of the times our family had a few cattle and Sunday barbecues. Those were special days."

"You seem to miss El Nido, even though you have come to the capital."

"Oh yes," Flor replied, "I had never spent a night anywhere but in El Nido until last Saturday night. I always thought that I would live and die in my village and be buried for eternal life there."

"Well, why did you leave?" further queried Doña Marta.

"It was Esperanza's doing. She saw no future for her son and herself after her terrible attack."

Dona Marta put down her glass and asked, "Attack?"

"Yes," continued Flor in a low, matter-of-fact tone. "You see, she wanted to be a teacher. She completed all the eight grades at the school in our county seat. In fact, she was at the top of her class. She had taken the entrance tests for the Chalatenango City High School and did so well that she was offered a scholarship."

Flor paused to take a drink. "Well," she continued, "She was very excited and arranged to visit the school and interview a lady who offered to provide room and board during the school year. The director of the high school approved her application and talked to her about becoming a teacher. Then. she visited the lady in whose home she was to live. She was so happy."

Doña Marta noted, "I wanted to go to that high school but did not pass the entrance exam."

Flor tapped Doña Marta's hand, as she lamented, "Our family fortunes had dropped so badly that I could only complete the first four grades. With only my brother and me left at home, I had to join my brother in working the fields and tending the animals when our father died."

Doña Marta touched Flor's hand this time. "Flor, tell me about the attack."

"Coming back from Chalatenango City, it was almost dark when she got off the bus and started to walk toward El Nido. Then, some drunken man jumped out of the brush, knocked her down, ripped off her panties and raped her. I suspect that she was so surprised that she did even realize what was happening. When she got home, she was badly-shaken. I tried to clean her up, even made poultices of herbs and plants to clean out her innards, as my great-grandmother had taught me, but to no avail. That drunk had impregnated her in season, and the baby took shape."

"When she went to the priest and school director, they blamed her for having sinned. They didn't believe that she had been raped. That was almost more terrible for her than the rape itself. She became bitter and decided that she did not want to live any longer in El Nido. In fact, I think she even thought about taking her life. So, I talked to my brother who owns the neighboring farm. He and his sons agreed to take care of mine, and I agreed to accompany Esperanza and her baby to wherever she chose to live. She chose San Salvador and here we are."

Doña Marta quietly absorbed Flor's words. "You have explained much about Esperanza. I knew she was intelligent from our first meeting last Saturday night. Now I understand her disappointment—and the reason for her being so driven to succeed. As young as she is, she has suffered deeply. Thank you for telling me."

Flor added. "You know, Doña Marta, my mother was the *Gran Curandera's* star pupil. She saw in Esperanza talents that I certainly don't have. She made certain Esperanza went to school. She saw to it that Esperanza joined her every day to learn about herbs and plants. She taught her how to use them in cooking and healing. When she died several years ago, she urged me to educate Esperanza because she had promised. So, I am trying to carry out my mother's request."

After sipping her horchata, Doña Marta said, "Saturday night you said my face was familiar. In fact you did see me several years ago when I took my husband to El Nido. He was gravely ill, and I hoped that your family still had the powers of the *Gran Curandera*. Your mother tried, but she couldn't cure my husband. We saw each other then. I think I also recognized you in the hall last Saturday night."

The two women sat quietly in the yard, drinking horchata until Doña Marta said, "Flor, I must prepare for dinner. The maids don't do anything unless I rouse them." As she started to get up, she saw Esperanza in the door of the kitchen calling for the kitchen maid to come to work. She turned to Flor, "Well, that's something I didn't expect. I'll take a look. I may even be back."

CHAPTER 11

T hat evening Esperanza prepared the menu that Doña Marta had given her without missing a beat. She prepared a *sopa de res*, with tenderized beef, diced potatoes, carrots and green beans, a *curtido* of cabbage and carrots, a specially flavored pot of beans and warmed tortillas that the ten guests ate with gusto. They complimented Doña Marta.

Doña Marta smiled not only for the compliments but also for the lack of pressure on her during its preparation. Esperanza had pressed the maids to help her prepare the food and get it on the table. She sensed the tension in the kitchen from the maids who were not happy taking orders from someone younger than they—and someone who insisted that they do as she ordered. *Well, I'll think about that tomorrow,* she said to herself. *Tonight the dinner was fit for a first-class hotel.*

Friday passed without incident. Esperanza was up at dawn and had breakfast on table without any instructions from Doña Marta. Lunch was routine, with only one or two guests coming back to eat. Once Doña Marta went over the menu with Esperanza, she took over and cracked the whip to prepare it and have it on the table on time. Doña Marta sensed that she might have to talk to Esperanza about how to deal with the maids tomorrow.

Doña Marta took Esperanza to the Central Market again on Saturday. Doña Marta and Esperanza carefully inspected all the remaining food on hand and made a list of what would be needed for the next three to four days. Doña Marta went to the bathroom while Esperanza got into the car. It was the same taxi as on Wednesday.

As Esperanza settled into the front seat, Chico, the driver quickly placed a hand on her knee. She knocked it away and sneered, "If you ever touch me again, I will use my knife on you." She took a large kitchen knife from under skirt and looked sternly at him and said, "I mean what I say."

The driver looked at her for only a split second before moving his hand back onto his own lap.

"Okay, don't blame me for trying," he managed to get out. He then looked straight ahead. Esperanza had established her relationship with the driver.

Doña Marta emerged a short time later. She settled herself in the back seat, "Chico, let's go. I want to get to the market before all the food has been picked over."

Then, she advised Esperanza, "I have only six guests who have reserved rooms for next week. I don't plan on having any guests for Sunday lunch or dinner tomorrow. I will be eating at my son's house Sunday afternoon, so we need not buy as much as we did Wednesday."

Esperanza cut in, "I checked all the food on hand in the kitchen and there is enough for the guests, the maids and my family through Monday breakfast."

"Are you sure Esperanza? Usually, we run out of food on Saturday."

"Yes, I am sure. If I remember what you told me yesterday, the maids will be off Sunday morning and return in the evening. That means I will only need to prepare meals for my family, and there is plenty to meet our needs."

The market routine was much the same as Wednesday's, except this time Esperanza carefully inspected each item the market women offered, making sure no leftovers were slipped into Doña Marta's baskets. Doña

Marta watched her closely, noticing how naturally Esperanza interacted with the women. Over the years, Doña Marta had learned that when the market women respected you, you received their best produce at a fair price—and Esperanza, almost instinctively, was doing everything to earn that respect.

When they reached the meat area of the market, Doña Marta greeted her long-time butcher and began looking over the available cuts of beef. Esperanza came up to her and said quietly in her ear, "The pork looks extremely good, and the price is well below the per kilo price for beef. You can change your menus and save some money, since there will be so few guests next week. My grandmother taught me several recipes for pork, and, with the herbs and spices we now have in the kitchen, I think I can prepare meals that your guests and you will enjoy."

Doña Marta was indeed surprised because none of the cooks she had hired over the years had ever bothered to help her save money. They usually encouraged her to buy more so that they could smuggle some of it out when they left for home on Sunday mornings. She followed Esperanza to the counter full of pork cuts and looked over the meat and the prices. She said quietly to Esperanza, "You are sure that you can prepare the dishes?"

"Yes, and I can use the pork in *pupusa* and a breakfast sausage."

When they left the market, Doña Marta had spent a good deal less than she had expected. She was quite pleased with herself and, frankly, very surprised by her teenage cook.

The following morning, after breakfast, the maids left for home with their pockets empty. Esperanza had given them small packages of food to take with them and made sure that they did not have access to the items purchased the day before. The new cook had made three enemies, because the maids usually went home with a couple of days' worth of food for their families.

Doña Marta had Sunday dinner with her two sons and their families at the home of the elder one. She loved her family and her grandchildren, but she saw them only once a week. Her sons wanted her to sell the pension and retire. Her older son had an apartment set aside for her, but Doña Marta loved her independence and wasn't really sure her daughter-in-law was eager to have underfoot.

When her son pressed her once again to consider retiring, Doña Marta smiled and replied, "I'm not sure this is the time. A new cook arrived last weekend from El Nido—you know, one of the villages near La Palma, where the *curandera* lived, the one who saved my mother's life. She came with her mother and baby son. For some reason, I don't know why, I let them stay. Her name is Esperanza Vasquez Choarti."

Doña Marta then recounted the young cook's story, adding, "A family member told her about my pension, so she brought her family here while she looked for a job as a cook."

Taking a sip of wine, Doña Marta continued, "She started looking last Monday but didn't have any luck. She even tried her cousin Carmen's restaurant near the Central Market but came home very disappointed. I should have warned her about Carmen. You know, money is thicker than blood."

She smiled and shook her head. "Anyway, Tuesday at 5:30 a.m., my cook showed up drunker than usual. I fired her on the spot, and Esperanza stepped in, working in exchange for room and board. She knows by heart the traditional recipes of her people in Chalatenango, which she learned from her grandmother, a daughter of the *curandera*. So far, my guests have been pleased with her cooking. She's a quick learner and has been a great help at the Central Market. She might just keep me going for a few more years."

Doña Marta smiled at her children and continued, "No, my children, I appreciate your concern because of my age, but I am pleased to have Esperanza and her family with me, and I will stay a bit longer at my sanctuary in Soyapango."

CHAPTER 12

It was just 5:30 a.m. the following Monday when Doña Marta opened the kitchen door and saw Esperanza hard at work preparing breakfast. As she looked around the room, she said, "Good morning, Esperanza. Where is your helper?"

"Good morning, Doña Marta. She and I had a disagreement, and I sent her to her room."

"What happened?"

"I found her stuffing spoiled pieces of yucca and overripe plantains on the platters for breakfast," replied Esperanza.

Doña Marta paused, "Well, I thought all those items would have disappeared yesterday when the maids went home. You see, I always buy a little more than I need when I go to the market, and then on Saturdays, I put whatever we didn't use on the bottom shelf of the refrigerator and in the vegetable bin—in three little stacks, one for each maid. They always take a little extra, but I expect that. In a way, those little packages save me from having to raise their wages."

"Doña Marta, I didn't know. I scolded them when I found them taking food out of the refrigerator and made them put it back."

Doña Marta reassured Esperanza, "You didn't know my plan, but now you do. I will talk to the maids and arrange to give them something to take to their families in the next couple of days. We have only five expected guests this week, so I'll give each one an extra afternoon off and leave around some food for them to take to their families."

Doña Marta smiled and began helping Esperanza prepare the platters for the dining room. Then, she stepped out the back door to the maids' quarters and brought the kitchen maid back, getting both the maid and the cook working together again.

When breakfast was over, Esperanza made her way through the dining room to her bedroom. She noticed that someone had left the daily paper on the table. She picked up the issue of *El Diario de Hoy* and read the headline, "The Japanese Take Manila." She was totally taken by surprise. Up until that terrible day on which she was raped, she had kept up with the war in Europe. It had been discussed at school, and she had known about the fall of France and the Battle of Britain. Now there was war in the Pacific and Asia—not merely just in Europe. She sat down and read the paper, page by page.

While she was reading, Doña Marta came out of her quarters in search of an invoice. She saw Esperanza reading the paper and asked, "What is new?"

"Oh, excuse me, but I saw the paper. We have had so little news in El Nido this last year. It was not like going to school every day where we tried to keep up with the news. I lost touch with what is going on in the world."

Doña Marta asked, "How long has it been since you saw a newspaper?"

Esperanza thought, "It must have been the day I went to Chalatenango City. I read the one in the director's office while I waited. That was in January 1941 and now it is March 1942. My goodness, I've lost a full year."

Doña Marta mused. "A lot has happened. Germany attacked Russia, Japan attacked the United States, El Salvador entered the war on the side of the United States. You didn't know we are at war. All the world is involved. I'll tell you about the year you lost when I have some time.

Right now, I must get my books caught up. You finish reading the paper. We'll talk later."

Esperanza said, "A lot has happened since I left school. Do you mind if I read the newspaper every day? When I was in school, I tried to read one whenever it was available."

Doña Marta smiled as she turned back to her suite, "Of course, Esperanza. It comes every day. Keep up with the news. I think you will find that the market ladies with whom we do business two or three times a week know as much about national news as the newspaper reporters."

The small-town girl from a village with no radio or electricity found herself reading the newspaper from cover to cover, beginning to appreciate how much she had missed during the terrible year since the rape and José's birth.

Doña Marta patched over the hard feelings of the maids toward Esperanza, but they never warmed up to her nor she to them. Esperanza was eager to learn, and they were content to get by. She chided them when they repeated mistakes or overlooked chores; they resented her badgering. That uneasy peace hung over the kitchen as Doña Marta spent hours teaching Esperanza how to operate the electric stove and properly keep the refrigerator functioning. The kitchen maid smoldered inside because Doña Marta had never spent much time with her when she was hired. She was jealous—she couldn't see the potential profits that Doña Marta saw from the cooking talents of her latest hire.

CHAPTER 13

The following weeks at the pension were a time of adjustment for Esperanza. Doña Marta carefully guided her through the use of the kitchen's modern conveniences: what to store in the refrigerator, how to operate the electric burners and oven, and the best ways to keep fruits and vegetables fresh while protecting them from rodents and roaches.

She helped her put all her spices into glass jars, with labels noting their names. Doña Marta systematically asked about how to use each one to enhance the flavor of the foods on the menu. Doña Marta noted how many guests told her how much they enjoyed their meals and, as a businesswoman, was pleased with her investment.

Doña Marta also found herself enjoying her relationship with the Choarti family. Almost every afternoon, she joined Esperanza's mother and son in the backyard. She estimated she was about ten years older than Flor and clearly more educated and experienced, but Flor was genuine—reminiscent of her own mother and the people she had grown up with in La Palma. With Flor, she could quietly discuss her own problems without fear of judgment or gossip.

It was now late April and San Salvador was approaching summer and the rainy season. On its 2000-foot plateau, San Salvador never suffered tropical heat, but became warmish, especially in the confines of the family room at the pension. Sitting under the tree in the backyard was a daily treat, both for Flor and Doña Marta. Each afternoon, Doña Marta brought out the pitcher of horchata.

Flor would say, "How nice of you. It is so much more pleasant here than in the room. The breeze is soft, and I have come to live with the aroma of the stockyard, but I remember the sweet air of El Nido."

Doña Marta would shake her head and comment, "I've been here so long that I can hardly remember the air in La Palma. Here is like the only reality I seem to remember. I guess I'm just used to it."

This afternoon, as Flor sipped her glass, she asked, "Why did you leave La Palma? Your family was well known. I recall, as a little girl, hearing your family name. I'm not sure but I think it was in connection with the purchase of our indigo crop. My that was a long time ago."

"Yes, Flor, you are right. My father and then my husband worked for the company that purchased the indigo crop in our region. Our ties go back a long time. It was because of the indigo that my grandfather took my mother to your grandmother, the great *curandera*, for the cure that saved her life. Yes, I guess that is why when I heard the name Choarti that I offered your family a room in the pension."

Flor cut in, "You had never told me that before."

"Well, I had never really thought about it before. Anyway, while the indigo business was profitable, our family did well. You see, my great-grandfather came from Galicia as a contract laborer to work on an indigo plantation for the company. He educated his children, and the company hired them in the office. My mother married an indigo company accountant, and they lived quite comfortably in La Palma until after World War I, when the indigo company closed its doors. My husband worked for a farm machinery company whose primary customers were farmers who raised indigo. When the indigo business dried up, his company transferred him to San Salvador. We came here over thirty years ago."

Flor asked, "Have you always lived here in Soyapongo?"

"No. When we first came to San Salvador, we lived downtown not far from the cathedral, in a house owned by the farm machinery company. I had my three children there—my two sons who now live in San Salvador and my daughter who died in childbirth in Santa Ana. My husband bought this building in the 1920's to be the headquarters of his own business. He planned to import American-made machinery for the coffee *fincas* when the great depression struck. All we had was this building, three teenagers, and no money. The pressure killed him. I took him to El Nido when the doctors here said there was no hope."

Doña Marta paused and took a sip of horchata before continuing. "When he died, I brought the children here and kept us alive running the pension. I managed and cooked. I sent the children to school every day and had them do chores for taking care of our guests before and after school. We had several tough years, but everything turned out well. My daughter met a wonderful businessman from Santa Ana who was a regular guest here—a very happy marriage until her death. The two boys got good jobs—one in real estate and the other with his father's old farm machinery business. And I ran the pension to bring in money to keep us all going through the bad times."

Flor observed, "Doña Marta, I so admire you. You were able to save your family during difficult times. I wish I had your powers. I remember the good times of my early years before the sacred indigo lost its value. Then, not only did the indigo die in the field, but we lost our last shaman, my great-uncle, and our great *curandera*, my grandmother. They tried to pass their powers to my uncle and my mother, but that didn't happen. As the story of the great shaman predicted, when the last shaman dies, the people of El Nido will die with him. Oh, my mother and uncle tried, but they didn't have the powers. You, Doña Marta, do."

Doña Marta responded with a hand on Flor's shoulder. "Now, we do what we must do. Let us hope that El Nido finds its way."

Flor confided, "Esperanza was my hope. You know, my grandmother taught my mother all about the herbs and plants and how to use them in curing people and making our simple food taste special. My mother was taught all the cures, but did not have the powers to use them. She could use the plants and herbs in cooking but not in curing. I have had six children—my oldest son Diego, four babies who died and then my sixth, Esperanza. It was my mother who named her. My mother's cures did not save my four babies, but she put all her faith in my sixth. Esperanza was a healthy baby, and my mother took charge of her."

Flor took a sip of horchata and then continued, "Esperanza is so unlike me—I never liked school or even learning from my mother about plants and herbs. I only wanted to tend the chickens and pigs and work in the field with the boys. After the fourth grade, I left school and was content to just stay around our village. That's how I met my husband when I was 14. We had no *colones* to give the church for our wedding, so my uncle married us according to the old traditions. I loved being with my husband and wept each time a child died. My mother tried everything she knew to save them. For my sixth, she told me that it would be a daughter and that her name should be Esperanza because she would be the hope of our people. And she was smart. My mother taught her all about herbs and plants. She was the star pupil at the county school—she never tired of learning. My mother died when Esperanza was ten, and she made me and my husband promise to keep her in school no matter the cost. My mother said that she would be the teacher of our family and people."

Doña Marta was surprised when Flor, who seldom spoke more than a few words at time, continued, "Esperanza had earned a scholarship to high school when she was raped. Her decision to leave El Nido hurt me deeply. My husband and I had to send our only living son from El Nido in search of a job. We had none in our village. He came home for a couple of years and shared his earnings with us, but he didn't come home two years ago when his father was ill. Now I have lost him and his father. And, when my Esperanza said that there was no hope for us in El Nido, I thought that I would die, but to follow her and take care of José as she is all I have left."

The two ladies just looked at each other. Flor said, "Now, I am almost glad that Esperanza brought us here. This new life is so strange. Please excuse me Doña Marta. I know that we are not of the same class, but I feel quite comfortable talking with you."

"You know, Flor, having you here has been a help to me. You and I have become friends, and watching José reminds me of when I watched my own children. Esperanza has eased some of my kitchen worries, though she still has a lot to learn. Life is tough for women, especially with so few jobs for us in this country."

José began fussing. Flor said, "I must go in. He needs changing again."

CHAPTER 14

It had been only three months since Esperanza rang the bell at the pension and Doña Marta welcomed them as guests—three months in which circumstances aligned to provide Doña Marta with the cook she had hoped to find and gave Esperanza a foundation on which to build a new life. The two seemed to complement each other perfectly.

Esperanza was learning what it meant to be a cook in the city. She quickly realized that the knowledge she brought with her from El Nido was not enough to secure a job in this new environment. Grateful for Doña Marta's guidance, she often thanked her gods that fate had led her to this woman at this time of her life. She was learning how to use an electric stove, properly maintain a refrigerator, and handle food with the care required in a modern kitchen. Determined to master these new skills and recipes, Esperanza appreciated Doña Marta's patience and teaching.

Doña Marta, who had trained many cooks in the fifteen years since her husband's death, saw something different in Esperanza. It wasn't just her youth or ambition—she was smart, eager to learn, and quick to absorb every word of instruction, following directions with precision. While Esperanza sometimes took charge—like a bull in a china shop—and her relationships with the maids were often chaotic, Doña Marta believed these issues could be managed over time. She dared to hope that she had finally found a cook she could truly depend on.

The routine was grueling. Esperanza was up at dawn to prepare breakfast. After an hour break, she was back preparing lunch. After two to three hours of rest, she was preparing dinner. Two to three times a week, she joined Doña Marta on the trip to the market and bargained for each and every item of food they bought. That bargaining included learning not only the cost of everything in the market but also each market woman, her personal life, her children, and her views of the local politics and the state of the economy. Doña Marta had learned over the years not only to survive but to prosper from what she learned from the market ladies.

One afternoon during that third month, Doña Marta called Esperanza into her office. She said, "I believe we'll be working together for quite some time, and it's time for you to take on more responsibility. I want you to help me plan the daily menus and prepare the market lists. I know how many guests we'll have over the next few days, and you've learned enough about their preferences to help me estimate the food we'll need. You can also suggest any changes to the menus that might appeal to them.

"You see, I have to be very careful with my spending to keep this place running—I can't afford mistakes. I'm asking for your help, and not just with the cooking or accompanying me to the market."

"Yes, thank you," nodded Esperanza.

"Here are my menus and my list of purchases. Look them over," said Doña Marta as she handed Esperanza several pages of hand-written notes. "These are my menus for the rest of the week, and what we need is on my market list. Look them over and tell me if my estimates of food look right. If you have suggestions to change menus or the market list, let me know now."

Esperanza carefully read the menus first, and she pointed out various changes she thought made sense. She suggested dropping some items, pointing out that they had been eaten at prior lunches or dinners. She also suggested changing some items from one day's menu to another because she thought the dishes might go better together.

Doña Marta considered each one of the suggestions and found most were sound and nodded her head. "Esperanza, I should have thought of those changes myself." Then the two ladies scoured the market list and made the necessary changes in produce and amounts. "I think we may have saved ourselves some money."

Doña Marta looked up at the clock and said, "It's time to get to the market before all of the good stuff is sold. Today I am going to give you another lesson in getting the best price possible. Don't merely check the produce for me but listen to how I deal with market women. I know them and they know me. We have been bargaining together for many years. I want you to know them and see how to bargain with them on terms they understand. Now get your *rebozo* and we'll head to the market."

When they reached the market, Doña Marta resumed her role as employer. She pointed to one of the boys standing near the front door and said, "You, yes you, come over here. You did a good job for me last week. Yes, I recognize you. Come here, you can help me today." He came running and picked up the baskets in the trunk of the car.

Doña Marta said quietly to Esperanza, "Remember, I want you to watch me carefully today."

Then, she strode into the main entrance of the market. The market woman at the large front stand called, "Doña Marta, I have some beautiful fresh chayote and beans from Coyapeque. Just right for you."

"Oh, good, I'll be by there later."

Another woman in a small stand to the left said, "Doña Marta, I have some oranges and melons just arrived from Antigua—just what your guests like."

"Very well. I'll be back."

As she walked up the aisle, Esperanza noted every gesture and greeting that Doña Marta made. She watched as if she had never seen the performance before. In prior weeks, she had been an assistant. Today, she was preparing to engage with a social center where knowing the people was just as important as the purchases she made.

Doña Marta finally stopped at a stand close to the back of the market and began looking over the cabbages, chayote, carrots and squash. Luisa, the seller, said, "Dona Marta everything is fresh from the fields today."

"Looks a day old to me," was the expected retort.

"How can you say that?" Luisa replied. "I picked it out myself at dawn this morning."

Doña Marta holding up a cabbage, asked, "How much?"

"How many do you want?" asked Luisa.

Turning to Esperanza, "How many do you think we will need for the next three days for *curtidos* and *sopas*?"

Esperanza felt the thickness of the cabbage and said, "With only five guests, I think two will do."

The market woman said, "For two, 40 *centavos* each one."

"That's highway robbery," replied Doña Marta. Looking down at the back of the stall, she continued, "I see the little ones are better. I see your girl looking up at me from the back of the stall."

"Oh, yes, she is better today. The syrup you suggested last week was good, and she is almost over the cough. Fortunately, her brother didn't catch it. I always appreciate your help." Then, looking back at the cabbages, she continued, "Well, if you buy two, you can have them for 35 *centavos* each."

"I know you need the money for the children. So, just because of that, I'll pay you 90 *centavos* for three."

The market woman looked dejected and then said, "I can't make a profit at that price. What else are you buying?"

"Oh, I have my regular list," said Doña Marta.

"Well then," said the market woman, "You're cheating me, but all right. Three for 90 *centavos*."

The same ritual unfolded with each purchase—carrots, green beans, chayote, and squash. With every item, Doña Marta introduced a new topic: the latest gossip from the president's office, the growing list of politicos in need of loans, or the whispered love affairs between military officers and market vendors.

When she got to the next stand that sold black and kidney beans, the particularly handsome young woman greeted Doña Marta with a big smile, "Good morning, Doña Marta."

"You look very happy this morning. Are you and that handsome lieutenant enjoying life?"

"Oh, yes, he is a fine man. He is very generous."

"Are you using the protection I told you about? You know you can't afford to have another child. He'll leave just like the last one did when you got pregnant. I'm not sure I can help a second time. You know I'm getting older, and business isn't doing well with fewer salesmen coming into the city because of the war."

"Yes, dear friend, I am taking precautions. I am using that IUD you told me about." She squeezed Doña Marta's hand.

Doña Marta asked Esperanza how many kilos of beans she thought she might need. Esperanza looked at her and requested a kilo or two less than she expected to need. "Only that little?" asked the young market woman.

"Well, I guess that will be plenty." They then quibbled over the price for a kilo or two until Doña Marta agreed to buy three or four kilos at a reduced price.

As they were about to leave the stand, the young lady whispered to Doña Marta, "The lieutenant told me last night that the Americans are going to set up a base at our airport and will soon send a detachment here."

"Oh," noted Doña Marta.

"Yes, you know the lieutenant's colonel is making the arrangements for the advanced group. The Americans always have money, and maybe they'll need a place to stay while they build their base."

Doña Marta smiled, "I know your lieutenant's colonel quite well. Thank you for the information. See you next week and do take care." She discreetly slipped a few extra *colones* to the young lady.

As usual, the final stop was the meat section toward the back of the market. On the way, Doña Marta asked Esperanza, "Have you ever roasted beef or pork?"

"I have roasted pig on the spit outside and cooked some loins over the wood stove. But I don't know if that's what you mean by roasted. I've never used the electric stove for roasting anything."

"All right, Esperanza, I'm going to buy some beef. You can make a soup and a stew. We'll see if it's tender enough to roast after we marinate it and add some of your herbs and spices. That colonel loves roast beef, and I want to train you to make roast beef and roast potatoes for a special meal. I'm planning it for that lieutenant's colonel."

Then Doña Marta led her party back to the main entrance, with the market lad carrying their baskets and burlap bags full of produce. Before she left, she stopped at the stand with oranges and melons. She bargained for a half dozen oranges and three melons, which she would serve as dessert for the next two nights. She also bought some carrots and green beans from the lady at the first stand to the right of the main entrance. As she led her party through the entrance, she commented to Esperanza, "That lady at the door is the most powerful woman in the market. She assigns the women their stalls every day. She is the mistress of the manager of the market. As long as she is his mistress, she has her spot. All the women know. And, if the manager tires of her and gets a new mistress, the faces change, but the order in the market remains the same. Each market may be a little different, but make sure you know who the top dog is and make sure that you never slight her."

Esperanza was learning. The size of the market, the variety of foods, and the tricks of the trade had been a lot to take in, but seeing the other side of market life was something she hadn't expected. Doña Marta was now becoming her teacher in the art of surviving in this new urban environment.

CHAPTER 15

Once back at the pension, Doña Marta sat Esperanza down and spoke to her almost maternally. "My dear, I've decided to keep you on as my cook. I will teach you everything I know about cooking and managing a kitchen. We're only at the beginning of the process. You've seen how useful and complex the electric appliances are, and how important the buying process at the Central Market is to running both the kitchen and the pension. This is just the start. If you have any reservations, tell me now. I'll let you stay until you find another job if you're unsure. But if you have no doubts, then plan on staying with me for some time."

"Doña Marta, I had no idea how tough coming to the city would be. I just knew there was no life for me in El Nido. I want to learn from you how to survive in the city. I promise to stay with you and do my best."

"Then we have a lot of work ahead of us," continued Doña Marta. "First, I want to get your mother, José, and you settled in permanent quarters. Taking care of José will become a more difficult job as he begins to teethe and learns to walk. We can't have his teething keeping up the guests, and we can't have the pension smelling of baby. Let me think."

Thinking out loud, Doña Marta said, "I don't want to create more problems for you with the other maids. I don't want them to begin asking me to allow their mothers and children to stay here because your mother and child are here. You don't like each other now, and I don't want it to get any worse."

"Yes, Doña Marta," a surprised Esperanza chimed in.

"Esperanza, I will talk to my son who is in the real estate business and see what we can work out. Meanwhile your mother, José, and you stay in your current room. I'll find a solution."

Doña Marta then looked at Esperanza and blurted out, "We will need to get some appropriate clothes. You can't continue to look like a country bumpkin. You are my cook now. My dressmaker will come over later this week, and I'll have her make some uniforms for you—maybe a dress or two for you and your mother. We'll see how much they will cost and how you can cover their cost."

Then she ran her eyes down to the sandals on Esperanza's feet, "Those sandals won't hold up for long. We will need to get some better sandals or maybe work shoes."

Esperanza looked at the sandals that she had bought at the store in the county seat before her trip to Chalatenango City. They indeed were beginning to tear apart at the seams.

"Esperanza," continued Doña Marta, "I want you to know how difficult it is for a girl to get a job in San Salvador. The only ones are for maids and prostitutes, unless you have a high school degree or a friend. Well, I have made you my friend. When you stepped in that Tuesday morning, you helped me at a critical time. Your help at the market is turning out well. I am giving you this job because you earned it. But you must earn it again and again by your performance. You can lose my friendship and your job if you cross me or cause me unnecessary problems."

Doña Marta looked squarely into Esperanza's eyes. "We all make mistakes. If you make one, just let me know. What I never tolerate is lying and cheating. If you need something, tell me. Never steal anything from me. You are a smart young girl whom I can help. In fact, I have come to like having you and Flor around. That can change easily if you lie to me or cheat. And I am not a forgiving person. Just remember those simple rules, and we will get along fine."

Esperanza acknowledged Doña Marta's words with a nod of her head and said, "I understand and appreciate the opportunity you are giving me." She smiled and left the office to clean up before she went to the kitchen to prepare lunch.

Doña Marta took out her ledger and began noting the costs of the food and other supplies she had purchased earlier. She went over her original lists and made sure that everything had been purchased at or below the price she expected to pay. Then she carefully entered them into her ledger. Above everything else, she was a businesswoman.

Doña Marta looked up from her ledger and smiled at the pictures of her three children—her two sons and a daughter. "Yes," she said to herself, "I reared them as a widow and protected them as best I could."

Looking at the photo of her late husband, who had passed away on the eve of the Great Depression, Doña Marta spoke softly, "My dear, you left me to provide for our family, and for the past fifteen years, I've poured every bit of my ingenuity into making it work. I think you would be proud. Both of our boys are in business and doing well. Our beautiful daughter—Jesus rest her soul—had a happy marriage before she died in childbirth.

"Now, I'm taking a bit of a gamble. I see a chance to help Esperanza and turn a profit in the process. It may succeed, or it may not—but it feels worth the risk."

Then, she picked up the phone and asked the operator to connect with her son, the manager of a construction and real estate business. The phone rang twice before he picked up.

"Ricardo, this is mother."

"Hello, dear, is everything alright?" he replied.

"Ricardo, you remember last Sunday at dinner, I told your brother and you about the young girl from El Nido? Well, I decided to keep her on. She has been making excellent meals. Her use of spices and herbs gives an extra dimension to the food. She is smart and a quick learner. And I can hire her at a very comfortable wage, little more than room and board for the next few months. Well, if I keep her, I have a problem of what to do with her mother and son. I don't want to set a precedent for any future maid or cook to expect that I would allow them to bring their parents or children to live at the pension. And I can't let the cook, her mother, and son live in one of the guest rooms much longer. I will need it for business."

"I see you have a problem. What do you want me to do to help?"

"Well, is one of the apartments in San Judas available?" asked Doña Marta.

"Mother, your young cook could not afford to rent a unit. I'm asking 230 *colones* a month. You'd have to pay your cook a lot more than you plan."

"Well, Ricardo, do you have any ideas?"

"I'll come by tomorrow morning, and we can talk. I'll do some thinking about a solution. You want to keep your cook, pay her as little as possible, and use her food to expand your business. I get your plan, don't I, Mom?"

"You take after your father!" Doña Marta intoned. "What time tomorrow?"

"How about 1:00 p.m.? I'm working on a building job in Escalón in the morning, but with the usual afternoon rains this time of year, I'll be wrapping up around noon."

"Fine. You can stay for lunch."

CHAPTER 16

Ricardo arrived about 1:30 p.m. for lunch. Doña Marta had Esperanza prepare a typical lunch—nothing special. She helped Esperanza use the electric stove for a *sopa de res* and a simple *curtido*, with *pupusas* on the side, and some fruit for dessert.

Ricardo ate his lunch with gusto and said quietly to his mother, "This is better tasting food than Carmen serves in her restaurant downtown. Your country girl is a jewel."

"I am glad you agree. Now, I need your help to keep her here."

Doña Marta went into the kitchen and told Esperanza that she had enjoyed the meal. She brought the young girl into the dining room to meet her son. Esperanza was very shy when she was introduced. Doña Marta said, "Just clean up and rest for the afternoon."

"Thank you," said Esperanza as she returned to the kitchen.

Then Ricardo and Doña Marta moved from the dining room to her office.

Ricardo said, "Mother, you have a money-maker, and you need to keep her under your roof as long as possible. If Carmen or the chef at the Astoria tastes her cooking, you'll have to fight to keep her. She is young, new to city ways, and dependent on you. Let's try to keep it that way for a while."

"But Ricardo, I have to avoid problems with the other maids. They don't like Esperanza, and Esperanza doesn't trust them. Whatever I do, I have to avoid a blowup in the kitchen."

"I agree with you that you cannot keep the cook and her family in one of the guest rooms. So, let's see what we can work out in the servant quarters."

He took his mother's hand, and they walked from her office through the dining room and kitchen to the area in which the maid's rooms were located. To the right of the door, which Doña Marta locked every night after dinner, were three small rooms and a bath. Two of the rooms housed the maids, and each one held two cots, a table, and two chairs. The third was a storage area. Ricardo looked them over carefully, and then led his mother back to her office.

"Well, Mother, as a construction adviser, let me help solve your problem. It might cost you a couple of thousand *colones*, and I'll do it for that, but I can redo the three rooms and build another bathroom that should make all your staff happy. I can open up one of the maids' rooms with a couple of windows, fix up a few broken armoires from storage, and paint the tables and chairs. I can move the inside walls of the maid's room and add a quarter of the storage space to the second maid's room so that the cook and her family can fit in there. I can get the job done in a week—and I have nothing scheduled next week because I'm waiting on materials for the house in San Benito from my supplier in Guatemala. Now, I guess the rest of the problem is yours."

"What do you mean, 'the rest of the problem'? I already have a big problem just trying to find the money to pay you a couple of thousand *colones* to help your mother out."

"Don't try to bargain with me, Mother. I know you too well. You know I'll do the job, and I'll add value to your property, no question. Your real problem is explaining to your maids why you are letting the mother and child stay. What you're saving by not paying Esperanza will just about cover the costs. And you'll have your guest room to rent."

He paused and looked at his mother's face almost burst into a smile. "Well, think of something the mother can do so that you put her on the payroll, and explain to the maids that you hired Esperanza as the cook and her mother for some other job."

Doña Marta's face burst into a full smile now. "Ricardo, you are a genius. I can hire her as my garden assistant. She can take care of the chickens, and we'll try a small home garden. Flor has told me that those were her chores in El Nido. She can do them for me here while she looks after José. Yes, you are a genius."

The work started not the following Monday, but Wednesday. Ricardo arrived with one carpenter and a laborer. No one bothered to prepare any plans or specs, Ricardo just told the laborer to clear out the storage area and the carpenter to tear down the existing interior wall, cut the size of one of the maids' room in half, put up a new wall, and line the walls of the storage area with shelves. Doña Marta then supervised the carpenter and workman.

A week passed before work began on building the new quarters for Esperanza and her family—a room with four windows for cross-ventilation and a wall of shelves to store their belongings. The wall separating the new room from the maids' room was replaced, which increased the space for the three maids by a quarter. Then the walls were repaired and whitewashed, and the restored armoires, chairs, and tables were painted. The three maids moved their cots and possessions into the new room while their original quarters were being fixed.

The work on the new room was finished the following Monday when a couple of laborers showed up to put in the windows and repair holes in the walls. On Tuesday, the carpenter returned to divide the room into three cubicles with shelves that allowed each maid her own storage area and some privacy.

It was in the fourth week that the carpenter completed the work. Then, Ricardo brought in a plumber to put in a second commode and shower, and he had his carpenter build a wall between the two facilities.

It took a month to complete the job that Ricardo had promised his mother to do in a week. And Doña Marta oversaw every piece of the operation and made sure that the work coincided with the images in her mind.

When the work was finished, Ricardo presented a bill to his mother that he said was mainly for labor. Doña Marta just smiled as she paid him. She knew that most of the lumber and other supplies had been paid for by the owner of the house under construction in San Benito.

She called Esperanza and Flor into her office and said, "I've built a new room for you to stay in. It's not quite as nice as a guest room, but it should be comfortable. Esperanza, I'd like you to agree to stay with me for the next year or two. Flor, I'd like you to take care of my chickens and food garden. In exchange, I'll provide room and board, allow José to stay with you, and pay you, Esperanza, 50 *colones* a month; and you, Flor, 30 *colones*. I'll also have my dressmaker make you some work smocks and get each of you a new pair of sandals. If you agree, you can move into the new room at the back."

Esperanza looked at her mother. Her mother was wide-eyed and smiling. She had never expected to receive so much money for a month's work—and room and board—new clothes and sandals. It was too good a deal to turn down. She said, "Yes, Doña Marta. I will agree to be your cook for the next couple of years and accept your offer."

It took only a few minutes for Esperanza to pack their few possessions and move to their new quarters. For Esperanza and Flor, their cots and facilities surpassed their primitive facilities in El Nido—and for Flor the door opening to the backyard was welcome and working with the chickens was like being at home in El Nido.

For Doña Marta, the new arrangement brought stability to her operation. No more drunken or lovesick cooks to manage. The staff seemed content, and it didn't cost her a single colón more than she would have spent on a less reliable cook.

CHAPTER 17

E speranza's life settled into a routine. Five days a week, she was up
at dawn to prepare breakfast, with an hour or two to rest before
getting lunch ready, which was served from 1:00 to 2:30 p.m. After a
short *siesta*, she would start preparing dinner, served from 7:00 to 9:00
p.m. Each morning, Doña Marta went over the day's menus with her
and allowed her to prepare the meals. The kitchen maid assisted with
food prep and washed the dishes in the cold-water sink, while the two
room maids helped dry the dishes after each meal. When they were in
the kitchen, they worked under Esperanza. However, none of the three
maids warmed to the fifteen-year-old country girl, who gave them terse
orders and often criticized their efforts.

Doña Marta found that under Esperanza's watchful eye, she only had
to make two trips to the Central Market each week. Occasionally, they
visited a farmers' market just to see what might be available.

On the weekends, the pension usually had only one or two guests. Most
arrived on Sunday night or Monday morning and left Friday afternoon
or Saturday morning. Esperanza prepared the usual breakfast on Saturday
morning and had the rest of the day off; Doña Marta served leftovers for
lunch and dinner. On Sundays, she prepared breakfast and dinner. There
was no lunch on Sundays. That was consistent with the practice in most

households, restaurants, and hotels in the city—a six-day work week, with a half-day off to visit family and friends.

Esperanza's attire had changed significantly. Doña Marta had her dressmaker prepare three work uniforms for Esperanza and two for her mother. With the new uniforms, they left behind their country bumpkin look. Esperanza persuaded Doña Marta to make their uniforms different from the maids', whose outfits consisted of black blouses and skirts with white aprons. Esperanza's new uniform was an indigo blue coat dress that buttoned down the front. Although Doña Marta complained about the cost, she agreed—after all, it was an operating expense. Esperanza and her mother folded up their country blouses and skirts, which they wore only when they left the pension for personal business.

For Esperanza and Flor, still strangers in the capital city, the routine was no great strain. They knew no one in the city, and their lives revolved around Doña Marta and the pension. Flor was delighted. She had three meals a day, a roof over her head, a cot better than the straw bed in El Nido, and the chance to do something she genuinely enjoyed. She took care of José while doing her chores, and she got paid for it.

Esperanza was saving a few more *colones* than she paid out for the upkeep of her family. Her mother watched her carefully hide her savings under the mattress. Almost without realizing it, her mother said. "When we have a little spare cash, can we buy a radio? The music in the front hall is so pleasant. I would like to have our own radio for our room."

The first purchase Esperanza made was their own radio!

Before she knew it, it was the first week of August, Salvador del Mundo week. The pension, like everything else in San Salvador, was closed for the entire week. There was no civic celebration. Everything just shut down, including churches. Neither mother nor daughter felt any strong connection to the church. Their family had been nominally Catholic since the arrival of the Spanish, with their shamans always advising them to live in peace with the Spaniards, attend church to show respect to Jesus and Mary, and privately revere their Mayan creators. This balance had kept them an independent people. With the decline of the indigo market, their family couldn't afford the church fees for marriage and baptismal rites. Even when they prayed at home to Jesus and Mary, it was almost in the spirit of their Mayan ancestors.

The week of Salvador del Mundo, Doña Marta closed the pension for the week. On the Saturday before, they had thoroughly cleaned the place. They aired, repaired, and spruced up all the guest rooms. They washed all of the bed linens, and on Tuesday, the two maids on duty busily ironed sheets and towels. Wednesday morning, Doña Marta inspected each room. When she finished her inspection, she told the two maids on duty, "You have done a good job. You may spend Thursday, Friday, and Saturday with your families. You have the three days off with pay, and I have a special package of food for you to share with your families. I expect you back by 4:00 p.m. next Sunday."

For Esperanza, the week was almost like a vacation. She had only a few meals to prepare each day—simple traditional dishes for Doña Marta and the two maids. When they went to the market on Tuesday, many of the market stands were closed.

On Thursday, after breakfast, Doña Marta told Esperanza, "I'll be staying with my daughter's family in Santa Ana for the weekend. I'll be back Sunday afternoon. No guests are expected until Sunday night. Esperanza, I'm leaving you in charge. I'll double lock the front entrance—only use the side door if you go out, and keep it locked at all times. The upstairs maid will stay with you until Saturday morning, but she prefers to spend Sunday with her married sister. So, you'll only have to look after her and your family until I return. I've alerted the policemen who guard the pension, and they'll be watching day and night. If you have any problems, just contact the policeman at the corner. His boss assured me there will be someone there twenty-four hours a day until I'm back."

On Thursday morning, Ricardo picked up his mother, leaving the maid, Esperanza, and her mother in the locked-up pension. After lunch, Esperanza and her mother, with José in his cradle, were resting under the mango tree in the backyard. Music played softly from their radio. Her mother spoke gently, "Are you holding up well? I'm worried about the routine you've fallen into. It's much harder than your life in El Nido. You seem to be working all day, every day. You're on your feet constantly—cooking or going shopping. Cooking and shopping."

"Mother, please do not worry. I know full well what I am doing. I am learning how to survive in this difficult city. I learned how little I really knew when we left El Nido. I had a lot of school and knew a great deal from books, but no one taught me much about life beyond our farm and our community. San Salvador is much more complicated. If I am to find out how I can keep our family going, I must learn how to make a living for us."

Her mother was clearly unprepared for this reply from her daughter.

Esperanza continued, "When we left El Nido, I thought that what Grandmother taught me about preparing and cooking food would be enough to make a good living for us here. Now I know it isn't. I believe the great shaman and my great-grandmother, the *curandera*, led us to Doña Marta's door and opened her heart to us. Through their grace, they created the situation where Doña Marta needed me, and they allowed me to respond well to her needs."

"Now she's teaching me not only how to cook for city people but also how to run a city house. I learn every time she prepares a menu. I observe how she handles the maids, and she's teaching me to hold my temper when they make mistakes—though I'm not very good at that yet. I learn something new every time we go to the market, not just about buying food, but about gaining the trust of the market women and having them share their special knowledge about what's happening in the city and country. Doña Marta also lets me read the newspaper every morning, so I'm keeping up with local and international affairs."

Esperanza paused to take a sip of the horchata she had made for the afternoon, before continuing, "And, Mother, I have learned how difficult it is for women like us to survive in the city—much more difficult than in our El Nido. There are lots of women like me and almost no jobs for them. The lucky ones are maids who live in the big houses with one afternoon off a week to visit their mothers and children. There are also the market women who have a permanent stand in the markets. I know a few of them now and how hard it has been for them to get ahead."

Her mother asked, "Where are the husbands?"

"I can't answer that yet. I've noticed that most of the market women and maids I've met are a lot like me—raising a child with no husband, while their mothers help care for the child. One market lady scoffed at something Doña Marta said a few days ago. Doña Marta asked her about her husband, and the market lady replied, 'You know my man is a sergeant. He comes around when he wants a favor. Marry him? Not on your life! If I did, he'd own me, my money, and my children.' I don't fully understand what she meant yet, but I will figure it out."

Esperanza cuddled her son and then placed him back in the cradle Doña Marta had lent them. She said, "Mother, we will stay here until I have learned how to make a better living for us. It isn't going to be easy. We will save every penny we can. We will make Doña Marta happy that we are with her. The time will come when our lives will have to change again. Maybe Doña Marta will retire to live with one of her children. Maybe, I'll have to find another job. Come what may, I am living for our future now. Maybe I can still find a way to become a teacher."

CHAPTER 18

In the months that followed Salvador del Mundo, Doña Marta carefully expanded her cook's knowledge. She taught her to prepare fish. Esperanza had fried river fish in El Nido, but she knew nothing of ocean varieties and different ways of preparing them for the table—from ceviche to sauteed sole to baked sea bass. Doña Marta showed Esperanza how to use her spices to bring out the flavors of her foods, to tenderize the beef, and how to bake a roast and prepare a tenderloin of pork. Doña Marta wanted to keep her teenage cook open to new recipes and new cooking experiences. As she told her older son Teodoro, "Esperanza is good cook, not a chef. She is as good as I will find for my pension, and I will keep her as long as she believes that I have more to teach her."

The rainy season, which began in late April, continued through the fall. It rained every afternoon for several months, with a couple of hurricanes from the Caribbean bringing days of continuous rain. The rain didn't significantly affect the guest rate, as Doña Marta still averaged eight guests per week. In mid-August, Doña Marta had Esperanza prepare a special dish each week—new additions to Esperanza's repertoire, most of which were well-received. By late October, Doña Marta began receiving inquiries from businessmen about her availability to cater special meals.

To which she would reply, "Thank you for asking. I'll have to think about it."

She had thought about it quite a bit. Her cook was making her pension well-known for its food, and Doña Marta had quietly raised the room rates. Doña Marta also began planning to offer her dining room to select groups for lunches. As she said to her younger son Roberto, "I seldom have more than one or two guests at lunch. That leaves me an almost empty dining room. A special lunch or two a month could work well for my finances. No dinners—my guests must come first. And, you know I can't overwork my cook."

In late October, Doña Marta called Esperanza into her office. "Please sit down, my dear. I want to commend you for the lunches and dinners over the past several months. The guests have told me how much they enjoyed them. You are doing a good job learning and preparing my special recipes. I have so many more to teach you if you wish to learn, from pastas to desserts."

Esperanza, "Yes, indeed, I like to learn and try out new dishes."

"Well, you know, my dear, we're approaching the Christmas season. Just like during the Feast of Salvador del Mundo and Easter, all of San Salvador will shut down. There won't be any guests at the pension. And, just like after Salvador del Mundo and Easter, we'll do a thorough cleaning on Monday and Tuesday. Each of the maids will get three days off—of course, on different days. I was wondering if you and your mother would like to go up to El Nido for the week."

"I haven't talked to my mother, but I doubt that we would undertake the trip right now. We would need to make arrangements with our family, and José has begun to teethe. I will talk to my mother before I give you a final answer."

"Well, do plan to be here next Sunday. I am planning a family dinner here for my two sons, my son-in-law, and their families. I would like to prepare a very festive event, with a special roast, roast potatoes, *tamales dulces, empanadas,* and any other festive dishes you might want to prepare.

This is the first time in many years that I have invited my family to dine here; normally I go to their houses. Do you have any problem with my infringing on your Sunday?"

"Oh, no, Doña. I see no problem in preparing such a meal. I can marinate the beef as you showed me and rub it down with my spices. It should be tender and tasty. The rest is no problem. You like my *empanadas, tamales,* and *pupusas."*

Little did Esperanza realize that Doña Marta was using her family as the guinea pigs in her plan to offer catered lunches.

When Esperanza returned to her room to tell her mother that Doña Marta had offered them a week off at Christmas to visit their home, her mother was excited. She thought about seeing her brother, the family, and neighbors—and working the good soil of her own land, instead of trying to coax beans and corn to grow in the harsh red clay of Soyapango. Esperanza, however, thought of the cost of traveling back to a place she wasn't ready to face, where the dark memories of the rape and the death of her dreams still lingered. "Mother, I'll look into the possibilities over the next week, and we'll talk about it later," Esperanza said, concluding the conversation.

The family lunch was a festive occasion. Doña Marta set out her finest linen and decorated the table with store-bought roses. Esperanza prepared the most special meal of her life, and every bite was eaten—there wasn't a single slice of roast, *tamale,* or *pupusa* left uneaten by the family. After lunch, Doña Marta brought her two sons, Ricardo—whom Esperanza had already met—and Teodoro, her eldest, whom she hadn't met before, to the kitchen to congratulate her on the meal.

More importantly, they had endorsed Doña Marta's new venture, to serve catered lunches for businessmen. She was satisfied that Esperanza was up to learning any recipe and producing any meal that she could design. She was convinced that she could keep the nearly sixteen-year-old in her kitchen for the next couple of years. Doña Marta's business instincts had saved the family during the Depression years, and now, in these uncertain times, they told her that she had a valuable asset to secure her nest egg for retirement.

Esperanza spent the next week investigating the cost of bus fare and other arrangements for spending Christmas in El Nido. She estimated that it would require her to spend all the meager savings that she had built up as Doña Marta's cook. She had added only 25 *colones* to the nest egg of 800 that she had brought with her from El Nido.

Esperanza was confounded. She was sure that she had saved more. Then she thought of the cost of new uniforms, the bras, panties, and slips she had bought at the nearby bazaar for her mother and herself; the formula, diapers, and clothes for José; and the radio. Even with room and board at the pension, the hundred *colones* that she and her mother received were barely enough to make ends meet. If she were to support her family, she had to earn more money each month—but how?

In late October, she had to tell her mother that there was no chance for them to visit El Nido that Christmas. They did not have enough money to cover the trips and buy presents for the family and friends. This year they would spend Christmas at the pension and make do as best they could.

CHAPTER 19

The year 1943 began as a busy one. The pension was fully booked throughout January, and there were two special luncheons that month—one hosted by Teodoro and the other by Ricardo. Both events were for ten guests, a mix of military officers and businessmen, and each required special preparations and elegant entrées. The luncheons meant extra hours of work for Esperanza, all under Doña Marta's careful supervision.

In February and March those extra lunches continued, and now Esperanza heard from the serving maids that there were American as well as Salvadoran guests at the table. They also noted in whispers that some of the guests in February were American military officers.

In early March, Doña Marta sent Esperanza to the Central Market alone. She handed her a list of produce to buy, carefully instructing her on which market women to approach for each item and to inform them that payment would be made on Friday when Doña Marta planned to visit the market herself. Esperanza navigated the task with ease, skillfully bargaining for high-quality goods. As she haggled, she engaged the market women in conversation about the growing presence of the American military and President Martínez's plans to build American bases in the country.

One of the women confided, "We hear that Doña Marta's sons are very close to the Americans. You know, they both speak English and know a lot about machinery and construction. They also have good friends among the Salvadoran military and are getting contracts to build the bases. Very few Salvadoran officers speak English, so Doña Marta's boys help them to work out the details." With a wink, she smirked, "You know what details I mean."

Another told her, "Doña Carmen of the big restaurant next door is mad at Doña Marta. It seems that some of the business lunches that used to be held at Doña Carmen's special room are now being held at Doña Marta's. That must make extra work for you, but I guess you know all about that. I think that Doña Carmen is really mad because the business deals that used to be made at her place are now being made at Doña Marta's."

Almost every woman she dealt with had some variation on the same theme. By the time she settled into the front seat of the taxi to go home, Esperanza began to think about how she might take advantage of the situation to increase her income. She knew she had proven herself to be a good cook. True, Doña Marta had spent long hours teaching her many new dishes and improving her skills, but Esperanza was realistic enough to know that she needed to learn more in order to earn more.

She waited until after the second lunch in March to approach Doña Marta. By then, she had come to know her employer quite well and didn't want to jeopardize their relationship. She listened carefully for any comments Doña Marta made about her plans for the periodic lunches. By the end of March, after the second lunch of the month, Esperanza was convinced that these lunches would become a regular part of her workload. So, she decided it was time to talk with her employer.

After the first lunch in April, she knocked on the door of Doña Marta's office and asked politely, "May I come in?"

"Of course," answered Doña Marta. "Come in and sit down. That was a fine lunch you prepared today. All the guests were pleased."

"Well, that is what I want to talk about." She paused before saying, "Doña Marta we agreed on my salary some months ago; I am grateful for your treatment of both me and my mother. I appreciate all the lessons you have given me. But now my workload is much heavier. Some of the guests tell me that they come back because of the food. And I hear that you are charging for the two special lunches each month. I think that it is time for you to increase my salary."

"Well, began Dona Marta, "I gave you and your family a place to live when you needed it. I have been training you to be a proper cook. I am not sure that you are ready for a raise."

The bargaining had started just as Esperanza expected. She responded, "Doña Marta, we are friends now. I stepped in when you needed me most, and I respect you and want to continue helping you. But you have to understand what I need to keep my family afloat, and the expenses my mother and I take on to help keep the pension running. For example, my mother has doubled your flock of chickens, and it has been quite some time since you've had to buy chickens or eggs at the Central Market. And . . ."

Doña Marta broke in, "Okay, I will raise your combined monthly salary to 125 *colones*."

"Oh, I don't think that's fair. I would like 5 *colones* for each guest at your special luncheons, along with an increase to 175 *colones* per month."

Doña Marta snapped, "Are you mad?" She looked shocked and then pulled herself together. "Well Esperanza, I guess I trained you too well. Let's agree on 150 a month and two *colones* for each special luncheon guest. That would bring your monthly salary to 190 *colones*."

Esperanza smiled meekly and countered, "Make it two hundred and we have a deal."

The two ladies smiled, "Two hundred it is," said Doña Marta. The two ladies nodded; both were pleased with the outcome. Doña Marta and her sons could continue to schedule their business lunches, and Esperanza would be building a stronger financial base for her family.

CHAPTER 20

Esperanza spent her teenage years, from 1943 to 1947, under the tutelage of Doña Marta. She emerged from her cocoon as a country bumpkin and became a competent urban household manager. She not only expanded her knowledge of cooking but also ran the kitchen with an iron fist, much to the dismay of the maids who worked under her. In addition, she mastered other aspects of maintaining the pension, from cleaning rooms and changing beds to polishing furniture and tidying up after guests. Doña Marta also introduced her to bookkeeping and maintaining a ledger.

The quality of her meals added to the reputation of Doña Marta's pension as a comfortable place to stay, and businessmen and army officers welcomed invitations to the biweekly lunches hosted by Doña Marta's two sons. After each lunch, the son hosting the event would invite the cook to greet his luncheon guests. That required Doña Marta to have her dressmaker make two more elegant uniforms for her cook, with frills that enhanced the young cook's appearance.

Esperanza was very realistic and carefully considered her situation. At twenty years old, with a mother and a son to support, her immediate value was tied to Doña Marta and the success of the pension. Doña Marta, meanwhile, recognized that she was aging. Her sons were doing well and wanted her to retire, but she had resisted their pleas. However, Esperanza noticed signs that Doña Marta had begun to entertain the idea of retirement.

Esperanza tried to save every *colon* she could. She wasn't sure what she would do when the time came to make a change, but she knew a change would come. She did not consider going back to El Nido. It would take too much of her small nest egg, which she kept hidden in her room. Even with the cost of taking care of José, she had more than 2000 *colones* in her hoard. She was very careful to hide it, even from her mother. She trusted no one.

She had tried to open an account at the local bank, only to be told that without a man to co-sign, she couldn't. The bank clerk explained that the bank wouldn't open accounts for women unless their husband, father, or brother co-signed or authorized it. Not long after, when Doña Marta sent her to the Central Market alone, she asked one of the women she had become friendly with, "How do you protect your profits? You told me that, like me, you live with your mother and children. You must have some savings. Where do you keep them? Do you have a bank account?"

The market woman just smiled. "I had to find a good place to hide it. Like every other lady in the market, I tried to open a bank account, but they turned me down because I wouldn't have a male co-signer. Too many of us have been robbed blind by men who co-signed accounts. If you let them co-sign, they'll spend it. Better to hide it. This world isn't made for women like us."

Esperanza was beginning to understand the ground rules of the urban world into which she had inserted herself. She became ever more convinced that she had to look out for herself. Her asset was that she was becoming quite a good cook. She absorbed Doña Marta's teaching like a sponge—one recipe after another. She began thinking about her future after Doña Marta retired. Maybe she could open a restaurant like her cousin Carmen. Perhaps hers could become the favorite dining spot for the rich and famous—she could build on the clientele from the biweekly lunches that Doña Marta's two sons hosted at the pension.

When she was introduced after the lunches, Esperanza made an effort to connect names with faces. She quickly noticed that many of the men attending were Americans, including several military officers. Their Spanish was limited, and they often responded with a simple nod or a polite "thank you" for the meal. However, she also overheard remarks like, "Salvadoran food is easy to eat, but it's so bland it doesn't compare to the international cuisine at the Astoria Hotel or the meals at the French Embassy.

Those comments strengthened her resolve to expand her culinary knowledge beyond the traditional dishes she had learned as a child. Later that day, while preparing dinner for the pension guests, Esperanza turned to Doña Marta and asked, "Have you ever tried cuisines other than Salvadoran?"

"Of course, yes, I have tried many."

"Are they very different from ours?"

"Yes," responded Doña Marta. "Our cuisine highlights the natural flavors of the ingredients, and while we use spices to enhance the taste, we don't rely on the strong spices or delicate sauces common in other cuisines. For example, Mexicans take similar ingredients but add hot peppers and rich sauces. The French and Italians use combinations of creams, cheeses, olive oil, and mushrooms to create flavors very different from ours. I don't know much about Chinese or Indian cooking, but I've heard they're both unique and quite exciting for the palate."

Esperanza was perplexed, "Are there schools in San Salvador to teach me how to cook those various styles?"

Doña Marta smiled and said, "Our schools barely teach the ABCs of reading, mechanics, or science. My sons, who have been to America, tell me that almost every city they visited has places to learn about the modern world, including cooking schools for various cuisines—but not here in San Salvador."

Then she added, "My pension caters to the taste of our people, but our wealthy neighbors in Escalon and San Benito who travel abroad and experience those other cuisines want much more variety than the rest of us. They often bring chefs from abroad to satisfy their palates and, occasionally, one of those working in the kitchen with those chefs learns their secrets. That is how Carmen's two cooks at her restaurant learned the recipes for the exquisite meals she serves." Then, Doña Marta half-scoffed, "She had to make them her partners to keep them."

"How can I get to America to take one of those courses?" Esperanza asked eagerly.

"Oh, my dear, you need to know English, have at least a high school diploma, and a lot of money. I suspect admission to those schools is very competitive. Don't count on getting to America. The best you can hope for is that, after the pension, you might secure a job as an assistant cook in one of the Fourteen Families' homes—the wealthy elite who control most of the land and power in this country."

Doña Marta saw the disappointment on Esperanza's face. She immediately thought of her own interests, as she said, "Esperanza you're only twenty years old. You came here five years ago with nothing. You have many years to learn other cuisines, and I will help as I can. Right now, concentrate on how we can present the most inviting dishes for the guests of the pension. You are making enough money now to keep your family safe and comfortable. Be patient."

Esperanza just nodded. She knew that her hopes were limited if she did not broaden her skills. She wanted more for herself and her family. She still yearned to be a teacher.

After her conversation with Doña Marta, she went back to her room with her mother and son. She sat on the discarded sofa that Doña Marta had allowed her to move into the room. Her mother, seated beside her, saw the worried look on her face and asked, "What is troubling you?"

Esperanza said, "I am worried about our future. This job with Doña Marta will not last much longer. Doña Marta is aging, and her sons will not keep the pension open when she retires. I am a cook for our people. I only know the recipes of our people. There aren't enough restaurants in the city to offer me much of a future as a cook. We don't have enough *colones* to open a place of my own in San Salvador, no matter how humble. And, you know that returning to El Nido is not a choice. No one there can afford a restaurant—the only cantina in our county seat makes its money on liquor, not food. And having been raped by a drunk, I want nothing to do with cantinas."

Her mother patted her gently on the shoulder and said, "My dear, you have made the right choices for us up to now."

"Mother, I have a lot of thinking to do. Thanks to some of my friends at the Central Market, I understand how difficult life is for almost every woman of our class—the lack of jobs and the sacrifices we must make to survive. I want more for us. I don't want to have to send José away just to help us get by, like you and Father had to do with Diego—and I've seen how much you ache to see him again. Oh yes, I know. I always ask if anyone has heard anything about Diego when I go to the market."

Her mother began to weep, and Esperanza embraced her.

The next time Esperanza had an afternoon free, she took the bus to downtown San Salvador and found a bookstore that had a book, *Basic English*. She told herself that learning what was in the book was her next step forward.

CHAPTER 21

During those years of learning under Doña Marta, Esperanza began to understand how everything in the city revolved around the military and how its decisions affected the rhythm of life, even at the pension. She had seen army officers regularly visit Doña Marta, leaving after a brief meeting with an envelope in hand. From what she overheard at the Central Market, nearly every shopkeeper and market woman experienced similar visits. A close friend at the market explained to her that the women paid for protection against the swarm of sneak thieves that infested the area.

So, Esperanza carefully told herself that, if she went out on her own, she would need to pay for protection, but to whom? She thought a minute and remembered that in school she was taught that the police were a part of the military. "Oh, well," she shrugged to herself, "Someone will approach me. I'll just have to wait for that person to show up. From what the women tell me, it doesn't take long, and the market women seem to get along okay, so long as the payments are made."

This experience cast doubt in her mind about what she had been taught in school about Salvadoran history and civics. She had learned that the Spaniards had brought God, civilization, and an enlightened way of life to the Americas for the indigenous people—of which she was one—and that she should be grateful. Then, the children of the Spaniards had broken away from Spain, the Mexican Empire, and the Central American Confederation to create an independent country. She recalled that independent El Salvador had been governed mainly by generals and wealthy landowners, who were portrayed as wise and just. There were mentions of a few tyrants and the occasional suppression of bloody uprisings, but the lessons emphasized trusting the military to take care of the people. Now, however, she was beginning to see how people truly lived and the price they paid to ensure the military system protected them. For an indigenous woman like herself, finding a decent job was difficult—and when she did, she might have to pay for protection.

Esperanza was receiving her education in the real world. She focused on what was going on and how it affected her and her family. It was no longer a school lesson. What happened in the government and the economy could help her or hurt her. So, as she read the daily newspaper and listened to the conversations at the market and in the pension, she constantly asked herself, *How does this affect me and my future?*

She knew that for almost all her life the president had been General Maximiliano Hernandez Martinez, the strong man whom her teachers lauded for ousting the first "communist" government in Salvadoran history and putting down its rabid supporters. His picture hung in every school and was the oracle for national good in the daily newspaper. Everything he said and did became national law.

It was in the Central Market that she began to understand that there was dissension behind the public imagery. When she first went to the market with Doña Marta, she had thought how silly it was for the women to talk about fruits and vegetables as if they were real people. Little by little, she came to understand that the women had developed a special lingo to discuss the local political scene among themselves, with each military and political leader being identified by a specific fruit or vegetable. She learned that General Maximiliano Hernandez Martinez was a bloody tyrant who tolerated no dissent in the military or by civilians. When the first moderate reform government in the history of the republic came to power in a free election in 1930, it threatened to modernize the state, give a voice to the indigenous people, and tax the wealthy landowners. She heard how the powerful Fourteen Families called in General Maximiliano Hernandez Martínez to oust the elected government and quash the reform movement. He was given a blank check, and he used it. He had massacred an estimated thirty-five thousand indigenous people, executed civilian and military opponents, and silenced popular discussion. He had ruled the country for a decade with an iron fist.

Then, dissent within the military began to fester. He rooted out the discontented, silencing them through exile or death. Under these circumstances, the women in the markets found special ways to protect their interests, regardless of their personal political inclinations. Some became repositories of the latest information about infighting in the barracks—sometimes from the police or military men they paid for protection, and sometimes from sexual partners. Esperanza observed how Doña Marta tapped into that information. Doña Marta was one of the few with such access—for reasons Esperanza never fully understood. Through Doña Marta, Esperanza became someone to be trusted. She listened and kept silent. She was getting her education in the true workings of governance in El Salvador.

1943 was a year of simmering struggle in the barracks. Around Easter time in 1944, came the uprising that resulted in the ousting of General Maximiliano Hernandez Martinez and the election of a new president in 1945, General Salvador Castenada Castro, and an era of continued dissension in the barracks. Doña Marta and Esperanza heard the inside information at the Central Market, not in the daily newspapers that carried only officially condoned reports.

The more Esperanza learned about the power struggle in the barracks and the inherent corruption in the socio-political order, the less she considered going into business for herself. She had to find a way to support herself and her family without having to pay for protection.

The more she learned about the reality of the marketplace, the more she wished that she could have gone on to high school and become a teacher.

CHAPTER 22

E speranza began to notice signs of Doña Marta showing her age. She guessed she was in her late fifties or early sixties. Doña Marta moved more slowly now, often staying in bed during breakfast hours and delegating the marketing entirely to Esperanza. It never occurred to Esperanza that this was a mark of Doña Marta's trust in her abilities.

Seeing the shift as an opportunity, Esperanza eagerly honed her supervisory and marketing skills. She also cultivated relationships with several sharp-witted market women, finding her trips to the Central Market increasingly significant. These outings became a window into the world beyond the pension, as she carefully listened to the gossip and assessed the implications of what was said.

By 1946, rumors about shifting political and economic dynamics were everywhere. The market women murmured about a brewing crisis: government revenues from coffee export taxes were reportedly falling short of the president's budget needs, and his plans to impose new taxes on income and property were alienating support from the Fourteen Families. Esperanza shared these whispers with Doña Marta, who nodded knowingly. "Yes," she said, "I've been hearing the same. My sons have warned me to be cautious—there could be unrest, even rioting, here in Soyapango."

At the biweekly luncheons, Esperanza observed a noticeable shift in the guest list. Younger Salvadoran officers were being invited more frequently, many of whom had served abroad and returned with a taste for the economic advancements they had seen in other countries. She also noticed an increasing number of Americans at these gatherings and occasionally overheard snippets of conversations in English, a language she barely understood. These guests were American military officers and businessmen, whom Doña Marta's sons, Teodoro and Ricardo, were actively trying to cultivate as allies.

When World War II ended in 1945, there was great uncertainty. After many a lunch Esperanza positioned herself in the pantry off of the dining room to listen to the conversations in Spanish and English. She had studied her book on basic English, memorized many words and phrases, done all of the grammar exercises and tried to train her ear, but the spoken word gave her real problems. Words in English were not spoken as she saw on the printed page. She listened to hear vowel sounds that resembled Spanish, but to no avail.

She did learn in the Central Market that there were some American families settling in the city. Most of them were working with the US Embassy, some were military, and some were civilian. She wondered what their home life was like and what they liked to eat. She remembered she overheard one of those aliens commenting how good, but bland, her cooking was.

It had been more than five years since Esperanza, her mother, and her son had rung the bell at the pension when Doña Marta called her into the office. Smiling gently, Doña Marta said, "Esperanza, I've decided to retire. I'll be closing the pension in August. An American company is purchasing the building and grounds. Teodoro has represented them for years, and they'll be using this space as their new office. I don't know all the details, but they've offered me a fair price. And, well, you know, I'm not getting any younger."

Esperanza hesitated, then replied, "I'm happy for you, Doña Marta, but this will mean big changes for my family. The pension has been our only home in San Salvador. I'll need your help to find a new place to live and a job."

Doña Marta nodded. "I know how much you've helped me over the years, Esperanza, and how essential you've been to running the pension. Don't worry—we still have two months before I close down. We'll have time to figure things out together."

"Thank you for being so understanding," Esperanza responded.

When Esperanza told her mother, she reacted with fear. Her mother had become quite comfortable in her routine. She seldom had left the security of the pension, and she had made its backyard area her domain with her chickens and her kitchen garden. She turned to Esperanza, "I somehow knew that we would not live here for much longer. I will help all I can in this move. You improved our life when we moved from El Nido. I did not want change then. But you led us here, and I am sure that you will find another haven for us."

CHAPTER 23

I n the three weeks after Doña Marta advised Esperanza of her decision to close the pension, Esperanza took several afternoons off to explore the house rental and job markets. Esperanza read each daily paper for listings and talked with her friends in the Central Market. She asked her cousin Carmen for a job at her restaurant and was offered one as an assistant cook at less than she made at the pension and without room and board. She looked at available apartments in various sections of town, many with rents beyond her income. Those within her price range were in unsafe neighborhoods. She became increasingly depressed and even began thinking about taking her savings and returning to El Nido.

As she finished up her breakfast chores, Doña Marta asked her to come to the office. After Esperanza took a shower, she knocked on the door of the office with trepidation.

Doña Marta responded, "Come in."

As Esperanza entered the office, Doña Marta smiled, "Sit down Esperanza. We need to talk. Would you like some coffee?" Esperanza sat and took a cup of coffee.

Doña Marta took a sip of coffee and looked directly at Esperanza. "I've been watching you closely since I shared my plans with you. I've seen how you have read the papers each morning and explored the market beyond the pension. I've listened to the questions you ask the women at the market. I know you're doing everything you can to prepare for life after the pension closes."

"Yes, I have a big responsibility, and the situation is very difficult," Esperanza responded.

"I know that there are very few jobs and not many decent places to live that you can afford. We Salvadorans are not ones to ask for help, let alone charity. We understand that the world is tough, and we must find ways to cope. You did exactly what I had to do when my husband died at the beginning of the Great Depression. I had three children and almost no resources except this building, and if it hadn't been for some help from my friends, I don't know what would have happened to me and my family."

Esperanza looked puzzled as Doña Marta continued, "You helped me at a critical moment—not in the same way your great-grandmother once saved my mother's life, but in a way that changed the course of my business. I'll admit something to you: before you told me your family name and connection, I almost denied you a room at the pension. Even after agreeing, I had my doubts—a poor country girl, her mother, and her son? It wasn't the kind of risk I was used to taking in over a decade of running this place. But that morning, when you stepped in to help after I fired the drunk cook, you proved I'd made the right decision. In that moment, it felt like you were sent to save me."

Esperanza was so pleased by those words because she had felt the same inner feeling that her coming to the pension had been predestined. She smiled and nodded.

"You and your mother have become more than my employees. You are my friends. Over these past five years, I have spent many afternoons with your mother and José in the backyard. They have been happy times and often helped me deal with the aches and pains of aging. Watching José reminded me of my own boys growing up. Oh, yes, I love those boys and their families, but they have lives of their own and José has been here all the time. I have a special affection for your family, and I want to help you with the transition to your new life."

Doña Marta looked intently at her cook, "I thought about having you move with me, but I am moving to an apartment at Teodoro's house—no need for more than a maid to keep me going, and the upstairs maid will go with me. So, I asked Ricardo to help me find a place for you to live. He owns several apartments in a block in San Judas, and he has agreed to rent one to you for 100 *colones* per month. It is a safe neighborhood with several neighbors you know from the Central Market—mothers raising their children by themselves. The apartment has two good-sized rooms, an indoor bathroom, a kitchen sink, and a fenced-in backyard area where your mother can keep a few chickens. I have arranged for a driver to take you there tomorrow."

The astonished Esperanza knew nothing more to do or say other than to hug Doña Marta.

Doña Marta continued, "If you like the apartment, you can take the furniture from your room with you. I'll arrange for Ricardo to move it. I also plan to sell the refrigerator, stove, and other appliances, along with all the furnishings. I'll give you first preference for any items you're able to pay for.

After she poured them each another cup of hot coffee, Doña Marta queried, "How has your search for a job gone?"

Esperanza replied, "I asked Carmen for a job. She offered me one as an assistant cook. Six days of breakfast, lunch, and dinner at 200 *colones* per month. No room or board. I also answered two ads in the *Prensa Grafica* newspaper, and the conditions weren't good. At one, the pay was 150 *colones* per month with Thursday afternoon off, and the other was at a coffee finca owner's house in Escalon with three maids from the finca and two teenage boys who ogled me as I walked out of the interview. I also got a few leads from our friends in the Central Market."

Doña Marta chortled, "Do take care with those teenage boys; their hormones have caused me more than a few headaches with the maids here."

The women exchanged a knowing look. Then, Doña Marta asked, "Have you thought of working for an American family? Ricardo tells me that several new families have recently arrived in the city. I know that you have been studying English. Would you like to work in one of their homes?"

"Well, I haven't seen much of them except at your lunches. They seem nice, even though they think my food is bland. I guess if the working and living conditions were right, I wouldn't mind giving it a try."

"I'll ask Ricardo to see if any of his contacts are looking for a cook. We can also ask around at the Central Market when we go there tomorrow. You still have six weeks to find a place to work before the pension closes. I'll write you a strong letter of recommendation that you can use at any interviews that come up."

When Esperanza left the office, she had hope for the first time in weeks that her problems could be overcome without returning to El Nido.

The following morning, Doña Marta and Esperanza went to the Central Market. When they asked one of the market women if she had any leads, one pointed to a blonde lady at a nearby kiosk and said, "She just asked me if I knew of any responsible girl who might be looking for a job. She doesn't speak much Spanish, but she seemed very nice."

Doña Marta motioned for Esperanza to approach the woman. Esperanza walked up to her and, in a sentence she had memorized from her English book, said in a barely understandable version of the language, "My name is Esperanza, and I am a cook." Running out of English words, she switched to Spanish, "I work at Doña Marta's pension in Soyapango." She pointed back at Doña Marta, "The pension is closing at the end of August, and I will be looking for a new job then."

Doña Marta told the market boy to guard her purchases and walked calmly to meet the blonde lady. She smiled and said in broken English,

"I not speak much English. I am Doña Marta." She continued in Spanish, "Esperanza has worked for me for over five years, and she is good."

The blonde lady said in not-too-understandable Spanish, "Good morning, ladies. My name is Elizabeth Holmes. My husband is Dr. Holmes, and we have just arrived in El Salvador to work with the Ministry of Health. We are renting a house in Flor Blanca, and I need some help. I have a maid to do the cleaning but need a cook. Could you visit me at home so that we can talk?"

Doña Marta smiled and said, "I will give Esperanza time off to visit with you. Just tell us the time and place."

Mrs. Holmes took a pen and paper from her bag and wrote the address and asked, "When will Esperanza be available—this week or next?"

"This week, no," Doña Marta shook her head. "I have big lunch tomorrow and Friday, many guests. How about next Monday afternoon?"

"Let's say 3:00 p.m. Monday."

"Agreed," said Doña Marta as she took the paper with the Holmes's address. She looked at the address and said, "My son Teodoro is your neighbor."

"Oh, I don't think I have met him. We haven't met many Salvadoreans yet." Mrs. Holmes replied in a mix of Spanish and English.

Mrs. Holmes and Doña Marta shook hands and they both smiled at Esperanza. Mrs. Homes turned and continued her shopping, and Doña Marta and Esperanza went back to finish up their business.

When Doña Marta and Esperanza were in the car on the way back to the pension, Doña Marta said, "You see Esperanza, we don't have many places in town to get news about who needs what. Very few people spend money to place ads in the newspapers. There is no place for an employer to find a worker except from a friend who knows a friend. There is no place to really find out when a house is for rent. Ricardo has some friends who tell him about prospects, and sometimes he is lucky. Everything is by word of mouth. And the best source of such news for now is at the Central Market—the housewives and the maids tell such news to the market women, and we see they are rewarded with our business when they share their news with us."

CHAPTER 24

M onday afternoon found Esperanza on her way to Flor Blanca. She wore her navy-blue dress uniform and a rebozo. Her mother wished her luck, and Doña Marta gave her a letter of recommendation to show to Mrs. Holmes. She walked around the corner to the bus stop for downtown San Salvador. She found a seat for the half-hour ride downtown. Then she walked toward the Hotel Nuevo Mundo and found the bus stop for Flor Blanca, a neighborhood of fine houses that had been developed in the past twenty years.

It was a twenty-minute ride, nearly to the end of the line. Finally, she saw the sign for the street where Mrs. Holmes lived. After getting off the bus, she checked the street address and saw she needed to turn right. The house was in the second block from the bus line, one of several two-story homes set side by side and a few feet back from the sidewalk. She checked the number again, then walked up to the front door and rang the bell.

A maid answered the door and looked her over carefully. "Yes?" asked the maid.

"I'm here to talk with Mrs. Holmes," replied Esperanza.

"Oh, you must be the cook she is waiting for," the maid noted in a not very friendly tone. Then she led Esperanza through an entrance hall, past the staircase, to a dimly lit room where Mrs. Holmes was waiting. "Come in Esperanza. I have been waiting for you."

Esperanza entered the room and said slowly in Spanish, "Good afternoon, Señora. I hope I am not late. The bus trip from Soyapango was longer than I thought."

"No problem. It is just 3:00 p.m. I asked my friend, Señora Clark, to join us. She speaks much better Spanish than I." Esperanza smiled at Mrs. Clark.

Mrs. Clark said, "I understand that you work for Doña Marta at her pension in Soyapongo. You are her cook?"

"Yes, Señora. I have been her cook for over five years. She asked me to show Mrs. Holmes this note." She handed it to Mrs. Holmes, and she and Mrs. Clark read it carefully, with Mrs. Clark explaining its content to Mrs. Holmes.

Mrs. Clark commented, "Doña Marta speaks quite highly of you and your cooking talents, but you are much younger than I expected. How old are you, and how did you learn to cook so well at such a young age?"

"Señora," responded Esperanza, "I am twenty years old. I come from El Nido in Chalatenango. My great-grandmother was a skilled cook, and my grandmother taught me as a little girl the recipes of her mother. I was hoping to go to high school in Chalatenango City when we had to come to the capital. A few days after our arrival at the pension, Doña Marta's cook arrived drunk at breakfast. I prepared breakfast for Doña Marta and have been her cook ever since."

Mrs. Clark quite surprised asked, "Do you cook the lunches at the pension to which her sons invite guests?"

"Of course," said an equally surprised Esperanza. "I have prepared them with Doña Marta for almost four years."

Turning to Mrs. Holmes, Mrs. Clark said in English, "My husband has been to several of the lunches. He is a friend of Doña Marta's son Ricardo, and he tells me that the food is among the best in town. He raves about the roasts and Salvadorean specialties." Turning back to Esperanza, she asked in Spanish, "Why are you looking for a job now?"

"Señora," Esperanza said softly, "Doña Marta is selling the pension. She's planning to move in with her son Teodoro. I support my mother and my son. I've looked for work as a cook in the few restaurants in the city, but I am a young woman, and the jobs and pay they offer me are nothing. There are few decent jobs for women here. I'm looking for a good job that will allow me to support my family."

Mrs. Homes interjected herself into the conversation, and in English, said to Mrs. Clark, "Jean, I understood most of the discussion. I believe that she would do the trick. What you think?"

In English, Mrs. Clark said, "I think that she is as good as you will get."

Then, turning to Esperanza, in her limited Spanish, Mrs. Holmes asked Esperanza, "Would you be willing to work here? My family here is my husband, my teenage daughter, and me. I plan to have only one maid and a cook. There are two maids' rooms out back. One will be for the maid, the other for you. There is a common bathroom. I will supply a cot and some other furniture, and a place to hang your clothes. I prefer that you eat what we eat, but will allow you to prepare tortillas, beans, and other local dishes if you wish. The most important thing is that I want someone who is honest and loyal to me. Everyone breaks something. Just tell me, don't lie."

Esperanza asked Mrs. Clark to repeat it in Spanish. She took a minute or two before replying, "Yes, I would, provided the pay is adequate."

"How much would you expect?" asked Mrs. Clark.

"My current salary is 250 *colones* a month," Esperanza explained, referring to the Salvadoran currency, with each *colon* worth about 40 cents in US dollars. "I could not support my family on less—especially now that I will have to rent a home for them."

Mrs. Holmes thought for a minute. She looked at Mrs. Clark. They seemed to agree. "I will pay you 250 *colones* a month. Do you need new uniforms?"

"No, Señora. I have five that Doña Marta made for me and two pairs of good work-shoes," Esperanza paused and then added, "Señora Holmes, I have been studying English grammar for three years. English looks so easy on paper, but it sounds so different from Spanish. If I help you with your Spanish, will you help me learn English?"

Both Mrs. Clark and Mrs. Holmes seemed totally unprepared for the question. Then, they both smiled. Mrs. Holmes said, "Of course."

CHAPTER 25

The pension closed in the last week of August. Esperanza and her mother carefully packed all their earthly possessions—they had some new clothes for José and themselves as well as two lamps and their radio.

Their possessions had accumulated. Doña Marta sold Esperanza her 1938 GE refrigerator for 200 *colones* and two well-worn armchairs, some faded drapes, and two well-used twin beds with mattresses for another 125 colones. She also gave them the items that had been in their room for the past five years: the lumpy sofa, three fold-up cots, an old kitchen table, three wooden chairs, and the armoire. Additionally, she gave Esperanza's mother all the chickens still roaming the coop—almost thirty prize egg-layers. This was quite a haul for the family, who had arrived in Soyapango five and a half years earlier with little more than the clothes on their backs and only enough *colones* to pay for ten days at the pension.

The Monday following the closure, Ricardo moved Doña Marta's office and bedroom furniture to Teodoro's house in Flor Blanca. Ricardo supervised the removal of all the remaining furniture, kitchen equipment, and supplies to purchasers who bid for them. Whatever else that was left over was given to a nearby school.

On Wednesday, Ricardo arranged to move all of Esperanza's goods to her two-room apartment in San Judas. Two of his workmen helped Esperanza's mother arrange the furniture in the apartment. Esperanza arrived late in the afternoon after she assisted Doña Marta and Ricardo with locking up the building.

It was only a few steps across the sidewalk to the front door of her new home. She rang the bell, and her mother peeked through the front window before opening the door. Esperanza glanced around the living room. To her left was a sitting area with the sofa and armchairs, and a wooden box that held the radio and a lamp. In the back left corner was one of the cots. The kitchen table and chairs sat in the center-right of the room, near the refrigerator, with some wooden boxes serving as storage shelves. A wood stove and the kitchen sink were also there. At the back of the room were three shuttered windows with iron bars on the outside, looking out at the small fenced-in backyard. On the street side, two draped windows, also with shutters and iron bars, faced the street.

To her right was the door to the second room and the bathroom. The two twin beds were on the far-right wall, with a wooden box between them. On the box was a lamp and the alarm clock. The armoire was set against the left wall, and one of the fold-up cots was set up under the shuttered, iron-barred back window of the bedroom.

Esperanza embraced her mother and said, "This will be our home for some time. I signed a lease with Señor Ricardo today that allows us to live here for five years at 100 *colones* per month. We will have to watch our expenses because I will make only 250 *colones* in my job with Señora Holmes, but we have a place to live."

Her mother smiled, "Yes, I believe that this is a comfortable place. I can shutter windows and lock the doors, but there is a cool breeze. The furniture fits well into the space. The yard is big enough for a few chickens, some bean plants, and a line to hang the wash. We have a fence around our yard, and it looks like all the neighbors do, too; and

I couldn't see any passageway to the street from the back area. I will meet our neighbors and see what they think about using the back area."

"Where is José?" asked Esperanza.

"He is next door. When we arrived, a boy about his age appeared at the door of the next house. He looked at José and José at him, and they smiled as if they had been together all their lives. His name is Pablo. Pablo's mother came to the door and asked if we were her new neighbors. I said yes. She invited José to play with Pablo while we moved in, and the two boys have been playing together since."

Her mother said, "It's wonderful. José has never had a playmate. He's been with us at Doña Marta's his whole life, and he has needed someone his own age to play with. We've been so lucky—he's been healthy, with almost none of the illnesses my other children had. We only had to ask for Doña Marta's help a few times when he got sick, and we were able to treat him ourselves. We've been fortunate. And now, he has a friend."

In almost a whisper, Esperanza broke in, "While José is playing, let us put away the money we have saved. Doña Marta took me to her bank again last Friday, and they would not allow me to open an account. So, I have all our savings in a napkin under my dress. And you know Doña Marta has promised to pay me a termination bonus of 250 *colones* for each year I worked for her. We will use that money to live on for the next several months—and we must hide our savings. No one should know about the money. There are so many thieves in the city."

Esperanza shook her head, almost in frustration. Then she continued, "Mother, I counted what we had hidden in our room in the pension, and it amounts to over 3,000 *colones*. More than we thought. I want to divide it up into packets of 1,000 *colones*—just in case. We can put 1,000 in the hollowed-out leg of the padded chair; another 1,000 under the top board of the armoire, and the rest where?"

Her mother interjected, "Maybe under one of the mattresses?"

"I'm not sure that is a good place, but let's check the beds," said Esperanza.

The two women inspected both beds, lifting the mattresses. Her mother noticed a loose board at the back of one of the bedsteads. "This is a good hiding place," she said. "I can slip 1,000 *colones* between the loose boards and tighten them."

With her cash reserves in their hiding places. Esperanza said, "You can go next door and get José. I will prepare dinner."

Mother went next door and was back in less time than you can imagine. She said, "Our neighbor has invited us to dinner. The boys have made us friends."

Esperanza smiled and said, "I need to go to the bathroom. Lock the door, and I'll join you in a few minutes."

After cleaning up, Esperanza stepped out of her front door, locked it, and carefully scanned the block before walking to the house next door. Still glancing around, she knocked. A young boy opened the door, smiling, and said, "You're my friend Pepe's mother. Come in."

Standing in the doorway, her eyes still on her locked front door, she replied, "Thank you, but before I come in, could you ask your mother if it's safe to leave my home unattended?

A smiling lady came into view and said, "Oh yes. We have Nico looking out for us. As I told your mother, he is like our special watchman. Please come in. Welcome, I am Patricia. You must be Esperanza."

Esperanza stepped into a comfortable parlor, furnished with a large divan and several armchairs. Two end tables flanked the divan, each with a tall lamp. To her left was a dining room table, set for five people.

"Yes," she replied. "I am Esperanza, and I thank you for the invitation. Today has been a long and difficult one for us. Moving after more than five years at the pension has not been easy."

Esperanza looked at her host, a very good-looking woman perhaps in her mid-thirties. She had light brown, wavy hair, soft blue eyes, and creamy white skin. She looked like she belonged in one of the houses in Flor Blanca or San Benito, not in an apartment in San Judas.

Her hostess said, "Please sit down. I have dinner almost ready. I am not a good cook, but I have put together a *sopa de res*, a few *empanadas* and *curtido*. Pepe tells me that you have been the cook for Doña Marta's pension."

Esperanza smiled, "Your dinner sounds fine. Yes, I have been with Doña Marta for over five years. Do you know her?"

"No, I don't know her, but some friends have told me about staying at her pension while in town. I also know that my landlord is her son." She then motioned to her guests to come to the table, as she announced, "Dinner is ready."

"Can I help you bring the food to the table?" asked Esperanza's mother. Without waiting for an answer, she followed her hostess into the walled off kitchen area, and the two women brought the food to the table. Without much formality, the new friends talked while they ate. They were just getting acquainted.

Esperanza's mother shared that they had come from El Nido over five years ago and had been with Doña Marta ever since. She explained how Esperanza became the cook and how their friendship with the pension owner had developed over the years. Patricia, in turn, mentioned that she had lived in her home in San Judas for over five years, ever since her son Pablo was born. She added that she was a dressmaker with several clients who kept her quite busy.

Pablo and José were fully engaged in bonding with each other. They kept a constant flow of gestures and sounds from one to the other. Their eyes seemed glued to each other as if somehow, they had always been meant to be together. Both boys had been reared, almost alone, by mother or grandmother. They had had little contact with other children. Now they seemed to sense that living next to each other, they had found something that they had never had before.

Patricia said quietly to Esperanza, "I think our sons like each other. They have been playing together without a fight all afternoon. It was

Pablo who asked your son his name. When he replied, "José," Pablo said, "All Josés are Pepes, and you are my Pepe. I am your Pablo."

When dinner ended, Flor helped Patricia clear the table and wash the dishes. Esperanza sat on the divan and watched the two boys play games with themselves, wrestling and having fun. When the two women emerged from the kitchen, Esperanza announced, "Tomorrow night, I would like Pablo and you to come to dinner. Please bring a chair because we have only four. I don't have my electric stove, but I still know how to cook on the wood stove and will try to prepare as delicious a meal as the one you served us tonight."

Patricia said, "Thank you so much. Tomorrow is Thursday and I have no appointments. I will be pleased to bring a chair. Before you go home, I want you to meet Nico. He is our night policeman. The carpenter on the corner made him a little stand where he can rest at night. He does his rounds and rests at the stand most of the night. To take special care of our block, we pay him five *colones* a week, and he knows how to get the word around the neighborhood not to bother this block."

Patricia opened her door and called to Nico, who came running.

"Good evening, Señorita," greeted Nico. He was a well-built, middle-sized man who resembled the people Esperanza had grown up with in El Nido. To Flor, he reminded her of her absent son Diego.

Patricia said, "This is Esperanza, her mother Flor, and her son Pepe. They just moved in next door today. I told them about you, and they want you to be their friend."

Nico smiled and said, "Nice to meet you. I'll stop by tomorrow to say hello."

CHAPTER 26

E arly the following Monday morning Esperanza, with a small card-board suitcase, took the bus to Flor Blanca to the house of Mrs. Holmes. The twenty-five-minute bus ride took her from one world to another. She walked the two blocks to the house rented by Dr. Holmes and rang the bell.

A young girl who looked like many in the countryside around El Nido answered the door; Esperanza said, "I am the cook. Is Mrs. Holmes at home?"

The maid said, "Yes. Please wait. I'll call her."

Shortly thereafter the maid reappeared and led Esperanza to the sitting room where she had met with Mrs. Holmes before.

Mrs. Holmes was seated on the couch and there was a man at the desk. The man rose as she entered the room and in good Spanish said, "Good morning, Esperanza. Mrs. Holmes and I are pleased that you will be our cook. I talked to Doña Marta and her son Teodoro about you at dinner just last night. I hope that we can all get along as well as you did with Doña Marta."

"Thank you, sir. I am pleased to meet you. Is Doña Marta well, and is she comfortable in her new house?"

"Oh yes, she is well and asked me to say hello to you." After a short pause, he continued, "I want to tell you what my wife and I expect of you in this house. We are very serious people and expect every member of our household to be clean, honest, and hardworking. We want a happy house, and friction between Altagracia and you will not be permitted."

He looked sternly at Esperanza as if Doña Marta had alerted him to her run-ins with the maids at the pension. She nodded her agreement.

He continued, "My wife plans to sit down with you every morning to plan the meals for the day. You may find that our diets are different from what you served at the pension. We plan for you to eat the meals that you prepare for us. However, we understand that your meals usually include beans and tortillas, and you may prepare them every day for your meals. The important thing is that my wife always knows what you are doing. She wants you to work with her as you did with Doña Marta."

Mrs. Holmes added, "I expect you to go to the market with me and help me with bargaining. Doña Marta tells me that you know the women and their ways."

Dr. Holmes continued, "We welcome you to our home and hope there will be no problems. Your job will not only include meals for the family, but occasional dinners for officials of your government. I am here to advise your government on its public health programs, and I will have dinners and cocktails for the officials with whom I shall be working. Doña Marta says that you are accustomed to preparing meals that they like. So, Mrs. Holmes expects you to help prepare menus for those dinners and cocktails."

Esperanza said, "Dr. and Señora Holmes. I am pleased to be working in your home. I will do everything possible to please you and to make this a happy house. I have been loyal and honest in all my dealings with Doña Marta and promise you the same."

Dr. Holmes turned to his wife, "I will go to the ministry now. Get Esperanza settled in, and I'll see you this evening." He smiled at Esperanza and exited through the front door.

Mrs. Holmes led Esperanza down the front hall, past the dining room, through a floor-to-ceiling black iron gate, to an open patio, through a back gate to the back patio and the maids' quarters. To the left were two rooms and a bath. To the right was a large kitchen. In the back was a high wall with bits of broken glass and other sharp metal objects to discourage intruders. There were several large earthen pots with decorative plants against the back wall.

Mrs. Holmes took her to the second room in the maids' area. It was much smaller than the one at Doña Marta's. It had two windows facing the back wall and one facing the kitchen. It held a folding cot, a bedside table, an old garden chair, a well-worn oaken bureau with three drawers and two poles with a rod between them for hanging clothes. There was a naked light bulb hanging down in the center of the room. It was far more than Esperanza had expected.

Mrs. Holmes said, "Let me show you the bathroom between your room and Altagracia's." She opened the door to reveal a shower, toilet and wash basin, "Do you need to freshen up?"

"No Señora. I am fine." Esperanza replied.

"Then just leave your things in your room and let me show you the kitchen."

The two women crossed the patio and entered a room with a two-spigot sink under the window adjoining a large counter, above which were a series of cabinets. In the rear was an electric stove. In the back of the stove was large round tank that she had never seen before. Mrs. Holmes asked, "Are you familiar with the appliances in these two rooms?"

Esperanza said, "At Doña Marta's, I worked on an electric stove and used the refrigerator. I need to know what is in the cabinets and how you want me to use them. Our sink only had one spigot and the tank in the corner is new."

"Oh, one spigot is for hot water, the other is cold water—the sink has both hot and cold water. And the tank in the corner is the hot water heater for the downstairs of the house."

"Hot water—you have hot water?"

"Oh, yes, indeed. I expect you to wash all the dishes in hot water—it is essential for public health."

"Señora I never knew that there was a tank and system for hot water. All I have ever done is heat water on the stove for cooking purposes. How do I turn on the tank to get hot water?"

"Esperanza, you do not touch the tank. It just heats the water, and the water then enters the hot water pipes and goes to the kitchen and bathrooms."

Incredulous, Mrs. Holmes asked, "You never had hot water in the kitchen at the pension?"

"No Señora. Never."

Mrs. Holmes showed her the contents of the kitchen cabinets—the pots, dishes, and some appliances Esperanza had never seen before, including an electric mixer, a coffee maker, a blender, and a waffle iron. She didn't even know their names. There were also baking tins, pots, and pans that were unfamiliar to her. These utensils were so different from the ceramic *ollas* and jars she had grown up with in El Nido, or even the kitchenware at the pension. And hot water in the sink—imagine that! Mrs. Holmes mentioned it was a health requirement. Esperanza wondered how many other homes in Flor Blanca had such luxuries.

"Señora, you will have to teach me how to use these objects. They are different from the pots and pans with which I am used to working."

On the left side of the kitchen was a white table and two chairs, which Esperanza assumed was the servants' eating area. Next to the table was a door with a lock on it that led to a small narrow room that held the refrigerator and several floor-to-ceiling cabinets, also with locks. This room opened into the dining room, whose door also had a lock.

Esperanza had been introduced into another new world, as different as Doña Marta's pension had been from El Nido.

When they left the dining room area. Mrs. Holmes led Esperanza back to the sitting room–office. "Sit down if you wish Esperanza," said Mrs.

Holmes. But Esperanza remained standing as she had with Doña Marta. "I want you to remember that the sink in the kitchen has a hot water faucet that you and Altagracia are to use when you wash the dishes. It is much healthier than cold water, which Altagracia doesn't seem to understand."

Esperanza nodded, even though using hot water would be a new experience for her. "Yes, Señora. We will use hot water."

"Good," said Mrs. Holmes. "I thought we should have a simple lunch and dinner today. Only Dr. Holmes and I are eating in—my daughter is invited out. Maybe only a sandwich at noon and meatloaf, baked potato, and a salad for dinner."

"Señora, let me ask you for some guidance. How many people should I be preparing meals for each day? Just Dr. Holmes, you, and Altagracia?"

"Oh, I do have more to tell you, don't I?" She half-smiled as she explained in her halting Spanish, "My youngest daughter is also with us. My older son and daughter are in the United States at universities. I expect them for Christmas and have rooms for them upstairs. My daughter's name is Catharine—we call her Kitty. She is almost seventeen and will be going to college next year."

Mrs. Holmes sipped some water before continuing, "We arrived last month and plan to be here for about two years. We come from Ames, Iowa, where my husband is a professor. We arrived a few days before I met you in the market and we moved into this house last week when our furniture arrived. We lived two years in Puerto Rico on a similar assignment before the War. That's where I learned some Spanish—though not as much as Dr. Holmes and my children. Kitty is fluent; she was a little girl then and learned fast."

"Now about the housework," continued Mrs. Holmes, "I expect you to do most of the cooking. Altagracia is to do the cleaning and washing. She is the niece of the maid at a friend's house and has only recently come from the country. Please help her if you can. She has such a warm smile, but really doesn't know much about housecleaning."

Esperanza smiled and said, "Yes, Señora."

Esperanza asked, "How would you like your sandwiches, and what do you want in them? Please show me how you prepare them, so I won't disappoint you. Also, what is meatloaf? Is it similar to roast or chicken? For dinner at the pension, I often made a roast—either beef or chicken—or one of my special *sopas* or *cazuelas*. I'm not sure I've ever made a meatloaf before."

Mrs. Holmes smiled and said, "I guess I will have to teach you some American cooking. I'll show you after lunch how to prepare a meatloaf and you can teach me some of the Salvadoran dishes."

Mrs. Holmes then took Esperanza on a tour of the house. She began by showing her the bedroom and bath adjoining the sitting room, which Mrs. Holmes referred to as the "master suite." As they moved toward the front of the house, Altagracia quietly joined them from the kitchen area.

Beside the front door to the right was a closet and guest bathroom. To the left, past a short wall, was the large living room with a fireplace at the far end. Between the living room and master suite was the staircase to the second floor, which housed three large bedrooms and two baths. Opposite the master suite was the dining room, which opened onto the patio on one side and into the pantry on the other.

The entire first floor was painted a light pink, with matching pink-tiled floors that extended throughout the space—except for the servant's patio, where the walls were white-washed and the floor cemented. Beyond the kitchen door in the patio, Mrs. Holmes pointed out the laundry room, which contained two large washing basins and a large, box-like appliance with a door on the top. Curious, Esperanza asked, "What is the box for?"

"That is a new washing machine," responded Mrs. Holmes.

"A washing machine? Doña Marta's had one on rollers with a wringer on top," commented a very surprised Esperanza.

"The new one is much more convenient. I'll show you later how to operate it." The door between the pantry and the kitchen could be locked on the pantry side.

After the tour, Mrs. Holmes freshened up while Esperanza prepared lunch. She found white bread in the refrigerator as well as packages of ham and cheese. She toasted the bread on the top of the stove and prepared a platter of the ingredients for the sandwich. It took her only one time to learn how Mrs. Holmes liked her sandwiches, her coffee, and all her other lunch and dinner specialties. She learned to use mayonnaise, mustard, and pickles; and she introduced the American to Salvadoran specialties that she adapted, when necessary, to satisfy American taste buds. That afternoon she watched Mrs. Holmes prepare a meatloaf and blend all the ingredients and then bake it. She also learned for the first time how Americans prepared salad with fresh vegetables—including how to soak lettuce with disinfectants to protect against amoebas and dysentery. She also peeled her first tomato for a salad, and she learned how to make salad dressings, which were very different from her native *surtidos*. These were the first of many American recipes that Esperanza would learn from Mrs. Holmes.

Before the first day in her new cycle of life, Esperanza had established a warm working relationship with her new employer. They respected each other and were keen to learn from each other. Esperanza helped Mrs. Holmes to find the right word in Spanish to complete an explanation, and Mrs. Holmes was helping Esperanza pronounce words in English, usually the name of a kitchen appliance or a food ingredient.

The relationship between Esperanza and Altagracia was firmly defined. Esperanza was the one who would train Altagracia to do her job to the standards Esperanza deemed necessary.

Lunch went very well. The sandwich met Mrs. Holmes's expectations.

CHAPTER 27

At 6:00 a.m. the following morning, Esperanza and Altagracia were seated at the table in the kitchen. Esperanza was clearly frustrated. She could find nothing to prepare for breakfast. There were no beans, tortillas, or plantains. Altagracia was trying to explain to her what the Americans ate for breakfast. She had shown her the boxes of flakes and nuggets that they placed in bowls and added milk. She pointed out the strange contraptions they used to squeeze the oranges for juice and toast their bread. A frustrated Esperanza could only manage to prepare coffee for the two of them until a family member arrived to give her further instructions.

About 7:00 a.m., the first family member appeared—the daughter, Kitty. She was a teenager, about Altagracia's age and just a few years younger than Esperanza. In the rapid cadence of Caribbean Spanish, she greeted them, "Buenos días, I'm Kitty."

Esperanza responded, "I'm Esperanza, your new cook. I am not sure what you want for breakfast. I am used to preparing for Salvadorans—and there are no beans, tortillas, or plantains like we usually eat. And I don't know how you like your eggs.

"Well, let me help you. We don't eat beans, tortillas, or plantains. My mom and dad have orange juice, warm cereal with milk, a piece of toast, and coffee. I like orange juice, cold cereal with milk, a piece of toast with jam, and milk."

"Please show me, Señorita, which cereal each of your parents and you prefer. And do you prepare the toast on the stovetop or in the oven?"

"First, please call me Kitty, not Señorita. Second, let me show you." She opened the freezer unit of the refrigerator and took out two cans of frozen orange juice. Then she opened a nearby cabinet and took out an appliance that opened on both sides. Then she reached into another cabinet and took out two tall boxes. Turning to Esperanza, while Altagracia looked on, wide-eyed, she said, "The orange juice is frozen in these containers. You pour the contents into a pitcher and cold water. Watch me."

Kitty went to the refrigerator, took out a large pitcher of water, and filled the container with more water before emptying it back into the pitcher, repeating the process. She said carefully, "Only use the water from the refrigerator, not from the tap. We boil all our drinking water to avoid parasites."

"If I understand you, the water is boiled on the stove before putting it in the refrigerator?" Esperanza asked.

"Oh, yes, we never drink the water from the tap. My father is a public health doctor and knows all about diseases that come from untreated water, and you will need to boil or disinfect any water that we use."

"That is all new to me, at Doña Marta's we just used the water from the tap. How long should I boil the water? And the bottles must also be clean?" asked Esperanza.

"I suggest that you let the water boil for a minute or two. And always make sure that the bottles are carefully cleaned with hot water before you refill them."

"Thank you, Señorita. I will do my best to keep the family well," Esperanza affirmed.

"Now, Esperanza, this is a toaster," as Kitty moved the appliance out of a cabinet. "You put a slice of bread on each side. Toast that side and then turn the bread over to toast the other side."

Esperanza looked at the contraption and asked, "How do I get it warm to toast the bread?"

Kitty just smiled and pulled out the cord and plugged one end of the cord into the toaster and the other into the wall socket. "You see what I did. That turns on the toaster. Pull the cord out of the wall socket and turn off the toaster. Here let me show you."

She toasted a piece of bread and handed it to Esperanza. "Butter it and you and Altagracia try it." They tried it, but it was not as satisfying as their tortilla.

Kitty then took three bowls from the cabinet in the pantry filled with dishes. She set them on the kitchen table. Then she opened the box of Quaker Oats, dished out several spoonfuls into a pot. Then she added some milk to the pot and turned on the heat. Esperanza watched very carefully—both the amount of milk added and the temperature on the stove. Kitty said, "That's the way you make my parent's hot oatmeal. Don't overcook it, just bring it to a boil."

Then, she took another large box of Post Toasties and emptied a large amount into the third bowl, added the milk and said, "And this is my morning cereal."

Esperanza absorbed the process and said, "You don't want any eggs, beans, or plantains?"

"Oh no. Too heavy for me." She then paused as if a light had just come on, "You girls aren't used to our breakfasts. You eat tortillas, beans, and plantains. And eggs?"

"Yes, Señorita for five years, I prepared breakfast at the pension with beans, fried plantains, tortillas, pupusas, and sometimes eggs and bacon. The guests loved my breakfast. I had planned to have one on the table for you this morning. I am sorry that I could not have your breakfast ready for you."

"Don't be upset. I understand. We had a similar problem when we went to Puerto Rico in 1939. I'll remind my mother that we need to buy your staples as well as ours. We expect you to eat the same food as we do, but we learned that you have certain foods that you prefer. Esperanza, prepare your breakfast today with what is available. I'll ask my mother if we can go to the market later this morning to buy some beans, plantains, and tortillas for your breakfast tomorrow. I'll just take my breakfast to the dining room table, and you get everything ready for my parents. They will be getting up about now."

"Thank you very much, Señorita. You have saved my day; I'll be ready to go to the market when you say. Do you have baskets for us to take to the market?"

Kitty pointed to several in the corner just as a monster cockroach jumped out.

Esperanza sternly said to Altagracia, "Get that insect and move the baskets to the patio. Scrub them. I want no roaches in my kitchen."

CHAPTER 28

T hanks to Kitty, breakfast went off without a hitch. Dr. and Mrs. Holmes had their breakfast just as they liked it. Dr. Holmes asked for some cinnamon for his oatmeal and Mrs. Holmes, some butter. They never had to ask again.

Kitty got her mother's approval to go to the market. Kitty and Esperanza took the bus downtown to the Central Market. They no longer had the luxury of the taxi. They did hire a boy to carry the baskets though. Esperanza convinced Kitty that it was insurance against sneak thieves. Esperanza introduced Kitty to all her market friends and taught Kitty how to bargain. As a result, they spent much less than Kitty had expected, even though Esperanza bought a supply of spices to season her foods, and some fruit to enrich the family's daily cereals. Kitty also found that the oranges in the market cost more than the cans of frozen juice. With full baskets, Kitty hired a cab to take them home.

After taking the items back to the kitchen area, Esperanza turned over the cleaning and storing of the purchases to Altagracia, and she observed how little Altagracia knew about food handling. As Altagracia worked at the kitchen sink, she emptied the baskets, throwing out the window any leaf or extraneous item she thought inedible.

"What are you doing, Altagracia?" Esperanza rang out.

"Oh, I am doing what the nuns taught me. I am separating out the bad stuff and throwing it out the window for the buzzards to clean up," responded Altagracia.

"That's not what we do here. You take those baskets into the patio, lay down some cloths, place the food on the cloths, then scrub the baskets and make sure there are no cockroaches before bringing the food to me in the kitchen. I will go over the various items and tell you what we'll keep and where to store them. Are you throwing out my spices?"

Esperanza glared at the younger girl as her voice got shriller, "I told you never to throw anything through the window into the patio for the buzzard to clean up. I am not going to tell you again. You will learn how to do things right, or I'll report you to the Señora."

There was a short pause before Altagracia started to cry, but Esperanza turned her back to her and went to the task of preparing lunch. Then she remembered what Doña Marta had told her so often, "Control your temper if you ever hope to train them. They grew up learning bad habits. You can't train them if you fight with them." Then she also recalled Mrs. Holmes' words about a happy household. She knew that she had to train Altagracia to satisfy Mrs. Holmes. Esperanza turned back to Altagracia and said, "No need to cry. I will teach you and things will work out." Altagracia wiped away her tears and nodded.

After supervising the cleaning and storage of the morning's purchases, Esperanza went to the sitting room to ask what Mrs. Holmes wanted for lunch. There she found her talking with Kitty. "Just some soup and a sandwich will do. Dr. Holmes is not coming today."

Mrs. Holmes went to a locked cabinet in the pantry and brought out two cans of Campbell condensed tomato soup—something Esperanza had never seen before. Kitty explained, "You make the soup from the cans. You just open the cans, pour the contents into a pot, add two cans full of water, stir the water into the mixture and then cook until it comes to a boil."

As she absorbed the instructions, Esperanza realized how Altagracia must have felt just a few minutes before.

"What would you like for the sandwiches?" asked Esperanza.

"Do we have meat left over from last night?" asked Mrs. Holmes.

"I don't think so, Señora," replied Esperanza.

"Then," turning to Kitty, "Let's open a package of ham in the refrigerator. Please show Esperanza where we stored it in the back of the refrigerator."

Esperanza cut in, "Señora, I make good beef, chicken, vegetable, and tomato soups. There is no need for canned soups. If you tell me in the morning that you want soup for lunch, I will have it ready for you. And, for the sandwiches, do you want the bread toasted and buttered or just plain?"

"We almost always have soup and sandwiches every day. Sometimes a salad," replied Kitty.

Mother said, "Kitty is right."

Kitty showed Esperanza where the ham was kept in the refrigerator. The ham was in a package prepared somewhere in the US. Kitty stayed with her as she prepared today's lunch. Lunch was served about 1:00 p.m., and Esperanza observed how little Altagracia knew about serving the table.

When Esperanza commented to Altagracia, "I need to teach you to serve table." Altagracia seemed more than confused. She was grumbling to herself.

Then, she blurted, "I served table for the nuns at my village since I was five years old. I am doing what the nuns taught me."

Esperanza let the matter stand through lunch. She supervised the cleaning and washing of the dishes in hot water, as Altagracia grumbled again about having to use hot water. She resisted Esperanza's efforts to help her.

Then Esperanza decided she needed to know what work experience Altagracia really had. "What jobs did you do at the convent besides wait tables?" Esperanza asked quietly.

"I swept out the halls and school rooms, scrubbed the floors, and wiped the walls and windows."

"Did you work in the kitchen?" was Esperanza's next query.

"Oh no. They never allowed us servant girls to work in the kitchen, but we did carry out the garbage."

"How did you dispose of the garbage—burn it or bury it?" asked Esperanza.

"Oh, we just piled up in the field next door. The nuns said that animals and vultures would dispose of it for us."

"Well," said Esperanza, "You are working in the city now, and you will have to learn, as I had to learn, new ways to work. And I will teach you—and that is what I am doing now. Neither one of us has ever used hot water to clean dishes. But that is the rule in this household—and we will wash the dishes very carefully in hot water. We will scrape each plate and put the garbage in those waste papers to take to the garbage bins outside. Then we must keep the bins tightly sealed to prevent rats and buzzards from opening them. That is the way Mrs. Holmes wants her home managed, and that is the way you and I must work. If we don't learn to do our jobs properly, we'll both be in trouble."

Esperanza thought of her old life in El Nido and realized that Altagracia had lived in an even less prosperous village. Rather than scold her, Esperanza resolved to teach her.

After dinner that night, Esperanza made a list of the duties that she thought Mrs. Holmes would expect Altagracia to perform. The next morning when she presented it to Altagracia to look over, the young girl said quietly, "I cannot read or write."

Very surprised, Esperanza said, "But you told me you had been with the nuns since you were five years old."

"Oh yes, I had lived and worked with the nuns since I was five, but they only taught reading and writing to paying pupils," was the response.

"Didn't you even try to learn from listening to the nuns or trying to read the books in the classrooms you cleaned?" asked Esperanza.

"Oh no, the nuns wouldn't let me," chirped Altagracia.

Esperanza seemed perplexed. If she had been in a similar situation with her inquisitive mind, she would have found a way. Then she thought of many of the young people she had known in El Nido at her elementary school, and she wondered if they would have done what Altagracia did or found a way to learn.

Later in the morning she accompanied Altagracia upstairs while she made the beds and tidied up. Altagracia really didn't know how to make a bed, and her use of the broom and cleaning rags was haphazard. Esperanza taught Altagracia how beds were made in Doña Marta's pension—how the corners were tucked in and the blankets shaken out. Then she introduced her to the Holmes' vacuum cleaner stored in the downstairs closet. Altagracia's eyes almost exploded when Esperanza turned on the device, and she asked, "Oh, what is that thing? What does it do?"

"This is a vacuum cleaner. It sucks up the dust from the floors and carpets. It is much better than a broom. Mrs. Holmes stores it in the downstairs closet. Just bring it up when you clean. It will make your job easier."

Then Esperanza turned off the vacuum and handed it to Altagracia to use. She showed her how to turn the on/off button and how to use it. She supervised Altagracia as she cleaned every inch of Kitty's bedroom.

She thought she had completed one aspect of Altagracia's training until she heard the young maid muttering in despair. Esperanza walked to the door of Kitty's room and saw Altagracia trying to work the vacuum cleaner in the hallway, but nothing happened as Altagracia moved the on/off button. Esperanza saw the problem immediately: she had forgotten to show Altagracia that she had to attach the cord of the vacuum cleaner to a wall plug.

Next, Esperanza showed Altagracia a mop and how to use it to clean up the tiled floors without getting down on her hands and knees as she had when she had cleaned the floors at the nunnery. Altagracia had never seen a wet mop before and required several lessons before she mastered the art.

One morning in the kitchen, Esperanza asked Altagracia, "Get me the box of Grape Nuts from the pantry closet." She heard the familiar muttering of a confused Altagracia—and then remembered that she couldn't read. "Never mind, I'll get it myself."

That led Esperanza to teach her the alphabet, a few key words, and how to sign her name. She came to realize how little Altagracia knew when she had joined the Holmes household—so much less than the eighth grade-educated Esperanza when she had started working at the pension.

It must have been in the first week at the Holmes' when Esperanza wondered if Altagracia had learned how to tell time. Esperanza heard her vacuuming the office-sitting across the hall. She knew it had a large electric clock on the desk. So, she called to Altagracia, "What time is it?"

There was a pregnant pause, the patter of feet, and the response. "It is 10:30, Esperanza."

Esperanza waited several minutes before crossing the hall from the pantry to the office-sitting room. She looked at the clock and felt Altagracia at her side.

"Was that the right time, Esperanza?" asked Altagracia.

"No, it is only 10:10 right now," responded Esperanza.

"Ay, Esperanza. I have such difficulty with those English-speaking clocks!"

Thus, Esperanza thought carefully about what training Altagracia would entail. It would be an ongoing process, as Esperanza had learned from Mrs. Holmes and Kitty what they expected from their household staff. She made sure Altagracia understood how the Holmeses wanted their house maintained, how often the linens should be changed, how the furniture should be arranged, what security measures had to be followed, and how guests should be treated. Esperanza took careful note of the Holmeses' standards and worked to instill those expectations in both her own work and Altagracia's.

CHAPTER 29

E speranza had Thursday and Sunday afternoons off, which were the two occasions each week she spent with her mother and son. Mrs. Holmes allowed her to leave after lunch and return by 10:00 p.m. Of her monthly salary of 250 *colones*, 200 went to her mother to cover rent, food, and other family necessities. Esperanza and her mother learned to carefully budget those precious resources to make ends meet.

Her mother decided that she needed to add a few more *colones* to the monthly income. She alerted her new neighbors that she was home all day and, for a few *colones* per day, she would babysit for those single mothers who needed to work. Almost every woman on their block had at least one child. By the third month, she was earning almost 20 *colones* a week—not much, but a little more to cover budgetary needs.

She also developed a close relationship with her next-door neighbor Patricia, thanks to the friendship between Patricia's son Pablo and José. The boys had become inseparable companions. Patricia and Flor took care of both boys, and their families soon began sharing dinners and intertwining their lives.

Flor also took care of the chickens that Doña Marta had given her when the pension closed. Those chickens seemed to love Flor and laid her a good daily quantity of eggs. She had a schedule for each hen to hatch a chick or two. Flor made a few more *colones* from selling eggs each week. She also planted a few vegetables in her small yard using seeds she had brought from the pension. After all, she had grown them for Doña Marta, so why not grow them for herself? She knew the soil was mostly clay, but by adding in garbage scraps and eggshells, she hoped to make it a little more fertile over time.

Flor was clearly adapting to her new circumstances. She had never wanted to leave El Nido or live at the pension, but here she was. She had learned to live with running water in the house, indoor plumbing, a radio, electric lights, a shower in her bathroom, a refrigerator, and even sleeping on a bed with a mattress—things she had never known existed when she lived in El Nido.

Now she was building a new life for herself, her daughter, and her grandson. She lived in a two-room home that required only minimal chores to maintain each day—and she had her radio. To her surprise, she found herself happier than she ever expected to be outside of El Nido. It wasn't that she didn't miss her own land and her own people, but she had found a way to create a new life that, somehow, suited her.

She knew that Esperanza would be home with them only two afternoons a week, arriving around 3:00 p.m. and leaving by 8:00 p.m. Esperanza had explained the bus schedules and how she spent time at the market on Thursdays before coming home. She knew that Esperanza had connections with women at the Central Market who sold her leftover vegetables, fruits, and meat scraps at special low prices. When Esperanza arrived, she would cook dinner on the wood stove, and the leftover food would last them another day or two. It was Esperanza who ensured they had delicious entrées and soups, supplemented with beans, plantains, tortillas, and eggs.

Mother also became responsible for all the apartment bills—the monthly rent, utilities, Nico the watchman's fee, and medicines from the corner pharmacy. Esperanza paid these once a month when home, but Flor grew increasingly aware of each family expense and made every effort to reduce costs so as to not deplete their small nest egg. She not only kept track of the bills but also kept the receipts. It was a stark change from life in El Nido, where her husband and brother handled such matters. Now, Flor was learning the importance of money to survive in the city.

Her mother knew that, despite all her efforts, Esperanza was central to sustaining her and her grandson's life. For Esperanza, those demands meant that Esperanza herself had little time to develop any real social life of her own. Her world revolved around the needs of those who depended on her—her mother, her son, the Holmes, and even Altagracia.

CHAPTER 30

E speranza settled into her new routine. Every weekday morning, she prepared the breakfasts that each family member preferred. Afterward, she met with Mrs. Holmes to discuss the menu for lunch and dinner before setting about preparing those meals. She grew accustomed to the different eating habits of her American employers, which were quite different from those of Doña Marta's clients at the pension. Esperanza absorbed the recipes for the special dishes that the Holmes family favored.

Purchasing food for the Holmes family was very different from Esperanza's experience with Doña Marta at the pension. Mrs. Holmes wasn't particularly interested in going to the market. She received cases of canned goods from the United States—fruits, vegetables, cereals, and canned meats. She seemed wary of many local products, and when she did buy something, she preferred the neighborhood's only grocery store, run by an American, which was stocked with higher-priced groceries and specialty foods.

The Holmes often went out to dinner with friends in the American community living in San Salvador—most were from the embassy or the US government. In turn, the Holmeses had dinner parties for those friends and the members of the Salvadoran government or local doctors with whom Dr. Holmes worked.

In their first couple of months, the daily fare included canned foods that Esperanza found quite bland. She slowly introduced the family to her soups and main dishes, especially the chicken and beef specialties she had prepared for Doña Marta's special luncheon guests, and then the canned soups and meats began to disappear from Mrs. Holmes's daily menus. When the Holmeses invited guests to dinner, Mrs. Holmes gradually began asking Esperanza to prepare one of her specialties—much to the delight of their guests.

By the third month of her time with the Holmeses, Mrs. Holmes allowed Esperanza to prepare the daily menu and grew fond of many of the local dishes Esperanza made. She stopped shopping at expensive stores and began letting Esperanza go to the Central Market to buy fresh local products. As a result, Mrs. Holmes noticed her food bills decreasing, and her taste buds were more satisfied than ever.

By the end of the third month, Esperanza and Kitty had developed a close relationship. Kitty spent a lot of time in the kitchen teaching Esperanza how to use the waffle iron, the mixer, the liquefier, and the popcorn popper. Kitty enjoyed practicing her Spanish and learning the Salvador slang. In turn, she helped Esperanza pronounce words and phrases listed in her basic English book.

Kitty enjoyed the atmosphere and experience of the Central Market and often accompanied Esperanza on her trips. She not only spoke Spanish with the market women but also asked them about their lifestyles and families. Kitty and Esperanza were quietly building a bond unlike any Esperanza had felt before. Although she had worked with Doña Marta for over five years and shared many experiences with her, Doña Marta was much older—it felt more like dealing with an aunt than with a friend.

Along with her friendship with Kitty, Esperanza never overlooked Doña Marta. Once a week, with Mrs. Holmes' permission, she walked two blocks to see Doña Marta in her suite at Teodoro's house. Sure, she talked to Doña Marta about her new life, the health of her mother and son, the gossip from the Central Market, and many other items of interest, but they never really touched the subjects that she and Kitty had begun to share about personal concerns and ambitions that churned inside her mind.

Esperanza realized that Kitty was genuinely interested in her, and she found herself equally interested in Kitty. Kitty shared stories about her life and plans for college, and she encouraged Esperanza to open up about herself. No one had done that before. Esperanza had kept everything inside since her grandmother's death—and even more so after the day she was raped. She had focused on survival and protecting the life she had conceived by doing what was necessary. But deep within, she had never lost the dream of being more than just a cook. She longed to express herself and do something meaningful, which was something her grandmother had instilled in her when she had taught her to cook and use the herbs and plants of her great-grandmother, the *Gran Curandera*. Esperanza wanted to emulate the *Gran Curandera*, and that ambition kept alive her dream of becoming a teacher. It was with Kitty, not Doña Marta, that Esperanza felt she might be able to share such intimate thoughts.

Sharing their thoughts seemed to come naturally, but it was Kitty who opened the door. After all, she was the daughter of Esperanza's patron, and she instinctively knew that Esperanza would be hesitant to express her opinions to her employer's daughter. Kitty had learned that in Puerto Rico, but she was also her father's daughter. He was a doctor who wanted to improve health services for the people, and she wanted to follow in his footsteps. He was an adviser to the minister of health and was interested in helping the Salvadoran people, and so was she. So why not share her thoughts with a Salvadoran woman around her age, someone she liked, and gain insights into the country where she was temporarily living?

On their second bus trip the Central Market, Kitty commented, "There are so many poor people in the city, even in our neighborhood."

"But these people live better than those in my village, El Nido," replied Esperanza.

"Really? I thought life in the villages would be easier and better. Afterall, you can produce your own food and have your own land," reacted Kitty.

"Oh no, Señorita, life in the villages is very hard. We live each day and hope to have food for the next. It is a dawn-to-dusk workday hoping to raise enough food for the family to eat. There are no cash crops anymore, and we have to use our seed carefully," continued Esperanza.

Kitty thought for several moments before saying, "I would like to talk to you about how you see things when we get home. My father is working with the minister of health, and I will be helping my father for the next few months before I go to Johns Hopkins University next year. I can't help my father very much unless I understand your country better."

Then Kitty asked, "Esperanza, how old are you?"

Esperanza replied, "I am almost twenty-one years old."

Kitty gasped, "I thought you were much older."

Esperanza said bitterly, "I was a teenager like you when I was raped as I returned from my acceptance at our high school in Chalatenango City. I had to abandon school to care for my child. I saw no future in El Nido and brought my mother and son to San Salvador in search of a likelihood to sustain us. Fortunately, my grandmother had taught me how to cook and to use the spices nurtured by my great-grandmother, the *Gran Curandera,* in enriching our food. My family for generations had lived in El Nido, and the indigo crop kept us living well. When the market for indigo dried up, so did our family income. So, with my misfortune, I had to come here for a new life."

Kitty asked no more questions en route to the Central Market. Once they got off the bus and were inside the Market, Esperanza took charge and bargained for all the items on the family shopping list.

When they returned from the Central Market, Kitty helped Esperanza carry the purchases to the back patio. Esperanza called for Altagracia and asked her to wipe down the meat, vegetables, and fruit, ensuring that any unwanted guests, like cockroaches, were washed off the food.

Kitty then went into her mother's sitting room and, in almost a whisper, said, "Did you know Esperanza is only twenty-one years old and that she was raped and has a son?"

"Of course I did," her mother replied. "I had a long conversation with Doña Marta, the owner of the pension where Esperanza worked, before I interviewed her for this job. Doña Marta told me the heartbreaking story of a bright, ambitious young woman who had earned a scholarship to study at the provincial high school but was raped by a drunk on her way home from the acceptance interview. She explained how, at just fifteen, Esperanza became a mother and decided to leave her ancestral home, knowing there was no future for her or her son if they stayed. She arrived at the pension and, within a week, became the cook after stepping in to help Doña Marta during an emergency. Yes, I knew all that, and it made me want to help her. And Kitty, you've seen how well she's been doing here. I'm glad she's with us."

Kitty added, "So am I."

From that day forward, Kitty and Esperanza talked not only about the world around them but about their ambitions and interests, too.

CHAPTER 31

The workload at the Holmes household was much less demanding than at the pension. Esperanza prepared three meals a day for three people, and the meals tended to be simpler and less time-consuming. She also learned how to make the dishes Americans especially enjoyed, such as fried chicken, chicken-fried steak, barbecued pork ribs, apple and cherry pie, and various cakes. She discovered how to use flour and instant rice from packages, which saved her hours of preparation compared to the traditional Salvadoran recipes. She spent about an hour each day overseeing Altagracia's work—often having to retrain her on basic tasks like peeling vegetables or making beds. Esperanza worked hard to provide Mrs. Holmes with the quiet, efficient home environment she had wanted.

As the weeks and months passed, Esperanza also saw real advantages to a career working with American families. The attitude toward servants was very different than in a Salvadoran household. She observed that the Holmeses were less demanding and intrusive than at the pension. The market women often told her tales of sexual favors expected of maids in Salvadoran households. She heard stories about the hierarchies in wealthy Salvadoran households, often built on long-time family retainers—life-long loyalty, an almost caste-like relationship, meager wages, and a steady stream of handouts and hand-me-downs. With the Americans, it was more of a business relationship, with better salaries and less uncertainty about the duration of a job—for each American seemed to be in the country for only a couple of years. Esperanza learned that to keep a job with an American employer, performance was key. In contrast, from what she had heard, with a Salvadoran family, it was often loyalty and submission that secured employment.

Esperanza decided she preferred working for an American family for as long as she could. She absorbed the lifestyle of her employers and resolved to truly learn English. One Wednesday morning, as the two girls headed to the Central Market, Kitty commented on the bus ride down, "Doña Marta told my mother at dinner the other night that you bought a book to learn English. How's it going?"

"Yes, Señorita, I actually have two books—one on English grammar and another on understanding English. I have read them several times."

"Oh really? Tell me what you know."

"Well, I have a lot of book knowledge. I can conjugate verbs. I know a lot of words and phrases, but I can't really understand how to speak or hear the flow of language because the sounds are so different from Spanish. Your vowel sounds confuse me. I listen to your conversations at dinner and catch a word or two. When I see the words on paper, I understand a lot but speaking and hearing are real problems."

"Yes," Kitty responded, "We have many vowel sounds, while Spanish only has five—and yours are always constant. In English, you have to learn by pronouncing words since the same vowels vary in different words. Would you like to spend some time with my mother and me learning how to pronounce and hear words?"

"Oh, yes, I would," responded Esperanza.

Thus began periodic sessions where Esperanza practiced speaking and listening to English. Over time, during her employment with the Holmes family, her English improved to the point that she could understand Mrs. Holmes' requests and instructions and respond in English. She even found that she could follow some of the conversations at the dinner table while serving meals. Esperanza borrowed books from Kitty and spent hours poring over the texts, asking Kitty to clarify passages she didn't understand.

It was sometime during the sixth month of Esperanza's employment with the Holmes family that she found herself preparing dinner just for Kitty, since Dr. and Mrs. Holmes were invited out to dinner. After dinner was finished, Kitty entered the kitchen and asked Esperanza to join her in the sitting room. Esperanza supervised Altagracia's cleanup before joining Kitty.

Kitty was reading a batch of papers. She looked up when Esperanza knocked on the door. "Please come in," Kitty said. "I hope you're not tired, because I would like to talk to you for a few minutes."

"No, Señorita, I am not tired. Dinner was simple and there were only a few dishes to wash up."

"Please come over here and sit in that chair. I have some questions about the reports I've been reading from the ministry," Kitty began, motioning to a hesitant Esperanza, who uneasily sat down. Then Kitty added, "Call me Kitty, not Señorita."

Esperanza seemed uneasy at the request to sit down and call her Kitty. She had come to know Kitty well, but she was still her employer and sitting down with her employer and calling her Kitty seemed as unnatural now as it had been when Doña Marta had asked her to sit down in the pension. She almost reluctantly moved into the room, but, this time, she did sit down and say, "Thank you, Kitty."

Kitty began, "You know that I have been working with my father. While his Spanish is good, I've been helping him review some of the papers and records at the Ministry of Health. He finds many of them incomplete, which makes his work harder. So, he's spending a lot of time trying to organize the ministry's record-keeping and standardize the reports coming in from the field offices."

"Oh, there are field offices of the ministry?" queried Esperanza. "I saw a health post at the municipality near El Nido. Would that be part of the ministry?"

"I think so," replied Kitty. "From what I've been reading, the ministry has offices in the capital city of each department, as well as hospitals, health posts, and clinics in many communities throughout the country. Each of these facilities reports to the ministry in San Salvador. They're designed to improve health care for the people of your country and are supposed to provide medical services, staffed by doctors, nurses, and assistants."

"I didn't know that," mused Esperanza.

"The reports from different departments are not standard and my dad is having great difficulty making sense of them."

"What do you remember about the health post in your municipality?" asked Kitty.

"Well, let me think," responded Esperanza. "My school was nearby and occasionally a lady came to talk to us. I think she was a nurse. The only doctors I heard of were in Chalatenango City, the capital of our department. I don't think I ever saw one in our municipality. Yes, the only hospital I know of was in Chalatenango City. I remember one of my teachers or the nurse at the post told us about it."

"You mean to tell me that's all you heard about the national health program in your eight years of schooling?" asked a startled Kitty. "In Puerto Rico, information about health services is built into the curriculum from the first day of school. So, you didn't have school nurses or courses on nutrition and good health practices?"

"Well," thought Esperanza out loud, "We were taught to brush our teeth, told about foods to eat—many of which we couldn't afford—and how to keep our bodies clean. We had some classes on biology. We were taught about mosquitos, rats, and bugs that cause diseases, but I can't think of much more."

Kitty continued, "The reports I'm reading indicate that infant mortality is very high."

"What exactly is infant mortality?" asked Esperanza.

"Oh. That is the death rate for babies," replied Kitty.

"Well, it is a lot," began Esperanza. "My mother lost four of her six children when they were babies. My grandmother always lamented that she was not like her mother, who was famous in our country for curing sick people with her herbs and plants. I remember many ill babies brought to our house and my grandmother and mother trying to treat them—many died. I don't know of anyone who went to the health post in the municipality."

"Well. You have been helpful. I see why so many records are incomplete. The ministry does not have a national child and maternal care program for one thing, and they probably need to set up a standardized reporting system and teach people in the departments how to fill out reports. That is going to be a big job for my father—if he can convince the minister and his military advisers that it must be done."

Kitty began writing a series of notes and then looked over at Esperanza, "I have a question that you may not want to answer."

Esperanza just shrugged her shoulders.

"According to the data I have been reviewing, a very large number of children born in the country are to unmarried parents. Many birth certificates, according to the report, do not contain the name of the father. You told me that you have a son—and that you were raped. Do you know many other women who are single mothers?"

This was a subject Esperanza did not prefer to talk about—the rape and her son and their impact on her dream to become a teacher. She hesitated a bit before saying. "Kitty, this is a subject I'd prefer not to talk much about, but I will with you."

Kitty responded, "I don't mean to get personal, just to understand the situation in El Salvador. Do you know of many unmarried mothers?"

"Well, I don't know of many mothers who are married. In my own family, my grandmother was married. My mother and father married themselves—they couldn't afford the fees for the municipality or the church. They simply said before my grandparents and his parents that they had agreed to marry each other. You see, in my village, we once had strong families because the indigo crop brought in enough money for us to stay together. As my grandmother told me, in those days, the whole family stayed and worked the farms together. They had enough money to tend the crops and live well. Then, as I learned in school, a German scientist discovered a chemical formula to produce indigo, and the market for our product dried up. With no income, the men in our families had to leave the village to find work. Like my older brother, Diego, they went to work the crops elsewhere. For a year or two, they sent money home, but then, like Diego, most disappeared. My mother still mourns for news of Diego."

Esperanza paused and then slowly continued, "We girls at home often have no one to marry. The men still at home are frustrated by the hard life and have no money. They drink, and often the women drink with them. The result is a lot of babies with no man in the house. I saw this when I was a little girl, and my grandmother told me to get an education and stay away from the men until I had my own life. I wanted to be a teacher before I became a mother. I don't know about other places or people, but, in El Nido, I saw lots of babies without a man in the house."

Kitty was visibly moved, said, "Esperanza, I didn't mean to pry."

"That's alright, Kitty. It doesn't hurt to tell you how I feel. And since I've started, let me tell you that most of the women we buy food from at the Central Market aren't married either, but for different reasons. There aren't many jobs for women in San Salvador, as I've learned. The best someone with a limited education can hope for is to become a maid in a good family, like yours, or to secure a spot in the market. Getting a spot in the market usually means giving favors to the men who run it. These men are usually married or have women of their own, but they still demand favors—whether it's money or sleeping with them when they want. I don't know a woman in the market who doesn't have a baby or two from these arrangements."

Kitty was shocked and almost trembled.

"I'm sorry, but you asked me—and I can only tell you what I've learned in the five years since I came to San Salvador. It's what I've gathered from the Central Market, other markets around the city, and in Soyapango. Let me also add that many of the market and working women don't want to get married. Under the law, once they're married, their husbands own them. The husbands take their money to drink and spend it on other women. They can control the children and run their wives' lives. Several women have told me never to get married and lose my independence."

Kitty thought for a minute about women's rights in Iowa and the struggle for equality in her country—and she understood the reluctance of Salvadoran women.

"Kitty, I've also met several women at Doña Marta's and in my neighborhood who are mistresses of powerful men—often military officers or coffee planters. They live on the money their lovers give them to support themselves and raise their children. None of them are married either."

Esperanza thought for a minute and continued, "I don't know what percentage of the children that may be, but it must be quite a few. I know rich people get married. They can afford it. But there are a lot more poor people in this country than rich. How it affects the numbers in your report I can't imagine, I suspect the more information you can pull together, the more children of unmarried mothers you will find."

Kitty said, "Thank you, Esperanza. The statistics I've read show that about four out of every five children born in the country are to unmarried mothers. I was questioning that, but now I need to look at them again before I talk to my father about these reports. You know, I think you should never give up your dream of becoming a teacher. You've taught me many things tonight."

Esperanza smiled for the first time all evening and said, "Kitty, would you like to have some milk and cookies before bed?"

"Only if you join me," was Kitty's reply.

The two young women walked together to the refrigerator in the pantry and prepared a snack before bed.

For Esperanza, this was the first night that she shared with another person some of her inner feelings and views of the world in which she was living. She had found a friend in Kitty.

CHAPTER 32

At breakfast the next morning, Kitty told her parents in English about her discussion with Esperanza the night before. They listened intently.

It was her father who first responded, "Esperanza has led an interesting life. She is so young and yet so old. She has taken the world on her shoulders and has learned how to cope with it. I can't imagine what it was like to have your dreams shattered at fourteen and end up moving your family to some unknown place to seek a future. Our lives, with all our problems, have not given us such complex challenges."

Mrs. Holmes nodded and said, "I was especially taken by her comments about the rights of women and the opportunities for them to make a decent living. It makes me wonder how I would have coped."

Dr. Holmes mused, "We know the struggle for women's rights in our country over the past half-century, and the terrible working and living conditions our women have faced. But what she described is far more harrowing. It makes my task even more challenging than I anticipated. How do I design a maternal and child care program that most mothers can actually afford in a country where government revenues are so limited?"

Kitty interjected, "What do you mean father?"

"Well, the ministry's budget is small. It has only a handful of trained staff and almost no experience in administering programs. Much of its available income goes to managing the few hospitals and clinics in the country. As of today, the country has almost no industry to create jobs for either men or women. Tax revenues are nearly all based on taxes from coffee exports and import duties. How can I advise the minister to set up a critically important program the country can't afford?"

There was a pause in the conversation as Altagracia removed the dishes, and then Dr. Holmes said, "I guess I'll find a way. But I do have to make the minister aware of all the institutional and personnel investments he needs to make to build a well-functioning public health program."

Trying to change the mood at the table, Mrs. Holmes interjected, "Kitty, I wonder what Esperanza can tell us about the herbal remedies of her great-grandmother."

Dr. Holmes piped in, "I learned during the war that some herbal medicines can work wonders. What if I arrange for Kitty to work with Esperanza to make a list of those she knows and how she uses them?"

"That would be a great idea," said Mrs. Holmes. Kitty nodded her head in agreement.

Dr. Holmes offered, "I will talk to her after breakfast to see if she is interested." His wife and daughter smiled.

Instead of heading to his car for the drive to the ministry, Dr. Holmes turned toward the kitchen patio and called to Esperanza, who appeared almost immediately.

"Good morning, Doctor, did you call?"

"Yes, I did," continued Dr. Holmes in halting Spanish. "I want to thank you for sharing your thoughts with Kitty last night, and to ask you if you would describe the herbs and plants that your great-grandmother used."

In her equally-limited English, Esperanza replied, "Thank you, Sir. I would be pleased to tell you."

"Oh, you know some English, good. Good," he responded in English. "I'll have Kitty talk to you." He smiled and turned back to the hall in route to the front door and his car.

A few minutes later, Kitty appeared at the kitchen door. The two usually spoke in Spanish, except when Kitty was helping Esperanza improve her English. She asked Esperanza, "When will you have time to tell me about the herbs and plants your great-grandmother used?"

"If your mother is not planning a dinner party, next Wednesday might work. We will have gone to the market on Tuesday, and Altagracia doesn't do the wash until Friday."

"Alright, I'll tell my father," nodded Kitty.

"You know, Kitty, I would like to include my mother in our talk. My great-grandmother showed her all the herbs and plants when she was a little girl. And maybe she knows better than I. She can help me remember them and their uses."

"I'll see if my father can arrange a car to take us to your home."

"We just have a small apartment in San Judas—in a building that the son of Doña Marta owns. It is very simple, but that is all we can afford."

"That doesn't bother me," said Kitty.

When Kitty told her father about Esperanza's suggestion, he arranged for an official ministry car to take Kitty and Esperanza to the apartment. Esperanza sent word to her mother through one of the market women who lived in the same San Judas block, letting her know that she and Kitty would be visiting on Wednesday afternoon.

That Wednesday afternoon, after midday lunch, the ministry car delivered Kitty and Esperanza to the front door of the apartment where Esperanza's mother was waiting. The apartment, with its hodge-podge of furniture left over from Doña Marta's pension, was dusted and in order.

Esperanza embraced her mother and introduced Kitty to her, "Mother, this is Kitty, the daughter of my employers, Dr. and Mrs. Holmes. I have told you about her. She is here this year before she goes to the university in the United States."

Her mother with her eyes cast down said, "I am Flor de los Angeles Choarti, and I am pleased to meet you."

"I am pleased to meet you, too," Kitty replied.

Flor seemed very uncomfortable with her guest—as if she didn't quite know what to say or do. Rather awkwardly, she motioned to Kitty to sit down on the well-worn sofa and asked, "May I bring you some *horchata*? I just made it for your visit."

Esperanza followed Kitty to the sofa and began explaining, "Mother, Kitty and her father are very interested in learning about the herbs and plants that the Gran Curandera used to care for our people—the ones that were passed down to us. We may never have the gift to use them as she did, but we did learn to identify them and how they can be used to improve our food and to help cure people."

Esperanza's mother just sat transfixed. She seemed very surprised that someone would ask for her knowledge. She was only a tender of farm animals and children. Quite humbly, with her eyes fixed on the floor, she responded, "Are you sure you want to ask me? I love herbs and plants, but I was never good at using them on people, just on my chickens and pigs. My mother was better than I—but, never like my grandmother, the *Gran Curandera*."

Kitty smiled as she said, "Señora, I want to make a list of the herbs and plants that you and Esperanza know about. Please help me. All I need is for you and Esperanza to tell me the names of those you remember, what each looks like, and what each is used for."

Esperanza said, "Mother, we can help a lot of people get well if we take a little time to remember what we learned—and we can honor the *Gran Curandera*."

Esperanza's mother just sat quietly, thinking. She rose from her chair and poured three cups of *horchata*. She brought two cups over to the sofa and handed them to her visitors. Then she retrieved her own and sat down. She took a sip or two before she said, "If you think I can help, I will work with you."

Esperanza moved to the small table and motioned for Kitty and her mother to join her. Kitty took several sheets of paper, a couple of pencils, and a Leica camera from the briefcase she had brought with her. She also produced some of the herbs and plants that Esperanza had on hand in the kitchen. She said, "Let's start by you naming each one of these and telling me their uses. I'll do the writing and picture-taking."

That was the first of many sessions over the next few months in which Esperanza and her mother identified and described the precious herbs and plants that the *Gran Curandera* had shared with her family. Esperanza found several more in the stalls of the Central Market. Kitty wrote down the names and took photos.

It was Dr. Holmes who provided the formal structure for Kitty's presentation. Each herb and plant was given its own page, headed by the name that Esperanza and her mother used. This was followed by a photo, a description of its color(s), known locations in El Salvador, and its uses in healing and cooking that Esperanza and her mother could recall. Dr. Holmes was interested in starting a program within the Ministry of Health to collect information about the country's resources for use in combating various diseases.

For Esperanza, it was the first time that she had ever participated in preparing such a report, and it taught her the disciplines she would need if she were ever able to continue her education.

By the time Kitty left for university, nearly fifty plants and herbs had been cataloged. Dr. Holmes was so proud of his daughter's work that he presented the findings to the minister of health, a military surgeon by profession. The minister looked them over and remarked quizzically, "I only know of one useful plant—it helps reduce the swelling of gunshot wounds, and it's not here. This is interesting, but it's not one of my priorities."

A very troubled Dr. Holmes walked out of the minister's office. He believed that El Salvador had an opportunity to develop herbal medicines to help treat its own people, but he had encountered an uninterested minister. Upon returning to his office, he had three copies of the report made, leaving the original in his office files. He sent one copy to the Washington headquarters and took the other two home—one for Kitty and the other for Esperanza.

The project strengthened the relationship between Kitty and Esperanza, making them lifelong friends. It also sparked in Kitty a lasting interest in herbal medicine. When she became a respected doctor, she was known for incorporating herbal remedies into her treatments whenever possible.

For Esperanza, it was life changing. It made her feel that she indeed had skills and knowledge beyond cooking. It revived her dream of getting more education and becoming a teacher.

CHAPTER 33

With Mrs. Holmes's permission, Esperanza spent an hour nearly every week with Doña Marta at her suite in Teodoro's house, just a block away. Whenever Esperanza prepared one of Doña Marta's favorite dishes, she would bring a portion for her former employer to enjoy. Each visit, Doña Marta seemed delighted to see Esperanza, almost as if it brought her back to life. Esperanza couldn't help but wonder if closing the pension had been the best decision for the older woman, even though it likely made good financial sense.

Each visit began with Doña Marta asking Esperanza about her week and the latest news from the Central Market. She was particularly interested in what the market women were saying about the political scene. Since his former stalwarts had abandoned the long-time dictator, President Hernandez Martinez, three years earlier, there was a power struggle among the colonels to see who would become the new strongman. Doña Marta was eager to keep up on the latest developments for the safety of her family and its economic future. The news from the Central Market always gave her some tidbits she and her sons could use to forward their interests.

Esperanza also told her former employer about her life with the Holmes family, especially her relationship with Kitty. Doña Marta shared that she had met Dr. Holmes during the war when he came to El Salvador to assist the leader of a US base near the Gulf of Fonseca.

Doña Marta recalled, "At one of those special lunches hosted by my sons, Teodoro brought Dr. Holmes. The American government had sent him to deal with an outbreak of yellow fever at one of the bases the US had set up near the Gulf of Fonseca. He contacted Ricardo to do some drainage work around the base to stop the breeding of mosquitoes. I remember him as very serious and proper. Ricardo told me that he knows his business and gets the job done. Both my sons respect him very much. You know, it was Ricardo who found the house for Dr. Holmes that you're living in and who installed the hot water system. Can you imagine—hot water!"

Esperanza told Doña Marta about her project with Kitty on the herbs and plants. Doña Marta encouraged her and was not surprised when she was told of the minister of health's reaction to the presentation by Dr. Holmes. "What other response should he have expected? The minister is one of the old warhorses who happens to be a doctor. He doesn't want to change the way he does anything—even if it might be better."

Esperanza was flabbergasted. At the pension, Doña Marta would never have uttered such a comment. Then Esperanza realized that in a place where she might have been overheard, Doña Marta would have been very careful in her choice of words. The military under the dictator-president Hernandez Martinez would not have tolerated such expressions, and one might suffer serious consequences, from exile to death.

"I had forgotten that the Americans had bases in El Salvador during the war," Esperanza ventured.

"Oh yes, they had several. Thanks to Teodoro's company relations with the Americans, Ricardo was contracted to help build those bases. Teodoro's company is a major supplier of equipment for the American military, and they recommended Ricardo. I am not sure where the bases were—Ricardo never talked about them specifically—only that he had lots of jobs at the bases. And he was well paid in dollars."

Doña Marta smiled and smugly continued, "You know, Esperanza, when my husband died and times were tough, I decided that my boys would learn English and look to America for their future when some of my friends looked to Germany, France, and Spain. Germany bought some of our best coffee beans, and France was our culture trove. But I knew that America was the place. I wasn't an old, blind warhorse." Half-laughing, she continued, "And I was right."

"Do you know what Dr. Holmes is doing now? Kitty tells me he is an adviser to the minister," asked Esperanza.

Doña Marta thought for a moment before replying, "I'm not sure, but Teodoro told me that the government wants America's help with some medical, agricultural, and educational projects that were started during the war. Teodoro explained that each of the bases needed local personnel and food. Most of the local people living near the bases had endemic diseases, and many were illiterate. So the US set up clinics and community health posts and opened schools to teach reading and writing. They also found almost no trained workers to help repair vehicles and equipment, so the bases created vocational courses. You know how hard it is to get competent repairmen even in San Salvador—and how few trained workers there were in Chalatenango. After all, there can't be more than two or three Catholic training centers in the whole country. I guess Dr. Holmes is working with the minister to create a national program to provide health services for the people—since, after all, he is a doctor."

Esperanza nodded her head and said, "There is so much our people need to know."

Dona Marta looked intently at Esperanza, "You really still want to be a teacher, don't you!"

Esperanza nodded slowly, surprised by how much the words still rang true. "Yes, Doña Marta. I do."

For a moment, neither woman spoke. Then Doña Marta's expression softened. "You have the heart for it. Don't lose that. The world may push you in different directions, but don't forget what you have always wanted."

Esperanza smiled faintly. The weight of her responsibilities had never allowed her to truly believe in her dream, but hearing those words from someone she respected sparked a flicker of hope.

As she rose to leave, she realized that her visits to Doña Marta were not just about sharing news or meals—they were a reminder of who she had been and who she could still become.

CHAPTER 34

I t was mid-November 1947 and more than six years since Esperanza
had left El Nido and several months since she had been employed by
the Holmes family. Esperanza had grown under Doña Marta's tutelage
into a better-than-average cook. And she was learning much more about
a different cuisine than she had learned from her grandmother and Doña
Marta.

It was about 10:00 a.m. on a Thursday morning. She and Kitty had
done the marketing at the Central Market the preceding day, and she
was preparing to spend her afternoon off with her mother and son.

Esperanza knocked on the door of the sitting room where Mrs. Holmes
was working on some papers. "Yes, come in," responded Mrs. Holmes in
her broken Spanish. "Kitty will be here in a minute."

Kitty appeared just as Esperanza walked into the room. There were
smiles all around as Kitty sat down next to her mother and Esperanza, as
usual, stood.

Mrs. Holmes looked up at Esperanza and happily advised her, "I am
hosting a traditional Thanksgiving Day dinner for the six other American
families here in San Salvador a week from today. I expect there will be
twenty people. That means a lot of extra work next week, and I must ask
you to take your day off next week on Friday instead of Thursday."

Esperanza seemed a bit confused, because she hadn't understood what Mrs. Holmes had said. Kitty saw the confusion on Esperanza's face and added in her fluent Spanish, "A week from today is one of our special days in America. It is called Thanksgiving Day—a national holiday to thank the Lord for all our blessings. We celebrate the day with a special feast, and my mother has invited the families of the other American technical advisers in El Salvador to come to our house for the feast. There should be twenty people."

Esperanza's confusion turned into a smile, as she asked, "What do you want me to do? Should we plan to buy special food at the market?"

Now it was Mrs. Holmes who seemed confused, so Kitty explained to her mother Esperanza's reply. Then Kitty and her mother spoke a bit in English, and Esperanza understood only a word or two. Kitty then looked up at Esperanza to report, "My mother has ordered most of the food from the commissary in the Canal Zone, and the US Air Mission is flying it to us."

Esperanza was surprised. She thought, *Flying in food with all that is available in the Central Market.*

Kitty continued, "We'll be getting two large frozen turkeys, yams, cans of pumpkin, jars of olives, and other special foods. My mother and I will help you with cooking the turkeys, preparing the yams, and making the vegetables. Another lady has agreed to bring pies for dessert. We'll need to plan carefully because our oven isn't very big, and we'll be cooking the turkeys, baking pumpkin pies, and preparing other dishes all at the same time. Next week will be very busy. We'll need you here on Thursday, so we're asking if you can take your day off with your family on Friday instead. My mother wanted me to let you know before you left today."

Esperanza thought to herself, *All the turkeys I have seen were basically wild, and their meat much less tender than chicken. Well, maybe the Americans like that taste.* But she said out loud, "Of course, I will change my day off next week to Friday, and I am ready to do whatever is needed."

Mrs. Holmes then took a cookbook from a nearby bookcase and showed Esperanza a page of recipes with pictures of what a Thanksgiving table looked like. Esperanza nodded. Kitty said, "I will help you read the recipes, and my mother and I will work in the kitchen with you next Wednesday and Thursday."

Esperanza said, "I will need your help in preparing such a special feast for the first time." After a pause, she added, "We will need at least two days to do the cooking because I doubt our oven is large enough to hold two turkeys at a time. And we can't always count on electricity—we have had several outages in the past few weeks. Should we cook one turkey on Wednesday and another on Thursday?"

Kitty said, "Mother, Esperanza has a good point. Maybe one of the other ladies can help us out."

Mrs. Holmes said, "Yes, I hadn't thought of those possible problems. Yes, Esperanza, we will cook one turkey on Wednesday and the other on Thursday morning."

The following Tuesday, an American military vehicle delivered several packages that filled the dining room table. Mrs. Holmes and Kitty oversaw the receipt and arrangement of the items, while Esperanza and Altagracia followed their instructions. Many of the food items were unfamiliar to Esperanza. What especially caught her eye were the two frozen Butterball turkeys, which were unlike any she had ever seen in the market. Her gaze shifted to packages of dried bread, cans of oysters and cranberry sauce, jars of olives and pickle relish, bags of frozen vegetables, and several cans of pumpkin. Esperanza realized she was about to learn how to prepare an entirely different type of meal, and the thought excited her.

On Wednesday, two other American ladies joined Mrs. Holmes and Kitty in the kitchen. The ladies divided up the work, but the turkeys were still defrosting and not ready for cooking. Mrs. Holmes and the other two ladies discussed their plan for getting the feast on the table, with Kitty translating for Esperanza.

"I'm sure the turkeys will be ready to cook by tomorrow morning," Mrs. Holmes said. "I'll prepare the stuffing tonight with breadcrumbs, giblets, and oysters, so all we'll need to do is put the turkeys in the oven and baste them regularly."

One of the other women chimed in, "I've been roasting turkeys for years, and I'd be happy to help. I love the smell of roasting turkey, and I can use the leftover giblets to make the gravy—that's my specialty."

Mrs. Holmes smiled as the woman took charge of one of the turkeys and some of the stuffing ingredients. The woman added, "I'll start roasting around 8:00 a.m. Thursday morning. Are you sure you don't want me to handle the yams too? I make mine with brown sugar and lots of butter—they're a hit every time."

Mrs. Holmes nodded. "That would be a huge help. You can bake the yams in the oven with the turkey if your stove is large enough."

"Oh, mine's the latest GE from Sears, about the same size as yours. I think it'll work just fine." The third lady chimed in, "You know, I cook a good turkey too, and I really want to help out."

Mrs. Holmes smiled. "I think you've got enough on your plate with the pumpkin pies. With twenty people, we'll need at least three or four. Feel free to take as many cans of pumpkin, spices, and condensed milk as you need."

The third lady nodded, clearly pleased with the plan.

Then, with Esperanza and Kitty as the audience, the three ladies went to work to get the food ready for the feast. With Altagracia doing the heavy lifting, the various items were placed in the cars of the other two ladies. When they left, Mrs. Holmes gave a sigh of relief and said, "Now we are ready to go to work."

On Wednesday night and into Thursday morning, Mrs. Holmes kept a close watch on the thawing turkey, deciding on the exact moment it would be ready to go into the oven. She prepared the oyster stuffing, adding celery and moistening it with a splash of bourbon. After stuffing the bird, she carefully stitched it up and placed it in a large roasting pan before sliding it into the oven. It was a process Esperanza had never seen before, and she made sure to commit every detail to memory for the next year.

Mrs. Holmes then showed Esperanza how to make her family's string bean casserole and candied yams with brown sugar, giving precise instructions on when to place the dishes in the oven and how long to bake them. Afterward, Mrs. Holmes left the kitchen to get dressed, but returned periodically to ensure the turkey was being basted regularly and the right spices were added to the gravy accumulating in the pan. Kitty joined Esperanza to help with the green bean casserole and to prepare mashed potatoes Iowa-style, for those who might not care for yams.

Esperanza set up a table in the pantry for the second turkey and the pumpkin pies that the other two ladies were preparing. She also guided Altagracia through each step of arranging the tables in the dining room and front hall—not outside on the patio, as November weather still made it uncertain whether the rainy season was truly over. Mrs. Holmes organized a buffet table in the dining room and gave detailed instructions to Esperanza and Altagracia on how she wanted the food displayed. Esperanza made sure that Altagracia knew how to keep the buffet table well-stocked throughout the meal.

Once the guest arrived, Dr. Holmes served drinks, and Altagracia helped him with ice and mixers. Dr. Holmes carved the turkey in the manner he had learned from his father. Mrs. Holmes kept coming into the kitchen to make sure that all was flowing well. The halls were filled with good cheer, and everyone seemed to be enjoying the food and company. It was a happy, lively feast.

And, once the guests departed, Dr. and Mrs. Holmes invited Esperanza and Altagracia to partake in the feast. Esperanza had never tasted food quite like that before. The turkey had a flavor so different from that of the wild turkeys of El Nido; and the yams, the dressing, and the pies were new to her palate. She truly enjoyed the new sensations.

Mrs. Holmes allowed Esperanza to take some of the leftovers home to her mother and son the following day when she took her day off. Her package included turkey, dressing, string-bean casserole, mashed potatoes, pumpkin pie, jars of pickle relish and watermelon rind, a can of olives, and some other odds and ends. Esperanza placed each item in a large net market bag and shepherded it on the bus to her dwelling in San Judas.

On arriving home, she set about to prepare a feast for her family. Her two-room apartment, with castoff furniture from Doña Marta's pension, was a stark contrast to the house of Dr. Holmes. The wood stove was no match for the electric stove of her employer, but Esperanza gloried in being able to introduce her family to the American tradition of Thanksgiving.

Esperanza made the old kitchen table as festive as possible. There were four rickety chairs at the table: her mother, Pepe, Pablo—whose mother was gone for the day—and Esperanza. She prepared the dinner and even made some gravy from the leftovers. Then, she heaped the plates with the delicacies, and the four ate one of the most sumptuous feasts of their lives.

"This is how the Americans thank God for their good life—by celebrating the feast of Thanksgiving," said Esperanza to her family.

Her mother asked, "Thanksgiving for what?"

"Thanksgiving to God for their bounty and well-being," replied Esperanza.

"Well," said little Pepe, "It is sure good."

Her mother added, "I never thought a tough old turkey could taste better than chicken, and those potatoes were better than anything you ever prepared at the pension. The green beans are different from ours, but very good." Then she paused and added, "I liked the pickles and olives. Their jars will make good drinking glasses, and I will use the can to plant a flower. Please thank Mrs. Holmes for sending us the food."

Esperanza just smiled.

When they finished dinner, Esperanza said to her mother, "When I left El Nido, I thought I was a good enough cook to support my family. Working with Doña Marta, and now with the Americans, I know how much more I have to learn before I will truly be an excellent cook."

CHAPTER 35

I n early December, Kitty gave Esperanza the exciting news that her two older siblings would come to El Salvador for the Christmas season, "The University of Iowa is on vacation for three weeks, and my dad has arranged airfare for them to come here to celebrate Christmas."

Esperanza reflected for a moment. Christmas in El Nido was always a festive time—all twelve days of it. The family had usually attended church in the neighboring county seat on Christmas Eve, followed by a family dinner on Christmas Day. Since it wasn't a busy season on the farm, they had often held small family gatherings. Many families created nativity scenes and adorned them with fresh flowers or greenery throughout the Twelve Days of Christmas.

Her mother and grandmother had often told her that in the old days, before the indigo market dried up, there was much more food and drink during the holidays. Families would decorate carts with green boughs or colorful cloths and head to the church for celebrations. By Esperanza's time, however, the festivities were much more subdued. Gifts were exchanged on Twelfth Night, January 6, when the magi were said to have reached the manger to adore Jesus. After the glory days of indigo, there was little money to buy presents—most were simple foods or hand-spun cloth. What Esperanza remembered most vividly was the drinking and dancing by the adults as they celebrated the season.

At Doña Marta's pension, there wasn't much of a celebration. Doña Marta would set up her family's crèche in the large front parlor by mid-December and decorate the hall and dining room with extra greenery. However, the pension always closed on December 23 and didn't reopen until early January, as it was customary in El Salvador to shut down the government, city, and businesses from Christmas Eve until January 3. Esperanza remembered how her mother, son, and she were always alone in the pension during Christmas, with little to give one another. At least, during those ten days, the only meals she prepared were for her family. She had managed to find small toys for her son and a bit of clothing for her mother.

Now, for the first time in her life, she was sensing a different kind of excitement. Mrs. Holmes and Kitty were searching through trunks to find special boxes for special Christmas items. Dr. Holmes brought home packages from the United States. Then, in the week before Christmas, everything in the house changed. The shift began with the arrival of the two older children, who came not only with their luggage but also with brightly wrapped packages.

Kitty introduced her older brother, Charles, and older sister, Janet, to Esperanza and Altagracia. Both spoke some Spanish, which they had learned when the family spent a year in Puerto Rico before World War II. Charles was about a head taller than Esperanza, with warm brown eyes and wavy brown hair. His face resembled his mother's. Janet wasn't as tall as Charles, but she had a striking resemblance to her brother. They looked like the picture-perfect American teenagers Esperanza had once seen in a magazine on Mrs. Holmes' desk.

Charles and Janet both nodded hello. Charles said in Spanish, "We won't be much trouble."

Esperanza and Altagracia smiled in response.

184

Esperanza asked in her not-so-fluent English, "We are pleased to meet you. Are you hungry after your trip?"

Janet said, "Oh, yes. I would love something. We have been flying for so long. Des Moines to Miami and then to San Salvador. It seems like forever."

Kitty said, "Let Esperanza prepare one of her Salvadoran dishes for you. It's not a hamburger, but you'll love it."

Kitty said to Esperanza, "Prepare a *sopa*, some *pupusas* and a salad. They will like that for now. You know my mother has a big dinner planned tonight."

That began three weeks of festivities like Esperanza had never seen before.

Later that afternoon, Dr. Holmes brought home a tree, which he had ordered from Guatemala. The family enjoyed a wonderful dinner before gathering in the living room to set up the tree and unpack ornaments and strands of flowered paper. Charles and his father started by testing the strings of little glass bulbs, which lit up in various colors. When one bulb didn't work, they replaced it until the whole string lit up. Following Mrs. Holmes, Janet, and Kitty's directions, they carefully draped the lights on the branches. Once the lights were in place, the three ladies began hanging ornaments and paper strands while the men chimed in with suggestions. Laughter filled the room as the family finished decorating the tree.

Esperanza and Altagracia stood in the hall, observing the spectacle and waiting for instructions in case they were needed.

Then, Kitty, being the youngest, was appointed to place a beautiful glass star on the top of the tree. She went up the stepladder that was usually kept in the front hall closet. After the ornament on top was set in place and Kitty was down from the ladder, Mrs. Holmes nodded, and Charles put a plug in the wall socket. The tree lit up. Esperanza and Altagracia were astounded—they had never seen anything like that tree before. They gasped with delight. Kitty turned to them and said in Spanish, "This is our family Christmas tree. We prepare it every year to celebrate Jesus' birth."

Mrs. Holmes said in Spanish, "Please bring us some hot chocolate and cookies."

That marked the beginning of a holiday season that Esperanza would never forget. Every evening for the rest of December, until Janet and Charles returned to university, friends dropped by to see the tree and leave brightly wrapped packages, which were arranged around it. While Esperanza and Altagracia had extra work each night, the joy of the Holmes family being together and sharing that happiness with their friends made the extra tasks feel rewarding.

On Christmas Eve, the Holmeses went to church—not the Catholic church downtown but to a Union Church for evangelical believers. Esperanza had learned of the Reformation and the Protestants in her history courses, and her Catholic instructors had called them heretics. She hadn't had time to think about this heresy until this very Christmas, and she wondered how such loving people could be heretics.

When they returned from church around midnight, Charles lit the Christmas tree again. The family then moved to the dining room, where Mrs. Holmes had asked Esperanza to prepare a pitcher of hot chocolate. As everyone gathered, Mrs. Holmes opened a tin containing a cake Esperanza had never seen before. Kitty explained that it was called fruitcake. When Altagracia brought in the hot chocolate, Dr. Holmes invited both Esperanza and Altagracia to join the family in celebrating Christmas. By custom, Esperanza and Altagracia participated in the Holmes family's annual celebration, despite being household staff.

The following morning, about 7:00 a.m., the family came downstairs and spent the next hour opening presents: shirts and scarves, books and perfume, blouses and unmentionables. There were even presents for Esperanza and Altagracia and their families. Doña Marta had always had a small gift for Esperanza's mother, her son, and her, but nothing like the English language book and table lamp the Holmes gave her. Christmas morning ended with Dr. Holmes giving Altagracia and Esperanza their *aguinaldo*, an extra-month's pay. That was tradition in Latin culture, but often overlooked when not required by law.

Kitty said, "My family asked me to thank you for all your help. We'd like you to spend the rest of the day with your family. My mother, Janet, and I will take care of things here. Go ahead and leave now but be back early tomorrow morning."

Altagracia and Esperanza were truly surprised. They were so surprised that they nearly cried. Altagracia said, "My family is in Ilobasco. I have only my aunt who works for a Salvadoran family nearby, and she has to work today."

Esperanza said, "Then come with me and be with my family today. Kitty, would that be all right?"

Kitty asked her mother, who nodded her agreement. Then, Mrs. Holmes and her two daughters went into the kitchen to send some food home with Esperanza for Christmas dinner.

Esperanza smiled gratefully as she and Altagracia hurried to the bus stop. The streets leading to Esperanza's home in San Judas were nearly empty, as most of the wealthy Salvadorans were away at their country villas or traveling abroad. Neither Esperanza nor Altagracia felt the need to attend church—they had just experienced the true spirit of Christmas with the Holmes family.

CHAPTER 36

Right after New Years, Charles and Janet flew back to Iowa. The Christmas tree was dismantled, and the old routine of life seemed to settle in again.

However, something had changed inside Esperanza. She felt a new awakening within her. Though she carried out her work with the same diligence, it was different—not like at the pension or even before Christmas. For the first time, she felt appreciated not just as a cook, but as a person. The way the Holmes family had treated her made her feel truly respected, something she hadn't felt since that terrible day when the drunk had assaulted her.

As she sat on her cot in the dimly lit servant's room, Esperanza reflected on how the entire family had taken a genuine interest in her life. It wasn't just Kitty, who had become a true friend, but all five members of the Holmes family. Dr. Holmes, the adviser to the minister of health, had seen real value in her knowledge of herbs and plants. Mrs. Holmes had trusted her with most of the food purchasing, confident that she would select the best ingredients at the right price. Kitty had not only accompanied her to the market, but she also encouraged her to study and learn every day, even helping her practice speaking English. Kitty had valued her family's knowledge of herbs and plants, worked alongside her and her mother to document it all, and shared it with her father.

Janet and Charles had even taken time to tell her about their university courses and life at the University of Iowa—as if she were about to join them. After all, she was almost their age—just twenty-one. Without the assault, she would have graduated from high school and earned her *bachillerato* by now, which would have qualified her for university. Had fate been different, she wouldn't have been just their cook. Yet, they had treated her as more than that.

Being at the Holmes' had reignited her innermost desire of becoming a teacher. For the first time since that terrible day, she allowed herself to imagine a future that extended beyond being a domestic servant—a future where she and her family could rise above their current circumstances.

That feeling was strengthened almost daily. Mrs. Holmes even talked to Kitty in Esperanza's presence about her experience doing charitable work at the city hospital, as if Esperanza were truly trained and capable of joining the effort.

Mrs. Holmes had just returned home from the city hospital, where she had spent the afternoon working on a project sponsored by the wife of the American ambassador. In English, she told Kitty and Esperanza, "There's so much to be done. There are so many expectant mothers that sometimes two women have to share a single bed. There are so many people to care for, and so few resources available. The way the hospital is run leaves much to be desired."

As Mrs. Holmes began her report, Dr. Holmes walked in and interjected, "El Salvador has very little experience managing modern hospitals. Traditionally, they were run by the church, but the church no longer has the resources to staff and operate a twentieth-century institution. Some of my colleagues say that when a wealthy Salvadoran falls ill, they head straight to the airport and catch the next flight to the United States. The Ministry of Health lacks the funds, programs, and personnel to properly manage hospitals, even though the law mandates they do so. In the hospitals I've visited, the facilities fall far short of international standards. I'm advising the minister on a plan to upgrade hospital infrastructure."

Esperanza had learned enough English to understand much of the conversation, and she knew from her experiences in El Nido and in the capital that health care was lacking. Her mother had often shared how difficult it was to find adequate care in San Judas, so she had used her own herbs to treat Pepe or Pablo when they were ill since there was little else to rely on. Fortunately, neither child had ever become seriously sick. Neither her mother nor Esperanza had ever needed extensive medical care themselves, and village midwives had been there to help them with childbirth.

Mrs. Holmes increasingly entrusted Esperanza with managing the household. After Christmas, Esperanza was often left in charge while Mrs. Holmes worked at the hospital, and Kitty accompanied Dr. Holmes to the ministry. Kitty assisted him with his Spanish, as they reviewed reports and drafted questionnaires about the country's medical resources, disease prevalence, and operating systems. Dr. Holmes implemented many of the same methods he had used in Puerto Rico before World War II. One evening, Kitty confided to Esperanza, "My father says there's even less reliable data here than there was in Puerto Rico when he worked there."

Becoming informed about the medical needs of her own country reinforced Esperanza's feeling that she should aspire to be more than a cook. She felt she was gaining part of the education she had missed because of the assault, one more relevant to her people's needs than what she would have learned at the high school in Chalatenango City.

She was also improving her English, which she thought was better than she could ever have learned in a classroom. Thanks to the Holmes family, she could now hold conversations in English about more than just marketing needs, and she could read recipes and cooking instructions with ease. Kitty had loaned her textbooks and a novel or two, and Esperanza found herself understanding more as she read. She was also picking up more and more of the conversations at the Holmes' dining room table, which sharpened her ear with each passing day.

At Easter, Mrs. Holmes informed Esperanza that she would be in charge of the house for the week. Dr. Holmes, Kitty, and Mrs. Holmes would be traveling to Antigua, Guatemala, for the special four-day festival. Mrs. Holmes added, "I hope you wouldn't mind skipping your Thursday and Sunday afternoons off while we're away, but we trust you and your judgment. You can take time off when we return."

Esperanza accepted.

Mrs. Holmes also informed her, "I've given Altagracia three days off to visit her family in Ilobasco. After all, she's been working here for almost nine months without a break to go home. We'll be leaving for Antigua on Wednesday and will return Monday afternoon. I'll give her an advance on her salary so she can buy a few things. That should make things easier for you over the weekend."

Esperanza agreed. Easter was not a busy season in El Salvador. The week before Easter, like at Christmas and for the celebration of Christ the Savior of the World in early August, everything in the country closed down—the government, mail delivery, phone service, and most businesses. The city's three movie theaters had only one showing a day. Most churches held only servants' masses, and they were early in the morning. Wealthy Salvadorans disappeared from the city for trips to their country villas or abroad. Hospitals ran on special schedules, because most of the doctors went abroad.

The Holmeses went to Antigua on Wednesday, Altagracia left for Ilobasco early Thursday morning, and Esperanza had the house to herself until Monday. She tried to read the first chapter of an elementary botany textbook Kitty had lent her, but her frustration grew as her limited knowledge of English made it hard to understand.

On Monday morning, Esperanza waited for Altagracia, but she didn't show up. The Holmeses returned later that afternoon, and Esperanza covered for Altagracia. On Tuesday, Esperanza cleaned the house and served lunch and dinner, but still no sign of Altagracia. Wednesday morning, Kitty and Esperanza went to the market while Mrs. Holmes stayed at home—but there was no Altagracia. Finally, late Thursday morning, just before Kitty and Mrs. Holmes were about to leave for a social event, Altagracia appeared—disheveled and reeking of *aguardiente*, El Salvador's sugar-based firewater.

"Oh, Señora, I am so sorry to be late. The water in the river rose, and I couldn't get across."

Kitty looked at her mother. One of the main topics of conversation among the American advisors had been the extended period of drought in the country and its possible effect on this year's crops. Both mother and daughter caught the smell of *aguardiente* at the same time—that sweet, heavy aroma that is like no other.

Mrs. Holmes looked sternly at Altagracia and said to Kitty in English, "She's hungover and has lied to us. I think I'll have to fire her right away."

Kitty nodded and, almost sounding like her mother, said in Spanish, "Altagracia, you are three days late. There hasn't been any flooding in the country, and you smell of alcohol. You've broken our trust. No, Altagracia, pack your things and leave the house at once."

Altagracia burst into tears and said, "Oh, no, Señorita I am telling you the truth."

Kitty and her mother were unmoved. Kitty asked her mother, "Doesn't the embassy instruct us to pay a month's salary if we fire an employee, something to do with a month's notice?"

"Well, just to be safe, I'll prepare a note for her to sign."

Then Kitty, in Spanish, repeated to Altagracia, "Go pack your things. You are fired."

A remorseful Altagracia quietly made her way to her room and packed her few personal belongings into a market bag. She tried to avoid Esperanza but inevitably crossed paths with her in the back patio. The strong scent of *aguardiente* hit Esperanza, instantly bringing back the horrifying memory of her assault. That smell was unforgettable.

"Altagracia, what did you do?"

"There was a party on Easter, and I danced and drank. I was having such a good time, and the men were so attentive. Now, I don't know. The patron has fired me, and I must leave."

At that point, Kitty came into the back patio with a pen and paper, and some *colones*. She said to Altagracia, "This is your notice to leave our house. We will give you a month's pay instead of notice. Please sign the paper."

Altagracia was flabbergasted. She just sobbed. She signed her name as Esperanza had taught her and accepted the money. Then Kitty escorted her to the front door and showed her out.

Shortly thereafter, Mrs. Holmes and Kitty departed to their social event.

On their return, Mrs. Holmes called Esperanza into her sitting room. She began, "You understand why I fired Altagracia. I could not trust her living in this house after her behavior."

"I thoroughly understand," replied Esperanza.

"Now, do you think you can handle both the cleaning and cooking alone, or do you want me to find a replacement for Altagracia?"

"I think I can handle the work by myself," was her reply.

"Then, let's try it that way. If the work gets too heavy, let us know."

Esperanza was almost relieved that she would never have Altagracia around to remind of that terrible *aguardiente* smell.

CHAPTER 37

S everal days later, after lunch, Mrs. Holmes settled down for a quiet afternoon at home. Kitty joined Esperanza in the kitchen. She helped dry and put away the lunch dishes, as she was used to doing at home in the States. When they were finishing up, Kitty asked, "Esperanza, have you ever been to the slum area on the far side of Flor Blanca?"

Esperanza glanced at Kitty and said, "No, I've ridden the bus with people who've told me they live in the ravine, but I've never had the time to see where they actually live. I usually only have enough time to walk to the bus and back to the house."

"Well," Kitty continued, "when I spent Monday and Tuesday with my father, we visited the terrible slum on the edge of our neighborhood. It's a maze of winding lanes with hundreds, maybe thousands, of hovels where people live. The ministry official who took us said there's no sewage, water, or health care services there. We walked through the dust and stench, and I'd never seen anything like it—a few adobe houses, one or two with cement walls and tin roofs, but most looked like makeshift chicken coops covered with cloth, cardboard, or tin. There were scores of little kids running around—many nearly naked. It was heartbreaking."

Esperanza half choked at the description, "My mother, son, and I would be one of them if it had not been for the luck of finding Doña Marta."

Kitty said, "I think you should see what's happening just a few blocks away. My father says it's a huge challenge for your government, and I think you should understand it too. You want to be a teacher, and seeing the level of poverty here will show you the challenges anyone faces who wants to make a difference in this country."

Esperanza was ambivalent, but Kitty insisted.

Kitty arranged with her mother for time to walk the five blocks across the bluff where Flor Blanca was situated. They passed the elegant, cement-reinforced homes designed to withstand earthquakes, continued beyond the few remaining empty lots, and reached the outer edge of the neighborhood near the ravine. As they walked by hills of carpenter ants and patches of crabgrass, they came upon a small path that led down the hillside into the slum below.

Esperanza tried to look away, but the sight deeply moved her. Hovel after hovel clung precariously to the sides of the ravine, with more scattered across the floor of the gap. Everywhere she looked, disarray and poverty dominated the scene. It was a stark reminder of how so many of her countrymen lived. A few women and children wandered through the sand and filth. In her mind's eye, Esperanza imagined the same scene during the rainy season, which would transform the landscape into muck and mud.

Kitty said, "I don't think we should go any further; but I can tell you, seeing it up close yesterday nearly brought me to tears. The conditions these people live in are heart-wrenching."

Esperanza stood, almost transfixed by the scene before her. She nodded in agreement to return to the Holmes' house, but, as she slowly turned, she said quietly, "It's my responsibility to make sure my mother and son never have to live like that."

CHAPTER 38

I n late May, the Holmes' house buzzed with noise and excitement as the two college students returned from Iowa for the summer. The workload was heavy when the entire family was at home, but they took three trips during the eight summer weeks: a week exploring the Guatemalan highlands from Antigua to Chichicastenango, a week in San José and the Costa Rican heartland, and a long weekend visiting Copan in Honduras.

When the Holmes family was away, Esperanza never left the house. Both she and the Holmeses knew that an empty home was an open invitation for burglars. There seemed to be an invisible network that alerted small-time thieves whenever a house was left unattended, even for a short morning errand or an afternoon social event.

Esperanza didn't mind being alone in the house. She organized her daily routine and always set aside time for reading the books Kitty had given her to improve her English—English training texts from the Salvadoran-American Cultural Institute (sponsored by the US government) and some of Kitty's old textbooks. She also bought high school textbooks in Spanish on geography and world history from a downtown store, hoping they would help her prepare for the Salvadoran high school exams.

When the Holmes family returned from Copan, Kitty told Esperanza that she would be leaving in early August with her siblings. She was headed to study at Johns Hopkins University in a city called Baltimore, where she would take a course to prepare for medical school. Esperanza was crestfallen, even though she had always known her job with the Holmes family and her friendship with Kitty—the first true friend she'd ever had—were only temporary.

In late July, Kitty accompanied Esperanza to the Central Market for the last time. Before heading there, however, Kitty took her to the main post office and purchased a post office box for Esperanza. For the first time, Esperanza realized that if anyone—especially her older brother Diego—was searching for her or her mother, they had no way of being found. They had never had an address in El Nido; they had simply lived there. She couldn't recall her family ever receiving mail—neither her grandmother, her mother, nor her uncles. All her communication as a schoolgirl had been through the school itself. As she stood next to Kitty at the post office, it struck her that she'd never even considered needing an address, because she had never expected anyone to send her a letter.

Kitty said, "Esperanza, I plan to write to you regularly from Baltimore, and you'll need a permanent address. The post office sells boxes where I can send letters. My parting gift to you is your very own post office box. I'll cover the rent for the first year, but after that, you'll have to pay it yourself. As long as you keep this box, we can stay in touch."

Esperanza started to cry. She and Kitty embraced. Esperanza said, "I am crying from happiness. I have never thought myself worthy of receiving a letter. But you do."

Kitty helped Esperanza to fill out the request to buy a post office box. Kitty handed it to the clerk, together with the *colones* needed to cover a year's rent. After reviewing the application, the clerk provided a stamped receipt and a key to a box. Kitty led Esperanza to the box with her number on it.

Kitty said, "My letters will come to you at this box, and, when you write to me, you can use this box number as your return address. Every year, you'll need to go to that clerk and pay the rental fee to keep the box. That way, we can continue our friendship."

Esperanza took the key and indelibly wrote the number in her mind. Kitty had given her an identity she had never felt before. She had a post office box of her own.

CHAPTER 39

By the end of the first week in August, the house was nearly empty—only Mrs. Holmes and Esperanza remained. Dr. Holmes had taken Kitty to enroll at Johns Hopkins, and the other two children had returned to Iowa. Before leaving, Kitty gave Esperanza her crane-necked study lamp and a box of stationery. Esperanza now needed Kitty's address, before she could write her a thank-you note.

Esperanza took care of Mrs. Holmes' every need and saw to it that everything ran smoothly. Mrs. Holmes gave her several extra afternoons off to make up for the weeks that Esperanza had stayed in the house while the Holmes family visited Guatemala, Costa Rica, and Honduras.

Esperanza appreciated the extra time she had now. Pepe had just started first grade, and she wanted to make sure he understood how important learning was. Her mother had never been very interested in schooling, so Esperanza knew it was up to her to instill that value in him. Her conviction had only grown stronger, especially since she felt it was her love of learning that had built her bond with Kitty.

Esperanza had only stayed overnight twice at the apartment in San Judas. Mrs. Holmes had always insisted that Esperanza return in the evening on her afternoons off. However, this time she allowed Esperanza to spend the night with her family in San Judas and arranged for a friend to stay with her while Dr. Holmes was away. Esperanza had left dinners and breakfasts prepared in the refrigerator and hurried back to Flor Blanca each morning after Pepe left for school.

During her overnight stay, Esperanza slept in Pepe's bed in the shared the bedroom with her mother, while he slept on a cot in the main room. As usual, when she spent her day off with her family, she prepared dinner on the wood stove. Pablo was always there to join them. His mother often had other evening commitments, so Pablo spending time with Pepe was a welcome blessing.

Each morning, at first light, Esperanza would hear a tap on the front door. She would open the door to see Pablo. Nothing seemed to keep the two boys apart. What Pablo liked, Pepe liked. What Pepe wanted to do, Pablo wanted to do. They learned together. They played football together. Pablo's friends were Pepe's friends, and Pepe's enemies were Pablo's, too. They shared their thoughts, their expectations, and their doubts. They had become inseparable.

Pepe would unlock the front door every morning, and Pablo would burst in. The two boys would embrace as if they'd been apart for ages. Then, Pepe's grandma would open her arms for her second "grandson" to receive his morning *abrazo*. Smiling, she would say, "I have breakfast ready for both of my boys."

Pablo and Pepe sat at the small table on the far side of the room as Grandma placed plates of food and cups of coffee in front of them. Smiling, she asked, "So, what are you boys doing in school today?"

"We have reading and writing and some other subjects," one responded. The other said, "It is so difficult to try to learn so much."

Grandma nodded and said, "It's important that you learn. You must prepare yourself for life—reading and writing are the base of all learning."

Pepe grabbed a tortilla almost before Grandma could set it down. "José, don't grab," Grandma scolded. "There's plenty for all of us today." Though his given name was José, everyone called him Pepe—except when he was scolded or called on in school. Grandma's scolding softened into a smile as she placed the plate of fried plantains and tortillas on the table. "No eggs today, boys—the chickens weren't cooperating yesterday."

Esperanza watched the scene unfold and felt almost like an outsider. She wasn't there every day to nurture her son, and she was so grateful to her mother for the care and devotion she provided. On those mornings in August, she joined the breakfast conversation. "You boys have no idea how important school is for building a life. The only way to get ahead is to learn and have a trade or profession to support your family. I'm a cook—and I get better every day because I keep learning. I wish I were a teacher, so I could help others learn and improve their lives."

The two boys and Grandma looked warmly at her. Grandma said, "My dear, you don't know how proud we are of you, and how much we appreciate you."

The boys just gulped down their food.

Grandma urged, "Now, my boys, don't get into trouble today. Study hard. Be home by four, because Pablo's mother is having dinner with us."

The two boys jumped up, and each gave Grandma and Esperanza a big *abrazo* before running off to the neighborhood public elementary school.

Grandma locked the door and adjusted the shutters over the iron-barred windows, which allowed a cool breeze to drift into the room. She sat down with Esperanza, finished her coffee, and enjoyed the rest of her breakfast. Looking around the room, she said to her daughter, "You know, you were right to bring us to San Salvador. You've worked so hard to give us this comfortable home. You've made our lives so much easier than they would've been in El Nido."

Esperanza smiled and said, "That makes me happy. My family is my rock. You, like Grandmother and Great-Grandmother, built this rock, and I'm working to protect it. And now, Mother, our rock has an address—somewhere people can find us. Maybe Diego will, someday. Kitty gave me a post office box—my own box, with my name on it—a place where people can reach us, you, Pepe, and me."

As she spoke those words, Esperanza realized she was more attuned to life in the Holmes household than her own. She spent six days a week immersed in the Holmes family routine and shared more of herself with Kitty than with her own mother. In fact, she had more in common with Kitty than with her mother or son. She knew more about Kitty's thoughts than those of her own child. For the first time, she admitted to herself that, since leaving the pension, it was her mother, not her, who was raising her son and giving him the affection he deserved. Working in someone else's home six days a week paid the bills, but the cost to her relationship with her mother and son was immeasurable.

Without saying a word, she rose from the table, put on her *rebozo*, embraced her mother, stepped out the door, and headed down the street toward the bus that would take her back to Flor Blanca.

CHAPTER 40

After Esperanza left, her mother cleared the breakfast table and washed the dishes in the cold-water sink. She then straightened Pepe's cot in the far corner of the living room and gathered his dirty clothes for washing. Entering the bedroom, she noticed that Esperanza had already made the twin beds before leaving. Smiling at the small favor, she brought out her broom and swept the floor, then lightly dusted the furniture. Afterward, she began her morning ritual in the bathroom. Once she relieved herself, she stepped into the cold shower, still marveling at the luxury of indoor plumbing.

She checked on her brood of hens, ensuring they were healthy, then fed them and collected any eggs laid overnight. Afterward, she inspected her squash and corn plants growing near the clothesline that the carpenter from the corner had installed—a service she paid for by caring for his two young children.

Back inside, the alarm clock on the end table next to Pepe's cot caught her eye. It read 9:45 a.m. A half-smile crossed her face as she recalled how they had saved colones to buy that clock while at the pension, and how it faithfully woke them each morning at 5:30 a.m. In El Nido, they had never needed a clock—they had simply risen with the sun. Her eyes then drifted to the other end table by the sofa, where her prized possession, the radio, sat. She remembered how there had been no radio and no electricity in El Nido. The discovery of the radio at the pension had been a revelation, and she still felt a rush of gratitude that Esperanza had gifted it to her as a Christmas present. Now, it was 10:00 a.m., time for her favorite soap opera, *Siempre María*. In El Nido, she would have had no radio—and she would likely be working in the fields.

With a fresh cup of coffee brewed on the wood-burning stove, she sat down in the chair beside the radio and let her gaze wander around the room. Everything in the house belonged to them now, which was a stark contrast to six-and-a-half years ago, when they had arrived with little more than the clothes on their backs. She recalled the fear she had felt leaving El Nido, yet now she was filled with a deep sense of contentment. Over time, she had come to know all the neighbors on her block, from the carpenter on the right-hand corner to the pharmacy owner on the left.

She had also learned how to earn money by being a good neighbor. The carpenter, for instance, had installed her clothesline and repaired the armoire in the bedroom in exchange for her care of his children. The pharmacy owner, too, had offered her medicines for Pepe in return for advice on the use of herbs and plants. *I was never interested in herbs and plants back in El Nido, but now I have time to recall the teachings of my grandmother and mother.*

At 10:00 a.m., she was on the sofa, listening to *Siempre Maria,* and sipping her coffee. She followed Maria's latest disappointment closely and empathized with her struggles. When the episode ended, a thought crossed her mind: *Maria's life is difficult, but so is ours. I want Esperanza to solve her problems, just like Maria is solving hers.*

Then, it dawned on her that most of her neighbors were facing struggles much like Esperanza and Maria. Many were single women raising children. She could think of only three married women on her block—the carpenter's wife, the pharmacist's wife, and the wife of a clerk. The rest were working mothers. Two had stalls in the nearby San Judas market, one was a dressmaker like Pablo's mother, and others did odd jobs. All of them seemed to have male friends, often military or police officers. Esperanza's mother had heard that some of these men helped pay the bills in exchange for sexual favors. She smiled to herself, remembering the *colones* she had earned watching children late into the night until the male friends left. Who was she to judge? After all, she and her husband had never had a legal wedding either. Only their families had officially recognized their marriage.

Every time she did a favor for a neighbor, she was rewarded. The market women brought her left-over produce for which she always found a use for—either feeding her family or her chickens. Her special neighbor was Pablo's mother, Patricia. They shared many a meal together, and Pablo always stayed over when Patricia's major came by. Patrica would eke out a new shirt, underwear, and even pairs of pants for both Pepe and Pablo from fabrics left over from items she made for one of her clients. Due to this, Pepe and Pablo often dressed like twins.

Above all, Esperanza's mother felt safe. The word on the street was that their block was off-limits to the petty burglars and pickpockets that roamed the inner city. Many of the women were girlfriends of officers—whether police or military. So criminals avoided causing any trouble that might provoke them. The jails were notorious for their treatment of prisoners. Her neighbors had reassured her that, with so many officers' lady friends living nearby, their block was protected. As Patricia had affirmed, "Crooks may pay off the police for some break-ins or assaults, but they know better when the victim is a family member or friend of an officer. And, you know, many of us on this block have such special friends."

Esperanza's mother had learned how to navigate life in the city. She carefully avoided unsafe areas and made it a point to show respect to the policemen who patrolled her neighborhood. She often offered small gifts, like a *pupusa* and coffee, when one stopped by the house. She had become "everyone's grandma," and her neighbors treated her with the respect given to the older women on the block. It reminded her of life in El Nido, where community members sought out guidance from the eldest woman in times of trouble. In many ways, she liked it that way.

CHAPTER 41

E ven after Dr. Holmes returned, the house felt unusually quiet without Kitty. The routine had become so simple. Esperanza only had
to clean the first floor, but going upstairs brought back memories of Kitty
and all the times they had spent together as friends. Preparing meals was
no burden. Dr. and Mrs. Holmes preferred simple fare and often dined
out two or three times a week. They hosted small dinner parties only
once or twice a month.

Esperanza's day began early. She had breakfast on the table by 7:30
a.m. and the dining room cleared by 8:30. She usually met with Mrs.
Holmes after 9:00 to go over the day's plans and decide on the lunch
and dinner menus. After that, she tidied up the house, focusing on the
sitting room, study, master bedroom, and bathroom. Every Wednesday,
Esperanza took the bus to the Central Market and carefully purchased the
food from the list she and Mrs. Holmes had prepared the day before. She
kept a detailed record of every purchase and accounted for each *centavo*
when she returned. Fridays and Saturdays were for laundry and ironing,
but with the General Electric washing machine and iron, the job was far
easier than in El Nido, where the women washed clothes in the river and
heated a manual iron on a wood-burning stove.

Dr. Holmes usually came home for lunch about 1:00 p.m., and Esperanza had the lunch laid out for him. There were days when Dr. Holmes was out on assignments, and Mrs. Holmes went to luncheons with her friends or had appointments at one of the charities that embassy wives supported. On those days when Esperanza was alone, she would prepare soup or beans and tortillas with coffee for herself. She developed a routine of reading in the afternoon—usually the newspaper, one of her textbooks, or some papers that the Holmeses had discarded.

Dinner was typically served at 7:00. Dr. Holmes often prepared cocktails for himself and his wife before they moved to the dining room for a quiet meal. Conversation was minimal, unless they had received letters from the children or had a special event coming up. After dinner, Esperanza would check all the locks and windows to ensure the house was secure. By 9:30 p.m., she was usually in her cot.

What a comfortable, easy life it had become!

Thursday remained her regular afternoon off. After lunch, she would take the bus to San Judas to spend time with her mother and son. On her way home, she always stopped by the post office to check her box. Almost like clockwork, there would be a letter from Kitty once a month. Each time she pulled out an envelope addressed to "Ms. Esperanza Choarti, Apartado Postal #421, San Salvador, El Salvador," she felt a surge of excitement. The letters were a constant reminder that she mattered—that she truly existed.

Kitty also sent her an occasional magazine—in English—that she thought Esperanza might be able to read and enjoy. Many an afternoon after lunch in the back patio of the Holmes' residence she wrestled with the meaning of words and the construction of sentences in those magazines. She kept all the magazines and letters in a special box by her bed in the San Judas apartment. To Esperanza these were the precious possessions that kept Kitty's presence alive.

On her afternoons off, she always prepared dinner for her mother, Pepe, Pablo, and, when available, Pablo's mother. Many an evening that autumn her dinners included left-overs and canned goods that Mrs. Holmes had authorized her to take home. Esperanza never took anything that Mrs. Holmes had not given her. Mrs. Homes, like Doña Marta, was generous but unforgiving if something was taken without permission. Esperanza took no liberties.

One afternoon each week, Mrs. Holmes allowed Esperanza a couple of hours off to visit Doña Marta, who had also become a friend of Mrs. Holmes. Often on a Wednesday or Friday afternoon, Mrs. Holmes would call Doña Marta, and say in her not-so-fluent Spanish, "*Buenas tardes*, Doña Marta. I hope you are well." After listening to Doña Marta's response, Mrs. Holmes would ask, "Would you be free to see Esperanza today?" Once confirmed, Mrs. Holmes would smile and say, "That's perfect. She'll be by soon." Then, she would tell Esperanza that Doña Marta was at home. Mrs. Holmes often asked Esperanza to bring Doña Marta a treat—some dish that Esperanza had prepared that Doña Marta particularly enjoyed.

Esperanza would put on her *rebozo* and walk to Doña Marta's house for an hour or so of conversation—just as if they were back in the yard under the tree at the pension. After an initial greeting, Doña Marta would ask Esperanza, "What is the latest news from the market? You know there will be elections next year, and I understand from my son that the colonels are bickering among themselves now that they have convinced the president not to run for re-election."

Esperanza had never been particularly interested in Salvadoran politics until she met Doña Marta. Growing up in El Nido, she had simply assumed that the army controlled everything. That's how it seemed, so she hadn't seen any reason to care. Now, however, she was beginning to understand that the wealthy coffee families had a significant influence over what the army did. While her primary focus remained on keeping her own family functioning, the importance politics held for Doña Marta had started to rub off on her. As a result, she began to make an effort to gather bits of information during her Wednesday morning trips to the Central Market.

"Well, your old friend Lupe asked me to tell you that a Colonel Osorio, who has been in Mexico, is gaining a lot of support from the younger officers. She said her major friend was impressed by his call for development and reforms, similar to what's happening in Mexico now. The major advised her to keep an eye on Osorio."

Doña Marta smiled and said, "What else did you hear?"

"Well, she said young men from important families were also rumored to be supporting this Osorio." She paused as she tried to remember the rest of Lupe's message. "Oh, yes, I remember, now. They are forming a new political party to support him. I think the name is PRUD."

"And," she continued, "your friend Maria asked me to say hello and that she still misses you. Her daughter is now in Texas for high school, because she couldn't arrange for a spot for her here. She said you know how picky the nuns are about having the daughter of an unmarried market woman in their school. She also said you know the family in San Antonio who arranged for her admission to the academy there."

"That is good for Maria. Her daughter is very bright—like you. Maria's long-time boyfriend, the son of a *finca* owner, had family members in San Antonio, and that should give Maria's daughter a good start for her life."

Esperanza continued, "Most of the women are really worried about the rise in assaults and robberies on the streets. Several of them mentioned that they never walk home alone anymore. Lupe even warned me about taking the bus back to Flor Blanca after dark. My mother told me that the policeman on our block advises everyone to be cautious, especially around San Judas, particularly near the cantinas."

Doña Marta added, "Ricardo has been telling me the same thing. Since President Hernández Martínez left, law and order has gotten worse. Ricardo believes that with so many unemployed men in the city, more people are growing desperate. He thinks the government needs to create jobs, but that requires money—something the government doesn't have much of. Most of its revenue comes from coffee taxes, and even that barely covers basic services and the military. We could be facing some tough times ahead."

Esperanza replied, "I worry sometimes about my family in San Judas. I know our block is fairly safe, but there are several cantinas not too far away. And from the reports I hear at the market and read in the newspaper, the number of killings every weekend is monstrous. All the men seem to carry knives and machetes, and, when they get drunk, they get mad and use them. It is so depressing that we haven't educated our people to do better."

"Yes, my dear," reflected Doña Marta, "Violence in the cantinas is a national disease. Our people can be wonderful friends or vicious enemies. And too much *aguardiente* seems to make them enemies. Those knives and machetes are as dangerous as guns." As an afterthought she added, "And we do have a lot of guns around."

After a long pause, Doña Marta looked at Esperanza and asked, "Do you still want to become a teacher, or have you settled into the routine of being a cook?"

"Yes," she replied. "I still want to be a teacher. To do that, I need to earn a *bachillerato* from high school. Kitty helped me buy some used high school books on mathematics and Spanish literature. I'm also studying English, learning to speak and understand it better. At the Holmes' house, I usually have time in the afternoons to study, but I don't think that will last much longer. From what I've heard them discussing at the table, they plan to return to America to be with their children."

Doña Marta replied, "Esperanza, you're a smart girl, and I think you're right. The Holmes family won't be here much longer. When they leave, I'll help you find a new job as a cook. You'll need the work to keep Flor and José going. But another job as a cook won't get you that high school degree. And in our country, it's not easy—there are so few high schools, and so many barriers for someone like you to get in. Let me think on it, and you keep studying. There may be a way."

Doña Marta had grown to care deeply for Esperanza. Perhaps it was because her own daughter had passed away, or because the *Gran Curandera* had saved her mother's life. Maybe it was Esperanza's grit and determination that had won her admiration. Or perhaps, over time, she had simply come to see her as a friend—someone dependable and caring, someone she could trust.

CHAPTER 42

During the Thanksgiving and Christmas season of 1948, Esperanza found herself alone in the Holmes residence. The family traveled to Iowa for Thanksgiving and then to Washington, D.C., for Christmas. Dr. and Mrs. Holmes were away for the week of Thanksgiving, leaving Esperanza with a well-stocked refrigerator and plenty of canned goods. Over Christmas, they were gone for two weeks. To help manage the household, the housemaid of one of Mrs. Holmes' American friends came by on Wednesday mornings to house-sit, which allowed Esperanza to go to the market. On Thursdays, from 10:00 a.m. to 5:00 p.m., the housemaid came again so that Esperanza was free to visit her family.

When the Holmes returned, they not only gave Esperanza her *aguinaldo*, the customary holiday bonus, but also brought gifts for her, her mother, and her son. Kitty had chosen a Timex wristwatch and a nylon blouse for her friend, a cozy sweater for Pepe, and a bathrobe for her mother. Along with these personal gifts, they included a tin of Christmas cookies and a box of chocolates. To top it off, they gave Esperanza three days off to spend with her family.

Esperanza filled her shopping bag with the gifts and made sure to express her deep gratitude to the Holmes before boarding the bus for San Judas. She had seen tins of cookies and boxes of chocolates passed around at the Holmes' dinner parties but never imagined she would be taking one of each home to share with her own family.

When she reached home, the first thing Esperanza did was hide the *aguinaldo* in the hollowed-out leg of the chair near her bed. She then sat down to write a thank-you letter to Kitty, all the while glancing down at her new Timex and marveling that it was truly hers. After posting the letter, she hurried back home to prepare a special dinner. It was the sixth of January, the day the Three Wise Men arrived at the manger with their gifts for the Baby Jesus. That night, as she served the meal, she felt like the Magi, bringing unexpected treasures to her own mother and son.

CHAPTER 43

The next three months settled into an almost monotonous routine. Then, in early April, Mrs. Holmes called Esperanza into the sitting room and, in a mix of Spanish and English, shared some important news: "Dr. Holmes has been transferred to Washington. We are very excited because it means we'll be close to our children. My son is going to graduate school at the University of Maryland in College Park, just outside the city. My daughter has been admitted to the School of Foreign Service at Georgetown University in the city. And you know Kitty is in Baltimore, only forty miles away. We'll be leaving in about a month."

Esperanza was not surprised, but she was uneasy with the news. Her thoughts immediately turned to the impact on her family. She was the breadwinner and, without a job, her small reserve would be gone in no time.

Mrs. Holmes said, "I see you are troubled. Well, don't be. Doctor Rand will replace my husband and is due to arrive by June. Dr. Rand has arranged with the landlord to rent this house. I have written to Mrs. Rand about you, and she has agreed to keep you on at your same salary. Dr. Holmes tells me that the Rands have three young children, and that he has been working in a similar post in Peru for the last two years."

The relief on Esperanza's face reflected her inner feelings.

"Now, I will need your help in packing up and preparing for the movers who are scheduled on April 28. Our routine will certainly change because we shall be eating most of our dinners out at farewell parties. Also, I expect to sell some of the items that I no longer need. I will have some people looking at those items starting next week."

"Oh, yes, I will be pleased to help out. Just tell me what you want done."

"Well, that will be all for now. I expect you will still need to go to the market once a week as usual and have your afternoon off on Thursday. The visits with Doña Marta may have to be put off. It all depends on our needs in getting ready for the packers."

That began a hectic month. That very afternoon she was given time to visit Doña Marta and, when she entered her sitting room, Doña Marta began, "I hear that your life is about to change once again. My sons tell me that the Holmeses are leaving San Salvador, and that Dr. Holmes has been chosen to head the US public health technical assistance aid program for Latin America. He is going to have a very important job."

"My goodness, you already know my news. I was just told this morning."

Doña Marta added, "It should be all over town. I also saw an article in the *Prensa Grafica* newspaper this morning."

She took a sip of coffee before continuing, "Well, that must be all your news?"

"Oh, no," responded Esperanza, smiling. "Mrs. Holmes has arranged for me to stay on in the same house with the new family when they arrive in June."

"Well, that is good for you. Now, what is the latest news from the market?"

"Lupe told me that the president and his colleagues in the barracks are squabbling, but the military is standing firm on not allowing the president to be reelected. Osorio's supporters are calling it the 'Mexican Plan.' She also mentioned that coffee prices are dropping, and that's bad news for all of us."

Doña Marta just nodded.

Esperanza continued, "There's more bad news about crimes. I'm start-ing to worry about my trips to the market and getting home safely. I also worry about all those poor people in the ravine down the street—will they flood into our neighborhood?"

Dona Marta said, "My sons tell me not to worry, but, like you, I am uneasy."

Esperanza took a sip of coffee and then showed Doña Marta her new wristwatch. "Kitty sent it to me for Christmas. And a sweater for Pepe, a bathrobe for my mother, and a blouse for me." Looking at her wristwatch, Esperanza added, "Isn't it lovely?"

Doña Marta smiled. "You really have made yourself a special friend."

Esperanza said, "I should probably head back. The Holmeses are going out to another farewell dinner tonight, and Mrs. Holmes might need me. This might be my last visit for a few weeks since I'll be busy helping her pack. She's selling some things she no longer needs."

"I'll tell my sons about the sale. They're interested in buying the Holmeses' car if he plans to sell it. Now go along, my girl. Good of you to come. See you soon, I hope."

The following day was Esperanza's day off. She stopped first at her post office box, and she found a letter from Kitty. She had just tucked it into her bra and started for the exit when she noticed a middle-aged clerk staring at her.

"Niña, you have a post office box?" he asked, eyeing her suspiciously.

"Oh, yes, sir, I do," she replied.

Still doubtful, he pressed, "What's your name and box number? People like you don't have boxes."

With confidence, Esperanza answered, "Check your records. I'm Es-peranza Choarti, and my box number is 421."

He scanned his records, visibly surprised. "You do rent that box, and it's paid up to date. Esperanza Choarti."

She lifted her head, met his gaze for a moment, then turned and walked proudly out.

Once home in San Judas, she opened her letter and read:

Dear Esperanza,

I guess you now know that my parents are leaving San Salvador for Washington. They are as excited as I am. College is very tough and having them nearby will be very helpful. I think I will spend my weekends with them.

My father's new job is as chief of public health at the Institute of Inter-American Affairs. He'll be responsible for overseeing public health technical assistance programs in twenty Latin American countries. As I'm learning in my class at Johns Hopkins, all these countries need significant help, and El Salvador is among the least developed in the hemisphere. It needs a lot of support. Can you imagine the responsibility my father will have, trying to create programs not just for El Salvador but for the other nineteen as well? His new position is part of President Truman's initiative to share our expertise with underdeveloped nations around the world. President Truman announced it in Point Four of his inaugural address last March. Isn't that exciting?

I'm doing well at school and already getting ready for final exams. The science classes keep getting more challenging, and the lab work takes up a lot of time. Now that my father has such an important job, I'm working even harder.

I hope you and your family are well. We'll keep in touch

after my parents leave.

Your friend, Kitty

That evening Esperanza told her family of the changes to come.

CHAPTER 44

The Holmeses had packed up and departed, leaving Esperanza in the nearly-empty house. On the one hand, she felt uneasy about the new chapter of her life that was about to begin. On the other, she felt comfortable in the familiar surroundings, with her own private room and bath. The Holmes family had left behind the refrigerator, stove, and washing machine for the Rands, and she was able to use them while waiting for their arrival.

May passed quickly. A friend of Mrs. Holmes stopped by once a week, which allowed Esperanza time to visit the market and check in with her family. Mrs. Holmes had also paid her a little extra beyond her monthly salary for giving up her usual time off, which was helpful. She didn't have anything special planned for May anyway, so the extra money came in handy.

Then, one morning in early June, the front doorbell rang. Esperanza answered cautiously, holding the door locked. "Who is it? What do you want?" she asked.

A man replied in clear Spanish, "I am Dr. Rand. We've just arrived from Peru."

Esperanza unlocked the door, still cautious. "Welcome, sir. I'm Esperanza. I always make sure I know who's calling before opening the door."

"That's sensible," he replied. "This is Mrs. Rand."

Esperanza looked at the couple. They were younger than the Holmeses and quite attractive. The man sported a neatly-trimmed beard and dark, wavy hair that framed his sharp features, though his warm brown eyes gave him a gentle expression. Beside him stood a striking woman with auburn hair swept back into a sleek ponytail, her fair skin lightly dusted with freckles. She invited them in and asked, "How can I help you?"

Mrs. Rand responded, "We'd like to see the state of the house. Our furniture will arrive by boat in the next couple of days, and we need to plan how to arrange it."

Esperanza led them through the house. As they toured both floors, Mrs. Rand made notes, commenting to her husband, "Mrs. Holmes was so generous to leave the draperies and Venetian blinds—and having the kitchen already set up makes it so much easier than when we arrived in Lima."

She turned to Esperanza, "Let me thank you for keeping the house in such good condition. Mrs. Holmes said you were a wonderful cook and very trustworthy. I can see that by the condition of the house."

Esperanza smiled.

Dr. Rand then said, "We hope everything will work out well with you. We will continue to pay you the same as Dr. Holmes did—with the same day off and your room. We have brought a Peruvian nanny to care for our three young ones. She has been with us for nearly four years, and the children adore her. She will be staying on the second floor with them, in the same room as our two-year-old son. We will see if we need another girl later on, but, for now, it will just be Numa and you. Do you have any questions?"

In fact, Esperanza was quite relieved. She hadn't been sure if she could manage cooking and looking after three small children, and the thought of dealing with another Altagracia hadn't amused her. She preferred working alone, and with the nanny living upstairs, she felt confident everything would work out. So, she replied, "Thank you, sir. I will do my best."

Two days later, the furniture arrived. Mrs. Rand directed the movers, ensuring that each piece of furniture was placed precisely where she wanted it on both floors. Esperanza offered water to the workmen and refreshments to Mrs. Rand. As the moving truck pulled away, Mrs. Rand surveyed the scene and said, "Well, it's all here. Nothing's missing—just a few damaged items. But that always happens when you move. I'll be back tomorrow morning with the children, and we'll start getting settled."

"Señora, I know a good carpenter if you need any repairs done. He lives down the street from my mother in San Judas, and he is responsible and does good work."

"That's good news. We do need some repairs. Thank you again, Esperanza." Mrs. Rand took another glance around before heading out to the family car, which had also arrived on the boat, and driving off to the hotel where the rest of her family waited.

The next day, the Rands moved in. The children and Numa settled upstairs, while Dr. and Mrs. Rand took over the master bedroom suite on the first floor. They hired the carpenter to repair the damaged pieces of furniture, and he did a good job. Life with the Rands went as smoothly as it had with the Holmes family, except there was no Kitty. Esperanza took care of the cooking and the first-floor cleaning, while Numa looked after the children and kept up the second floor.

It was an easy routine for Esperanza, but not for Numa. She kept busy, but she was sad and uncommunicative. Numa showed little interest in getting to know Esperanza and focused entirely on the care of the three children, to whom she seemed deeply devoted. She barely ate—only picking at her food—and she almost never left the house.

Esperanza tried to engage her in conversation, but Numa, whose speech pattern and choice of words were quite different from the Salvadoran vernacular, seemed reluctant to respond. She stuck to her duties and ignored Esperanza's attempts to connect. Their interactions were limited to Numa picking up and returning meals, and, even then, they hardly exchanged a word.

Several weeks after the Rands had settled in, Esperanza noticed that she was running low on the cereals the children liked for breakfast and needed to order more. She was unsure which ones the children preferred, so she made her way upstairs to Numa's room. Just as she was about to knock, she heard soft sobs from within. Concerned, she knocked gently and asked, "Numa, are you alright?"

Numa came to the door and her eyes were red from crying.

Esperanza asked again, "Are you alright?"

Numa said, "I am sorry that you see me like this. I am just homesick. I miss my family, my homeland, and my way of life. Everything is so strange here."

Esperanza was surprised, "You say everything is so strange here. You haven't left the house very much. You hardly know us. Why do you think your country is so different from El Salvador?"

"Oh, yes," Numa replied. "You dress differently. Your diet is so different, and you even talk differently than my people in Lima."

"Really? I had no idea. I understand how much you must miss your family," Esperanza said softly. "Even though mine is just an hour away, I find myself quite often wondering what they're doing. But this is what I have to do to keep them going."

Numa nodded, her voice barely above a whisper. "Oh, I understand that. I'm here because we need the money too. Every penny I earn is sent to my family back home."

"Is there anything I can do to help?" asked Esperanza.

"No, but thank you," replied a stoic Numa.

"Well, if I can help, just tell me." As she turned to leave, she remembered, "Which brand of cereal should I reorder for the children? Do they prefer Post Toasties or Quaker Oats?"

"We will need both. The four-year-old likes Post Toasties, but the others prefer warm Quaker Oats."

That conversation seemed to break the ice, and Numa and Esperanza gradually became friends. Numa shared stories about her life in Lima, and Esperanza could feel the depth of her loneliness. Though Esperanza wanted to console her, she instinctively understood that she couldn't provide the kind of comfort Numa truly needed. Still, she offered warmly, "If you'd like, I can arrange for you to meet my mother. I think you'd like her, and maybe you could spend some of your afternoons off with her."

Numa half-smiled and nodded.

So, Esperanza arranged with her mother to meet Numa, and they did spend time together. Her mother tried to assuage Numa's homesickness—or at least offer a place to visit on her afternoon off.

Even with her mother's help, the relationship between Numa and Esperanza never truly warmed. The two women had little in common. Their upbringings, outlooks on life, and interests didn't align. Though both were indigenous, they came from different environments and shared almost no common ethnic identities or values.

Life in the Rand household was very different from that with the Holmes. Mrs. Rand stayed close to home and entertained very little. She seldom went to parties. Her life revolved around her children. She spent hours with Numa and the toddlers on the second floor—she never seemed to tire of reading to her little ones or teaching them games. The oldest boy enrolled in the American school, and she took him every morning and picked him up each afternoon. The return from school was always followed by cookies and milk with his siblings.

Dr. and Mrs. Rand had breakfast together every morning at 8:00 a.m. Then, he would leave for work and rarely return for lunch. Unlike Dr. Holmes or Kitty, Dr. Rand seldom discussed his work at home and hosted only one or two social events with his American and Salvadoran colleagues during the two years they lived in the house. From the conversations she overheard at these events, Esperanza gathered that Dr. Rand was advising the Ministry of Health on establishing rural health posts and maternal and childcare services.

Esperanza had never felt more like a servant than in the Rand household. Her role was clear: to serve the family and follow Mrs. Rand's instructions. She kept a steady routine, prepared three meals a day, seven days a week, and handled the household chores as prescribed. Every Wednesday morning, she took the bus to the Central Market and returned by taxi with her purchases. On those bus rides, she encountered people who lived in the ravine in makeshift homes, and she often marveled at how they managed to survive in such conditions.

Like clockwork, every Thursday on her afternoon off, she stopped at the post office. She walked eagerly from the bus line over to the post office. Was today the day she would receive the monthly letter from Kitty? She sent a letter to Kitty almost every other week, and she would wait in line to get an airmail stamp. Then, she would make her way to her post office box, take out the key and open it carefully to see if a precious letter from Kitty had arrived. If there was a letter, she would tuck it into her shirt, like a piece of gold, and hurry home to San Judas. Frequently, she stopped at the window for dispensing post office boxes to make sure that the payment for her post office box was up to date.

Kitty remained Esperanza's beacon of hope for the future. Her letters painted a picture of a life dedicated to learning, and Kitty never disappointed her. She wrote long, informative letters and even arranged for her father to include a textbook or manual for her in his periodic shipments to Dr. Rand. Among those books were basic English textbooks on botany, biology, and history, as well as two Spanish novels by Lope de Vega. Dr. Rand encouraged Esperanza to read and study. In that, he offered her a small—but welcome—sense of support.

During those two years with the Rands, Mrs. Rand allowed Esperanza to visit Doña Marta periodically. The Rands had met both of Doña Marta's sons, who had helped them settle in. They were among the few Salvadoran friends the Rands invited to dine. Doña Marta's sons shared the story of their mother's close relationship with Esperanza and how much joy each visit from her brought to their aging mother.

Almost two years to the day after their arrival, Dr. Rand alerted Esperanza and Numa that he and his family were returning to their home in the United States, and that they would be vacating the house. Not surprised but concerned, Esperanza asked, "How soon do you plan to depart?"

"At the end of this month," was his reply. "Will you need a new job?"

"Oh, yes, indeed. My salary keeps my family going."

"Well, our friend, Mrs. Jones, needs a cook. I'll ask her to come and talk with you."

"She lives on a side street off Avenida Roosevelt, just a few blocks up the hill from where the hospital Bloom is being constructed. If you are interested, I'll ask her to drop by to meet you."

"Thank you for your concern. When may I meet with Mrs. Jones?"

"Mrs. Rand and I will be seeing her later this week, and we will arrange a time for you to meet with her."

"Again, my thanks. And would it possible for you to allow me to take an hour or two this afternoon for me to inform my friend, Doña Marta, of the news you just gave me?"

"I know Mrs. Rand plans to be home, and I'll check with her."

That afternoon after cleaning up after lunch, Esperanza walked around the corner to Doña Marta's. After the usual *abrazo*, Esperanza began, "The Rands are leaving. They are giving up the house and are arranging for me to meet with another American lady. What do you think?"

"Esperanza, I am sad to hear the news. I have really enjoyed having you nearby, and I always look forward to your visits. We know the Americans don't stay for long, but they do pay better than we Salvadorans. You know how hard it is to find a well-paying job as a cook. It seems like you enjoy working for the Americans, so just meet with the new lady and see how it goes."

"You know if you need me, you just have to let me know," Esperanza interjected.

"I know. I know," replied the older woman.

Then they talked about the news from the market women, which always stimulated Doña Marta. They discussed the new President Osorio and the three civilians in his cabinet—three men who promised real changes for the country: Dr. Galindo Pohl in education, Dr. Jorge Castellanos in economy, and Dr. Mario Hector Salazar in labor.

Doña Marta opined, "The military let some civilians in this time. Let's hope it's a sign of better times. And the new political party PRUD is calling for real improvement in the standard of living for the people. Let's hope it's more than just the usual words."

Esperanza helped Doña Marta get up from her chair and they walked out into the garden. Doña Marta just smiled and said, "You know, you remind me of my daughter. I appreciate the time you spend with me." Then, she gave her a long hug before saying, "Look at the time. I fear that you must be getting back to the Rands."

Mrs. Jones came to lunch the following week. She was a tall, buxom woman from Indiana who had lived in Puerto Rico and Panama for several years. She spoke Spanish well, and she was delighted by the meal Esperanza had prepared. After lunch, they spoke, and it was agreed that two weeks after the Rands' departure, Esperanza would start as the cook at the Jones household. She would receive the same salary. Mrs. Jones handed Esperanza a note with her address and invited her to visit the house the following Thursday. That visit went smoothly, and Esperanza secured the new job.

Then came the packing again. Mrs. Rand and the children left before the furniture was moved out. Numa returned to Peru the day after Mrs. Rand. Only Dr. Rand remained with Esperanza until the furniture was crated and hauled away. His departure was very formal. There was none of the warmth or sadness that she had felt when the Holmes left. No *abrazos* or tears.

Esperanza packed the bedside table and lamp that Kitty had given her, neatly folded up the uniforms and other clothing in boxes and wrapped up the books and other items she had acquired in the nearly four years of living in the same room. She paid a few *colones* to her San Judas neighbor, the carpenter, to come by in his truck to drive her and her possessions back to the apartment in San Judas.

When she arrived home, she carefully placed the lamp and her books on the bedside table, arranged her clothing neatly on a shelf in the armoire, and then sat on the bed.

She glanced around the room, and took in all that had been accumulated over the four years they had lived in the two-room apartment. She compared it to what her two American employers had. A wave of frustration washed over her. Despite working at a good salary, she wasn't satisfied with the results. On the verge of tears, she lamented, *What real future is there for me and my family? I work seven days a week with almost no time for them. I feel trapped. What do I need to do to change this life?*

She pulled herself up from the bed mechanically and reached for the chair beside it. Turning it upside down, she unscrewed one of its hollowed-out legs. She carefully counted the five hundred *colones* of termination pay Dr. Rand had given her. Then, she pulled out the wads of bills she had already saved. After counting, she realized she had five thousand, five hundred *colones* stored away—money she kept hidden because no local bank would allow her to open an account. She rolled the bills up carefully, placed them back inside the hollow leg, and screwed it tightly in place. Then, she set the chair back in its innocent spot beside her bed.

Then, for a moment, she worried about her family. Her thoughts went to the ravine at the edge of Flor Blanca, and she shuddered, realizing how close they were to living there themselves. She pulled herself together, knowing that, at twenty-two, she had no one but herself to depend on.

She then thought: *My family and I are so much better off than so many others in this city.* She half-smiled, pulled herself together, and said to herself, *I'm worth a present. I'm going to ask the carpenter on the corner to build me a bookcase for my books.*

Then she took the two-week vacation with her family that Mrs. Jones had given her—her first since leaving El Nido. Her first undertaking was to write a long letter to Kitty about her change in employment, her feelings for Doña Marta, and her concerns about the future.

CHAPTER 45

E   speranza arrived at the front door of the Jones' house at precisely the date and time that had been agreed upon. An older—and not very friendly—maid opened the door. Then Mrs. Jones appeared and took Esperanza and the maid into the dining room. She said with a professional air, "I am pleased to see you arrived on time. I hope you had a pleasant vacation with your family."

"Yes, thank you," said a business-like Esperanza.

"I want you and Maria to get along. I don't want any discord among my servants," the lady said firmly. "You will both be sharing the maid's room. We've already agreed on your salary as the cook, and you'll have two afternoons off each week—Mondays and Thursdays. Maria's afternoons off are Wednesday and Saturday. On your days off, you may leave after breakfast, but you must return to prepare dinner."

She paused before continuing, "I expect you to wear a black uniform at all times, just like Maria's. If you need a new one, I'll have my seamstress make it for you. Now, settle in, and I'll tell you what I want for lunch at 11:30."

Maria then took Esperanza to the maid's room. It was so different from her room at Flor Blanca. There was a solitary cot, some wooden boxes arranged to look like a bureau, and a pair of poles with a wire on which

233

to hang clothes. On her cot were some linens, a blanket, a washcloth, and a towel. Maria watched Esperanza for a reaction, but Esperanza said nothing. She just placed the market bag with her clothing on one of boxes and changed into her black uniform. They did not exchange a word.

At 11:30, Mrs. Jones showed Esperanza around the kitchen: the electric stove, her refrigerator, other appliances, and the kitchen equipment. Then she showed her the cabinets in which she kept her supplies, the sideboards in the pantry, and dining room cupboards that held the dishes and flatware. Then, she showed her a locked closet in the front hall in which she kept canned goods and other staples from America. Mrs. Jones said sternly, "I have the key to this closet. Come to me if you need anything. And never to try to open this closet without my presence."

Esperanza thought to herself, *How could I open it since you have the key?*

Mrs. Jones then loosened up and smiled warmly. "Esperanza, I'm really glad you're here. Mrs. Rand has told me wonderful things about you. She said that you're a skilled cook and very reliable. You know, I also enjoy cooking. I love spending time in the kitchen, and I'll be joining you often to prepare some of my favorite dishes."

Esperanza returned the smile, "I learned many dishes from Mrs. Rand and Mrs. Holmes, for whom I worked before Mrs. Rand."

Esperanza noted that Mrs. Jones spoke much better Spanish than either Mrs. Holmes or Mrs. Rand, but she did not speak as fluently as Kitty.

Mrs. Jones said, "Let me show you around the house, and then we will go into the kitchen to prepare lunch."

The house was located on the left side of a paved street, just a short distance from Avenida Roosevelt. It was a single-story home with no interior patio. A long entrance hall stretched forward, leading to the main living areas. On the right, it opened into the living room, dining room, pantry, and kitchen. To the left were a coat closet, a bathroom, and the entrance to the garage. Further down the hall on the left were three bedrooms and two bathrooms. At the end of the hallway, a large window overlooked the backyard, where several vibrant Bougainvillea plants bloomed. In front of the window stood a large desk with several armchairs, while bookcases lined the wall to the right. Esperanza guessed that the maid's room was located just beyond the back wall of the hallway.

Mrs. Jones said, "Maria keeps up the house. I have also taught her how to serve table, and she is to help you clean up dishes after meals. You see, I like to entertain. I have dinner parties and afternoon bridge games with the ladies all the time. I need Maria and you to work together."

Then, Mrs. Jones led Esperanza back to the kitchen. "Now, I will be eating by myself today. I just want a bowl of soup and a sandwich. I'll get a can of Campbell's soup, and you'll find some cheddar cheese in the refrigerator."

"What do you want to drink with your lunch?" asked Esperanza.

"A cup of tea would suit me fine," replied Mrs. Jones.

That began a not-always-pleasant year with the Joneses. Maria and Esperanza never seemed to find a way of working together, but they kept the Joneses very satisfied.

CHAPTER 46

E speranza adjusted to her new routine, which was unlike any she had experienced before. She lived and worked alongside Maria in a tense, but manageable, peace. Maria resented that the younger cook, just twenty-two, often received praise from Señora Jones. It stung even more that Esperanza earned a better salary than she did—a woman in her thirties, with a household to support, struggling to make ends meet. This only deepened the resentment she felt toward Esperanza.

Mrs. Jones truly enjoyed entertaining, and she introduced Esperanza to a variety of casserole and pasta dishes that Esperanza had never encountered before. Mrs. Jones loved cooking and often did so alongside Esperanza. She shared recipes that she had learned from her mother and grandmother in her rural Indiana kitchen. She explained how they used everything that the farm produced and made it last, which reminded Esperanza of the families in El Nido. Mrs. Jones combined ingredients in ways that were unfamiliar to Esperanza. She also cooked with milk and dairy products, which Salvadoran campesinos used sparingly—primarily to nurture babies. Mrs. Jones, however, used milk in everything from potatoes to breaded meats, casseroles, and even homemade ice cream, all of which were delicacies typically reserved for the wealthiest Salvadoran families.

Esperanza quickly absorbed every recipe. Mrs. Jones only had to show her once, then Esperanza could prepare an evening meal just as delicious. Together, they even made ice cream using local Salvadoran fruits like mango, mamey, and guava. By the time Esperanza left the Jones household, she had mastered ten new casserole dishes, including those with tuna and seafood, as well as chicken-fried steak, potato salad, and Indiana-style fried chicken, made with a cream-based batter.

Something unexpected happened involving Mr. Jones. One morning after breakfast, he left some brochures in Spanish on the dining room table. That day, while clearing the table, Esperanza began reading them. The brochures described the new Farm Extension Service and its program to support small farmers. The work of the research station outside San Salvador showed how the program would benefit the farmers.

That evening, before dinner, Esperanza handed the brochure back to Mr. Jones, "You left this on the dining room table this morning. I read it, and I found it very interesting."

"Thank you, Esperanza." Mr. Jones replied. "You found it interesting?"

"Is this the first agricultural research station in the country?" asked the cook.

"Yes, they are researching ways to increase productivity and diversify farm crops. The extension service helps farmers by providing improved seeds and introducing more effective farming practices," Mr. Jones replied.

"That is very interesting," observed Esperanza.

The following Saturday morning, as Esperanza served at the table, she overheard Mr. Jones say in English to Mrs. Jones, "I'm so pleased that I have no work this weekend. I'm going to relax, stay in my favorite chair, and let the day drift by."

When she brought him his second cup of coffee, Esperanza asked, "*Señor*, may I ask you a question about your work?"

Quite surprised, he responded, "I didn't know that you were aware of what I was doing."

"I hope I am not out of order, but after I read the brochure that you left on the table, you told me about the research station and the extension service. And I saw your picture as the marketing adviser. Well, you see, I come from a small farm in Chalatenango and wondered how my family might participate in it."

Even more surprised, Mr. Jones said, "Go on."

"In the time of my great-grandparents, our family lived very well. We grew indigo. My grandmother told me that our family had been cultivating indigo since we first settled in El Nido many years ago. But then, someone invented a chemical process for making anil, and the demand for indigo disappeared. My uncle still produces indigo on his land and my mother's, but few people buy it now, and our community has almost no income."

Now, Mr. Jones was interested.

"When I was in the eighth grade, we studied geography, and I learned about different countries and their crops. I found out that El Salvador's main crops are coffee, cotton, and sugarcane, but we used to be a major producer of indigo. No one came to help our community plant new crops, and most small farmers barely scraped by. In my village, we're all part of the same family. My grandmother said that we tried to survive by growing the food we used to buy, but it wasn't enough. Most of the young men had to leave El Nido to find work, and, after a few years, they stopped coming home. My brother, Diego, was one of them. You know how men are."

Mr. Jones asked, "Where is El Nido?"

At this point, Mrs. Jones bustled back into the room, "What's this all about? Is Esperanza bothering you, dear?"

"Oh no, she saw one of my brochures and is asking me about my work and how it can help her family out on a farm in Chalatenango," responded Mr. Jones in English.

"Now you know you need a day off. I have some chores for Esperanza to help me with since Maria has left for the afternoon. You finish your coffee, dear, while Esperanza comes with me."

"All right, but I want to continue this talk with Esperanza. I want to learn more about her family and see if the *servicio* can help them."

Then, he turned to Esperanza and said in Spanish, "I want to continue our conversation later. I want to know more about your family and the community's struggles. Right now, Mrs. Jones needs you."

"Thank you, *Señor*," Esperanza said to Mr. Jones. She smiled at Mrs. Jones, "Let me put these dirty dishes in hot water, and I'll be back."

It was several days later before Mr. Jones asked Esperanza to meet with him in the back hall, which he used for his home office. When she arrived, he invited her to sit down. She nodded her thanks but remained standing.

"Esperanza, the other day you told me you came from a farm area in Chalatenango that was once prosperous from the indigo."

"Oh, yes, *Señor*. My grandmother told me of those days."

"What do you grow today?" asked Mr. Jones.

"I've been away for ten years, but, from what we hear, nothing has changed in El Nido. They still mostly grow the food they need to eat and sell any surplus for a few pennies to the truck drivers who pass by every few days. They also grow a little indigo for some villagers who use the dye in their traditional fabrics, which brings in a few *colones* each year. But really, they live on what they raise."

"The *servicio* for which I work has programs to help small farmers improve their production and livelihood. Let me see if we can help yours."

The statement awakened her curiosity, "What does the *servicio* do?"

"We work with the Ministry of Agriculture. We have established a research station to identify new cash crops suitable for this region. We collaborate with farmers to plant these crops, and I assist them in finding markets where they can get good prices for their produce."

Esperanza blurted out, almost in disbelief, "The government has a program to help farmers? I never knew it was interested in helping farmers."

Mr. Jones looked quite surprised, "We have been working here for several years now. The United States has three *servicios* that advise your government in health, agriculture, and education."

"You mean you're doing a job like Dr. Holmes and Dr. Rand, but focused on agriculture?"

"Yes," smiled Mr. Jones, "Now, can you tell me how I can look into El Nido to determine if the *servicio* can help your family there."

"Well, my family is Choarti. All the people in El Nido are my relatives by blood or marriage. It is on the main highway from San Salvador to La Palma. We are part of a municipality whose main town is just across the highway."

He showed her a map of Chalatenango, and she ran her finger down the highway from La Palma and found El Nido. "This is it."

Mr. Jones took out a red pencil and circled it.

"*Señor*, we are a very poor village. We are good people, and we had hoped that we could improve ourselves. But we have no real money. You'll see. My community needs new crops to sell. They need something that keeps their men home. When I was in the eighth grade, I read about agricultural programs that bring in enough cash to keep farm communities growing. Well, that was once true of El Nido with indigo. Maybe your research can find a new crop."

Mr. Jones looked up at Esperanza and asked, "Did you complete the eighth grade?"

"Oh, yes, I finished elementary school with honors and even earned a scholarship for high school. But on my way home from Chalatenango City, I was raped and became pregnant. I still dream of becoming a teacher, though, and I study high school subjects whenever I have spare time."

Mr. Jones looked up at Esperanza as he absorbed her revelation. After a pause, he asked, "Is there someone I should look for in El Nido?"

Esperanza thought for a moment before suggesting, "Ernesto Choarti. He's my uncle, and he's farming both his land and that of my mother. He knows everyone in El Nido. My mother got a message from him last year. He sent her a few *colones* and mentioned that he's managed to keep his two eldest sons working on the farms."

"Thank you, Esperanza. That's helpful. I'll make sure to reach out to him when I visit El Nido."

As she was about to leave, Esperanza asked, "Would you like anything to eat or drink?"

"No, I'm fine," he replied. Then he added thoughtfully, "I might bring a soil scientist with me to check the quality of the land in El Nido. It could help with crop planning."

CHAPTER 47

After the conversation with Mr. Jones, Esperanza felt a deep unease. She kept asking, *Why is Mr. Jones so interested in El Nido?* The thought unsettled her. Her family had a long history of resisting outside influence, and she couldn't shake the feeling that his curiosity might lead to something more. Her grandmother's words echoed in her mind: *"Never trust outsiders. They always want to take, not help."* The wisdom passed down through generations made her wary, and now she wondered if Mr. Jones's intentions were as harmless as they seemed.

She worried that the Americans might be like the Spaniards, who, as her grandmother said, "came in the name of God and then took our land and enslaved our people." Was Mr. Jones really interested in helping, or was he just scouting land for his own purposes? The thought gnawed at her. Unlike in the time of her ancestors, there was no shaman to protect the village. No one was wise enough to engage with Mr. Jones while steering clear of falling into a predatory deal. Her shaman ancestor had once extended a hand to the Catholic priests and pledged his people's allegiance to the Spanish faith in exchange for autonomy outside the feudal *encomiendas* controlled by the Creole families. Now, she couldn't help but wonder if she had said anything to Mr. Jones that might threaten the existence and traditions of El Nido as a free community.

She became more concerned the more she thought about it. However, she felt that she could not approach Mr. Jones. After all, he was her patron, and, if she was not careful, she could lose her job and undermine the security of her family.

It must have been weeks after the conversation that Mr. Jones called Esperanza to his office.

"Please sit down," he began.

"Thank you, sir," but she remained standing.

"I have arranged to visit El Nido next Thursday. A soil scientist and an extension agent will be coming with me. I would appreciate it if you could write a note to your uncle as an introduction," Mr. Jones requested.

"May I ask you what you plan to do in El Nido?" she asked.

He looked at her a bit puzzled before continuing, "I'll be assessing the soil and terrain, as well as the farming practices and crops the community is currently growing. Then, I'll consult with my colleagues to see if the conditions are right for developing a plan to work with your uncle and the other farmers. The goal is to help them plant crops that not only increase production and income but also nurture and sustain the soil."

"Why do you want to help us?" she queried in a very firm voice.

"Well, it's the policy of my government to help your government improve agricultural production," Mr. Jones began. "And, as for me, I come from a small family farm in Indiana. My parents, my brothers, and I worked hard to keep it going. We didn't have much until my government started helping us. The county agent advised us on the best planting and harvesting methods, the seeds and fertilizer to buy, and the machinery that might help. He even gave us the crop information that the bank needed to lend us money. The government also helped to bring electricity to our farm. Now, I want to see if I can help your government set up similar services to support your uncle and other farmers here in El Salvador."

"You mean you came from a small farm like me and my family?"

"Oh, my, yes. My family lived from hand to mouth. Every day was a challenge just to keep going. We had very little cash and grew just about everything we ate."

"And your government helped you?"

"Yes, I'm part of the US agricultural team that is trying to help your government build a similar program here," Mr. Jones responded. "We have been working for about five years to build an agricultural research and extension service. Your government had nothing, and we are training local staff. The men who will accompany me to El Nido are Salvadorans in training."

"Well, then, why are you going to El Nido?" Esperanza asked again in a more cautious tone.

Mr. Jones paused and considered his words carefully before responding. "Well, up until now, most of the farmers I have worked with are wealthier with large commercial operations. They are mainly coffee planters or sugar growers, and they have the resources to invest in new techniques. Small farmers, like my own family back in Indiana, usually don't come to us for help. I want to see if there's a way to reach farmers like your uncle and the others in El Nido. I want to find out if we can help them improve their farms, too."

Esperanza thought before commenting, "My family has never had time since the indigo crop days to do more than work to keep us alive and eating. The bankers don't welcome us anymore. We just sell what we can to the truckers who go to Chalatenango City or San Salvador. The cash we get from them is our money for the year."

"They sound like my family before we got help. I want to see if I can help your family like my family was helped."

"Why my family?" queried Esperanza defensively.

"Because you asked me some questions. The other maids didn't. The workers we hired at the research station don't. Small farmers close to the large landowners we service haven't. So, I thought that your family might give me a chance to help."

Esperanza absorbed Mr. Jones's words. They reassured her that Mr. Jones meant no harm to El Nido. Then she said, "I will talk to my mother tomorrow and ask her about your plans. She also knows my uncle better than I do, and she'll tell me if he might be interested." Then she paused and looked down, "Thank you for caring."

The following day, on her afternoon off, Esperanza made her way to the post office. She mailed a letter to Kitty, which shared her conversation with Mr. Jones and asked for her thoughts. Afterward, she stopped by a store to buy a new pad of airmail paper and some envelopes before catching the bus to San Judas.

Her mother greeted her with an *abrazo* and, before Esperanza could say anything, said, "I had to go to the school this morning because Pepe and Pablo got into trouble for teasing a couple of girls. I assured the director that Pablo's mother and I took the matter seriously and that we will discipline the boys. We will need your help this evening. I've noticed their bodies are changing. They grow up so quickly. I remember having similar problems with Diego and my brothers—only, I think they were older when their troubles began."

"What should we do?" asked Esperanza. "Should I talk to Pablo's mother?"

Her mother responded, "I spoke to Pablo's mother, and we agreed to give them a good scolding. We want you to be firm with them. We have told them that they need an education to live better lives and make money to live in nice houses like the ones where you're working. Since keeping them in school is expensive, we have to make them understand that education costs money. We are barely getting by now with the cost of rent, food, and utilities. I make a few extra *colones* every month by babysitting, selling eggs, and doing favors. But it's tough, dear Esperanza."

"Mama, we must keep them in school, even if we have to spend our reserve. And what I want to talk to you about might help us make a few more *colones*."

After Esperanza detailed her conversations with Mr. Jones, her mother asked, "Are you sure that we can trust Mr. Jones not to steal our land?"

"I hope so. I sent a letter today to Kitty asking her the same question."

Her mother thought for a few moments before replying, "You've worked so hard for us since we left El Nido. All we have besides your work is our land and the ties to our community there. If Mr. Jones truly wants to help our people, maybe we could return home someday. When you write to my brother, Manuel, include the special name I always used for him—Mango. He'll know it's from me and understand that Mr. Jones comes in peace. Let's write the letter together, and we'll both sign it."

The two women wrote a long letter to Mango that not only introduced Mr. Jones but also told them of their life in San Salvador and her mother's affection for him.

Mr. Jones took that letter with him the following week when he led his team to El Nido.

CHAPTER 48

A very tired Mr. Jones returned late for dinner the next Thursday night. He had taken his team on a twelve-hour trip to El Nido and was covered in dust and grime from both the highway and the farmlands he had inspected. After a long shower, he came to the dining room for dinner.

Thursday afternoons were Esperanza's time off, but this Thursday she had come back early because she wanted to hear Mr. Jones' news.

When he entered the dining room, Mrs. Jones was already seated. She nodded hello and said, "Esperanza came back early and helped me with dinner. Do you want to chat with her this evening or wait until tomorrow?"

Mr. Jones responded, "Dear, I am not that tired. Let Esperanza come in after we eat. I had a pleasant day, and her family was very open and inviting." Mrs. Jones moved to get up, but Mr. Jones said, "Just wait. I'm sure that she will be serving dinner tonight."

At that moment, Esperanza appeared and smiled, "Good evening., Mr. Jones. Did you have a pleasant day?"

"Indeed, I did. I bring warm greetings from your uncle and the whole family. They were delighted to receive your note, and they asked me about you and your mother. I suggest that right after dinner you come in, and we can have a chat. I'm sure Mrs. Jones will enjoy hearing about the day, too."

Esperanza served them her special *caldo de res*. It was full of pieces of beef, potatoes, and vegetables. She also brought in the tossed salad that Mrs. Jones had prepared. After a dessert of flan and coffee, Esperanza reentered the dining room and asked, "Did you enjoy your dinner?"

Mrs. Jones said, "There wasn't one mouthful left. Your *caldo* was wonderful. Why haven't you served it before?"

"Oh, I thought that you preferred American foods. So, I just followed your daily menus. If you like, I can prepare Salvadoran dishes for you. I know quite a few, but we will need to buy some spices at the market the next time we go."

Mr. Jones chimed in, "I enjoyed my dinner very much. I would enjoy trying more of your Salvadoran dishes." Turning to his wife, he said, "I think our guests would like to try them, too."

Then Mr. Jones refocused on Esperanza, "Your family welcomed us warmly. We spent most of the day walking through different sections of El Nido. We took soil samples to test at our lab, looked over the crops, and inspected the few milk cows the villagers keep. We also visited the special field where they still grow indigo. Your uncle showed us the woods by the stream where the herbs and plants are protected. My assistant tested the water from the stream as well. We asked a lot of questions about the seeds they use, and how they plant, fertilize, and water their crops. We didn't have enough time to gather all the information on harvesting and selling, so I arranged with your uncle for one of my men to return in a few days. If your mother and you don't mind, he could stay at your home. Your uncle has it all ready for the day you both return."

That was a lot for Esperanza to absorb, but she immediately reacted, "Of course, your man can stay at our house. I know that our straw beds may not be comfortable for him, but they served us well until we came to the city."

Mr. Jones responded, "We have comfortable bed rolls with innerspring mattresses for field trips, so he'll just use your house as a shelter. No need to worry about him being a burden." Then, almost thinking out loud, he added, "Your uncle and cousins work hard, but they're using very primitive practices and equipment. Their production is quite low. My team and I will need a few weeks to analyze all the information before we can figure out how to help. Whatever we come up with, it's going to take time, a lot of hard work, and a good deal of investment."

Esperanza didn't know what to say except, "Thank you, Mr. Jones." No one had ever shown any real interest in how her family lived or what their future might be. Her experience had shown her that life in El Nido was far less comfortable than in San Salvador, but when Mr. Jones referred to their farming methods as "primitive," she wasn't sure what that meant. She recalled her history teacher mentioning primitive peoples in jungles and deserts, but how did that relate to her own people? Then she thought of Mrs. Holmes, who had explained that the electric current in Peru was different from that in El Salvador. As a result, the Rands had sold their old appliances in Peru and bought those the Holmeses had been using. Mrs. Holmes even planned to purchase all new appliances when she settled in Washington. Was that what "primitive" meant? Or was it more like the way of doing things in El Nido was as outdated as old appliances?

Mrs. Jones said, "I think that Mr. Jones needs some time to relax now. So, please tidy up. We will talk more later. And that was a lovely dinner."

CHAPTER 49

The next week went by very slowly. Esperanza was hopeful but concerned. She saw a flicker of hope for her family and village, but she still didn't understand what Mr. Jones meant by "primitive." She knew that her family had no money to make changes. She wrote another letter to Kitty to ask her what she thought about Mr. Jones' visit and report.

She took Mrs. Jones to the Central Market and introduced her to the native spices she used in her cooking. She also introduced Mrs. Jones to the market women she had known since her days with Doña Marta. The women gave Mrs. Jones better prices than those at the Santa Tecla market, which Mrs. Jones usually preferred. As they left, Mrs. Jones smiled and said, "Esperanza, you made quite a deal today. We'll have to come back here once in a while."

Mrs. Jones also encouraged Esperanza to prepare more Salvadoran dishes, so she prepared *caldos, surtidos, empanadas, pupusas,* and *gallo en chicha* for them to savor. At first it was just for them, but then they began to ask her to serve the dishes for guests at their luncheons and dinners. "It is time for them to taste local foods instead of living on canned goods from the commissary," Mrs. Jones said to her cook.

The new menu required many more days of marketing at the Central Market.

Each Thursday afternoon, Esperanza continued her routine of stopping by her post office box on her way to San Judas. For the past three Thursdays, she had sent her weekly letter to Kitty, but her box remained empty. In her letters, she had shared her mother's joy at hearing from her brother and told Kitty about the Jones family's discovery of Salvadoran food. There wasn't much else to write about until she heard from Kitty.

Finally, a month after Mr. Jones' visit, a long letter from Kitty arrived. Esperanza carefully tucked it into her shirt and headed home to San Judas, eager to read it in the quiet of her own space.

The letter was two pages long and typewritten instead of handwritten. It read:

Dear Esperanza,

I received both of your letters, but I've been so busy with schoolwork, long hours in laboratory classes, and a lot of homework that it's taken me longer to respond than usual. I also wanted to wait for some information from my father, which I just received yesterday. I've also started spending a lot of time with a friend named Damon. I think he might be someone I can be really serious about, but I'll tell you more about Damon after I share what my father said about Mr. Jones.

My father said to tell you hello and mentioned that he and my mother miss your cooking. It turns out he does know Mr. Jones. They worked together in a very poor part of the U.S. called Appalachia in the 1930s. My father was focused on a maternal and childcare project, while Mr. Jones was involved with an agricultural project aimed at helping farm families boost their production and income. My father says Mr. Jones genuinely cared about the families he worked with. Even though his main expertise is marketing, he always tried to help in any way he could. He was well-liked and made a lot of friends in the community.

My father said that Mr. Jones was born on a small farm in Indiana and that his folks barely kept their heads above water. He has a couple of brothers who stayed home working on the farm to put him through college. My father said that Mr. Jones never forgot his roots and wants to help other poor farm families improve their lot. So, I think that you can trust him if he says that he wants to help your family.

Last weekend, I went down to see my family. That's when I asked my father about Mr. Jones. I took my friend Damon to meet my family. I didn't tell you about Damon before because I wasn't sure that I really liked him or whether he was just a good lab partner. You see, we met on a project in our biology lab. We worked together last semester and this one, too. He is very smart and nice-looking. He has dark brown hair and big brown eyes. We worked well as a team, and then, a few weeks ago, he asked me out on a date. And, oh, it was a fun date—we went dancing and spent an hour talking—then he kissed me, and I liked it. We have been going out almost every night since. We spend a couple of afternoons each week in the lab, get together to study in the evening, and usually end up hugging and kissing by the end. I really like being with him.

So, I arranged for him to meet my parents. We drove

down to Arlington where my parents live. My parents liked him too. So, maybe Damon is my soul mate. We haven't made love yet, but I am getting very interested. You're the first person I am sharing these feelings with. I'll keep you posted.

Hope all is going well for you. I enjoy hearing from you about your life and things in San Salvador. I have to run. I have a class with Damon, and he is picking me up.

Lots of love,

Kitty

Well, thought Esperanza, *Kitty has put my mind at ease about telling Mr. Jones about my family and El Nido. If Kitty's father trusts him, then I can too.*

However, her major concern was about Kitty and Damon. Had Kitty really found a man she could enjoy being with? She wished Kitty well, but the memory of her own sexual experience with a man—the rape that had shattered her dreams—kept surfacing. Her only friends since then had been women. She had built a protective wall against men and feared the thought of letting anyone get close. Kitty had never experienced anything like what she had, and part of her wanted to warn her. Yet, the Holmeses, Rands, and Joneses had shown her that happy, respectful relationships between men and women were possible. Those glimpses of love reminded her of the joy her mother and father had shared, even in difficult times. Yes, she remembered their happiness, despite the hardships. Maybe, just maybe, a measure of happiness could be found in a relationship with a man. If Kitty could find love, perhaps there was still someone out there for herself too.

Then she froze. She remembered the pain and terror of her rape—the smell of *aguardiente* and stale body odor—and its consequences. The barriers went up again.

CHAPTER 50

Weeks turned into months. Life at the Joneses fell into a routine. Mr. Jones would tell her every few days that his team was working on a plan for the El Nido area. An Agricultural Extension Office had been opened in Chalatenango, and the Salvadoran technician assigned there visited El Nido to collect further samples and study their traditional farm practices. So far, however, there hadn't been any action—only planning and studies.

Her afternoons off seemed repetitive. She took the bus to the post office. Sometimes there was a letter, sometimes there was not. Each letter sang the same song of heavy college demands, hours in labs, dates with Damon, and the occasional query about life in San Salvador. Then, Esperanza went on to San Judas, where she saw her mother and her baby boy, whom she barely knew. He was growing into a young man and, along with his buddy Pablo, was already preoccupied with girls. Esperanza kept thinking, *He is not even 11 years old.*

After over four months since his visit to El Nido, Mr. Jones asked Esperanza to join him in his office after dinner. When she arrived, he nodded and said, "My team and I have gathered enough information to talk to your uncle and his neighbors about a long-term plan to improve and diversify their production. It will take several years and require the farmers to learn new methods, use improved seeds, shift away from some of their traditional practices, dig irrigation canals, and build new storage facilities."

Esperanza gasped.

Mr. Jones continued, "If your uncle and the neighbors agree, my team will teach them the new practices and, next spring, work with them to put in experimental fields of new and improved crops. Then they will, with the help of the extension agent in Chalatenango, move forward on their own."

"Where will they get the money to buy the seed and fertilizer? And will you provide them with any tools or equipment to do the work required?" asked the cook.

"I am working on a plan for experimental plots to test multiple crops for year-round production," Mr. Jones continued. "The assistance package would include seeds, fertilizer, some modern tools and equipment, and canals to bring water from the river to the experimental plots. If the plots increase production as I expect, we should be able to secure some low-cost loans to help the farmers in El Nido replicate the success of these experimental plots by the third year."

"Mr. Jones, even if the experimental plots are productive, banks won't help people like us. They won't even let us open accounts to deposit our money."

Mr. Jones wasn't surprised and just said, "Well, I want to try anyway."

It was a very sober Esperanza who wrote Kitty a long letter that night. Mr. Jones had unwittingly dashed her hopes. Her sulky mood hadn't changed when she told her mother the following Thursday. Her mother listened carefully and then said, "Why don't you tell Doña Marta? I went up to see her a couple of weeks ago, and she was as warm and caring as ever. She misses seeing you and your reports about life in the Central Market and her old friends there. Yes, I think that she might have some ideas about how to help El Nido and us."

Esperanza said, "Mother, I didn't know you have been visiting Doña Marta! I guess I have just fallen into the routine of living near Avenida Roosevelt. And Mrs. Jones hasn't given me afternoons off to go to see Doña Marta in Flor Blanca."

Flor continued, "Oh, yes, I have often taken the bus to Flor Blanca to visit Doña Marta—and yes, I even visited that sad ravine with all those people crowded together. Don't think for a moment that I am not grateful to Doña Marta and you that I am living here and not there. Truly, I am grateful, and I've learned how to live in this city and make a few *colones* each month to keep us going. I still miss my life and friends in El Nido, but I'm doing my best here. I would love to go back to my home in El Nido if it were possible. I'm glad Mr. Jones is trying to help. I think Doña Marta would be interested—after all, she's from La Palma and knew of my grandmother, the *Gran Curandera*."

Esperanza's eyes lit up for the first time in days. "Mother, you are so right. Doña Marta would be interested. Why hadn't I thought to tell her about it? Since she doesn't live around the corner anymore, I guess I just forgot. I will ask Mrs. Jones for time next week to make a visit. I am sure she is home every afternoon."

Her mother nodded, "I just take the bus, and she is always waiting. We have horchata and sandwiches and talk about the days in the pension. And she raised two fine boys, so she gives me advice about handling Pepe these days. She says a lot of affection and patience pays off."

CHAPTER 51

Mrs. Jones had a bridge party the following Wednesday, for which Esperanza had to prepare lunch and afternoon tea, so she was not able to visit Doña Marta. However, Mrs. Jones finally gave her time off on Friday afternoon. She had baked a chocolate cake for dinner the night before, and Mrs. Jones allowed her to wrap up a piece for Doña Marta.

Doña Marta was delighted when Esperanza appeared. "I've missed our weekly visits since you moved from Flor Blanca. Your mother has kept me up to date on your family, but that is not like having you here to chat about so many things that interest me. Come sit here."

Esperanza smiled, "I am so glad to see you looking so well. The last time I was here you were so pale, and I was concerned about your health. Well, you look so much better today. Here, I baked a chocolate cake for dessert last night, and Mrs. Jones allowed me to bring this piece for you."

"So you have learned new recipes from your American patrons. I'll order some coffee, and we will enjoy it together." Doña Marta called for her maid and ordered a pot of coffee. "Now, Esperanza, tell me about the market and my friends. I still miss seeing them every week. I rarely go out anymore except for dinner with Ricardo and his family. I am getting lazy."

Esperanza smiled as she said, "Mrs. Jones likes the market in Santa Tecla. It is smaller, and she has made some friends there. For several months, we didn't go downtown. Then, one night I made them *caldo de res.* They had only eaten American dishes until then. You would like the Joneses; they are very nice people. Well, they liked the *caldo* and Mrs. Jones asked me to prepare more of our traditional Salvadoran dishes. I said that I would need to get a supply of spices at the Central Market. So we go Santa Tecla two or three times a month and at least once to the Central Market. So, I have a chance to catch up on our old friends."

The maid brought in a pot of coffee and two plates. As they enjoyed the treat, Esperanza filled Doña Marta in on the latest news—not only about the people in the market but also the gossip surrounding the Osorio government, the political intrigues in the barracks, and some juicy new love affairs.

As they were finishing the coffee, Esperanza changed the subject. "Doña Marta, I want to ask your advice. It's about El Nido, and it's very confusing."

Doña Marta seemed quite surprised. Esperanza and her mother had not talked of El Nido for some time. She nodded her interest.

"Well, Mr. Jones is an adviser at the Ministry of Agriculture. I didn't know that when I took the job. I started to notice that many of the papers he left on the dining room table dealt with farming. So, I asked him about them. I told him that I came from a farm in El Nido. He asked some more questions, and I told him about growing up there. I was concerned that I had told him too much—you know, you can never trust an outsider. I wrote my friend Kitty—you remember the Holmes daughter who has become a good friend. She told me that her father said Mr. Jones came from a small farm, was genuinely interested in helping small farmers, and could be trusted."

Doña Marta gazed intently on Esperanza, "Are you telling me that the American is interested in El Nido?"

"Yes. He is. He took a team to El Nido several weeks ago. My mother and I gave him a letter to my uncle, Manuel, to show that we knew him. He looked over all of the lands of El Nido and did some soil tests. He watched my uncle and some other farmers work their fields. He told me that the soil is good, but the farm practices are primitive. I don't really understand what he means by primitive, because I only remember primitive from the way it was used in my school books."

Doña Marta interjected, "By primitive, he means old-fashioned—the ways Mayans have traditionally worked their fields. They don't use technologically advanced methods to protect the soil and increase production."

"Oh, thank you. That helps me understand what he is planning to do," mused Esperanza. "Mr. Jones told me that he is working on a plan to help the El Nido farmers. He sent some of his men back to check on some things, like the flow of the stream and work in the off season. I told him that, as I remember, we grow only one crop a year. He wants to ask my uncle and other farmers about that."

"You mentioned that Mr. Jones is an adviser to the minister of agriculture. My son, Teodoro, works for an American company that imports and sells farm machinery, among other things. I'll ask him if he knows Mr. Jones. Let's see what I can find out, and then we can talk more about what's happening. You know, I have a special place in my heart for El Nido because of your great-grandmother, the *curandera*, and how she healed my mother."

Esperanza smiled as she replied, "I would be so grateful, because my people say that we should never trust an outsider. I would be much more comfortable knowing your opinion. Mr. Jones told me that he genuinely wants to help small farmers, as he came from a poor, small farm himself. He said the only people in El Salvador who currently take advantage of his program are rich people; he wants to find ways to help families like mine."

Doña Marta put the last piece of chocolate cake in her mouth and took a sip of coffee. "Esperanza, that cake was delicious. I may go back into business just to sell it. But first I am going to find out about Mr. Jones and El Nido. It sounds very interesting, and, remember, I still have family in La Palma—maybe it is worth introducing them to Mr. Jones."

Esperanza finished her coffee before saying, "Thank you, Doña Marta. Visiting you always lifts my spirits. I will try to come back whenever I have some time off, just as if I were still living around the corner."

"I would welcome that."

As Esperanza gave her a farewell embrace, Doña Marta repeated, "Mr. Jones, an adviser to the minister of agriculture."

CHAPTER 52

A few days later, when Mr. Jones arrived home from work, he walked into the kitchen and said, "I had a visit today at the research station from Teodoro Romero. He mentioned that his mother, Doña Marta, told him about our conversation and my interest in El Nido. Mr. Romero works for the representative of an American company that sells farm machinery. I've been trying to set up a meeting with his boss for some time, but we could never align our schedules. Then, out of the blue, Mr. Romero walks into the office asking for me—all because you mentioned my interest in El Nido to his mother. I have to say, I was surprised."

Esperanza was not sure how to react, "I hope I didn't cause a problem by telling Doña Marta about your work in El Nido."

"No, quite the contrary. I am very pleased. I invited him, his wife, and Doña Marta to dinner next week."

Now Esperanza was surprised.

"After dinner, I want you to tell me all about him and his family."

The smiling cook said, "Yes, sir."

After dinner, Esperanza knocked at the entrance to the office in the hall. Mr. Jones looked up from the papers on which he was working and said, "Come in."

Mrs. Jones appeared at the door and said, "I am going to sit in, because I need to know more about them, too."

"Well, tell us about the Romero family."

"Doña Marta is the reason that I survived the move from El Nido to San Salvador," Esperanza began, and, in a matter-of-fact way, told the Joneses the story of her young life for the first time. "I graduated elementary school with honors and was awarded a fellowship for high school in Chalatenango City. On the way home a drunk raped me, and the school officials blamed me for getting raped. So, I decided there was no future for me in El Nido. My grandmother had taught me all the traditional recipes of our people, along with the herbs and plants that give them flavor. I thought that would be enough to get a job as a cook to take care of my mother and son. A relative had given me the address of the pension in Soyapango run by Doña Marta—and she took us in. Doña Marta is from Chalatenango and my great grandmother, the *Gran Curandera*, had cured her mother. I couldn't find a job, but when Doña Marta had to fire her cook, she gave me a chance—and for five years, I worked and learned from her. That's when I discovered that there are different types of cuisines. Doña Marta taught me some European and other recipes, and Mrs. Holmes and you, Mrs. Jones, have introduced me to American ones."

Esperanza continued, "Doña Marta sold the property and closed the pension. She helped me find our apartment in San Judas, and her two sons even helped us move, providing some old furniture from the pension to furnish it. Doña Marta has been a widow for many years and ran the pension to support her family after her husband passed away. She had three children—her sons Ricardo and Teodoro, and a daughter who died after childbirth. She and her sons are very close. While she has her own apartment at Teodoro's in Flor Blanca, she often visits Ricardo and his family in Escalón. She also helped me find my job with Mrs. Holmes. Since Teodoro's house was just around the corner from the Holmes,

I visited her almost every week during the four years I lived in Flor Blanca."

The Jones listened very carefully. "I don't know much more about the sons or their work. I know they like and respect their mother. And she is a very wise lady who tries to keep informed about people who matter and what goes on in the city. She introduced me to the women in the Central Market who know about such things and to this day I tell her what the women tell me."

Mr. Jones nodded and said, "Well, thank you for telling us about your life and Doña Marta. Do you know how she feels about helping farmers?"

"I know her family once had an indigo farm, but they live in the town in La Palma now. And she knows how hard farm life is, and that small farmers like my family need a lot of help. But we never really talked about that."

Mrs. Jones said, "I want you to prepare her favorite dishes for dinner next week."

Esperanza smiled, "She would love a *gallo en chicha*, one of Mrs. Holmes' tossed salads, and your chocolate cake."

Mrs. Jones said, "We have our menu. You and I will go to the Central Market to get the right ingredients."

The week leading up to the dinner was special for Esperanza, because this was the first time since the pension closed that she had prepared a dinner especially for Doña Marta. She wanted it to be right. For Mr. Jones, it was a time to prepare for a discussion with Teodoro about the plans for El Nido. Mrs. Jones' goal was to create a warm and friendly environment for making new friends. Mrs. Jones told Mr. Jones, "We have invited the Romeros to dinner as guests, not for a business meeting. So, use the time for us to get to know them and they, us. If we can build a friendship, you'll have plenty of time to talk business later."

The Romeros arrived at 7:00 p.m., which is an early hour for most Salvadoran upper-class dinner parties.

In the living room, Mr. Jones prepared scotch and sodas for his guests as they settled in. Mrs. Jones, in her best Spanish, welcomed them to her house, "Welcome. I am so pleased to have you in my home, and I guess I have Esperanza to thank for my good fortune."

Doña Marta smiled, "Thank you for having us. Yes, Esperanza told me about you both and of Mr. Jones' interest in El Nido."

"The pleasure is ours. Esperanza told us about you, Doña Marta, and your importance in her life. She is an excellent cook and very reliable. I have you to thank for this. And, you know, when we came to your country a year ago, I was apprehensive. We are from Indiana—both of us grew up on farms, just family farms—and living outside of America was a new experience. We lived in Puerto Rico for three years before coming here, but, really, this is our first experience in a foreign country."

Doña Marta reflected, "I come from La Palma in Chalatenango and coming to San Salvador with my husband was like moving to a foreign land. Everything was so different from the routine of my hometown. And then, when my husband died, I had to find some way of caring for my family in a city I barely knew. I think I can appreciate how coming here must have affected you."

Through cocktails and dinner, the conversation remained very focused on the people at the dinner party. The Joneses talked about their university years and their families. The Romeros reciprocated. Yes, the party referenced El Nido several times, but only in passing. When they finished eating dinner, everyone was on a first name basis.

As the evening came to its end, Mr. Jones made an appointment to meet with Teodoro and his boss, and Mrs. Jones had an invitation to play bridge with Mrs. Romero and friends. Doña Marta went to the kitchen to congratulate Esperanza and give her a warm *abrazo*.

Mr. Jones said to his wife, "What a wonderful dinner party. Such nice people. I had tried so hard to meet Mr. Romero through formal channels. Now, we call each other by our first names."

Mrs. Jones smiled, "My dear, in Puerto Rico, I learned that you get more things done by getting to know people and, when they are your friends and trust you, they'll do business with you. It is up to us to know the people we are dealing with, and whether we can trust them before we do business with them."

Mr. Jones gave his wife a loving kiss as they prepared to turn in for the night.

CHAPTER 53

It was almost two weeks later before Mr. Jones asked Esperanza to come to his home office again. He started, "Let me thank you again for your help in getting to know Doña Marta and her family. We have become friends, and his company has agreed to meet with my boss and me about how we might work together."

Esperanza said, "Does that mean good news for El Nido?"

"It may well be. We have a lot of planning to do, and then there will be discussions with your uncle and the other farmers. It won't be fast or easy. Their farming practices are so basic that we have a lot of work ahead to train them in adopting more productive systems and using more efficient farm implements. And they are so poor—they lack the working capital needed to make the necessary changes. In many ways, outside of coffee production, El Salvador is one of the least developed economies I've encountered."

"America is so rich. Why can't you give us the money we need?"

"Our program is to share our knowledge with you, so you can benefit from new technology. But it's up to your country to raise the funds needed to put that technology to use. The United States has a policy called 'Point 4,' through which we share our scientific and industrial advances with developing countries, like El Salvador, but implementing them is your country's responsibility."

Esperanza seemed confused as she asked, "How can a poor farmer use the new practices if he doesn't have any money to change from the old ways?"

Mr. Jones added, "That is what has been bothering me and my colleagues, and why we have wanted to talk with people, like Teodoro and his boss. Unless we can find people with resources to work with us, only wealthy farmers can use our knowledge. And most of them already know about it if they choose to use it."

"Can't you change your program?" asked the cook.

"Well, I can make recommendations, but the decisions are made by my bosses in Washington. Here in El Salvador, we have an annual budget of about one million dollars. That covers salaries, training grants for Salvadorans to study in America, and a few demonstration projects. This budget also supports the three *servicios* in El Salvador: the one for health, the second for education, and mine, in agriculture. Each *servicio* advises your government on designing new programs and improving those already in place. But it's up to your government to fund those programs. Poor countries with limited resources and few trained personnel face real challenges," he paused, adding, "A million dollars isn't much for the work that needs to be done, especially when powerful interests resist any changes to the current situation."

"You mean like the bankers who won't let me deposit my money," Esperanza mused.

"Yes," he said. "Like the banker who told me that he would approve a loan for one of my projects, if I provided 125 percent collateral—even with a *servicio* crop plan and oversight."

Mr. Jones sat for a minute looking at the floor, before saying, "Thank you again, Esperanza. I'll tell you when I have news about El Nido."

Esperanza just turned and left the office.

While it was several weeks before Mr. Jones talked to Esperanza about El Nido again, Doña Marta raised it each time Esperanza visited her. The week after the dinner party, no sooner had Esperanza entered the room, than Doña Marta greeted her with, "So glad you could come by. Teodoro talked to me about El Nido and Mr. Jones—and I want you to know how difficult things are."

"First, I brought you some mousse that Mrs. Jones just taught me to make. I think you will like it for dessert tonight."

"Thank you, and I must say that I never enjoyed a *gallo en chiche* as much as yours. You have become a fine cook."

Esperanza adjusted her rebozo and sat down.

"Teodoro tells me that he and his boss have had initial discussions with Mr. Jones. He says Mr. Jones is a good man who genuinely wants to help small farmers like your uncle. But his program mainly offers technical advice to the ministry—it doesn't come with much funding beyond demonstrating how to plan and organize a project. The primary focus is on running a research station and setting up an extension service to teach farmers about new crops and the benefits of adopting better farming practices. But any actual changes require funding, which has to come from either the ministry or the farmers themselves. Teodoro says the ministry has little money beyond paying salaries. And, to make matters worse, the minister seems more interested in helping his friends—who already have money. Mr. Jones is pushing the minister to do more, especially by supporting a national program to help small farmers adopt modern practices and bring them into the national economy. He hopes that the El Nido project will demonstrate how much agricultural production can increase when small, struggling farmers are trained in these new methods."

Esperanza commented, "I know how hard it is for little people like me. I couldn't find a bank to let me make a deposit. And I remember how the schoolteachers wouldn't believe me about the rape. I wouldn't have my post office box if Kitty hadn't applied for it. I wouldn't have my apartment if you hadn't asked Ricardo. I know that people like me just don't seem to count."

"That's the truth. I know how hard it was for a widow to keep going," nodded Doña Marta in accord. Then she paused for a minute as if in thought, "I have asked Teodoro to see if he can help Mr. Jones. You see, I like both Mr. and Mrs. Jones. I think he is right. The economy needs small, poor farmers to improve their production and make money. Too many of our men can't find jobs and work only as seasonal farm labor. Then, as we both know, they abandon their women, while they move from farm to farm. We need to get back to the way it was in Chalatenango when indigo was profitable—lots of small farmers, like my family, working together to get the crops planted and harvested and enough income to keep families together. I think that is what Mr. Jones wants to do, and I want to help him."

Esperanza's admiration for the older woman lit up her face with a radiant smile.

"It will take some time. I hope Mr. Jones doesn't give up. He has Teodoro and me in his corner."

CHAPTER 54

The next several weeks crawled by, marked by the usual routine—six days of following Mrs. Jones's daily calendar and menus. Wednesdays meant trips to the market, either in Santa Tecla or downtown San Salvador. Each day, Esperanza tried to carve out an hour to study English or review a textbook for a high school course. All the while, she shared her time and space with the other maid, Maria, whose interests didn't include English or studying.

Esperanza tried to focus on her work and push aside thoughts of her family and dreams. Earning the *colones* that kept her family going was her priority, and she felt trapped by reality. There was no time for dreaming. The hope she had seen in Mr. Jones's plan for El Nido faded away. Her life centered around her daily routine: ensuring Mrs. Jones was satisfied and maintaining a calm relationship with Maria. She let the routine become her world.

Then came the night, just before dinner, that Mr. Jones walked into the kitchen and said, "Come to the office after dinner—I have some news."

As soon as she and Maria finished cleaning up in the kitchen, Esperanza headed to the hallway office where Mr. and Mrs. Jones were reviewing some papers. Mrs. Jones noticed her in the doorway and said, "Come in, we've been waiting for you."

"Yes, Esperanza, thanks to Doña Marta, I met with one of Teodoro's colleagues today, Pedro Martinez. It seems that Mr. Martinez was the superintendent of a large coffee finca before he joined Teodoro's company. His former employer was Nicolas Borakas, the director of all the Suarez Moncada holdings. Mr. Borakas has been diversifying from *fincas* to other agro-industrial projects. I explained to him my plan for the development of El Nido, and Mr. Martinez was interested in the prospect that it might bring more small farmers into the market economy."

"You mean there is some hope for finding funds for your plan?" asked Mrs. Jones. "You were so disappointed when the *servicio* director said that it was beyond the scope of the *servicio's* mandate to consider it."

"Yes, Gladys. There is some hope. Mr. Martinez has agreed to ask for an appointment with Mr. Borakas. My *servicio* director said, 'More power to you. If you can find the financing, I will find a way to support you with all the technical resources that the *servicio* has available."

Turning to Esperanza, Mr. Jones explained, "You might be a bit confused, Esperanza. My wife is referring to my work with the U.S. agricultural *servicio* that advises your government on agricultural policies and programs. As I mentioned before, the *servicio* is a joint effort between our governments. The U.S. provides technical advisers to share our research, technology, and experience, while your government supplies the organization, personnel, and funding to carry out the policies. But since your government doesn't have the funds for my plan in El Nido, I have to find another way to secure the money to make it happen."

Mrs. Jones added sarcastically, "I've seen little evidence that the ministry wants to help the little guy. The minister seems to be interested in only taking care of his friends."

Mr. Jones scowled, "Gladys, that's enough."

"Well, it's true, isn't it?"

Esperanza just listened.

Mrs. Jones, looking up at Esperanza, said, "I've invited the Martinezes to dinner next week. I'll arrange a time for you to talk to them about El Nido. And you can prepare one of your special Salvadoran dinners."

Esperanza nodded, "Thank you for the information. I'll prepare a special dinner. Is there anything else tonight?"

"No, not right now. Good night, Esperanza," said Mrs. Jones.

The following week, Mrs. Jones took Esperanza to the Central Market for the spices and food items Esperanza needed for her *empanadas, caldo de res,* and *pudin de cacao.* That Friday night, the Martinezes savored every mouthful. Mrs. Martinez, Josefina, said to Mrs. Jones, "The dinner was simply delicious. Where did you get the recipes?"

"Oh, no, I didn't cook dinner. It was my cook, Esperanza, and it is the recipe that she learned from her grandmother in El Nido, the community that our husbands talked about during dinner." Turning to Mr. Martinez, Mrs. Jones asked, "Would you like to talk to Esperanza about El Nido?"

Mr. Martinez said, "Yes, I would like to meet her. I have an appointment to work with a client next week, and I plan to stop by El Nido and look around before I talk to Mr. Borakas."

"Fine" said Mrs. Jones. "I'll ask her to come in after we finish our dessert." Mrs. Jones had pre-arranged the meeting, and provided Esperanza enough time to fix her hair and put on a clean outfit. This was the first time since leaving the pension that Esperanza had ever been invited to talk to a guest after dinner.

Upon entering the living room, Esperanza was struck by how much the Martínez family reminded her of the people she had grown up with, except that Mrs. Martinez stood out as possibly the most beautiful, tan-skinned woman she had ever seen. Her graceful features and striking green eyes were captivating.

Mrs. Jones introduced her, "This is Esperanza Choarti, the cook of our sumptuous meal. As you know, she is from El Nido. My husband met her uncle and the family when he visited El Nido some time ago."

Mr. Martinez smiled and noted, "I will be going to El Nido next week. I have a client outside La Palma and plan to stop by before I come back to San Salvador."

"I am pleased to meet you. I understand that you work with *Señor* Teodoro."

"Yes, it is he who introduced me to Mr. Jones and told me about your friendship with his mother. Doña Marta has become our friend too."

Esperanza thought, *This is like meeting an old friend. He is one of us.*

"Could you give me a note to give to your uncle? Mr. Jones said that it might make it easier to talk with him."

"Of course. I will prepare a letter before you leave tonight. His name is Manuel Choarti. My mother calls him 'Mango.' He is farming both his land and ours. We are children of the great shaman who led our family to El Nido ages ago. We brought the indigo plant with us, and it served us well until they discovered how to make anil chemically. We have lived in hard times since then." Esperanza suddenly realized that she sounded like her mother.

"I would appreciate that. I would like to see the land and the crops and meet your people. Knowing them will make it easier when I talk about Mr. Jones's plan."

"Would you like me to tell you more about us before I write the letter?"

"That isn't necessary. Doña Marta has told me about your talents and your aspirations to be a teacher and about your great-grandmother, the *Gran Curandera.* I think my wife and I feel like we already know you."

"I'll be right back," said Esperanza as she hurried to her room for pen and paper. Mr. Martínez had given her hope that maybe she could have a future role in El Nido, perhaps as a village teacher. She could be a leader, like the shamans and *curanderas* before her. He looked and acted like people she knew, and she sensed that he might be an advocate for her community.

CHAPTER 55

The following Friday, Mr. Jones stepped into the kitchen before dinner and said, "Pedro Martínez called me this morning. He visited El Nido and spent the morning with your uncle and several other farmers. He asked them about their interest in my plan and what resources they could offer to help implement it. He also inspected the land and checked a few more factors. He plans to reach out to his former employer, Nicolás Borakas, from the Suárez Moncada Coffee complex, to see if he's interested in participating in the development of El Nido. Apparently, Mr. Borakas is diversifying into other agricultural ventures besides coffee."

"Thank you, Señor. I've read about Mr. Borakas in the newspaper. He is a very important man."

"That's what I understand. I have never met him. We'll have to wait and see what happens."

Esperanza felt it was important to share this information with Doña Marta and get her thoughts on Pedro Martínez's connection with Mr. Borakas. She asked Mrs. Jones if she could take an afternoon off in the coming days to visit Doña Marta. Since Mrs. Jones had no plans for the following Wednesday afternoon, Esperanza took the bus to Flor Blanca that day.

After all the formal greetings, Esperanza got right to the point. "Mr. Jones told me that Mr. Martinez visited El Nido last week and is planning to ask Mr. Borakas of Suarez Moncada about his possible interest in Mr. Jones' plan for El Nido. Did you hear about that?"

"Yes, Teodoro told me that Pedro was very impressed with your uncle and Mr. Jones' plan."

"Really?" said a very surprised Esperanza.

"Yes, let me tell you about Pedro and his wife, Josefina. Their story is very interesting," said Doña Marta as she took a sip of her horchata. "Pedro was born on the largest finca owned by the Suarez Moncada. Teodoro believes that one of Pedro's great-grandfathers was a Suarez Moncada. You know the stories of finca lords and their affairs with the women on the fincas."

She hesitated for a moment before continuing, "Well, I suppose you should know. When Felipe, one of the senior Suárez Moncada's sons, was a teenager, he fell in love with a beautiful girl from a finca named Josefina and got her pregnant. Felipe's father sent him to Spain and arranged for her to marry Pedro. Their oldest son, Carlos, is actually Felipe's child. It turned out to be a good marriage, but Felipe never stopped loving Josefina, even after his parents arranged his marriage to a daughter from one of Guatemala's prominent families."

"How does that affect Mr. Jones's plan for El Nido?" Esperanza asked.

"Patience, my girl, you'll see," Doña Marta replied. "During the Great Depression, Felipe's father fell into debt and lost control of the *fincas*. He salvaged what he could by arranging a marriage between Felipe's sister and Nicolas Borakas, from the Borakas international banking family. Nicolas took over managing the Suárez Moncada *fincas*, and he and Felipe became close friends. They treat each other as brothers and business partners. They saw Pedro's potential and sent him to the Salesian Brothers School for technical training. Eventually, they made him the first native-born superintendent of the *finca*.

"Teodoro tells me that Pedro did a fine job, He boosted productivity and profits and even tried to improve conditions for the workers and their families. But the workers felt that Pedro wasn't fully on their side, so he had to be replaced. It was Felipe who helped arrange a new position for Pedro with Teodoro's boss, and Nicolas made sure it happened. Teodoro's boss has never regretted it. Pedro has become a highly respected manager and technician, and he is in demand across the country."

"So, Pedro really does know Mr. Borakas and might be able to interest him in El Nido," mused Esperanza.

'Oh, yes, I think so. And Teodoro told me that he is impressed by Mr. Jones and his plan for El Nido. Teodoro also told me that his visit to El Nido went very well. Pedro was impressed by your uncle and the other *campesinos* he met. Pedro told Teodoro that the men in El Nido were so different from those on the *finca*. They have different mindsets. The *campesinos* on the *fincas* always lived dependent on the owners and looked to him to make all the decisions that mattered. In El Nido, they never had to live under the *finca* system, so the *campesinos*, no matter how humble, seemed interested in considering what they could do for themselves."

"Is there anything I can do to help?" asked Esperanza.

"I think that you need to wait to hear from Pedro. He will probably contact Mr. Jones." After taking another sip of her horchata, Doña Marta looked intently at Esperanza and warned her, "Don't get your hopes too high."

"What do you mean?" asked Esperanza.

"I learned long ago that people like Mr. Borakas act in their own self-interest. Their primary interest is in profits and how a deal is to his advantage. I doubt he will let sentiment color his decision. He will only react favorably to helping El Nido if he sees some way to profit from it."

Esperanza nodded her understanding. When she left Doña Marta's, she wrote a long letter to Kitty that ended with, "Maybe this will be my road back to El Nido and being a teacher."

Two weeks later, Mr. Jones came home with a package of books from Dr. Holmes. He called Esperanza in from the kitchen and said, "Dr. Holmes sent these for you. His note mentioned preparing you for a possible return to El Nido to work on my project, which caught me by surprise. I haven't informed anyone in Washington about it. But here they are—training manuals from the Government of Puerto Rico, designed for community health technicians who manage the daily operations of rural health posts."

He shook his head as he asked again, "How did he hear about my project?"

CHAPTER 56

Several more weeks passed before Mr. Jones mentioned El Nido again to Esperanza. She had read every manual on the health posts at least twice, and she had even begun to visualize herself working in one. She was dreaming wide-awake.

Another experience at her San Judas home brought Esperanza back to reality. On her last Thursday, after checking her post office box for a letter from Kitty and ensuring she had paid the rent for the box, she took the bus back to San Judas. When she arrived, she found the two boys at home, and her mother was out. The boys seemed just as surprised to see her as she was to find them there—they should have been in school.

"What's going on? You should be in school."

"Oh, we were let out early because of a teachers' meeting" replied Pablo.

She looked at them suspiciously. Pepe chimed in, "Yes, Mother, that's it."

Rather than begin preparing dinner, she sat down beside them and asked, "What classes will you be missing this afternoon?"

"Nothing important," said Pepe. "Just some social studies and Spanish literature."

"But they are important for you, so you can understand the world you are living in."

The boys were visibly unimpressed and tried to cut off the discussion. She sized up the situation. As she got up and turned toward the bedroom, she opined, "I think I should talk to your teachers next week when I'm here at home."

The boys looked guiltily at each other.

Shortly after she lay down, her mother entered the bedroom. She greeted her daughter with, "I think the boys cut school again today. It first happened a couple of weeks ago. The school director sent Patricia and me a note, so Patricia talked to her major, and he smoothed things out. The major only lightly chided the boys. He will have to warn them sternly when he takes them to the beach on Saturday. Patricia tells me that the major is arranging for them to be accepted at the new vocational high school when it opens."

Her mother added, "The boys are growing up fast. They are talking more about girls and events happening at the neighborhood cantina than about schoolwork."

"I thought they were lying to me when they told me that they were let out early because of a teachers' meeting. I am going to their school to talk with their teachers. Education is too important for their future."

For the first time, it dawned on her. She spent her days working in someone else's house to support him, yet she barely recognized the young person he was becoming. She realized, almost bitterly, that her commitment to supporting her mother and son had denied her the time and ability to shape his values or guide his life choices.

On the bus back to the Jones', she thought to herself, *Is this how I want to spend my life?*

Esperanza was too disciplined to break her routine, but those thoughts persisted. She began to think about what she needed to do to change her relationship with her son before he was too old to listen to her. Then it came to her. If Mr. Borakas were interested, she could take her family back to El Nido. That way she would have her mother and son with her all week long and play an active role in their everyday life. Suddenly, what Pedro Martinez was doing took on a new significance.

Her spirits soared when Mr. Jones told her that Mr. Borakas had agreed to discuss El Nido with him.

However, her spirits fell again when, on the following Tuesday, Mr. Jones, in the home office, told her, "Mr. Borakas listened and asked several questions about the soil, the crops, productivity, and logistical considerations. He said that he would have to think about the project. My impression is that he isn't very interested."

Esperanza was crestfallen, but she thanked Mr. Jones for the information.

She decided not to wait any longer to visit the boys' school and find out for herself what and how they were doing. On Thursday, she would go from the post office to the school.

It was almost 2:00 p.m. when she entered the main school door. She walked down the central hall, past several classrooms before she saw the office of the director. She resolutely opened the door.

A man looked up from his desk and—somewhat surprised—asked, "Yes?"

"I am the mother of José Choarti, and I want to ask you about his studies," ventured Esperanza.

"José Choarti?" asked the man.

"Yes. José Choarti. He is in the seventh grade. I am concerned about his grades." She paused and then added, "I am more concerned about his interest in learning. I know he needs education to make something of himself, and I am concerned that he is not committing himself."

The man put down his pen and looked inquisitively at his visitor.

"Last week I arrived home early and found José and his buddy Pablo in the living room. I asked them why they were not in school, and they told me that they were let out early because of a teachers' meeting. Frankly, I did not believe them. So, I decided to consult with you."

The director shook his head, "There was no teacher's' meeting. They skipped school again. I am glad you came to see me, because his teacher has advised me to recommend their expulsion."

"That concerns me deeply. I want both him and Pablo to receive a solid education. I understand the importance of education—I once dreamed of becoming a teacher myself. Their ability to make a decent living depends on their education, so I will talk to Pablo's mother and my mother tonight, and we will talk to the boys. I will do everything possible to prevent their expulsion."

The director said, "The major spoke to me about Pablo and José the first time they were truant, so we took no disciplinary action. But our patience is thin."

"I understand," replied Esperanza. "I will try to prevent another incident. You see, I love learning and still aspire to be a teacher."

"You do impress me, Mrs. Choarti. I think you might indeed have made a good teacher. It is a tragedy that with our country's limited facilities, adults like you cannot be admitted to high school."

"What do you mean there is no way?" queried Esperanza.

"Our country has no provision for an adult to be admitted to high school. Attendance is limited to children under nineteen. Unlike what I saw on my training grant in America, we have no night school courses for adults like you to obtain high school diplomas."

"You mean that I have no opportunity for further schooling?"

"Not in the public school system. The only possibility is if you can afford private schools," was the reply.

A greatly disturbed Esperanza said farewell to the director and went home.

By dinner time, Esperanza had talked to her mother and Patricia. They had agreed to cancel the visit to the beach with the major. And the major talked to both boys about skipping school and lying. The action, coupled with strong words from both the mothers and from Grandma Flor, led the chastened boys to agree to cause their parents no further concern. They kept their word.

CHAPTER 57

It must have been another month before Mr. Jones reported, "Mr. Borakas has asked his brother-in-law, Felipe Suarez Moncada, to accompany Pedro Martinez and me on a visit to El Nido. We have scheduled the visit for next Tuesday."

That day, Mr. Jones was up before dawn and Esperanza served him a hardy breakfast. He returned after dark, too tired to do more than eat a few mouthfuls of dinner, take a shower, and crawl into bed.

It was Thursday before Mr. Jones, at breakfast, told Esperanza, "The visit did not go well at all. I am not sure that Mr. Suarez Moncada was interested. He listened carefully to my plan and asked some questions. He talked to your uncle and other *campesinos*. He brought his son, Luis, along, and the friction between Pedro Martinez and Luis made it difficult for me. Every time I tried to make a point, Luis would undercut me. And every time Pedro tried to clarify or reinforce one of my points, Luis lit into him. It certainly wasn't a good day."

Esperanza said, "I'm sorry that it didn't go well."

"I'm going to see Pedro tomorrow and see how he feels."

Friday night, when Mr. Jones came home, he seemed much more optimistic. Before the Joneses went out to a dinner party, he stepped into the kitchen and said, "Pedro talked to Felipe Suarez Moncada on

Wednesday and Mr. Suarez Moncada is interested in discussing the project with me next week."

The next week came and went. The meeting never took place. Then 1953 crawled by. Each time Esperanza looked to Mr. Jones for some news, he would shake his head sadly or say, "Nothing new."

Then, in late January 1954, Mrs. Jones called Esperanza and Maria into the dining room and announced, "Mr. Jones is being transferred to Peru, and we will be leaving San Salvador at the end of March. The next two months will be very busy as we say goodbye to our friends here and pack up. I want you both to know how much I appreciate your good work and loyalty. I shall miss you and will try to help you find jobs with one of the other American families, if you wish."

The news saddened both Maria and Esperanza. For Esperanza, the news extinguished the last glimmer of hope she had carried that there might be some other way to sustain her family.

Later that day, Esperanza asked Mrs. Jones for permission to visit Doña Marta and tell her the news. Mrs. Jones said, "I am going out to lunch and play bridge on Wednesday, and I won't need you until dinner. So, you can plan on taking a couple of hours off then."

On Wednesday afternoon, Esperanza took the bus to Flor Blanca for a visit with Doña Marta.

As she entered Doña Marta's sitting room, Doña Marta looked up, "I have been expecting you. Ricardo tells me that his company has received an order to pack up the Jones' house, and that they are going to Peru."

"Yes, you already know. I only learned Monday," responded Esperanza.

"Well, you know those Americans come for a couple of years and then get transferred. They hardly have time to understand us before they move on."

"I'm especially disappointed because his plan for El Nido gave me hope that I could do more than cook and clean all my life."

"You poor girl. Mr. Jones didn't have a chance—no matter how good his plan might have been. We are not ready for it. The fourteen families and the military leaders don't believe that poor farmers are capable of helping themselves. They convinced themselves that the rich and powerful have a God-given right to make decisions for the rest of the people. I know. I had to survive on my own—for my children's sake. They wanted to give me charity, I wanted to be my own person. Yes, my dear, I do understand your disappointment."

For the first time in many years, Esperanza sobbed.

Doña Marta gently patted Esperanza's head as she spoke. "Mr. Jones had a solid plan, but we weren't ready to embrace it. He wanted to teach the poor *campesinos* in El Nido how to become capable farmers and businessmen. Imagine that, making them able to stand on their own. Well, Teodoro told me that Felipe Suarez Moncada understood the vision and wanted to support it. But Luis is from the old school of thought that says, "We have to do it for them." When Felipe and Luis returned from El Nido, Luis called some of his military friends—the ones who want the dictator back. He told them that Mr. Jones aimed to create a cooperative for the farmers in El Nido. Luis painted it as a Soviet Russian idea, which is a tactic that Arbenz and his communist allies in Guatemala are using to undermine the powerful families and the military. I don't know what Luis thinks or knows, but Teodoro says that, in America, there are powerful capitalist agricultural cooperatives that help small private farmers thrive and make good profits. Teodoro's company even works with some of them."

Esperanza had no idea what a cooperative was, but she knew now that Mr. Jones was a wise man, and that, if he thought a cooperative would be good for El Nido, it would be good for El Nido.

Doña Marta didn't skip a beat, "Well, Luis sabotaged his father. His cronies got to the minister of agriculture first. The minister told Mr. Jones' boss in the *servicio* that the government wasn't interested in El

Nido. That ended the El Nido project and probably led to Mr. Jones' transfer."

Esperanza shook her head, "Poor Mr. Jones, he didn't seem to know."

"Yes, poor Mr. Jones and poor Pedro Martinez. Teodoro thinks Luis is a very spiteful man, and his resentment stems from the past. Remember that I told you how Luis's father, Felipe, fell in love with Josefina when he was young, and that his love for her never faded? And that Carlos is really Felipe's son? Now, Carlos is about to graduate with honors in engineering from the University of California, Berkeley. Meanwhile, Luis, who was expelled from the University of Salamanca for misconduct, refuses to acknowledge Carlos as his half-brother. He undermines Pedro at every turn, just as he does to his own father. And now, Mr. Jones, El Nido, and you are caught in the middle of this family tragedy."

"Mrs. Jones says that she will help me find a new job. I have to go on supporting my family. I see no other way now."

"Are you still studying high school subjects?"

"Oh, yes," responded Esperanza. "I've bought used textbooks on botany, biology, advanced algebra, and world history. I've also read some of the required novels by Lope de Vega and Cervantes for the advanced Spanish literature course. I think my English is improving since I can follow most of the conversations at the Jones' dining table. And Kitty tells me that my letters in English are good. Yes, I really want to earn my high school diploma."

"Don't lose hope, dear Esperanza. You have come a long way from the fifteen-year-old who rang the bell at my pension so many years ago. Keep your head up. Keep learning. You will find the way."

CHAPTER 58

T he Joneses left their house on March 29, 1954. Mrs. Jones had spent most of March packing and used the hallway that served as Mr. Jones' office as a storage area. She had boxes ready to send to her sons in the United States—sons whom Esperanza only knew through photographs, as they had never visited their parents in San Salvador. "Too busy working and raising their young families," Mrs. Jones had remarked.

The main pile was marked with instructions to send to Lima, Peru. Mrs. Jones did much of the packing by herself, but occasionally asked Maria or Esperanza to help her move a box from the room in which she was working.

In February and March, the Joneses had one farewell party after another. Just about all their American and Salvadoran friends had dinner parties to bid them bon voyage. Mrs. Jones hosted her luncheon bridge parties every Wednesday until mid-March, and the Joneses invited their friends to an open house the next-to-last Saturday in March. It was a month in which Esperanza prepared mainly breakfasts and light lunches. She had lots of time to wonder what life had in store for her.

Moving out was a complicated process. All the electrical appliances were sold because, in Peru, the electric current differed from that in El Salvador. To avoid confusion, the buyers of the appliances were scheduled to take possession on March 30 and remove them from the house themselves. Since Mrs. Jones had no idea what her new house in Peru would look like, she sold all her rugs and draperies. By March 28, the windows and floors were bare.

They also sold their family car for a price above its listed used car value in America. The new owners picked up the car on March 30.

By the afternoon of March 29, almost all the furniture was packed up and in the moving van. Mrs. Jones called Maria and Esperanza to the empty living room. "Thank you both for your help over the past two years. Mr. Jones and I will be staying with the Masons for the next two days. You know where they live and can reach me there. Our plane for Indiana leaves on April 1. Mr. Jones and I will miss you." Almost tearful, Mrs. Jones then handed each of them a letter. "Here are your letters of recommendation and your termination pay."

With that done, she stoically walked out the front door to the family car, which sat on her next-door neighbor's driveway.

Esperanza had arranged for her San Judas carpenter neighbor to pick her up at 4:00 p.m. When he arrived, he helped her move her boxes of clothes, table lamp, and household items. Maria had already departed. Esperanza checked the house to see that all the windows were closed, and the doors locked. She walked out the back gate and locked it securely before climbing into the carpenter's car. She looked back at the empty house and whispered to herself, "You are unemployed for the first time since Doña Marta hired you that first week you arrived in San Salvador."

After she arrived home, she opened the letter from Mrs. Jones, and she was happily surprised. Mrs. Jones had doubled her termination pay from five hundred *colones* to a thousand. It would help tide her over until she found a new job.

That evening, Patricia invited her to dinner next door. It was a real luxury to not have to prepare dinner for one night.

The two families sat down at the table at 7:00 p.m. Patricia prepared a simple *caldo de pollo*, a *surtido* and *pupusas*. Pablo and Pepe ate everything in sight before running into Pablo's bedroom to complete some homework. The three ladies joined forces in cleaning off the table, washing the dishes, and putting them away. Flor and Patricia seemed to know the exact routine.

Patricia smiled at Flor, "You are such a dear. You always clean up for me." Turning to Esperanza, "You will never know how much I appreciate having Flor next door. She is like one of my own family."

Flor cut in, "My dear, you are like another daughter. And you let me feel useful, especially now."

"Oh" interceded Esperanza. "Why especially now?"

"Haven't you noticed? Patricia is six months pregnant."

"No, I didn't know," replied Esperanza.

"Well, I've wanted to have a daughter for some time, but my major has been hesitant. He has his own family to support, and, after Pablo was born, I agreed not to have more children. He and his wife have three daughters, and maintaining their household doesn't leave much for him to help with Pablo and me. He took me to a doctor who gave me contraception, which I've used ever since. So, when we make love, we enjoy each other and don't worry about my becoming pregnant."

Esperanza gulped at such frank talk about a subject that she had carefully avoided.

Patricia continued, "So, when I told him that Pablo is growing up, that soon he'll be looking for his own life and his own place, and that I'd be left alone without a daughter to care for me, he softened. He understands that his resources are limited, and he knows I'm not the young girl he first fell in love with—and we both know that men often seek younger women as their partners age. We've always been honest with each other, and, over these thirteen years, we've tried never to lie to one another. And he understands, just as I do, that in our culture, it's the daughter, not the son, who truly looks after her mother."

Flor interjected, "You know, back in the old days in El Nido, we women had our husbands to take care of us and our families. But when the indigo money dried up, the men left to find work—and many never came back, like Diego. Now, the men leave their women and children to fend for themselves. The old way of life is gone. Here, in San Judas, we live among a block of women without husbands. These women have to rely on themselves while the men become little more than parasites."

Esperanza was visibly surprised. She had never heard her mother say anything like that before. "Mother. What are you saying?"

"Daughter, I have been living in this block for nearly six years. I know everyone on the block. Most of my neighbors are unmarried women with a child or two. Some of them, like Patricia, have men, like her major, who are long-time partners—married men with their own families who love them but can't marry them. They have a home away from home. But most women are not so lucky. They land men-friends who want the women to support them and their drinking. I sometimes wonder why the women tolerate them. Oh, yes, I remember those wonderful nights of love with your father—and I still miss them. But is a night of love worth what those poor women have to pay?"

Flor paused for a moment before continuing, "At least, they're smart enough not to marry them. Yes, not marry them, because I've come to see how poorly our laws treat married women. Under the law, once we're married, the men own us—body and soul. Husbands can take everything their wives earn, and they have complete control over the children. So, I understand the unmarried women on our block who change partners from time to time, or even stop having men around once they have a daughter. Yes, Esperanza, your mother understands this world more than you might think. And I see why Patricia wants a daughter. Do you realize that you work so you can support your mother, who in turn cares for your son? You and I are part of this system—and I'm not the only grandmother on our block taking care of grandchildren while the daughters are out earning the income."

Patricia added, "You know, I'll soon be thirty-five, and I will need an adult daughter when I am your mother's age. My major may decide that he wants a younger mistress and just disappear. I can support my daughter with my work as a dressmaker if that happens. But what happens to me if my major leaves me, and I have no daughter to help me."

Flor innocently suggested, "And Esperanza, you may also need a daughter yourself. I don't know if you have thought about it. I know how the rape deeply hurt you. But you may need to consider having another child—for your own sake and mine. We can't depend on Pepe any more than Patricia can rely on Pablo."

Esperanza was shocked, "I have never thought about men except as monsters to be avoided. That drunk destroyed my dreams and forced me to become a cook in someone else's house to sustain the son who was forced on me. Now you are telling me that I must submit myself to another man to have a daughter to take care of me in my old age?"

"Yes," said Patricia, echoing Flor. "We women always have to take care of ourselves. In our world, unless we have some special skills, our body is our primary asset. And we must use it to our advantage."

Flor added, "You know, Patricia, in El Nido, I never had such thoughts. I loved my husband and loved being with him whenever he wanted me. I never thought of myself—it was always of him. I always thought it was my duty. Now after six years on our block, I am not so sure. I never thought of contraception, but now I do. I had children and watched them die, because we couldn't afford medical care. I long for each one I lost. But now I think it would have been better if I had known of contraception and avoided having children that we couldn't afford to take good care of."

Suddenly, the two boys rushed into the room. Pablo was chasing Pepe, and they were both laughing and teasing each other. They stopped and looked around at the three women who were conversing so intently.

Flor said, "I think it is getting late. There's school tomorrow, and we must be up at 6:00 a.m. We will have plenty of time to talk while you look for a job."

Smiling at Patricia, she continued, "Come over for dinner tomorrow night. Esperanza can cook us a feast."

CHAPTER 59

E speranza woke up in the well-worn twin bed that Doña Marta had given her when the pension closed. It was the first time in over two years that she'd slept in that bed overnight. Mrs. Jones had always expected her back before bedtime. She glanced at the alarm clock on the bedside table—a relic from the pension. It read 6:30 a.m., time to get up and make breakfast. She noticed the other twin bed was empty. Her mother was already up. As she became more aware of her surroundings, it struck her—she wasn't at the Jones household. She was in her own apartment, preparing breakfast for her mother and son, not for the Joneses, the Rands, or the Holmeses. Then the realization hit her again: for the first time since her fifth day in San Salvador, she had no job to go to and no assured income to support her family.

Then, she said quietly to herself, "Mrs. Jones gave me enough money to take a few days off and be with my family. Today is Friday. I'll start looking for a new job on Monday."

She rose, put on a clean skirt, blouse, and underwear, adjusted her sandals, and made her way to the bathroom. Then, she looked out at her mother feeding the chicken and collecting the eggs. She looked over at the far corner of the main room and smiled at Pepe, who was still asleep on the cot that she had bought from Mrs. Rand. It was the cot on which she

301

had slept while working for the Holmes and Rand families. Her mother looked up and nodded to her. Esperanza had not begun her day this way for many years.

Her mother was cradling a basket of eggs as she entered the main room. She said quietly, "Give Pepe a few minutes more while I divide up the eggs for my customers. I'll deliver them while you make breakfast. My chickens did very well. We have enough for my customers and four for us today."

As she separated the eggs, she said, "I'll get the tortillas at the corner while I deliver the eggs. Pepe usually wakes up when he smells the plantains cooking. He eats everything in sight."

Her mother slipped out the front door, and Esperanza decided to make a four-egg omelet with left-over peppers, potatoes, and pork in the refrigerator as well as some onion and spices. Just opening the refrigerator awakened Pepe, who looked up and seemed surprised to see his mother rather than his grandmother. He jumped out of bed and Esperanza noticed that Pepe wasn't a child anymore—he tried to hide an erection while he slipped into his pants. She immediately remembered the conversation with Pablo's mother the night before. Pepe and Pablo were becoming men, and, like men they would soon be looking for women of their own. Maybe she would have to think about having a baby girl. Maybe that was as important as finding a new job.

Mother returned with a couple of *colones* and a dozen fresh tortillas. Pepe went into the bathroom to shower—his grandmother insisted that he take one every morning except when he might be late for school. Then, came a tapping on the front door. Her mother opened the door to let Pablo in—he always ate where Pepe ate.

"Good morning, Grandma" he said to Flor. "Oh. He's still in the bathroom." They both smiled. Seeing Esperanza, he said, "Good morning to you, Mrs. Choarti. You're fixing breakfast today? Looks good."

Pepe appeared right on schedule. The two boys embraced as they did every morning and sat down at the table. In no time there was nothing left but dirty cups and dishes. They gave the two ladies hugs and raced out the door on the way to school. Esperanza realized that they were in the seventh grade, only one year from high school. Her consciousness focused again on the reality that they would soon be having women of their own. It had been an abstract thought when she was at the Joneses. Here it was a reality.

After breakfast, Esperanza walked to the San Judas market a few blocks away. The route was unfamiliar, and she felt uneasy as she turned the corner and passed street carts piled with shoddy goods, cantinas blaring loud music, and the lingering smell of *aguardiente*. After skirting the penitentiary, she finally reached the market. She spotted a familiar face—one of her neighbors who lived around the corner—so she went directly to her to make her purchases. Her neighbor cautioned her about pickpockets, saying, "Don't take out your purse. I'll stop by your house later today, and you can pay me then. That's what I do with your mother when she comes by. And be sure to leave the market through the back entrance, so the pickpockets lose track of you."

Esperanza, with her sack of vegetables, didn't make any additional purchases. She would go to the Central Market tomorrow, where she felt much more comfortable. The bus ride would also help her avoid the lines around the penitentiary of family members waiting to visit inmates and the smell of the cantinas.

She hurried back to the safety of her block. She passed a small Catholic church and one for Baptists. Esperanza had not noticed many churches in the city other than the National Cathedral. She had not been to church since she had come to the city, and all of her American employers had been members of the Union Church, of which she knew little. Kitty had told her that it was not Catholic, but Protestant. Esperanza had been told in school that Protestants were heretics, but the protestants she had met had all treated her well. *One day, when I have time, I'll learn more about the differences between Catholics and Protestants.*

That night, she prepared one of her signature *caldos*, using a chicken from her mother's flock, along with potatoes, green vegetables, onions, and white beans—enhanced with her special blend of spices that brought out their rich flavor. She made a mango pudding for dessert. Patricia, her mother, and the two boys ate every bite. Then the boys went next door to Pablo's room while the ladies cleaned up.

They sat down in the living room on the worn-out furniture that Doña Marta had given them from the pension. Esperanza couldn't help but compare her own furnishings to those of Patricia's next door. Esperanza's pieces seemed so drab in comparison to those of Patricia. She didn't envy Patricia; rather, she reflected on how little she had achieved, even after eleven years of relentless work—eleven years of laboring nearly every day, leaving hardly any time for herself, her family, or the pursuits that truly mattered to her, like learning and becoming a teacher.

That evening, Esperanza talked about her trip to the San Judas market. Her mother noted, "I seldom go there. I don't like the neighborhood. I have an arrangement with a couple of market women who live nearby. I just tell them what I need, and they come by on their way home. I pay them as you did this afternoon."

Patricia said, "I prefer the Central Market. I take the bus and deal with the same women I have known for years. One of the market boys helps me to the bus, and I'm home in no time. Marketing is not one of my favorite chores. I prefer eating here with Flor and the boys."

Then, they relaxed and listened to the radio, with very little talk.

The next day just seemed to come and go. She hadn't had much time for reflection when she was at work, but today was different. She was in what was her home. It was not as primitive as in El Nido, but it was certainly shabby compared to the three houses in which she had worked for the past six to seven years. She questioned herself, wondering if she could have done more or better, but she sadly concluded that, with her limited education and lack of family connections, this was likely the best she could do. The Americans paid double what the Salvadorans paid for a cook, and they gave her more time for family and friends.

She and her mother shared an occasional word as they did their chores, but the day passed mostly in silence. They each took a midday siesta before preparing dinner. Her mother took charge of arranging the table and dishes, and Esperanza prepared a simple casserole that Mrs. Jones had taught her.

It was about six in the afternoon when Patricia and the two boys joined Esperanza and her mother. The radio was playing classical music—*is it Bach, Mozart, or Schuman?* Esperanza didn't care. It added some enjoyment to the evening. At seven, they sat to dinner. There was nothing left by 7:30. The ladies cleared the table. The two boys ran next door to Pablo's room.

Almost unconsciously, Esperanza said aloud, "This has been a difficult day for me. I have been thinking how little we have to show for eleven years of work, and where do I go from here?"

"This life isn't easy for people like you and me. I never expected it to develop as mine has. And I know from my talks with your mother that you had hoped to finish high school and become a teacher," commented Patricia.

"Really, I thought that your life has been so much better than ours?" opined Esperanza.

"Oh, dear Esperanza, I had hoped for so much more when I was younger. My mother's parents had a small finca outside Santa Ana. My father was an officer of the IRCA railway. I was educated at the elite convent school when the Great Depression wiped out my grandparents' finances and reduced my father's income. Without a dowry, a good marriage was impossible, so I worked with my mother to make clothes for my former classmates. To get by, my mother, my father, my brothers, and I all had to earn money. My brothers were older, and they left home to work in Guatemala with an uncle who fared better than my grandparents.

They sent some money for a couple of years, before they got married and had to keep it for their own families."

Flor broke in, "In all our talks these past years, you have never told me this."

"No, but I want Esperanza to know that there are far too many women in this society who feel just like she did today."

Esperanza asked, "How did you get to San Salvador?"

"Well, it was in late 1939 that my mother and I got an order to make a wedding gown for the daughter of a colonel. We made the gown, and I met the handsome lieutenant to whom she was about to be married. Well, after the marriage, I made several other outfits for her and occasionally would see her husband. Then, in May 1941—I remember it as if it were yesterday, the lieutenant and I were alone at his home, and it happened. He told me he had been attracted to me at first sight, and I let him kiss me. It was a whirlwind. We had several trysts, and we tried to be very careful to avoid pregnancy. But after nearly a year, I became pregnant."

Flor broke in, "You took precautions to avoid being pregnant?"

"Oh, yes. My lieutenant took me to a doctor who had been in France, and he fitted me with a French IUD," replied Patricia.

"A what?" inquired Esperanza

"An IUD is a preventive device that the doctor inserts into the vagina to prevent conception. I have used one for years, and it has prevented me from getting pregnant. Pablo was a mistake. We expected to keep our love affair secret. But something went wrong, and I got pregnant with Pablo—and oh, I love Pablo, and I am so glad that I have him. We both love Pablo. He is my major's only son, and, except when they are being disciplined, my major takes Pablo and Pepe out once or twice a month. He is my husband and Pablo's father in all ways but in the sight of the law and probably God."

Patricia paused before saying, "When I told my family that I was pregnant and who the father was, my father and my brothers were furious. They have never forgiven me, but my grandmother and mother understood. Before word got around in Santa Ana about my condition, my grandmother arranged for me to move to San Salvador. My lieutenant arranged for my apartment in San Judas and grandmother sent me furniture from the *finca* that she had in storage. My dressmaking skills helped me build up a clientele here, and my lieutenant never left me. He is now my major. I convinced him that I needed a daughter to take care of me in my old age—especially if anything should happen to him."

"How different your life has been from mine!" exclaimed Esperanza. "And yet, in many ways, we find ourselves in much the same condition. Single mothers with sons. You have your major. I have my mother. We both know that our future depends on us—no one else. Yet, we are so different. Until our talk the other night, I really hadn't known you, how much we have in common, and how fragile our futures are."

Esperanza paused, looking down at the floor before continuing, "Up to now, I have lived to earn enough money to take care of my mother and son. Now you are making me think beyond today, and I am troubled. What should I do? My only experience with a man is a terrible memory. I hate even thinking about it. I have nothing but contempt for men and don't want them near me. You love your man and can't wait to have him with you. To have a daughter is to allow a man to abuse me once again. It scares me."

Flor broke in, "Daughter, I know what you have gone through, but I also lived with your father for many years and know the joy that true love brings. I only hope that you find a good man to love. My husband was like Patricia's lieutenant."

The conversation was broken off when Pepe and Pablo burst through the door, "Father just arrived and is looking for you. He brought us some chocolates and some roses for you."

Patricia said, "Oh, I must run. I don't want to let my major wait long."

Flor, almost instinctively, said, "Pablo and Pepe can share the cot tonight. You say hello to your major for us."

CHAPTER 60

E speranza spent the weekend enjoying life. She relaxed on the back porch and talked with her mother. Pepe and Pablo went to the beach in La Libertad with Pablo's father. It was their reward for getting good grades and promising to graduate and go to the new vocational high school. There were no big meals to prepare this weekend, because Pablo's father would feed the boys before they returned home. The three ladies only needed a simple dinner. The day was a long siesta as she looked out on her mother's garden and chickens. In her siesta, she could shake her concerns about finding a new job and having a daughter.

On Sunday, she resolved that finding a job was her top priority. First thing Monday morning, she would spread the word that she was available. In San Salvador, everything was done through word of mouth—there was no central place to go to look for work. She might place an ad in one of the newspapers, but few foreigners read the dailies, and the Salvadorans who did read the papers paid wages she could not live on. Foreigners told each other about good cooks and reliable servants. Sometimes they might ask a market woman whom they trusted, but mainly it was one lady telling another.

She planned to visit her friends at the Central Market on Monday morning, then go to the US Embassy and US Operations Mission on

Avenida Roosevelt, which was the headquarters of the Point 4 operations. Dr. Holmes and Mrs. Jones had taken her to both, and she knew they had message boards on which she could post her availability. She carefully wrote a note in English, explaining that she had worked as the cook for the Holmeses, the Rands, and the Joneses. She mentioned that she had recommendation letters from them and included the telephone number of the pharmacy on the corner as a way to contact her. Finally, she would call on Doña Marta—dear Doña Marta, whose sons seemed to know most of the foreign community in San Salvador.

She spent Monday and Tuesday carrying out her plan, including a long visit with Doña Marta. She got no responses for two days, and then, on Friday, Ricardo knocked on the door of the San Judas apartment.

Esperanza answered, and she smiled when she saw Ricardo.

"I called the pharmacy," he said, "but no one seemed to know you. So, I drove by."

"Welcome Señor Ricado. How can I help you?"

"My mother told me that you're looking for a job, and she asked me to assist you. There's a new chief of the U.S. Military Mission, and I'm helping him settle into a house in Escalón. I think he'll need to hire a cook since the previous chief's cook found a position at one of the embassies. I haven't discussed it with him yet, but if you meet me at my mother's house tomorrow morning at 10:00 a.m., I can take you to meet the colonel."

Esperanza dressed in her navy-blue uniform that buttoned down the front and her best rebozo. She was in Doña Marta's sitting room when Ricardo arrived at ten the next morning. He embraced his mother, and Doña Marta smiled as she said to Esperanza, "Good luck with the colonel. You are exactly what he needs."

Fifteen minutes later Ricado drove into the circular driveway inside the high-walled and iron-gated property in Escalón. Esperanza noted that, inside the wall, there was not only the large house in front but also a smaller two-story building behind it. *Perhaps a guest house.*

She followed Ricardo as he got out of the car and walked around to the back of the main house to a terrace overlooking the garden and the second building. An American in army fatigues was seated at a wrought-iron table carefully going over a pile of papers.

"Good morning, Colonel," Ricardo greeted him in English.

Without looking up, the colonel responded in English, "I've been waiting for you. We need to go over the plans for changes in the guest house. I see some easy fixes to accommodate the enlisted men who will be quartered there."

When he finally raised his eyes, he caught sight of Esperanza. "Who is she?"

"She is the lady who can be the cook you have been looking for," replied Ricardo in English.

Looking squarely at Esperanza, the colonel responded curtly in English, "I don't think that she fits the bill. She is too young, and she is a woman. I need someone who can not only cook my family meals but who can also arrange large barbeques for my Salvadoran counterparts and provide the rations for my enlisted men. No, I need a man."

Esperanza interrupted in English, "I can do all those works." She grappled to find the right words.

The startled colonel asked, "Do you speak English?"

Haltingly Esperanza said, "I study English for several years. I work for three American families for six years. I not practice English much, but I understand and read books as well as recipes."

The colonel's expression changed, and he smiled, "Tell me about yourself. What is your name?"

"My name is Esperanza Choarti. I come to San Salvador from little town in Chalatenango. I work as cook for Doña Marta at pension. Oh, Doña Marta is mother of Ricardo. I cook meals three times a day, seven days each week. I make barbecues and parties for Doña Marta and American families. You want American, Salvadoran, French food—I prepare it. You not worry."

Ricardo said, "Esperanza, I didn't know that you knew so much English."

She nodded, "Colonel, you want to taste. I cook for you now?"

The colonel said, "Ricardo, bring her back next Wednesday. My wife and my sergeant will be here. I never decide such serious questions without their opinion. Esperanza, you can cook for us then. And we will see if you can fit the bill. Meanwhile don't take another job."

"Okay," said Esperanza "I wait. I need work, but I wait."

Esperanza decided to take the next few days off. She relaxed with her mother and the boys, took walks around downtown San Salvador, and looked into the stores with their conglomeration of farm equipment, pumps, and Rosenthal China displayed right next to each. She bought herself a new pair of Bata shoes and even went back to the school where Pepe and Pablo were studying. She compared the facilities to those she remembered at her county school. How different the facility was from her own!

On Wednesday morning, Ricardo picked her up at 9:00, and she was in Escalón by 9:30. When they walked to the terrace at the rear of the house, a lady was seated at the table on the terrace. She looked up as they approached.

"Morning, Ricardo. Is this the cook? Does she speak any English?"

It was Esperanza who answered in English, "Yes, Señora. I know some English, and I cook."

Quite surprised and pleased, the colonel's wife breathed a sigh of relief.

"Señora, these are my letters of recommendations by Ricardo's mother where I work at her pension for five years and from three Americans where I work for six years. I cook American, Salvadoran and French. I hope you understand me—I practice saying all that in past days."

The colonel's wife smiled, "I understand you. Your name again is?"

"Esperanza—which mean Hope in English."

"I'll show you around the kitchen, and you will see where everything is."

The lady introduced Esperanza to a set of brand-new kitchen appliances, including the largest refrigerator she had ever seen; a freezer stocked with frozen meats, ice cream, and bags of vegetables; an electric stove with four burners and a grill; and a double oven with precise temperature controls. There was also a liquefier and mixer. She explored cabinets and drawers filled with cooking essentials, pots and pans, as well as dishes and glassware. The colonel's wife then led her to the pantry, where Esperanza spotted locked cabinets containing fine china, crystal goblets, and a cutlery chest. She also noticed a locked closet, likely filled with canned goods. The kitchen was more spacious and elegant than any other she had ever seen.

The colonel's wife then said, "Esperanza, do you have any questions?"

"No, Señora. I think I see everything. I need to try to use."

"Then please settle in. Lunch will be at noon. Four for lunch. Just prepare something simple." A few seconds later, she said, "Hamburgers, French fries, and a salad."

Esperanza nodded and asked, "What vegetables do you want in your salad?"

"There is lettuce, tomato, and cucumber in the fridge."

"Where do you keep the—" Esperanza paused, searching desperately for the right word, "drops for the lettuce?" she finally continued.

"Oh, yes, you mean for treating the lettuce. The bottle is over there, next to the vinegar and olive oil."

"What dressing you want?"

"Vinegar and oil for me and ranch for the colonel and sergeant. I don't know what Ricardo prefers."

"And what drink?" added Esperanza.

"I think iced tea would be fine. It is such a warm day."

"Where are your trays stored, and where do you plan to eat?"

The colonel's wife showed her the area in which the trays were stored and told her, "We will eat on the terrace today."

Esperanza prepared the meal and set the table on the terrace. She put jars of ketchup, mustard, and salad dressing on the table just before noon. She drew on what she had learned from her former American employers to prepare the food. Her French fries were thin, like the Joneses preferred, and the iced tea had lemon slices, as the Holmeses had requested. Her broiled hamburgers were juicy and topped with lettuce slices that she had perfected with Mrs. Jones. She warmed the buns, and carefully lined the interior with mayonnaise before adding caramelized onions, a hamburger patty, and a slice of tomato and lettuce. She had lightly seasoned her lettuce, tomato, and cucumber salad with basil and dill, just as Mrs. Rand had preferred.

At noon, she went to the terrace and asked the señora if she wished to be served. Once she served the table, she sat down in the kitchen and ate some salad and a hamburger while she awaited the ring of the bell on the table on the terrace.

When it finally rang and she returned to the table, it was the colonel who said, "That was a fine meal."

His wife added, "I think we would like you to work for us. It will not be easy because you will be cooking for my family and the sergeants. They love to eat—and the sergeant thinks his men will like your cooking. Eh, sergeant?"

The sergeant grinned as he added, "They are Latinos like me and will like her Salvadoran meals."

Esperanza smiled, "Thank you, Señora. I would like to work for you. I must support my family. You understand?"

"Yes, we do," said the colonel. "We would expect you to work six days a week. We can offer you Thursday off. You can leave after breakfast and return by lunch on Friday. Since you will be cooking for my family and my staff, we offer you 300 *colones*, room and board. We will also offer you two new uniforms and two pairs of shoes a year. How does that sound?"

"Thank you, Señor. That would be fine."

"When can you start?" added the señora.

"Tomorrow morning, if you like" replied Esperanza.

"Then, sergeant, when we finish lunch, please show Esperanza the maid's room and make the necessary arrangements for her coming on board," said the colonel.

"Yes, Sir," said the sergeant.

The colonel then turned to Ricardo, "Let's get on with the changes in the guest house. We should be finished in about two hours."

After Esperanza cleared the table, the sergeant showed her the maid's room. It was good-sized with a window that looked out on the back garden. It was furnished with a standard metal GI army cot, an army mattress with bedding and towels on top, a typical GI bedside table and lamp, a three-drawer bureau, two poles with a strong cord between them that held several hangers for clothes, and a chair. A naked light fixture hung from the ceiling. The bathroom had a shower, toilet, and wash basin—and hot water. Everything was brand new. Esperanza nodded at the sergeant to signal that it would do.

Ricardo drove her back to San Judas. He reminded her of the bus route to Escalón. She said, "I will be at work tomorrow morning. Thank you for your kindness. And please tell Doña Marta how grateful I am. It was her idea to get me this job, wasn't it?" She told her mother, Patricia, and the two boys of her new job at dinner that night. Then she wrote a long letter to Kitty. She had a new job, but she was no closer to becoming a teacher.

CHAPTER 61

T hus began Esperanza's job for the colonel and his wife. It was a tour of duty in which she prepared meals three times a day, six days a week. In the house were two other maids who kept up the main house and supported Esperanza in serving table and cleaning up. They lived together in a room next to hers. They lived their lives, and Esperanza lived hers. Unlike in her previous jobs with American families, she was never sure how many meals she needed to prepare every day. Salvadoran counterparts frequently invited the colonel and his wife to diplomatic dinners. However, she still had to feed the three sergeants, and occasionally, additional officers and men on special training assignments.

Working for the colonel and his wife was very different from her other jobs. They never came to the kitchen. It was the master sergeant who delivered the menu every day, who commended her or complained about a meal, and who arranged for her periodic visits to the Central Market. A Salvadoran soldier always drove her to the market. It was the master sergeant who delivered the food flown in every couple of weeks from the commissary in Panama or Tampa and worked with her in storing the frozen, canned, or fresh foods.

Unlike her previous experiences with American families, she did not come to know her employers and their family. She seldom saw them.

When their teenaged children came for summer visits, they would occasionally drop in for a bite, but they never spent time with her as had Kitty and her siblings.

Everything was by the book. She prepared the meals that the colonel and his wife ordered. She took her days off as scheduled. She had two weeks off that year—with pay—when the colonel and his wife went back home for Christmas with their kids. Her monthly pay was delivered, not by the Señora, but by the master sergeant. If she had a special need, such as visiting Doña Marta or attending a school event for Pepe, it was arranged through and by the master sergeant.

She came to like the master sergeant. His name was Mario Martinez. He was married with three small children at home near Fort Bliss. Mario loved his family and talked about them to Esperanza and the other maids all the time. He was a strict taskmaster, and the two other sergeants under him knew that and respected him. No doubt about it—he was in charge. Esperanza observed that the colonel frequently consulted him.

At the end of her first month with the colonel, Mario entered the kitchen carrying the monthly paychecks for the staff. He handed an envelope to each of them and said, "Please check the amounts inside. If everything is correct, sign this form." They each checked the amount in their envelope and then signed the form.

The two maids hurried away to their room. Esperanza turned to Mario and asked, "Would you like a cup of coffee?"

"Yes, please," he replied. He sat down at the kitchen table.

Esperanza brought two cups. "I wish to thank you for your help during the past month. You have made my job so much easier."

He smiled.

She said, "You know my name is Esperanza. You always call me Miss Choarti. Please call me Esperanza."

"Okay, Esperanza," he replied.

"Where are you from? My friend, Kitty, lives in Baltimore," continued Esperanza.

"I'm from New Mexico, but my family—my wife, mother, and three children—live in Texas, outside Fort Bliss."

"That's a big family," she commented.

"Just fine for me. My wife is a teacher, and my mother takes care of the kids," he continued.

"Someday I hope to be a teacher, too" she added. "Do you miss your family very much?"

"Every day, but my job is so demanding that I don't have much time to think about home."

"I notice that you and the other sergeants are up at dawn and away most days."

"Yes. Our job is to train Salvadoran troops. The colonel and the three of us are the regular mission and, as you will see shortly, additional officers and men will be coming for a week or two at a time to help us. That's why we have the additional barracks in the guest house. The short-time trainers will stay there. You will have to feed them as well as our permanent troop."

Esperanza smiled, "That will be a challenge with all that you and the other sergeants eat."

"Well, we like your food. You are a great cook—your food is much better than our usual army fare," was his reply. "Thanks for the coffee. It's time for me to move on. Have a good day." He was up and out the door.

Esperanza thought, *He is a nice man, and he is good looking. I like his features, and he is well-built and strong.* She began to see him as a special man and a friend. Her abhorrence of men somehow did not include him. Somehow, he was different from the other men she had observed—certainly she saw him in a different light than the other two sergeants. He had manners, and he never made passes at her or the other maids as the two sergeants sometimes did. Day-by-day, she relaxed more and more in her dealings with him, and she saw that he became more relaxed in her presence as well. She had never before had a friendship with a man. She wondered, *could Mario become my first boyfriend?*

For the next several months, Esperanza cooked for the sergeants, and every few weeks, an additional contingent of hungry men joined them. They ate in the area just off the kitchen. When officers visited, they dined with the colonel and his wife or were honored at dinners outside the house. However, the enlisted men were her regulars, and they devoured everything she put on the table. Mario never stopped praising her cooking.

At Christmas time, the colonel and his wife left to spend the holidays with their children in the U.S., and they closed the house in mid-December. The three sergeants also returned to their families. The colonel gave Esperanza and the maids time off to be with their own families, too. Master Sergeant Mario delivered a schedule for their time off, along with their paychecks and an *aguinaldo*—an extra month's pay. Esperanza was off from December 23 to January 2. Her *aguinaldo* allowed her to buy presents for her mother, Patricia, Doña Marta, and the two boys.

When she returned to work after her Christmas vacation, she was genuinely pleased to see the Master Sergeant as he entered the kitchen with the menu for the day. She allowed him to give her an *abrazo*. It was the first time in a long time that a man had embraced her. She liked the feel of his body against hers.

"Did you have a good Christmas with your family?" Esperanza asked Mario.

"Oh, yes," he replied enthusiastically. "My son is ten now, and he has grown so much. My daughters are just beautiful, and being with my wife was a joy. She earned a teaching certificate and will start teaching on the base this month. I'm so proud of her. When I retire from the military, I plan to become a teacher, too. Here, let me show you some pictures I took of my family over Christmas." He pulled out his wallet, which was filled with photos of his family.

"What a handsome family you have! And your wife has a good job as a teacher. I have always wanted to be a teacher. When I completed the eighth grade, that was my goal, but fate intervened. Now, I am still trying. I just bought the third-year high school texts on geology, biology, and Spanish literature as Christmas presents for myself." Then as if catching herself, she added, "You know I have no pictures of my family—my mother or my son."

"That's a pity. I would like to see them. I didn't know about your family. You never talk about them. And you have a son?"

"Yes, he is twelve years old and finishing the eighth grade," she responded.

"And your husband?" asked Mario.

"That is a long, sad story," replied Esperanza, who was now quite uneasy. It was a subject she did not want to discuss with Mario. She paused before rather awkwardly saying, "Well, I guess I better get back to work."

"So, do I," said Mario as he turned to leave the kitchen.

In the weeks that followed, each day, when Mario delivered the daily menu or arranged for Esperanza to go to the market, they talked a little more. Esperanza welcomed his smile and occasional *abrazo*. They chatted about their plans for the day or a pending event, such as the arrival of a special training group, an unusual assignment, or a dinner or barbeque that the colonel and his wife had planned.

That morning in April, just before Holy Week, the colonel's wife asked Esperanza to prepare a dish that required spices and avocados that she didn't have on hand. Mario drove her to the market and helped her with the purchases. On the way back, as they sat in the car, his hand brushed against hers. A spark shot through her. It was something she had never felt before. He seemed to feel it too, and he glanced at her as if seeing her for the first time. Despite maintaining his composure while driving, she sensed a change in him. When they arrived back at the house, he carried the groceries into the empty kitchen. Then, suddenly, he kissed her and began to explore her body with his hands. She didn't resist—instead, she found herself giving in. For the first time in her life, she wanted to be with a man. She was twenty-seven, and he was married.

Mario caught himself. He kissed her gently and left the kitchen. She pulled herself together and went back to preparing the meal.

Over the next few days, Mario and Esperanza slipped back into their usual routine. They met each morning when he brought her the menu. They exchanged pleasantries like nothing had happened. Yet, Esperanza couldn't shake the memory of that electric moment and the desire it had awakened in her. She also recalled Patricia's advice about having a daughter. *If I was to have a child*, she thought, *Mario would be an ideal choice as the father*. He was committed to his wife and family back in America, which meant that he wouldn't make any demands on her or the child. In fact, he likely wouldn't even be in El Salvador once the colonel was reassigned, as all American advisers eventually were. The added benefit was that Esperanza genuinely felt something for him—whether it was love like the feelings Patricia had for her major, she couldn't be sure. In either case, it was a feeling she had never experienced with another man. Thus, regardless of what Mario truly felt, she decided she would encourage him to make love to her, in the hope that he might give her the baby girl she believed she would need when she could no longer care for herself.

Those thoughts reechoed in her head for several weeks, and they weighed against her desire to be a teacher. If she had a baby, she would be close to forty years old before she could begin to think again about being a teacher. She liked Mario, but did she like him enough to seduce him into fathering a child? She felt that she was facing the crisis of her life.

As the weeks went by, Esperanza wrestled with her thoughts and feelings. June arrived, and so did the colonel's eldest child, Stephen, who was about to start his senior year of high school. He had a huge appetite and quickly grew fond of Esperanza's cooking. Despite his father's instructions that the master sergeant handle the daily snacks, Stephen often snuck into the kitchen, where Esperanza always had something he liked ready for him to devour.

Just as she had with Kitty, Esperanza developed a special bond with Steve, as all of Stephen's friends called him. Within two weeks, they were chatting mostly in English, since Steve's high school Spanish hadn't quite stuck with him.

"Hi, Esperanza. Don't tell Sarge, but I am hungry," he usually began.

"Well, Mr. Stephen, I think that I have some leftovers from lunch," Esperanza would respond.

"Please just call me Steve like my friends do, and you are my friend now," Steve would reply. "Do you have any cake or cookies to go with a glass of milk?"

While she fixed his snack, Esperanza would ask him to tell her about the courses he took in high school.

One day, Steve replied in a whisper, "I want to study law. My father would like me to follow my older brother to West Point, but I want to go to a liberal arts college. My favorite courses are history, economics, and civics, which are the ones that teach me how our government and society function. And those teachers make me think. I want to help people. I am not into military stuff very much. I want to avoid wars."

"You like your teachers?" Esperanza asked.

"Good ones are like gold. They get me to think and want to do positive things. Some are better than others. But, in my school, most of them are good. My English literature teacher really helps me understand the characters and the problems they are facing. Good stuff."

"Do you think teaching is a good profession?" Esperanza asked.

Steve shook his head affirmatively as he exclaimed, "Golly, this food is good."

The other two older children arrived in late June. The eldest son was a cadet at West Point, and the daughter had just completed her first year at Brown University. Steve proudly brought them to the kitchen to meet his friend, Esperanza. Occasionally, they would join Steve for a snack, but Steve remained her regular visitor. He always engaged her in conversation and impressed her with his genuine interest in learning and deep respect for good teachers.

Esperanza found herself thinking often of Kitty and Steve and their shared love of learning echoed in her mind as clearly as the voices of Patricia and her mother. She saw Mario every day and kept measuring her feelings for him. Esperanza knew she needed to be certain before making a decision—because whatever path she chose now would shape the rest of her life.

CHAPTER 62

I t was the middle of July, deep into the rainy season. Each morning brought muggy weather, followed by cloudbursts in the early afternoons and warm—sometimes hot—yet pleasant evenings. The house was bustling with the colonel's three teenage children, and there were all the regular meals to prepare. The colonel and his wife hosted several dinner parties, but it was the three young adults who added the most to Esperanza's workload—not just with their hearty appetites, but because they ate dinner at home even when their parents were out for the evening. Whether it was a day of swimming or tennis at the *Deportivo*, or a night of parties, they always returned to the house hungry. Esperanza always had something special ready for them, and she used those moments to talk with them, in English, about their schooling and life in America.

Three months—or was it four?—had passed since Mario kissed her. She continued on with her routine of preparing three meals a day, six days a week. Mario met with her every morning with the plans and menus for the day and at almost every meal. He made the arrangements for her to go to the Central Market and for visits to Doña Marta. Everything between them was formal—by the book.

However, the electric feeling and the kiss had happened. She didn't tell her mother or Patricia about it, but she wrote a long letter to Kitty. Kitty had written a terse reply and reminded her of her choices. It was not a lecture, but it was a reminder of her ambitions. Esperanza tried to let her work push aside her concerns, but she kept remembering. She was at war with herself.

It had been an especially busy day, but now Esperanza was finally able to sit down in a chair at the table in the alcove off the kitchen and continue rereading one of her favorite books, *Mujeres y Criadas* by Lope de Vega. It was then that Mario entered the kitchen.

"Is there anyone here?" he called out.

"I'm here at the table," replied Esperanza.

"It's almost ten o'clock. I saw the lights on in the kitchen and wondered if there was a problem."

"No," said Esperanza. "I was reading Lope de Vega, and the light here is so much better than in my room."

"Lope de Vega. He's one of my wife's favorite authors. A bit heavy for me," commented Mario. He paused before adding, "Just remember to turn off the lights when you finish."

"I thought you and your men had the evening off? You weren't at dinner, and the colonel and his family ate out. I only fixed dinner for the maids and me. I finished early and just wanted to do some reading before going to bed."

"You know, there's not much for the men and me to do in San Salvador," Mario reflected. "The only two decent restaurants, the Hotel Astoria and Carmen's, aren't exactly welcoming to enlisted men. There's just one decent movie house at the Teatro Nacional; the others are fleabags. And most of the movies are Mexican westerns—they all feel the same after a while. So, my guys and I usually grab a bite and a drink at one of the cantinas, but I try to leave early. There are too many machetes, guns, and mean drunks around—*aguardiente* is dangerous stuff. Tonight, I got us out early when I noticed some rough types coming in. The colonel wouldn't be too happy if we got into trouble."

"What do you think of San Salvador? I only really know El Nido, where I was born, Chalatenango City—which I visited once—Soyapango, and San Salvador," Esperanza asked.

"Well, it's not much compared to the places I have been in Germany, France, and America. No real business districts, no family entertainment places, like amusement parks. It's just for rich people who live behind thick walls. I don't even see many schools and hospitals. I don't know, but I sure wouldn't want to be stuck here for long," was Mario's meandering reply.

"Hmm, that's very interesting. So, there are places that are better. Is there much more opportunity for people to make something of themselves in America?" Esperanza asked.

"I can't say for sure, but I think so. From what I've seen, there are very few jobs outside of farm labor here. That's what the enlisted men in the Salvadoran army tell me. It seems the army is the best place to learn a skill since there aren't many schools. A lot of the boys we're trying to train can't even write their names, so my men and I are teaching them to read and write so they can understand the army manuals."

"You know that I wanted to be a teacher, like your wife. We had no school in my village. We had to walk to the county school several kilometers away. I went through the eighth grade. I was the only one in my village who went past the fourth grade. My grandmother insisted. I finished first in my class and was awarded a scholarship to go to the high school in our capital city, Chalatenango. Then, fate intervened, and here I am," reflected Esperanza.

"What do you mean 'fate intervened?'" asked Mario.

Esperanza thought carefully for a minute before she responded, "This isn't easy for me. On the way back from Chalatenango City—where the director of the high school had welcomed me with a scholarship and arranged a place for me to stay—I was raped by a drunk on the way home. Sometimes, I still smell the odor of his drunken breath. He raped me and no one believed me—not the local school director, not my teacher, not anyone. I had my son when I was barely fifteen, and I moved with my mother and son to San Salvador because I could see no future for me in my village, El Nido. I left countless generations of my family out of bitterness. I wanted to go to high school, get my degree, and be a teacher. The rape destroyed all those dreams. And I never let another man touch me until you—and why I let that happen is very confusing."

Mario was surprised. He seemed at a loss for words. Then, he asked, "Why?"

"I have worked for the last dozen years as a cook to support my mother and son—thanks to Ricardo's mother, Doña Marta. She trained me. My grandmother taught me how to make all our native dishes, but Doña Marta taught me to be a real cook. She ran the pension in Soyapango that my uncle had told me about and to which I went on my first night away from El Nido. She saved me from the life of a girl in a cantina. She arranged for my apartment in San Judas. I truly respect and love her."

She sighed before continuing, "I'm twenty-seven years old, and I have a son who is about to become a man. And, in Salvador, a woman cannot count on a son to support her in her old age. A man finds his own way to his own woman. A woman needs a daughter to take care of her as she gets old, and a woman knows that she must take care of her daughter's children—so few of us get married. You know, the laws give husbands the right to all that a woman earns. Husbands even have the right to her children. Well, my mother and my only friend in San Judas think it is time for me to have a baby girl. I thought that you, as one of the most decent men I have ever met, might be the ideal father. You have a family of your own in Texas. You'd be gone before you knew I was pregnant, and I could work as a cook for American families for another fifteen years while my mother raises my daughter. No problems from you, only maybe a pleasant memory of a brief affair."

Mario practically gasped at her frankness and was about to get up and leave.

"Mario, please let me finish. I am attracted to you, but I also want to have you as a friend. I want to know your wife as a fellow teacher. And, above all, I want to be a teacher. My American friend, Kitty Holmes, is in medical school. I think it is called Johns Hopkins. I worked for Dr. and Mrs. Holmes when he was here, and Kitty became my first female friend. I share everything with her. She reminded me that, if I have a daughter, my dream of becoming a teacher is over. El Salvador has no program for adults, like me, to get their high school degrees, but Kitty tells me that you have programs in the United States. Just now, while talking to you, as much I find you attractive, I decided that I really want to be a teacher and not spend the rest of my life like this."

Mario settled back in his chair as she said earnestly, "Please don't tell the colonel or his wife what I just said."

Mario thought for a while before replying, "You've had a tough life. Life for Mexicans, like me, isn't easy in America. There's a lot of prejudice, so our lives aren't easy. But, from what I see here, there is more opportunity to make a better life for oneself in the U.S. than here. And, if you really want to be a teacher, and the system here is closed, you should take the risk. But if you go to the United States, how will you cover the needs of your mother and son?"

"That's why I need time, Mario. Money is my problem. Even with the little I've saved, I can't put it in a bank. People like me aren't welcome at the banks, not even to make deposits."

Mario glanced at his watch and said, "Esperanza, it's almost eleven. Mornings come early. We should wrap this up. I don't really know what to say—you've shared so much about yourself and your feelings. You've shared things I can't even talk about with my wife. But know that I am your friend."

He left, and she closed her book, rose from her chair, turned out the light, and walked to her room. She had finally made her decision.

CHAPTER 63

The following Thursday, Esperanza left the house right after breakfast, eager to reach San Judas before the midday rains. She needed to mail her long letter to Kitty, in which she shared her decision to pursue her dream of becoming a teacher instead of having another child.

Two weeks later, a letter arrived—not from Kitty, but from Dr. Holmes. She tucked it into her shirt and hurried home to read it.

Dear Esperanza,

Kitty has shared your decision to become a teacher with Mrs. Holmes and me, as well as the challenges you face in achieving that goal in El Salvador. We want to help you come to our country, where the opportunity exists.

In our city, there's a college that offers a program for adults to complete their high school education and then continue with university courses to complete a degree in education. When you graduate, you'll receive a teaching certificate. It will take six or seven years, and the studies will be challenging.

If you're ready to make this commitment, Dr. Rand and I are prepared to support you. I've also informed Mr. Jones of your interest and asked if he would like to join Dr. Rand and me in helping you.

You will need a student visa to come to America, and Dr. Rand and I are ready to provide you with the necessary Affidavit of Support. Additionally, Mrs. Holmes and I will offer you room and board in our home and ensure you receive an allowance to cover your expenses while you pursue your studies.

I have also spoken with a close friend, the dean of admissions at a local college, and, on my recommendation, he has agreed to admit you. Upon arrival, you will need to complete a series of exams so the college can determine if you need to take any additional courses before you pursue your degree. Please understand, if you do not meet the college's standards, you will have to return to San Salvador. I also mentioned that you're an excellent cook, and the dean is open to considering you for a position in the college commons.

Please consider this opportunity carefully. If you decide to accept, Dr. Rand and I will prepare the necessary documents for your student visa and arrange to send them to you.

To proceed, you will need to schedule an appointment at the U.S. Embassy in San Salvador to apply for your visa. Visit the consular section for detailed instructions on the application process. Additionally, you will need to obtain a Salvadoran passport from your government.

Let me know your thoughts on this offer. Wishing you and your family all the best."

She read it twice more to ensure she understood each paragraph and its potential impact on her life. The letter offered her a chance to achieve her dream, but it also meant six to seven years away from her family, during which she wouldn't be able to contribute income. She weighed every factor she could think of—then decided to accept the offer.

She rose from her chair in the bedroom and walked into the living room. She found her mother listening intently to a soap opera, with a glass of horchata on the small table beside the sofa. Her mother smiled when she saw her daughter come through the door.

"You are early today. I didn't expect you until two."

"I received a letter from Dr. Holmes today and rushed home to read it. He has made me an offer, which we must discuss before Pepe and Pablo get home."

"Fine. But let's wait until my program ends."

Esperanza just smiled her agreement. She checked the refrigerator to see what was available for dinner. Then, she walked back over to her mother and sat down next to her on the sofa and promptly dozed off.

Her mother awakened her when the soap opera ended. She asked, "Esperanza, I suspect that you have something important to tell me?"

Esperanza roused herself and began to explain the situation. She had rehearsed it several times since reading the letter, "Mother, you know I have always wanted to be a teacher. You know that, ever since the rape, I have worked hard to support you and Pepe, but I have never given up on my dream. Well, Kitty and her family are offering me a way to reach my dream, and I have decided to take it."

Her mother nodded, "Yes, I've known for years that you were a cook simply out of necessity. I've watched you with your books. It's been seven years since we moved here from the pension, and, in all those years, every spare moment, you were reading and taking notes. You didn't have to say anything—I saw it in what you did."

"Yes, I love learning. Each textbook I read opens new vistas for me. The new ideas and understanding of the world in which I live help me to escape from the reality of what has happened to us as a people and to me as a person. I want to turn my life around, and I want to help other people understand our world and help them deal with their reality."

"I have been thinking about how to take care of you while I am away," she added. "I can take you back to El Nido, and we can ask Patricia to allow Pepe to stay with Pablo until they finish vocational high school and get jobs. Doña Marta's son, Ricardo, can help them find good jobs. We have nearly 6,000 *colones* that we have saved; you can take one-third to El Nido to help you get along, we can give Patricia one-third to help pay for Pepe, and I can take one-third to help me get by in America."

Her mother almost laughed, "My dear, I have no intention of going back to El Nido. It was one thing to consider if Mr. Jones's plan had gone through. With electricity, funds, and improvements to our home, maybe then it would have made sense. But I'm not going back to a straw bed, no shower, and no radio. I like my life here. I know all the neighbors on this block, and I have small businesses with many of them. Do you think we live only on the 200 *colones* you give us each month? We can't. I make another 200 *colones* by babysitting, selling eggs, and doing odd jobs. I get free meals for Pepe and me, and sometimes, I host neighbors for meals I prepare. I've even learned some of your recipes, and people pay me a few *colones* to cook for them. I visit Doña Marta at least twice a month, and I know she owns our apartment and charges us much less than the neighbors pay. They don't know what I know—and neither do you. So, if you think I'm surprised by what you've just told me, don't be. I know my daughter better than she thinks, and I am not surprised."

Esperanza almost cried as she embraced her mother. She had expected a contrite, trembling woman concerned about her life being ruined.

Her mother continued quietly, "We have much to discuss. I'm staying here in San Judas, and you are going to America. We will not have your 200 *colones* each month to support us. We have to keep Pepe in school until he finishes his degree. We'll have to plan together how to make this work. Then, we'll need to speak with Doña Marta and Patricia for their help—Doña Marta to keep the rent low, and Patricia to hire me to care for her new baby, just as I helped raise Pepe.

After a sip of horchata, her mother asked, "How much time do we have? When your father died, I had almost no time to figure out a way to work and live. Do we have a month or a year? When do you expect to leave your job and go to America?"

Esperanza looked at her mother with a deep respect she had never given her before. "Well, I am not sure, but it will be months. I need to a get a passport and visa. I don't know how long that will take. Then I have to give the colonel and his wife at least one month's notice. I have so much to do before I can leave for America."

"Fine. We'll talk this out today. The only person who needs to know what you are hoping to do is Doña Marta. She must hear it from you. We need her on our side. No need to tell anyone else until we know how much time is involved. We will worry about the money after we know exactly what you need to do and how much is involved."

Her mother's strength and clarity caught her off guard once again. "Mother, I thought you were urging me to have a daughter, so I could keep supporting you for another dozen years."

"Well, that was one possibility Patricia and I considered. It was her only option. She loves her major, and her ambitions are very different from yours. I know how much you've hated men ever since that drunk attacked you, but I wasn't sure if you had given up on becoming a teacher and settled into being a cook. Now you've given me your answer, and you can count on me to support you, just as you've supported me."

Esperanza gave her mother a heartfelt embrace. She suddenly realized how much her mother had meant to her survival and now, her dreams.

CHAPTER 64

It was only five the following morning when her mother awakened Esperanza. She said, "My dear, we must talk before Pepe wakes up. He has to leave for school by 7:30 a.m., and you need to be back at the colonel's for breakfast. Take your shower. The water is warm-ish. I'll be waiting on the back porch."

"Yes, I will be quick."

Her mother had a cup of coffee and a warm tortilla ready for Esperanza when she tiptoed onto the porch. Her mother said, "I will arrange for you to meet with Doña Marta next Thursday. I will go to the pharmacy and call Ricardo and ask him if she can see you next Thursday afternoon. I want to make sure that she is free. She is still a busy lady. She tells me about the business deals she makes. You know that she really runs Ricardo's business for him. I keep telling her that she needs to let him do things for himself. She tries, but she can't really give up—even though she's over seventy."

No longer surprised by her mother, Esperanza said, "Okay."

Her mother smiled, "What is 'okay?'"

Esperanza smiled, "That is what Americans say to each other when they are in agreement."

337

"I know that. They say it all the time in my soap operas, but you have never said it to me before."

Esperanza just hugged her mother again and ran out the front door to catch the bus.

A couple of days later Ricardo came by to let her know that his mother would be waiting for her the next Thursday morning after eleven. Her respect for her mother moved a notch higher.

She was in Doña Marta's sitting room at eleven the next Thursday. "Dear Esperanza, it so nice to see you. It's been several months. Your mother tells me that you are doing well at the colonel's."

"Oh, I am sorry that I haven't come to see you sooner. I have been busy. Every day there are three meals to prepare for the family and the enlisted men—even when the colonel and his wife are invited out. And it is so different from the other Americans. I almost never see the colonel and his wife. Even her menus are delivered by the sergeant."

"Ricardo tells me that the colonel and his wife are very formal people. They do everything by the book. He also tells me that they all like you very much, especially the sergeant."

"Mario has been very kind to me. He has shown me pictures of his family. His wife is a teacher."

"Mario. Well, are you sure that it is nothing more?"

"Oh, it might have been. He is the only man who has kissed me, and I let him do that. He didn't have the smell of *aguardiente* of the man who raped me. But he is married—and married to a teacher. And, above all, I want to be a teacher. I decided that I will do nothing to disrespect his wife, a teacher."

Doña Marta smiled, "I wanted to support my family and keep it together when my husband died. I had to fight to do it. But I never disrespected my husband. Many a man tried to take advantage of my situation, but I have let no one climb into my bed since my husband died."

"I have a chance to be a teacher. There is no path for me to do that in El Salvador. I'm too old to get into high school here, and there is no night school for adults. But I can finish school in America. You remember Dr. and Mrs. Holmes and their daughter Kitty?"

Doña Marta nodded in recollection.

"Well, they offered me an opportunity. I can live with them and go to college to finish high school, then continue studying to become a teacher. They will let me live with them while I'm in school."

Doña Marta listened carefully.

Esperanza shared, "My mother and our neighbor, Patricia, talked to me about having a daughter to take care of me in my old age, like so many of us poor people do. For a moment, I thought the sergeant, Mario, might be the right person for that. I even felt something when he kissed me, but my desire to be a teacher is stronger than anything else. I told him, and he understood."

Esperanza paused and reflected before adding, "I told my mother about my decision last week. I even offered to take her back to El Nido and arrange for Pepe to stay with his buddy, Pablo. But my mother made it clear that she has no desire to return to El Nido. I realized she's changed—she's become a city woman and has become comfortable with life in San Judas. So, I need to ensure she can live comfortably in her new life."

Doña Marta leaned back, "And that is where I come in?"

"Mother and I know that you have been very good to us these past seven years—more than you ever had to be. We are truly grateful. We don't want to impose, but I need to ask for one thing: please allow my mother and son to continue living in the San Judas apartment while I study to become a teacher."

Doña Marta thought for some time before saying, "I think you will be a good teacher. We need teachers. Education is the only way out of the problems we face. My boys are doing well because I educated them and made them responsible. If that is what you want to do, then I will continue to lend a hand. It's still like that morning so long ago when you walked into my kitchen after I fired my drunken cook."

Doña Marta smiled at Esperanza and said, "Your mother will be able to stay in San Judas. I'll make sure of it. She's my friend, and we will look out for each other while you focus on becoming a teacher. Now, have a cup of soup with me before you head back to San Judas, before the afternoon rains start."

CHAPTER 65

J uly turned into August, and the rains paused for a remarkable week of warm, balmy weather. The rains resumed the following week, just as the colonel's children packed up and returned to their schools in the United States. Those were busy and anxious weeks for Esperanza. Each Thursday, she hurried to the post office, hoping for a letter from Kitty. Each time, she walked home and wondered if she had made the right decision.

Then, on the third Thursday of August, she found a notice in her box indicating that a registered letter was waiting for her. She went to the front desk, where she regularly paid for her box, and handed over the notice.

"Do you have your *carnet* to identify yourself?" the clerk asked.

"My *carnet*?"

"Yes, your official identity card, the one the government issued you. I can't release a registered letter without your *carnet*."

Esperanza thought carefully and tried to remember where her *carnet* might be. It came to her suddenly: the county elementary school had taken her photo and placed it in a small, red-covered document, which she had last used when meeting the high school director in Chalatenango City. She had brought it with her to San Salvador and placed it in the white box with a copy of her school records. That white box was safely stored in the drawer of her bedside table, and she had recently seen it there. She had wondered what it was for, and now she knew.

Esperanza smiled at the post office official. "It is at home. I will be back soon."

The official scolded her, "You should always carry your *carnet* with you. It is your official identity if anything should happen." He handed her back the notice of the registered letter.

"You are right, sir," she responded as she ran for the bus to San Judas. She had never really known the importance of that document before. She knew of no one else in El Nido who had a *carnet*. *My, my,* she said to herself, *I should carry it with me all the time. It is my identity.*

When she got to the apartment in San Judas, she called out to her mother as she hurried to the bedroom, "The letter has arrived. It is registered. Can you imagine me receiving a registered letter? Well, I need my *carnet* to retrieve the registered letter."

"Your what?" asked her mother.

"It is my official identity card that the government issues. I got mine in the county elementary school," she shouted from the bedroom.

Yes, she found it in the white box. She tucked it into her shirt and headed back out the front door. "I'm going back to the post office to get my letter."

At the post office again, she gave the desk clerk her carnet and notice, and she received in return a large packet from Dr. Holmes. She carefully tucked it under arm and made the return trip to San Judas.

Her mother was still listening to her soap opera when Esperanza entered the front door and laid the packet on the dining room table. She cleared the table of dishes and other food items. She wiped the tabletop clean and rushed to the bathroom. On returning, she said to her mother, "I hope this is what I have been waiting for."

She carefully opened the sealed packet and found several letters and certified documents. On top was a brief letter from Kitty. It read:

Dear Esperanza,

I hope this is the first step toward you joining us in Virginia. My father spoke with a friend who is a consular officer at the State Department, who advised him on the documents needed for your visa application. He has prepared and no-tarized everything required for the consul in El Salvador, including an affidavit signed by Dr. Rand and my father, as well as a bond from my father to guarantee you have funds for your stay. There's also a letter from the college confirming your admission, along with letters of support from Dr. Rand and Mr. Jones. Now, go to the embassy and request an appointment with the consul. Show him the documents my father prepared, and he will let you know if any further paperwork is needed for your visa. We are hoping to see you soon—hopefully next year.

The following Thursday, she went to the embassy and was instructed to get in the line around the corner where visa applicants waited to get an appointment to see the consul. It was almost two hours before she reached the desk and was given an appointment for the last Thursday in September.

That night, a concerned Esperanza told Patricia and her mother about her situation. Patricia urged her, "Tell your colonel now of your plans. He may be able to help. My major says that the colonel knows everyone at the embassy."

Her mother said, "I will see Doña Marta. She will talk to her sons. They also know people at the embassy."

The following day, Esperanza confided to Mario, "The letter from my friend, Kitty, arrived a week ago. Yesterday, I went to the embassy and made an appointment to see the consul. He'll see me on the last Thursday in September. I think I should inform the colonel and his wife now of my plans and of the appointment."

Mario nodded, "I think you should, too."

"You see him all the time. Could you please help me arrange a time when they can see me."

The next morning, after breakfast, Mario told her, "The colonel and his wife are waiting for you in the dining room."

After adjusting her uniform and wiping her hands, she hurried to the dining room. The colonel looked up as she entered and said, "We understand you wanted to speak with us."

In her best English, she began the statement that she had rehearsed for days. "Thank you for this time. I want to tell you myself. Since a small child, I want to be teacher. My great-grandmother was the curer of my people. She was great teacher. My grandmother always tell me to learn and be like her mother. But some bad things happened, and I had to leave school and become cook to care of my son. My mother take care of son while I work. Now, I have opportunity to become teacher again.

My first work with American family was with Dr. and Mrs. Holmes. Their daughter, Kitty, is my good friend. She study medicine at Johns Hopkins. We write letters every often. I find out I am too old to get into high school here. Kitty find out in America there is college program. So, Dr. and Mrs. Holmes offer me chance to live with them and go to college. Once I have high school diploma, I can go to college for teachers."

Esperanza continued, "Two weeks ago, I receive many documents from Dr. Holmes, and he tell make appointment American consul to apply for visa. Apply new word for me. This Thursday I get appointment for final Thursday September. I know I must wait many months. I hope you will let me stay on as your cook while I wait for visa. But I not want to surprise you or cause problems. So, I want you to know what is going on."

The colonel's wife said, "I am glad you told us. And you can keep your job while you wait for the visa."

The colonel nodded his accord and turned to his wife, "Maybe we can help speed up the review of her application. I suspect Elsie Baldwin will be the one to see Esperanza." Then, turning to Esperanza, he asked, "Can you let me see the documents from Dr. Holmes, so I know what to say to Ms. Baldwin?"

Esperanza queried, "You want me to bring you the documents from Dr. Holmes?"

"Yes," said the colonel. "You really do know a good deal of English."

"Okay, I bring them next week after me off Thursday," agreed Esperanza.

The colonel thought a bit before telling his sergeant, "You arrange a day when you can run her to her home. I would like to see the papers before we have dinner with Ms. Baldwin." Then he asked his wife, "Is she on our guest list next Tuesday night?"

"Yes, dear, I think she is. I know the consul is away, and she is acting for him," replied the colonel's wife.

"So, Mario, have one of the men drive Esperanza to her home today to pick up the papers. We want to go over them."

"Yes, Sir. I will, right after I go over some work with you on assignments for next week."

On Sunday morning, the colonel and his wife read the packet of letters and documents that Dr. Holmes had sent to Esperanza. They discussed the implications of Esperanza's possible departure and then added a letter of recommendation of their own before returning the packet to Esperanza.

On the following Tuesday night, they received Elsie Baldwin as one of their dinner guests. After enjoying one of Esperanza's typically excellent meals, Elsie remarked to her hostess, "That dinner was especially delicious."

The colonel's wife smiled, "Thank you, I agree. I'm not much of a cook myself, but we are blessed with an excellent one, Esperanza." After a slight pause, she continued, "Elsie, you may be seeing her on a visa matter the last Thursday of the month. She has an appointment at the consulate."

"Really?" responded the vice consul.

"Yes," continued the colonel's wife. "Three of her former employers, all former technical advisers here, are recommending her for a student visa. Dr. Holmes, who is the chief public health adviser for Latin America at the Foreign Operations Administration, is posting a bond and offering his home to her as her US residence. He will be sponsoring her admission to a college education program in Virginia."

"That's very interesting—and quite unusual. We seldom get applications from someone like your cook. What is her name again?"

"It is Esperanza Choarti. By the way, we have also added a letter of recommendation of our own. She hasn't missed a day or a meal since we hired her. She cooks for the enlisted men who are living in the guest quarters out back, as well as for us. Our children were here for the summer, and they left wanting to take her with them. For the colonel and me, it is not only her food, but her organization and sense of responsibility that make her so valuable. That's what we have pointed out in our letter."

"Well, you know, it's just the consul and I who handle visas, and there's a high volume of requests. Usually, we prioritize cases with political or business interests, and a case like hers would start with our Salvadoran local staff. Given the volume and the background checks we need to conduct, the preliminary process can take months, if not years, depending on the visa type. Now that you've flagged her case, I'll mark her appointment and see her personally. By the way, do you know if she speaks any English?"

"Yes, she can read and speak some English. She is mostly self-taught. I understand that few of the maids here do, so Esperanza is a bit unique. And thank you for taking the time to see her; the colonel and I believe she deserves the opportunity."

"I'm glad you brought it to my attention," Elsie replied, pausing for a moment. "Please remind her to bring her passport, a letter of good conduct from the police, and a school transcript, along with her application and the letters you mentioned. We have a long wait time for immigrant visas, but educational visas have a shorter waiting period."

The next morning, the colonel's wife personally relayed to Esperanza the essence of her conversation with Ms. Baldwin, and emphasized the importance of bringing her passport, the letter from the police, and a transcript to the interview.

Esperanza tried to absorb the information from the colonel's wife. She understood the letter from police and the transcript, but the passport raised a question: Is my *carnet* my passport?

When she saw Mario later in the day, she asked him, "The señora told me this morning that I should bring my passport to the interview at the American embassy. Is my *carnet* my passport?"

Mario shook his head no, "A passport is different. It is a document from your government that says to all the countries around the world that you are a citizen of this country. You need a passport to visit another country. Your *carnet* is useful only inside your country."

"Oh" mused Esperanza. "Where do I get a passport?"

"That I'm not sure. You better ask around."

"Mario, would you ask the colonel if I could take some time off tomorrow to visit my friend Doña Marta? I want to ask her for help in getting a passport."

Mario agreed, and the colonel agreed to let Esperanza take the following afternoon off to consult with Doña Marta.

When Esperanza arrived at Doña Marta's, Doña Marta was taking her afternoon siesta. It was almost 3:00 p.m. before Doña Marta entered her sitting room. She gave Esperanza a warm *abrazo* and commented, "I understand that you have an urgent problem."

"Yes, Doña. Thank you for seeing me. It is about a passport. You know about my opportunity to study in America. Well, I have an appointment for the last Thursday of the month to apply for a visa. The colonel's wife told me that I need to bring with me a passport. Where do I get a passport?"

"The Ministry of Foreign Affairs."

"Where is that?" Esperanza asked in confusion.

"Let me talk to Ricardo," replied Doña Marta. "One of his close friends works there. I'll ask him to help you get an application and explain to you what you need to do to get a passport. You said you need it by the last Thursday of the month? That's only three weeks away. The ministry usually takes much longer than three weeks to process things, so we'll need to get some special attention."

"Oh, I didn't know."

"Well, we will give it try. I think you also need a letter of good conduct from the police—both for your passport and the American Embassy. Can you get that quickly?"

"I think so. Patricia's major seems to know the right people."

Doña Marta thought aloud, "The Americans are going to want to know if you have been a good student. A transcript from your school will be important to them." Looking at Esperanza she asked, "Do you have a transcript from your school?"

"I have a copy of the letter that I took to the director of the high school in Chalatenango City. It lists all my grades and commends my work."

"That would be useful, but I doubt it is an official transcript. The Americans will want something more official," opined Doña Marta.

"I can write to the director of the county school," responded Esperanza.

Doña Marta shook her head, "You don't have enough time. That would probably take months. I know how much time it takes for one of our officials to act unless he is under pressure. Oh, no, not just a letter. The director must be instructed to send a transcript immediately. Do you think Patricia could get her major to help?"

"I can ask."

"Well, then, we have a lot of work for the next few days. I will talk to Ricardo tonight. You get to Patricia for the major's help. I want you to get your visa and become a teacher."

Doña Marta sat quietly for a minute and reflected on what she had just said. She didn't usually lend her support to many people. Her generosity normally only extended to her immediate family. Then, she realized that she had let the poor, little ragamuffin from El Nido, as well as the girl's mother, become part of her inner circle. She realized that she really cared about them, and she did really want to help Esperanza achieve her dream.

Smiling to herself, she asked Esperanza, "Do you want something to eat or drink before you head back to the colonel's?"

"No," smiled Esperanza. "How can I thank you?"

In just three weeks, everything came together like a miracle. Ricardo's friend provided instructions for the passport application. The major responded to Patricia's request and helped expedite both a police report of good conduct and a copy of Esperanza's school transcript, all within a week. With friends in the right places, tasks that usually took months were quickly accomplished.

CHAPTER 66

E speranza arrived at the embassy an hour before her scheduled appointment with Vice Consul Baldwin. The afternoon rain was relentless, and her rain cape offered little protection against the downpour. She was drenched from head to toe, and despite her efforts to tidy up once inside, she could do little to improve her appearance. Feeling uneasy about her disheveled appearance, she sat in the waiting area, anxiously anticipating the moment her name would be called.

Esperanza was guided toward an office with the name *Ms. Baldwin, Vice Consul* on the door. Feeling tense and uncertain, she knocked lightly and heard a firm, "Come in." She entered to find a well-dressed, composed professional seated behind a tidy desk, seemingly unaffected by the rainstorm outside. Ms. Baldwin glanced up from her papers and, in clear English, said, "Please sit down, Miss Choarti."

"Thank you," replied Esperanza in English.

"I enjoyed your meal at the colonel's last month," added Ms. Baldwin. Esperanza smiled as she sat down.

"Looks like the rain got you. It is a nasty day," said Ms. Baldwin, trying to ease Esperanza's apparent tension. "Please hand me your application, the letters and documents you have to support your application, your passport, a letter of good conduct from the police, and, if you have it, a transcript of your grades."

Esperanza produced each item in the order requested. Ms. Baldwin meticulously reviewed each one, making notes on a separate yellow pad of paper. It seemed like hours for the nervous Esperanza, but it was only ten to fifteen minutes before Miss Baldwin said, "You have provided me all the documents we need to consider your application, and I have some additional questions to ask."

Esperanza said, "I try to answer."

"Your application says that you have a son. Are you married?"

In a matter-of-fact voice, Esperanza responded, "I never married. I graduate elementary school with chance for high school. I was raped by drunk. I had son, so not go to high school in Chalatenango and bring mother and son here to work as cook. I hope my English good enough to explain."

Miss Baldwin asked, "You have not been to high school? Where did you learn your English?"

"I listen to people talk at pension, get English book. Listen and learn. Kitty Holmes help me listen and talk. I know not much, but I try."

"Yes, I hear. What do you want to be?" asked Ms. Baldwin.

"I always want be teacher. My great-grandmother was the great curer of our people, my great-uncle our last shaman. Grandmother teach me. I want to help our people. So many not read or write. So sad. But in El Salvador, an old person like me," searching for a word, "not permit study—only young people can go high school. I think too few high schools. You understand."

"Yes," said Ms. Baldwin. "So, you agree to live with the Holmes family until you complete your teaching degree? You understand that you cannot stay in the United States if you violate any conditions of your visa?"

"Oh, yes," was Esperanza's clear response.

"You also understand that Dr. Holmes is providing a bond to assure the government of the United States that you have the money needed to cover the expenses required for you to obtain your degree, and that you have an obligation to him. If you fail to observe the conditions of your visa, he could lose a lot of money."

"Yes, I understand I owe him a lot. I will not,"—again, searching for a word—cause him hurt."

"And what about your family? Who will take care of your mother and son here?" queried Ms. Baldwin.

Somewhat confused by the question, Esperanza finally answered, "My mother has jobs. Doña Marta Romero help us with rent. Son to go new vocational high school. Most money we save since I work will be with mother. We talk and have plan."

Ms. Baldwin nodded and said, "Thank you, Miss Choarti. We will now carefully review your application. We will contact you if we need further information or documents. Should I contact you at the colonel's?"

"Yes, please contact me at colonel's house. I be there every day except Thursday," noted Esperanza.

Miss Baldwin said, "I think I need one more signature on the application. You swear that all the information you provided me is true?"

"Yes, I swear," Esperanza affirmed as she accepted the pen from Ms. Baldwin and signed the document where she indicated.

Ms. Baldwin also returned the passport. "Take good care of your passport."

"Thank you," said Esperanza as she rose from her chair and bowed her head in appreciation before turning and leaving the office.

CHAPTER 67

T he day after the interview, Esperanza wrote a long letter to Kitty describing her experience and emotions. She was hopeful but not optimistic. She wrote to Kitty: *I have learned that the system in this country is not intended to help people like me. Without the influence of people like Doña Marta and you, I would be living on the street, doing God-knows-what to survive. I have been blessed by friends. I know that I am not alone. I want to pay you all back by doing good.*

Before her trip to the post office the following Thursday, she wrote three short letters of thanks to Dr. and Mrs. Holmes, Dr. and Mrs. Rand, and Mr. and Mrs. Jones. She tried her best to express, in English, her appreciation for their support in her quest to become a teacher and promised to do her very best. She put them in the letter to Kitty and asked Kitty to pass them on, because she didn't know their addresses.

To the colonel and his wife, she wrote another note of appreciation and had Mario deliver it. To Mario, she gave a cordial, sisterly embrace.

Then, she waited until the rainy season ended. Pepe and Pablo graduated from eighth grade, and the colonel allowed her to take time off to attend the ceremony.

In the second week of December, the colonel and his wife went to America to spend Christmas with their children. Mario and the two enlisted men took advantage of space available on an air force plane to fly to Texas to spend Christmas with their families. The large house was almost empty. The Salvadoran security guard kept a watchful eye on the premises. Before he left for Texas, Mario gave Esperanza and the two maids a check from the colonel for Christmas and a schedule for each of them to take week-long vacations during the nearly month-long absence of the colonel and his wife.

Esperanza's vacation time fell on the week before Christmas. It gave her time, not only to prepare for the holiday, but also to visit the new vocational high school that the boys would attend. Although the school was closed, Esperanza and the boys walked around its exterior, peering through the barred windows to glimpse the layout of the rooms and some of the new equipment inside. She said to the boys, "What a gift for you to attend this high school. It's a solid foundation for building a good life."

Preparations for Christmas were special. Esperanza knew this might be their last together for some time. The family put together a traditional *creche* and hung some colored papers across the living room. She took her mother and son shopping in the small street bazaars around the city to find presents. They joined forces with Patricia and Pablo. They planned for Christmas Eve with sweet tamales and hot chocolate as had been the custom in El Nido. Esperanza prepared a feast of *gallo en chicha* for midday on Christmas. Patricia had delivered her second child—another boy—who was the spitting image of his father. The hope for a girl was not fulfilled.

Despite this, it was a joyful time for the two families, who had gradually become one through the bond forged between Pepe and Pablo. Esperanza's mother took charge of caring for Patricia's newborn son, and Patricia's major provided a weekly fee for her help. She embraced the role of grandmother and guiding spirit for all three boys and stepped into the role of Patricia's absent mother. She directed Esperanza in the household duties and meal preparations, encouraged Patricia to rest, and supervised her recovery. She also ensured that the boys behaved well and stayed focused on their schooling.

The day after Christmas, when Esperanza returned to the colonel's house, she felt a sense of relief. If her visa was granted, she could leave without guilt, knowing her family would be well cared for. Her mother had reassured her that their extended family in San Salvador could manage on its own.

Through the first weeks of 1955, Esperanza waited for word from Ms. Baldwin. She dared not approach her for fear of a negative reaction. People like Esperanza had to know their place and wait for those in authority to approach them.

It was mid-February when Mario let Esperanza know that Ms. Baldwin had left a message for her to come to the embassy the following Thursday. Esperanza thought it a good sign that Ms. Baldwin had remembered that Thursday was her day off.

"Come right in and take a seat," said Ms. Baldwin after Esperanza appeared at the door to her office.

"Good afternoon, Ms. Baldwin. I am so glad that you see me," replied Esperanza in her best English.

Ms. Baldwin began, "Ms. Choarti, your application for a student visa has been approved."

"Ms. Baldwin, that is what I dream to get. I want to study to be teacher, nothing more. I want to help my people learn and do better."

"A student visa does not allow you to work to support yourself—except in very limited ways tied to your studies. Be sure to read the instructions carefully and understand exactly what those limitations are."

Then, she asked, "Did you bring your passport with you?"

Esperanza shook her head, "No."

"I suggest that we set an appointment for you to bring your passport so that we can place the visa in your passport."

"May I tell Dr. Holmes the news?" asked Esperanza.

"Yes, indeed. I suggest you also inform the colonel," replied Ms. Baldwin.

"Can you see again next Thursday?" asked Esperanza, "Then I will come with my passport."

Ms. Baldwin looked at her calendar before stating, "Yes. See you next Thursday at 1:30 p.m."

CHAPTER 68

The letter to Kitty was written that very afternoon. Esperanza poured out her excitement:

Dear Kitty,

Today, I get visa. Now I plan to come to America. Ms. Baldwin give me student visa. No work. Just study. Thank you, your mother, father, and Dr. Rand. Without you no chance.

Tell me when I should come to begin school.

Do you need me bring something?

So excited. I can't believe real.

See you soon!

All my love, Esperanza

Esperanza was elated as she rode the bus to the post office, carrying the letter that would set her plans in motion. After mailing it, she continued to San Judas, eager to share the exciting news with her extended family and celebrate over a special dinner. The following day, she shared the news with Mario, who then informed the colonel and his wife of her plans. Esperanza assured them she would give a month's notice, allowing them time to find a new cook and ensure a smooth transition.

With the visa process done, Esperanza began making lists of everything she needed for the trip. She first needed to figure out how to get to Virginia, including how to pay for her airfare. She also planned to give her mother enough savings to support the family for at least the first year. Her list grew: a suitcase, suitable clothes, books—each item reminded her of the financial burden she faced. *Money, money, money,* she thought.

Then she remembered an ad she had seen about a year ago in *Prensa Gráfica* for an airline that offered special low fares for students. She resolved to look into it as soon as she received her visa.

The following Thursday, after Ms. Baldwin added the visa to her passport, Esperanza hurried to the airline office to ask about the student fare. She presented her passport and student visa to the agent, who confirmed that the special fare was still available. The cost for a ticket to Washington, D.C., was 750 *colones*, or $300 USD.

Excited, she rushed back to San Judas and gathered all the *colones* she had carefully hidden in various spots around her apartment. She counted the money several times and organized it into three piles: one for the airfare, one for her mother, and the third for her expenses during the trip to America.

To her relief, she realized she could pay for her ticket, take $500 with her, and still leave nearly 3,000 *colones* for her mother as a safety net. The sense of security this provided gave her peace of mind—she knew that her mother and Pepe would have a financial cushion as she pursued her dream in the United States. With this settled, she felt a renewed sense of determination as she prepared for the next chapter of her life.

Doña Marta solved another item on her list when she sent two old leather suitcases.

The following Thursday, when she opened her post office box, she found a letter from Kitty:

Dear Esperanza,

My parents and I are delighted. My mother says the room is ready for you when you arrive. My father reports that the college will begin its summer program on June 15, and that it has you enrolled in its high school diploma program. I think you should arrive no later than June 1.

I don't think you need to bring many books or school supplies. They are readily available here. No need to bring more than your clothes and you.

Write me as soon as you have made your travel plans. See you soon.

Now, she knew that the only things she needed to pack in the leather suitcases were her clothes.

Although June 1 was less than three months away, Esperanza decided that would be the day she would travel. She went to the airline office, made the reservation, and promised to return within an hour with her passport and the money. The die was cast.

The following day, she informed Mario of her plan to travel on June 1 and that she would be leaving her job on May 15. This gave the colonel a full two months' notice. The time flew by. The colonel's wife found a new cook who would be free in mid-May, once the embassy family she worked for was transferred. Esperanza stayed on for four days after May

15 to help the new cook settle into the job. The colonel expressed his appreciation by giving Esperanza an extra month's pay, which provided her with a bit more money to take on her journey.

June 1 dawned with bright sunshine—warm and humid. Esperanza woke up in her bed in the San Judas apartment and fully realized that today was the day she would leave for America. She glanced at the clock; it was 5:00 a.m. She needed to be at the airport by 8:00 a.m. The carpenter from the corner had offered to drive her in his panel truck, and her mother and the two boys would accompany her for the send-off.

Esperanza jumped out of bed and found that her mother was already up and preparing breakfast before waking Pepe. She took a quick shower, combed her long black hair, and tied it into a neat braid. She dressed in the chic tan linen suit that Patricia had made for her as a bon voyage gift. Before leaving the bedroom, she checked her two suitcases to ensure they were securely locked. Inside were all of her belongings: three pairs of underwear, four button-down uniforms—white, lavender, navy blue, and black—two flowered skirts, four white blouses, two pairs of walking shoes, two pairs of sandals, three pairs of hosiery, four pairs of socks, two nightgowns, and a sleek black dress Patricia had also made for her. She had also packed a couple of Lope de Vega novels that had always provided her comfort during difficult times.

All of her remaining books and possessions she entrusted to her mother and son. She took special care to discuss her books with Pablo and Pepe, and, to her delight, the boys showed genuine interest in science and algebra texts. She was pleasantly surprised by their grasp of the equations and the thoughtful questions they asked about biology and botany. Her mother joined the conversation as well, and Esperanza noticed that she seemed almost as intrigued by the subjects as the boys were.

They ate breakfast together as a family at 6:30 a.m. At 7:00 a.m., there was the familiar rat-a-tat of Pablo at the door. When Pepe opened it, he found not only Pablo, but also Patricia, the carpenter, and Mario. Mario explained that the colonel had given him permission to drive Esperanza to the airport. Quickly, they loaded the suitcases onto the carpenter's panel truck, and the boys hopped in. Esperanza's mother carefully gathered Patricia's new baby and joined Patricia and Esperanza in Mario's vehicle. The two cars made their way down the hill toward Ilopango airport.

Only Mario had been to the airport before, so he guided the group to the airline's booth for departing passengers. Esperanza felt a bit nervous as she handed over her ticket, *carnet*, and passport to the attendant. The attendant issued receipts for her suitcases and assigned her a seat, then directed her to the official booth where her passport and police record would be checked before boarding. Everything went smoothly, and, once cleared, she rejoined her group in the departure lounge for final words and heartfelt *abrazos*.

Then, the flight was called. Esperanza smiled, stepped through the door, and ascended the stairs to the plane. Before entering, she turned back for one last wave, her heart swelling with a mixture of hope and resolve. This marked the beginning of a new chapter—one that would be even more transformative than her departure from El Nido. As she took a final look at her loved ones below, she made a silent promise: the next time she returned, she would come back as a qualified teacher.

www.ingramcontent.com/pod-product-compliance
Lightning Source LLC
Chambersburg PA
CBHW060411030726
47495CB00003B/532